Fairfield Hall

Margaret Dickinson

Fairfield Hall

MACMILLAN

First published 2014 by Macmillan
an imprint of Pan Macmillan, a division of Macmillan Publishers Limited
Pan Macmillan, 20 New Wharf Road, London N1 9RR
Basingstoke and Oxford
Associated companies throughout the world
www.panmacmillan.com

ISBN 978-1-4472-3728-0

A CIP catalogue record for this book is available from the British Library.

Typeset by Palimpsest Book Production Limited, Falkirk, Stirlingshire
Printed and bound by CPI Group (UK) Ltd, Croydon, CR0 4YY

For Zachary and Zara

ACKNOWLEDGEMENTS

The setting for this story is inspired by the beautiful National Trust property, Gunby Hall and Gardens, near Skegness in Lincolnshire, which appears on the cover. My sincere thanks to Astrid Gatenby and all her team of helpers for all the help and encouragement I received on my visits there. Also thank you to four of the volunteer room guides who took the time to meet me and chat about the history of the house: Jane Hughes, Judy Morgan-Anstee, Veronica Stonehouse and Rose Williams.

I am very grateful to Gordon Smith of Grimsby for his kindness in allowing me to visit his home to see a film about the Grimsby Chums. Gordon and the late John Robinson came up with the idea for the film, which was made by Terry Marker, with the help of the Grimsby Branch of the Royal Lincolnshire and Royal Anglian Regimental Association. The Grimsby Chums was the 10th (Service) Battalion, The Lincolnshire Regiment, a 'Pals Battalion' formed at the outset of the Great War from volunteers from Grimsby and the surrounding district. The film is a moving tribute to those men.

A great many sources have been used for research, but I must give particular acknowledgement to Peter Chapman's superb book *Grimsby's Own: The Story of The Chums*, published by the *Grimsby Evening*

Telegraph and the Hutton Press 1991). Much of the material from his book also helped in the production of the film, as did information from the Imperial War Museum.

My love and thanks as always to my family and friends who are my constant source of encouragement and support as are my agent, Darley Anderson, and his staff, my editor, Trisha Jackson, Natasha Harding, Fergus Edmondson and all the team at Pan Macmillan.

Prologue

Tiffany parked the car at the side of the road and climbed the gentle slope of hill towards the grand house at the top. She dared not bring her little car any further, for the day was bleak, the road slippery and she feared losing control of the vehicle. *Beatrice* wasn't good on icy roads, never mind any kind of hill. As the ground flattened out, she paused to catch her breath and look around her. To the west, lay the wolds, undulating gently and covered in a frost that had not melted since morning. Directly below, Fairfield village nestled in a shallow vale. The light was fading even though it was still early afternoon and already lights flickered in several of the windows of the cottages lining the one main street. Beyond the village, she could see farms dotted on the hillsides. At one end of the village street stood the church with the vicarage beside it. She could close her eyes and imagine herself back in time; Tiffany doubted that the scene had changed much in the last hundred years, except, of course, for the cars parked on either side of the road – a necessity when the nearest market town was five miles away. And there was now only one village shop that sold everything instead of the butcher, the grocer and so on, who would all once have been able to make a living even in this small community. Now the villagers would head into the nearest town – Thorpe St Michael – to the supermarket for their weekly shopping, using the local village store only for emergencies. Even the smithy-cum-wheelwright's that had once been the heartbeat of a rural community would be long gone, unless, of course, the blacksmith's business had survived by making bespoke fancy wrought-iron work.

She turned to look up again at the house standing sentinel over the village and resumed her walk, shivering a little. March opening times, she'd read in a leaflet about Fairfield Hall, were Sundays and Wednesdays and today, Mother's Day, it seemed fitting that she should visit.

She was breathing hard by the time she'd walked along the curving driveway, lined with lime trees in their winter nakedness, though she knew they'd be a lovely sight in summer. She paused a moment, before passing beneath an archway into a courtyard. In front of her were stables and to her left, three coach houses. Completing the square were other buildings, which once, she guessed, might have housed the laundry and workshops. In the centre of the courtyard was a magnificent beech tree and, to her right, she could see the side entrance to the house. Nearing it, she saw the notice: PLEASE USE THE FRONT ENTRANCE. Passing through a small gate, she wandered round the corner of the house and climbed the steps. The impressive three-storey square house, with its front door positioned centrally, faced to the west with six windows on the ground floor and seven on the upper storeys. Closer now, she could see that there was also a basement partly below ground level. Attached on the northern side was a lower building – only two storeys high. The smooth lawn in the front of the house sloped down towards the village. To the side she could see more gardens and guessed that behind the house there was perhaps a kitchen plot that would have grown produce to help feed the household. Beyond the grounds belonging to the house were cultivated fields where, in summer, there would be ripening corn bordered with bright-headed poppies. She waited for what seemed an age before the door was opened slowly by an elderly man, dressed strangely, she thought, in a morning suit. He looked like a butler stepping out of the pages of a history book. But his wrinkled face beamed and his old eyes twinkled. 'Good afternoon, miss. How nice to see a visitor. Please come in.'

Tiffany stepped into the hall and wiped her feet on the square of thick matting. 'I expect you don't get many in the winter and especially on a day like this.'

The old man chuckled. 'Not many, miss, no.'

To one side of the hall, a log fire burned in a pretty fireplace lined with blue and white Delft tiles and Tiffany, drawn by its warmth, held her cold hands towards it.

'Would you like me to give you a guided tour,' the man asked, 'or would you prefer to wander through the house on your own? It's clearly marked where you're allowed to go, so . . .'

'I'd like the guided tour, please.'

He smiled again. No doubt he was delighted to be needed.

'Whenever you're ready, then, miss. I don't think we'll get any more visitors today, so you have my undivided attention.'

'That's nice,' Tiffany murmured sincerely. 'Thank you.' There was so much she wanted to know about this house and she was sure she'd found the right person to tell her.

'This is the entrance hall, of course,' the guide began and then he led her into the room on the left-hand side of the hall. 'This was once the housekeeper's room so that she could see who was coming up the drive – the family returning home or visitors arriving – and warn the rest of the servants. In the late 1890s it was used as the estate office. Beyond it we have what would have been the drawing room, but in later years, we understand it became known as the music room. Isn't it magnificent?'

Paintings and portraits lined the oak-panelled walls; in one corner stood a grand piano, in another an oak long-case clock solemnly ticked away the hours as perhaps it had done for over two hundred and fifty years.

He led her out of another door and along a corridor. 'Those rooms are just a modern kitchen and sitting room and this,' he said as they passed a staircase on the right-hand side, 'is what the servants would use, but *this*,' he emphasized as they passed once more through the entrance hall and to the southern end of the house, 'is the main staircase.' The walls above the oak staircase were again lined with family portraits. There was such a history to this house. Tiffany's heart beat a little faster.

'We'll go upstairs in a moment,' her guide said, 'but first let me show you the library here to the right of the stairs . . .' The room – as she had imagined it would be – was lined with shelves of books. 'And then this room to the left is what used to be the morning room. It faces to the east at the back of the house so it always gets the morning sun. Sadly,' he smiled at her, 'we haven't any today.

'Now, upstairs we have the family's private sitting

room and straight opposite are the best bedrooms. Further along, you will see that the living-in servants also have bedrooms on this floor.'

'Really?' Tiffany laughed. 'I thought servants were always confined to the attics?'

'Not in this house, miss.' He smiled. 'The top floor has the nursery and probably a room for a nursery nurse or governess and also a couple of very nice guest bedrooms.'

I wonder where she slept? Tiffany thought as they retraced their steps downstairs. *I'd like to think that I've been standing in her bedroom.*

He showed her the huge kitchen in the basement and other, smaller rooms that were used for different purposes: a wine cellar, a game larder, a still room and the butler's pantry. He even showed her the row of fourteen bells, which summoned the servants.

'And now I'll take you back to my favourite room in the house. I've deliberately left it until last.'

When they entered the dining room, where portraits of the more recent family members were hanging, Tiffany's interest sharpened.

'The main part of the house was built in the early 1700s by the Lyndon family in the style of Sir Christopher Wren and the two-storey extension to the north was added much later,' the guide told her. 'It's strange to find such a house as this in the countryside, isn't it? It's more suited to a town house.'

Tiffany said nothing, willing him to go on with the stories of the family. That was what interested her.

'The hereditary title, the Earl of Fairfield, was granted to Montague Lyndon at the end of a distinguished military career in 1815 and thereafter each generation sent a son into the Army, usually the second son, if there was one, so that the title was safeguarded. The eldest son always inherited the title and he was expected to run the estate.' They moved on slowly down the line of portraits, the guide pointing briefly to each one. 'That's the second earl, the third, the fourth and the fifth, and now we come to the sixth Earl of Fairfield, James Lyndon.'

Tiffany gazed up at the full-length portrait of a man in military uniform. He was tall with brown hair and dark brown eyes that, strangely, seemed to stare coldly down at her. There was no smile, no warmth in his face.

'As you can see,' her guide said, 'James was a soldier, too, and, by all accounts, a very good one. He was the second son and should never have inherited the title but his elder brother, Albert, died young.'

Tiffany took a step forward and then stopped, her gaze held by the picture of a young woman hanging on the opposite side of the fireplace to the one of the sixth earl. Her hair was as black as a raven's feathers. She had dark violet eyes and flawless skin. She was dressed in a blue satin gown with a necklace around her graceful neck. Tiffany hoped the artist had painted a true representation of her.

She bit her lip, hardly daring to ask. 'Who is this?'

'Ah, now that is Lady Annabel, James's wife. Isn't she lovely?' They stood a moment in silence, in awe of the woman's striking beauty. In answer to Tiffany's unspoken question, he added, 'And she was every bit as lovely as her portrait.'

Tiffany glanced at him. To the twenty-year-old girl, her guide looked ancient, but even he couldn't be old enough to remember Lady Annabel, could he? But it seemed he was.

He smiled. 'My grandfather worked here as a gardener and he used to talk about her. In fact, you couldn't get him to stop talking about her. I only saw her twice and she was getting on a bit by then, of course, but she was still striking. And everyone loved her, except,' he sighed heavily, 'the one person who should have loved her the most. Poor lady.'

'Tell me about her – please.' Tiffany couldn't help the pleading tone in her voice and, sensing it, the man smiled down at her.

'It's a long story.'

'I'm in no rush. It's – it's what I came for. I'd love to learn as much as I can about her, but only if you've time.'

'Oh, I've time. But let's sit down, my dear. My old legs aren't what they used to be.'

They sat down on two chairs near the fire, but facing the two portraits.

'Well, now, where to begin?' He fell silent for a moment, his gaze still on the enchanting face in the painting, and then he murmured again, 'Where to begin?'

One

Grimsby, Lincolnshire, January 1896

'Please can we go home, Miss Annabel? It's freezing.'

'Just another five minutes,' Annabel murmured, staring through the gloom of the winter's evening, watching the road ahead.

They were sitting in the horse-drawn chaise on the seafront at Cleethorpes, not far from the pier that stretched out into the cold sea. There were no holidaymakers today, no visitors walking its length. Although the chaise offered a little more shelter than an open trap, the wind blew in from the sea, stinging their faces and chilling their bones.

'If you're late for dinner, your father will ask questions. And you know I can't tell lies. I go bright red and he knows straightaway.'

'I don't expect you to tell lies for me, Jane.'

The maid shivered. 'The horse is getting cold too. See how he's pawing at the ground.'

The chaise rocked dangerously as the restless horse moved.

'Miss Annabel,' Jane said firmly, 'he's not coming and we're both going to be in such trouble when we get back. What will Mrs Rowley say if I'm not there to help with the dinner? You know I have to help out in the kitchen.'

The Constantine household had few staff: a butler, Roland Walmsley, who also served as valet to his master, a cook-cum-housekeeper, Mrs Rowley, a kitchen maid, Lucy, and Jane, who was everything else; housemaid and lady's maid to Mrs Constantine and to Miss Annabel. The only outside staff were a part-time gardener and a groom, Billy, who looked after the two horses and usually drove Annabel or her mother wherever they wanted to go. But today, Annabel had insisted upon driving the chaise herself with only her maid for company.

Annabel sighed and took up the reins, saying, 'Gee up.' The horse, glad of some activity at last, lurched forward and the two girls clutched at the sides of the vehicle.

'He'll have us over,' Jane muttered, but the sure-footed horse began to trot happily towards home. A little way along the road into Grimsby, Annabel pulled on the reins so that the horse turned to the right. Prince hesitated, yet he obeyed his mistress's instructions.

'Where are you going, miss? This isn't the way home.'

'Isn't it?' Annabel's tone was airy. 'I thought it was. Oh dear, we're lost.' She flicked the reins so that the horse picked up speed, taking them even further away from the road they needed to be on.

'Miss Annabel—'

'I think it's a short cut.'

'No, it isn't. You know very well it isn't. You're going towards the docks,' Jane said, 'and if you've some madcap notion of trying to find him, then – then . . .'

Annabel pulled gently on the reins bringing Prince to a steady walking pace. They reached a crossroads and, skilfully, Annabel turned the horse so that they were facing back the way they had just come. Prince began to trot again, more hopeful now that they were really going home to his warm stable. His speed quickened even more when he recognized Bargate, the road where the Constantines lived.

The house was a square building with a central front door and a bay window on either side. It had a small front garden but a larger one behind the house where their gardener cultivated both flower borders and a kitchen garden. As a young girl, Annabel had been allowed to help in the grounds and in the greenhouse, but as she'd grown older, her father had dictated that she should apply herself to more ladylike occupations.

'It is not fitting for you to be grubbing about in the dirt with only a servant as a companion.'

And so Annabel's love of the land was only satisfied on her visits to her grandparents who, unbeknown to her father, allowed her to help about the farm.

'There's Billy waiting for us,' Jane said as the chaise came to a halt. She climbed down and then turned to help her young mistress alight, whilst Billy hurried to hold the horse's head.

'Good evening, Billy,' Annabel said with a forced gaiety she was no longer feeling. 'I'm so sorry we're late. We got lost.'

Beside her, she heard Jane pull in a sharp breath but her maid said nothing. Annabel knew the girl would follow her lead and realize that her mistress had given her a ready-made excuse should she be questioned.

'You go in the back way, Jane. I'll go to the front door. Mr Walmsley will let me in. And remember' – she lowered her voice as Billy began to unhitch the horse from the shafts – 'we got lost.'

'Yes, miss.' Jane bobbed a quick curtsy and scurried in through the back door.

Annabel walked around the side of the house and rang the front door bell.

'Good evening, Mr Walmsley,' she said smoothly when the butler opened the door.

Despite having been told to do so on numerous occasions, Annabel flatly refused to address their servants by anything other than their full name or, for the younger ones, their Christian name. She abhorred the use of mere surnames and the butler had long ago given up trying to get her to change. Even her disciplinarian father couldn't enforce the rule with his wayward daughter.

Hearing her voice, Ambrose flung open the door to his study and strode into the hall. He was a short, portly man in his early fifties with a florid complexion and bristling sideburns.

'Where've you been?' he barked.

Annabel turned towards him as she removed her cape, hat and gloves and handed them to Roland Walmsley.

'Out for a drive in the chaise, Father, but I took a wrong turning in the dusk and I got a little lost. I'm so sorry I'm late for dinner.' She turned back to the butler. 'Mr Walmsley, please tell Mrs Rowley that it's my fault Jane is late, not hers.'

Roland Walmsley bowed and hid his smile. He could guess where his young mistress had been, though wild horses would not drag it out of him, nor would he question Jane. She was utterly loyal to Miss Annabel, as were all the servants.

Ambrose glared at his daughter. 'We've held dinner back for half an hour and Mrs Rowley is *not* best pleased.' Mrs Rowley was the only person who warranted – in Ambrose's opinion – a courtesy title.

'You'd better get changed – and be quick about it.'

'Yes, Father.' Annabel bowed her head meekly and hurried towards the staircase. Ambrose watched her go, his eyes narrowing. Had his ruse worked? he wondered. Annabel's expression gave nothing away. As he watched her climb the stairs, he fancied he saw her shoulders drooping in disappointment. But he couldn't be sure. His daughter was difficult to read. He'd interrogate the maid, he decided. She'd give herself away at once.

But this time, even Jane's resolve proved difficult to break. After dinner was over, he called her to his study. She faced her master fearlessly with wide, innocent eyes. Pulling herself up to her full five feet two inches, she straightened her shoulders and explained calmly, 'We got lost, sir. Miss Annabel took a wrong turning in the dark and then it was difficult to turn the horse round. By the time we got to the right road again, sir, oh, I reckon half an hour or more had gone by.'

Ambrose frowned. 'Did you meet anyone, girl?'

Her eyes widened even more. 'Meet anyone, sir?'

'Don't act stupid with me, girl. You know very well what I mean. Did Miss Annabel have an assignation?'

The girl shook her head vehemently. 'Oh no, sir. We didn't meet anyone.'

Ambrose stepped close to her so that his bulbous red nose was only inches from her small, well-shaped nose. In a low, threatening tone he said slowly, 'If I find out you've been lying to me, girl, it'll be the worse for you. You understand?'

Jane nodded vigorously. 'I wouldn't lie to you, sir. Honest, I wouldn't.'

Ambrose grunted as he stepped away. He still didn't believe her. In his experience anyone who used the word 'honest' to emphasize whatever they were saying, was usually lying.

Jane scuttled back to the kitchen, her cheeks flaming. She hoped that was the last questioning she would have to face from the master, but there was always the mistress to contend with. She was almost more fearsome than Mr Constantine.

'*Now* what have you been up to?' Mrs Rowley frowned. 'Are you in trouble? Because if you are, I want to know about it.'

Oh no, not you an' all! Jane thought. 'Nothing, Mrs Rowley,' she said aloud. 'I was out with Miss Annabel and we were late back. That's all.'

'Oh aye.' Even Mrs Rowley's tone was sceptical. 'And where were you "out", might I ask?'

No, you may not ask, Jane wanted to reply, but she knew that any cheeky retort would earn her a severe reprimand. Instead, she said calmly, 'Just out for a drive, Mrs Rowley. Miss Annabel took a wrong turning in the dark.'

'She shouldn't be out in the dark on her own.'

'She wasn't on her own. I was with her.'

Mrs Rowley rolled her eyes. 'And a fat lot of good you'd have been if there'd been any trouble.'

'What sort of trouble, Mrs Rowley?'

The cook said no more on the subject, contenting herself with a glare and a sharp, 'Get on with your work now you are here. There's a pile of washing-up to be done and Lucy's already drooping with tiredness having to do your work as well as her own while you go off gallivanting.'

For the next few hours there was no time to think, but later that night as she lay in her narrow bed in the attic room she shared with Lucy, Jane thought over the

13

problem she faced with her young mistress. She was devoted to Miss Annabel and would do anything for her – anything – but she was very afraid that what they had been doing over the past few weeks and months was about to be discovered.

Two

Annabel, too, was lying awake.

Why hadn't Gil come to meet her? Was it all over? Didn't he love her any more? Had all his ardent declarations been false?

She had first met Gilbert Radcliffe on a tour of her father's business offices near the fish docks. That day, Gilbert, as the office under-manager, had been deputed to show the boss's daughter around. At only twenty-five he held a surprisingly high position within the company and was well thought of by his immediate superior, the office manager, Mr Smeeton, and her father too. But Annabel was under no illusion that should their secret meetings over the weeks since then be discovered, the young man would no longer be held in such high esteem. Ambrose had big plans for his daughter and they did not include marriage to one of his employees.

Ambrose Constantine was a self-made man. He had been born in one of the poorer areas of the town, the third son of a deck hand on trawlers. He, too, had begun his working life at sea as a deckie-learner, but Ambrose was ambitious. He soon worked his way up to the position of Mate, working hard and enduring the vicious conditions of life at sea to earn good money and save every penny he could. Oh, how he saved his money. But by the time he was twenty, his father and two older brothers had been lost at sea. Broken-hearted,

15

his mother died the following year, leaving Ambrose alone, though the loss of his family only hardened his determination to succeed. He left the sea and became a fish merchant and by the age of twenty-four was employing ten men in the fish docks. He first saw Sarah Armstrong across the aisle of a church, when they were both attending a funeral in late May 1874. She was no beauty, but she was tall and walked with a haughty grace that appealed to Ambrose. She had a strong face and a determined set to her chin. At the gathering in a nearby hotel after the service, Ambrose contrived an introduction to her and found himself gazing into her dark blue eyes and wanting to know all about her.

'How do you know Mr Wheeler?' he began, referring to the deceased, whose coffin they had just watched being lowered ceremoniously into the earth.

'I didn't know him well, but I've accompanied my father today. He used to do business with him and felt he should pay his respects.'

'So – is your father in the fish trade?'

Sarah had laughed. 'No, no, he's a farmer, but he met Mr Wheeler on market days.' Abraham Wheeler had been an auctioneer throughout Lincolnshire, conducting sales of anything from fish to sheep and cows.

Curious about the fair-haired, stocky young man who, she knew, had deliberately sought an introduction to her, Sarah asked, 'And you? How do you know him?'

'The fish markets.' He smiled. 'He was very helpful to me when I started out.'

'And where have you finished up?'

'Oh, I haven't finished yet, not by a long way.'

Sarah's eyes gleamed as she heard the fire of ambition in his tone. She liked that. She had always bemoaned

16

the fact that she'd been born a girl; men could do so much more with their lives than women, who seemed destined to be wives and mothers and housekeepers. Her father's farm would one day be hers – she was an only child – yet she had no interest in the land. Every summer brought her hay fever misery and even getting too close to a horse could set her sneezing. Each June she spent time near the sea, which seemed to ease her symptoms.

Crossing her fingers at the lie she was about to tell, she said boldly, 'I'm coming to stay in Cleethorpes next week.' She paused, knowing instinctively that he would suggest a meeting. And he did.

Their romance – if it could be called that – progressed swiftly, much to Sarah's parents' dismay. It was more a meeting of like minds, of shared ambition, than a passionate love affair.

'I don't like it,' Edward Armstrong said to his wife, Martha. 'And I don't like *him*. But what can I do? I've talked to her, pleaded with her, even raged at her, but she's set on marrying the fellow. She's twenty-one next month and I suppose if they're really in love . . .'

Martha had put her arms around her husband and laid her dark head against his chest. 'Is it because of the farm, my dear?'

'Only partly. I wanted to pass it down the generations.'

As she heard the heavy sigh deep in his chest, Martha had raised her head and said, with a twinkle in her violet eyes: 'Never mind, perhaps Sarah will give you a grandson who will one day take over Meadow View Farm.'

But Sarah had only given them a granddaughter, Annabel, and it was on her that Edward now pinned all his hopes. He had never agreed with the belief that genteel young ladies should spend their time drawing, painting, sewing and playing the piano. Instead, he had instructed his daughter, Sarah, in the basic rudiments of accountancy and had introduced her to the precarious delights of buying and selling shares. At the time, he could not have foreseen that her quick mind and intuitive head for business, together with all that he had taught her, would equip Sarah not for running the farm as he had hoped but for helping her husband run his growing business.

Grudgingly, Edward was forced to admit that Ambrose was a clever and successful man. In 1883, Ambrose had been the first owner of a steam trawler and by the time Annabel reached adulthood, he was the biggest steam trawler owner in the Grimsby docks. Seeing that Sarah was well provided for by her prosperous husband, Edward made his will in favour of his granddaughter, leaving his five hundred-acre farm in the Lincolnshire wolds to her. One day it would all belong to Annabel, but for the moment, Edward and his wife remained in good health and continued to run Meadow View Farm themselves. And on her frequent visits, Edward delighted in the young girl's intelligence and her capacity for learning quickly. He was heartened that she seemed to possess nothing of the ruthless ambition of her father and – it had to be said – of her mother. She soon knew all the farmhands by their first names and, as a youngster, played with their children. But it was when riding on horseback around the fields with her grandfather that Annabel's face shone and she chattered with a multitude of questions. In turn, Edward was thrilled by the girl's enthusiasm and growing love for the land. His farm would be in safe hands and he began to teach

Annabel, too, the rudiments of bookkeeping and the ups and downs of the stock market. He introduced her to the stockbroker he used in Thorpe St Michael, Henry Parker, and together the two men guided and schooled the young girl until she was old enough to deal for herself.

What Edward didn't know – and for a long time neither did Ambrose – was that it was on these journeys to visit her grandparents that Annabel and Gilbert Radcliffe began to meet. Only Jane knew and now the burden of knowledge was too great for the young maid to endure. But she need not have worried that she would be questioned or even blamed; word had already reached Ambrose from his office manager, who had heard the gossip and noticed that his young protégé's absences from work coincided with Miss Annabel's visits to her grandparents.

Ambrose had acted swiftly.

'Father, I'd like to pay a visit to the docks. It's quite some time since my last visit,' Annabel said at breakfast the following morning.

Ambrose was a familiar sight on the dockside in his dark suit and bowler hat inspecting the most recent catches laid out neatly in containers. Annabel loved The Pontoon, the covered fish market where the early morning catches were auctioned. Whenever Ambrose could be persuaded to take her with him, she stood quietly watching and marvelling at the speed of the auctioneer conducting sale after sale. He seemed to know what each of his customers would want. But, much to Annabel's disappointment as she grew older, Ambrose forbade her to go so often. He didn't like to see the fishermen eying his lovely daughter. The docks, he decreed, were no place for a lady.

'But I'm not a lady,' Annabel had argued futilely.

'Ah, but one day you will be,' had been her father's only reply.

'Of course, my dear,' Ambrose agreed smoothly now. 'What would you like to see? The ships? The fish docks? Of course, the herring girls aren't here for some months yet. I know you like to watch them, but—'

'Your offices, Father. I'd like to visit your offices.'

'Then you may come with me this morning.'

'That won't be necessary. I can make my own way there.'

'No need,' he replied, deliberately keeping his tone mild. 'I should like you to drive with me.'

Annabel had no choice but to bow her head in acquiescence.

Ambrose wanted to shout at her, to roar his disapproval of her actions, but he knew it was not the way to deal with his strong-willed daughter. The path he had chosen was far better and was already bearing fruit, if his suspicions regarding the previous evening's escapade were correct. Instead of causing a confrontation, he smiled across the table at her. 'It pleases me that you should take an interest in the business. I thought you were all set to become a farmer.' They all knew the terms of Edward's will. Ambrose's tone sobered as he said warningly, 'One day you will be a very wealthy woman. Not only will you inherit your grandfather's farm, but also my company. You do understand that, don't you?'

Annabel smiled. 'But not for many years yet, I hope, Father.'

'I hope not, but your grandparents are both in their sixties. Just remember that. And now' – he rose from the table – 'I have a little paperwork to do, but I'll be ready to leave in about an hour.'

Ambrose closed the door of his study and went to stand before the window looking out on to the garden behind the house. He was pensive for a few moments before sitting down at his desk, picking up his pen and beginning to write a letter.

Dear Lord Fairfield . . .

When they arrived at her father's offices, not far from where the dock tower stood guardian over the forest of masts and funnels as the trawlers jostled for position to unload their catches, Annabel hurried to the manager's office. She knew that Gilbert occupied a desk in the same room. Ambrose followed his daughter at a more leisurely pace, deliberately allowing her to go ahead of him. A small smile played on his lips. In the outer office sat a middle-aged man at a desk and in the corner a young woman tapped at a typewriter.

'Good morning,' Annabel greeted them both and then turned to the older man. 'Is G— Mr Radcliffe in?'

The man blinked, but before he could answer the door to the inner office was flung open and Mr Smeeton, the manager, appeared.

'Ah, Miss Constantine, please come in. Is your father with you?'

'Yes, he's coming.'

She moved quickly into his office and glanced around. There was no sign of Gilbert. Neither was there any sign of his desk on the far side of the room where it had once stood.

'Please sit down,' Mr Smeeton said kindly. 'Would you like some tea?'

'No, no, thank you. Mr Smeeton—?' she began urgently, but her question was interrupted by the sound of voices in the outer office. The door opened again and her father entered the room. Annabel cast a beseeching glance at Mr Smeeton, but said no more.

'Good morning, Smeeton.'

'Sir.' Mr Smeeton gave a tiny deferential bow towards his employer and moved a chair for him to sit down.

Ambrose looked about him and asked casually, 'No Radcliffe this morning?'

'No, sir. He – um – he's left.'

A startled gasp escaped Annabel, but with amazing self-control she bit back her question. Instead, it was Ambrose who raised his eyebrows and said, 'Really? That was rather sudden, wasn't it?'

'Very sudden, sir. He didn't even stay to work out his notice.'

'How come?' Ambrose asked quite calmly, laying his hat and cane on Mr Smeeton's desk and pulling off his gloves whilst Annabel watched and listened with growing alarm. She gripped the arms of the chair and bit down hard on her lower lip.

'It seems,' Mr Smeeton went on, 'that he came into a sum of money very unexpectedly and he's – um – used it to emigrate to America, I believe.'

'Emigrate?' Annabel gasped, no longer able to keep silent. Nor could she stop the colour rising in her face. Gilbert gone? Without a word to her? 'For how long?'

Mr Smeeton avoided meeting her gaze. 'I presume for good, Miss Constantine.'

'But what about—?' she began, but managed to stop the words just in time. Instead, she finished rather lamely, 'his family?'

'I don't think he has much in the way of family. His

22

parents are dead. He has one brother, I believe . . .'

Out of the corner of her eye, she saw her father frown and Mr Smeeton added hastily, 'But I don't even know where he lives. I understand they never saw much of each other.'

Annabel dared not say more, dared not ask any more questions – not in front of her father. But somehow, some time, she would interrogate Mr Smeeton further.

'Now, my dear,' Ambrose said smoothly, 'you said you wanted to look around the docks.'

'Of course, Father,' she said meekly and rose, though she found her legs were trembling. She felt faint with shock. Gilbert had gone, had left her without a word.

'Are you all right Miss Constantine?' Mr Smeeton asked gently, with genuine concern. He had noticed how the girl had flushed on hearing the news about Gilbert Radcliffe, but now she had turned very pale.

Annabel lifted her chin. 'I am perfectly well, thank you, Mr Smeeton. Now, Father, where shall we begin?'

Three

Annabel endured a cold walk around the docks, trying to show an interest as her father pointed out the ships he owned, pausing now and again to speak to a skipper, asking if the morning's catch had been good. Then they walked to the market. Most of the day's trading was coming to an end already, but Ambrose rubbed his hands gleefully when he heard that the fish landed that morning had fetched a good price.

'A good morning's work,' her father murmured and Annabel could not know that the satisfaction behind his words had far more significance than the good catch and the price it had fetched. 'And now we'll go home for lunch, my dear.'

Ambrose led the way towards the brougham, driven by Billy, without giving her any further chance to speak to the office manager or even to the two people in the outer office; perhaps they knew something.

How was she to find out?

Back at home, she went towards the staircase, with the excuse of changing from her outdoor clothes, but as soon as her father's study door had closed behind him, she picked up her skirts and went swiftly towards the door leading to the kitchens.

'Where's Jane?' she demanded of Mrs Rowley.

'Oh, Miss Annabel, you made me jump. Jane, you say? She's upstairs cleaning the mistress's bedroom.'

Annabel whirled round and ran upstairs, bursting into her mother's bedroom unannounced. 'Jane—' she began but then realized that the maid, who was making the bed, was not alone in the room.

Sarah Constantine turned in her seat at the dressing table. 'Whatever's the matter, Annabel? Is the place on fire?'

'I'm sorry, Mother.'

'A little more decorum wouldn't come amiss for a young lady in your position.'

'My – position?' Annabel frowned. 'What do you mean, Mother?'

Mrs Constantine turned away but held her daughter's gaze through the mirror. 'Your father is determined to launch you into society. His earnest desire is to have you presented at court.'

Annabel gasped and sank down into a chair. 'Presented! To the Queen? But don't you have to know someone who's previously been presented for them to act as a – a, well, whatever they call it?'

'A sponsor. So I believe, but your father is working on that,' Sarah said calmly and now, avoiding eye contact with her daughter, she omitted to say exactly what else her husband was scheming. 'What was it you wanted Jane for?'

'I – er – um – just wondered if she'd be free this afternoon to go out.'

'Of course,' Sarah said blandly. 'As long as you're not late for dinner again.'

'No, I won't be. I promise.'

'By the way, your grandmother has written to ask if you'd like to spend Easter with them. Shall I reply that you would?'

Normally, such an invitation would have delighted

Annabel, but now her mind was filled with where Gilbert was and what could have happened to him. 'Yes – yes, of course I'd love to go,' she said half-heartedly. As she turned away to leave the room, she didn't see her mother's grim expression through the mirror as she watched her go.

But Jane saw it.

'We're going to be in such trouble, Miss Annabel,' Jane said, as she climbed into the chaise beside her mistress whilst Billy held the horse's head. 'You should have seen the look on your mother's face this morning after you left the room. Something's up. I reckon they know.'

'How can they possibly know? We've been so careful.'

'Your family's very well known in these parts and it's likely that maybe someone's seen us. Besides, there's all them men at the docks that work for him. You know how gossip gets around.'

'I can guess,' Annabel murmured, as she took up the reins and Billy let go of the horse. 'All I want to find out is where he's gone and – more importantly – why.'

Jane held on to the side of the vehicle as the horse gathered speed, trotting down the short drive, out of the gate and along the road. 'Where are we going, Miss Annabel?'

'Back to the fish dock. I need to see Mr Smeeton.'

'I don't think you should do that. He'll tell your father.'

'There's always that chance,' Annabel had to admit.

'And if you ask him not to,' Jane said sensibly, 'then he'll smell a rat and be all the more suspicious. And then – he *will* tell him.' And she'd probably be sacked,

Jane thought, when they found out she'd been going along with all this, but she didn't voice her fears aloud.

'Then I won't ask him that.'

'But what excuse are you going to make for visiting the offices again? You were only there this morning. *And* you're going without your father this time.'

'I've got you with me.'

'That's what worries me,' Jane said dolefully.

Annabel laughed and patted her maid's hand. 'Don't worry. I'll look after you.'

But who is looking after you? Jane wanted to say. I do my best, but you're a difficult little madam to control when you want to do something. But she held her tongue and concentrated on clinging on as her mistress flicked the reins and the horse went faster.

As she drew the chaise to a halt in front of the offices bearing the name Ambrose Constantine, Annabel turned to face Jane. 'Now, just go along with anything I say.'

'Yes, Miss Annabel,' Jane said meekly, feeling very anxious. Her stomach was churning with nerves. She was sure that, this time, there'd be trouble. Yet she followed Annabel into the building and to the manager's office.

The older male clerk, sitting at one of the desks in the outer office, rose as the two young women entered. In the corner the female typist looked up and smiled.

'Good morning, Mr Mabbott. I wondered if I might have a word with your typist?'

The man blinked and glanced at the woman whose eyes widened. 'Might I ask why, Miss Constantine?'

Annabel smiled winningly. 'Of course you may. I'm very interested in young women in the workplace and I wondered if Miss –' She paused and Mr Mabbott said helpfully, 'Tate.'

'– if Miss Tate would be kind enough to answer one or two questions.'

Mr Mabbott turned towards the typist and raised his eyebrows in question.

She inclined her head. 'Of course.'

'How very kind of you.' Annabel smiled, drawing off her gloves and sitting down in a chair opposite Miss Tate.

'Does your father know about this?' Mr Mabbott asked.

'No, but I'm sure he wouldn't mind.' Annabel put her head on one side coquettishly. 'He's always saying I should learn about the business that is one day going to be mine.'

The man seemed to be facing a dilemma. 'I – I'd ask Mr Smeeton, but he's not here at the moment.'

Annabel waved her hand airily. 'No matter, I wouldn't want to cause any trouble for either of you.' She took a small notebook and a silver pencil from the embroidered reticule she carried and smiled at the girl. 'Now, tell me how you came to work here? It's unusual to have women working in offices, isn't it, though I read that the Government have employed female typists for a few years now?' Miss Tate was quite a plain-looking young woman, but smart in a black tailored costume, a white blouse and with her hair pulled severely back from her face into a bun. She wore no adornment of any kind – no jewellery, not even a pretty piece of lace at her collar. She was unassuming and quiet, but it seemed to Annabel that she was efficient in her work. 'Did you have to undertake any training?' Annabel prodded her pencil towards the black typewriter. 'I notice that you type very fast and use all your fingers. Tell me, how did you learn to do that?'

As if now satisfied that the reason Annabel had given for her visit was genuine, Mr Mabbott excused himself from the room. 'I'll go for my lunch now and leave you to it.' As he left, Jane sat down in his chair, marvelling at Annabel's ingenuity. She would even have fooled Jane if the girl hadn't known of the ulterior motive.

'Now he's gone,' Annabel said, leaning towards the girl and lowering her voice, 'tell me, what is it like working with men? I presume there are no other female office workers here?'

'No – just me. It's all right really. They're very courteous and considerate.'

'All of them?'

'Yes, especially Mr Radcliffe, but he's gone now.'

'Who was he?' Annabel asked with wide-eyed innocence and Jane stifled nervous laughter.

'The under-manager. He was ever so nice, but – but he left very suddenly only last week.'

'Did he?' Annabel was still managing to keep her tone casual. 'Do you know why?'

The girl pursed her lips and glanced towards Jane. 'Not – really.'

Annabel lowered her voice. 'Anything you say to me, Miss Tate, is in complete confidence. And you can trust Jane. She's completely loyal to me.'

'There was a big row,' Miss Tate whispered, nodding her head towards the door that led into the manager's office. 'Raised voices. We could hear every word.'

'Really? What were they saying?'

Miss Tate pressed her lips together primly. 'Oh, I don't think I should repeat anything I heard, Miss Constantine. Not even to you. It wouldn't be right. I was told when I first got this job that I must never repeat anything I heard in the office.'

'Quite right,' Annabel said promptly. 'I apologize for asking. But you say the upshot of this argument was that this – er – Mr Radcliffe, was it?'

Miss Tate nodded.

'– has left the company?'

'He went that very day. That minute. He stormed out of the office' – she jerked her head towards the door into the manager's room – 'and we haven't seen him since.'

'Where's he gone?'

Miss Tate shrugged. 'Rumour has it that he's gone to America.'

'I – see,' Annabel murmured and was thoughtful for a moment. She realized that Miss Tate wasn't going to tell her any more – even if she knew more – but she had to round off her questioning by getting back to the supposed subject.

'So, tell me a little more about the training you had to do.'

They talked for a further ten minutes by which time Mr Mabbott appeared and Annabel stood up, closing her notebook. 'Thank you, Miss Tate; that was most informative. And thank you, Mr Mabbott, for allowing me to take up her time.'

'Our pleasure, Miss Annabel.' He held the door for Annabel and Jane to leave. When they were safely out of earshot, he rounded on Miss Tate. 'What did she ask you and what did you tell her?'

The girl blinked and stammered, 'Just – just about my job and what training I'd needed. That sort of thing.'

'Anything else?' he almost barked at her.

Miss Tate flinched but she returned his gaze steadily. Some instinct made her keep quiet about Miss Annabel's other questions. For her own sake Miss Tate didn't want her superior to think she had been gossiping and she also had the feeling that Miss Annabel's interest in the young and handsome Gilbert Radcliffe was a little more than casual.

'No, Mr Mabbott,' she answered him calmly. 'Just about my work.'

The man grunted and turned away to sit down at his desk whilst the girl began to tap away at her typewriter once more. She was sorry not to have felt able to help Miss Annabel further – she looked nice. The quarrel had indeed been about Mr Constantine's daughter – her name had been mentioned – but Miss Tate had not dared reveal what she'd overheard. The young typist had to protect her own position in a world of men. One foot wrong and she would be dismissed.

Just as Mr Radcliffe had been.

Four

'I wonder if I should see Mr Smeeton?' Annabel murmured aloud as they sat for a few moments in the chaise.

'No, Miss Annabel, please don't. He would definitely tell your father. And besides, you might get that poor girl into trouble.' Jane was sensitive to a fellow employee's position. 'I think she's already told you more than she should have done.'

'Perhaps you're right,' Annabel conceded. She sighed and picked up the reins. As they drove out of the yard, the tears began to flow and once they were well away from the docks, Annabel pulled the horse-drawn vehicle to a halt and began to cry in earnest. 'He's gone, hasn't he? Left me without even saying "goodbye" – without even telling me. All those declarations of true love – he didn't mean a word, did he?'

Jane put her arms around her young mistress and Annabel clung to her. She was mystified and bereft. Gilbert Radcliffe had been so kind, so circumspect. No doubt her parents would have been horrified that she was meeting one of her father's employees in secret, but Gilbert had never asked for anything more than a chaste kiss, a touching of hands and all the while Jane had been just out of sight but always in earshot. She had done nothing to be ashamed of, Annabel told herself.

32

'Don't upset yourself so, Miss Annabel, please. Just let's get home. If we're late again . . .'

With a supreme effort, Annabel sat up, dried her eyes and took up the reins once more. When they arrived home, Jane said, 'Come in through the kitchen and up the back stairs. And if anyone asks what's the matter' – Annabel's face was still blotchy from weeping – 'I'll tell them we had a bit of a scare in the chaise and it upset you.'

Annabel laughed, but there was a note of hysteria in the sound. 'You're getting inventive with your fibs.'

Jane grinned and dared to say, 'I've had a good teacher. Now, come on or else you won't be ready for dinner.'

'What's up with her?' Mrs Rowley wanted to know as Annabel hurried through the kitchen to the staircase the servants used.

'Nothing really. We had a bit of an incident. Nearly tipped the chaise over and it shook us both up. I'll make some tea and take her a cup.'

'Very well,' the cook agreed reluctantly, 'but come straight back down. There's work for you to do in the kitchen and Mrs Constantine will need you in about half an hour.'

'Yes, Mrs Rowley,' Jane said docilely and breathed a sigh of relief.

By the time Roland Walmsley sounded the gong for dinner, Annabel had managed to compose herself and appeared at the table with a smile plastered on her face. She was careful to talk as animatedly as she always did.

When Jane had come to help her finish dressing for dinner, Annabel had confided, 'Jane, I'm going to tell them where we've been this afternoon – that I was intrigued by Miss Tate and wanted to talk to her.'

'Oh miss, do you think you should? Your father—'

'If Mr Mabbott tells Mr Smeeton that I visited and then Mr Smeeton tells my father – as he surely would – it'll be far worse for us than if I tell him myself. By so doing I'll – what's the phrase? – take the wind out of his sails.'

There had never been a rule of silence at the table in the Constantine household, even when they did not have company to dine. Ambrose took the opportunity to quiz his wife, and particularly his daughter, on what they had been doing and often the conversation centred on the business. Sarah was still heavily involved and often visited the offices herself to look over the books. So, as the meal began, Annabel said brightly, 'Father, I hope you don't mind. I went back to your office this afternoon.'

Ambrose seemed unsurprised. 'Oh,' he said smoothly, 'and why was that?'

'When we were there this morning,' her hand shook slightly as she drank her soup, but she continued bravely with the story she had concocted and played out, 'I was so interested to see a young woman working in your offices. A typist. I wanted to find out more about her.'

'And did you?'

'Only about the kind of work she did and what training she'd undertaken – that sort of thing. She was very firm that she couldn't divulge anything confidential – and she didn't.'

'I'm pleased to hear it.'

'Why have you employed a young woman in your offices? It's unusual, isn't it?'

Ambrose wrinkled his forehead. 'A couple of years

ago I heard that the Treasury had experimented with women typists and they'd proved efficient and economical.'

'Economical? How do you mean?'

Ambrose smiled. 'We don't pay women the same rate as men.'

Annabel stared at her father, railing against the unfairness of it all. But, just now, she did not dare to cause an argument. Instead, she murmured, 'I see.' She paused and then added, 'You didn't mind, Father, did you? Miss Tate won't get into trouble, will she? I wouldn't want that to happen on my account.'

'Of course not. It sounds as if the young woman handled herself admirably. But in future, I'd be glad if you didn't undertake such trips on your own. Either your mother or I ought to be with you.'

In an unguarded moment, Annabel answered, 'I wasn't alone. Jane was with me.'

Ambrose frowned and glanced at his wife. 'I think perhaps our daughter is spending too much time with servants. We should endeavour to help her mix with young people of her own class.'

'I quite agree, Ambrose,' Sarah said. 'We must increase our efforts to arrange for her to be presented at Court. I have heard from Sir William's wife that she would be delighted to act as sponsor for Annabel. She has already put Annabel's name forward. As soon as we hear something, we can begin making arrangements.'

Sir William Carruthers had been a great supporter of Ambrose when the young man had been fighting his way in the world of business and both he and his wife, Cynthia, were Annabel's godparents. Ambrose smiled. 'And haven't your parents asked Annabel to stay with them over Easter? Perhaps it would be better for her to go there now since she has nothing better to do than ride around the countryside in the company of a servant girl and involve herself with one of my employees.' Annabel gasped and knew that the colour had drained from her face. Had her father found out about her trysts with Gilbert? But at his next words she breathed more easily. 'I don't think a typist is the sort of person you should be encouraging.'

'But, I didn't, Father. I merely—'

Ambrose held up his hand to silence her. 'Enough. The matter is closed.'

The meal continued without further conversation and Annabel found her appetite had completely deserted her.

Five

A week later, Billy, driving the brougham, took Annabel to her grandparents' home in the Lincolnshire wolds. This time, Jane had not been allowed to accompany her.

Annabel sat rigidly upright, determined not to let her inner misery show. There had been no word from Gilbert and she had been unable to find out any more. All she knew was that he had had a huge quarrel with his immediate superior at work, had either been dismissed or had walked out, and that, allegedly, he had gone abroad, financed by an unexpected windfall. But she couldn't get him out of her mind; his fair curly hair, his merry blue eyes and the sweet promises he had whispered. By the time the carriage drew into the farmyard, Annabel could not stop the tears from flowing. She fell into her grandfather's arms.

'There, there, my lovely,' Edward Armstrong held her close, 'tell your old gramps what ails you. Come along in. Your granny's waiting with a nice dinner for you. Les will bring your trunk into the house and upstairs to your room.'

Here in the countryside, dinner was the midday meal. Farm labourers who worked from first light needed a substantial meal by then. Tea or supper was taken in the late afternoon or the early evening. Sometimes both. Tea would be at five o'clock in Edward and Martha

Armstrong's house and maybe a light supper at nine o'clock after which they would soon retire to bed, for they rose at six every morning, summer and winter.

Edward Armstrong was in his mid-sixties, a burly, well-built man, still strong and muscular for his age. He had worked hard all his life and continued to do so even now when most folk of his age would be putting their feet up in front of the fire. And he still had quite a head of hair, though it was grey, turning to white, now.

Annabel dried her eyes and smiled wanly at Les Tindall. She had played with Les and his younger sister since she'd been a child and now she could see the anxiety in his eyes when he saw her tears.

'I'm fine,' she tried to reassure both men, but her voice trembled and she knew she had not convinced either of them. Les said nothing as he started to unload her trunk. Edward, his arm around her shoulders, led her into the house where her grandmother waited with arms stretched wide in welcome.

Later, after the evening meal, as they sat together before the roaring fire in the kitchen range, Martha took Annabel's hand, her look warm and loving. 'Now, my dear, we can see you're troubled. Won't you tell us? You know we will keep your confidence.'

Annabel stared into her grandmother's lovely dark violet eyes; eyes that were so like her own. Now, the once black hair had turned white and wrinkles lined Martha's face, but her loving nature still shone in her face and a smile rarely left her lips. Had life not pitched her into the class of society it had, Martha could have taken the London Season by storm and, no doubt, would have had a string of suitors. But she had wanted nothing more out of life other than to marry the man she adored, work side by side with him on the farm and bring up their family. They both loved children and had hoped to have a large family but only one child, Sarah, had come along. After her birth, which had been a difficult one, Edward had been advised that there should be no more. Their hopes had been centred on their only daughter; they wanted her to marry a farmer and one day run the farm. But that day had never come, nor would it; Sarah had hated the country life, not seeing beyond the cold, the wet and the long, arduous hours for little return. Her eyes and her heart were closed to the joy of tilling the earth, of watching growth and rebirth every season. She couldn't appreciate animal husbandry nor find contentment, at the end of a long working day, in watching a glorious sunset. Her sole ambition was to rise in the world and she had spurned the simple life. The meeting between Sarah and Ambrose Constantine had brought together two ruthlessly ambitious minds and now their sole endeavour was to see their daughter married into the upper echelons of society. It was a plan of which Edward and Martha were, as yet, unaware.

'I know,' Annabel whispered in reply. 'But – but you might think badly of me.'

'Never,' Edward declared and Martha even chuckled. 'Whatever it is, my dear, we will stand by you. There's always a home here with us. You know that.'

Annabel bit her lip and decided that she could confide in them. 'I – I've been meeting a young man, Gilbert, who is – was – employed as under-manager in Father's offices.' She hesitated and then took a deep breath. 'In secret.'

The two elderly people glanced at each other, but they didn't seem surprised. 'Why in secret?' Edward asked.

'Because Father wouldn't approve.'

'Why not? What's wrong with him – the young man, I mean?'

Annabel smiled wryly. 'He's not high enough up the social ladder, Gramps.'

Edward made a noise that sounded suspiciously like a snort of contempt. 'And who does he want you to marry? Lord Somebody-or-Other, I suppose.'

'I wouldn't be at all surprised.'

'And this young man?' Martha prompted. 'How did you meet him?'

'Father sometimes takes me to the docks and I met Gilbert on one of those visits. He took me round, showed me everything. He was so kind and courteous and when the visit ended, he asked if he might call on me. I – I said I would meet him somewhere as I wasn't sure what Father would say – although, of course, I did know *exactly* what would be said – by both Father and Mother. But I didn't want to hurt Gilbert's feelings.'

'Wouldn't it have been kinder to have refused him there and then?' Martha said gently.

Annabel sighed. 'I liked him, Gran. Really liked him – I still do – but I've never been allowed to mix with other young people – not girls or boys. I – I suppose I was bowled over by his – attentions.'

'Aw, lass, you haven't got yourself into trouble, have you?' Edward asked, with a break in his voice.

Annabel shook her head and said firmly, 'No, Gramps, I may be a silly young girl whose head has been turned by the first man to pay compliments to her, but I'm not stupid. He kissed me – yes – but that was all. I promise.'

Edward sighed with obvious relief. 'In your father's eyes, I expect even that would be bad enough. Just be careful, love, there's a good girl.'

Tears sprang to Annabel's eyes as she blurted out, 'Gilbert's gone and I can't find out what's happened to him.'

'What do you mean – gone?'

'He was supposed to meet me a week ago but he never came. The next day I went to the office with Father but Gilbert wasn't there. I went again on my own – well, not quite on my own; Jane was with me.'

'Where is Jane? She usually comes with you.'

Annabel grimaced. 'She wasn't allowed to this time.'

'That's a pity,' Martha murmured. 'I think Les is rather sweet on her and she's such a help to me in the kitchen.'

'And what happened on your second visit?' Edward prompted and Annabel recounted the details ending, 'The rumour is that he had a big row with the office manager – Mr Smeeton – that he came into some money unexpectedly, and that he's gone to America. He – he could have said "goodbye" even if he wanted to end our – our friendship.'

She saw the glance that passed between her grand-parents and the little nod that Martha gave. Edward took Annabel's other hand into his huge, calloused paw. She was comforted by his warm touch as he said softly, 'We guessed you were meeting someone sometimes when you stayed with us.'

Annabel's tears flowed again. 'Oh, I'm sorry. I – I shouldn't have deceived you.'

'You didn't. You're a grown young woman and have every right to come and go as you please. We trusted you and besides, Jane was always with you.'

Martha chuckled. 'We didn't have chaperones, did we, Edward?' The old man's eyes twinkled. 'Indeed, we didn't.' The love still flowed between the elderly couple and Annabel smiled, heartened to see it. How she longed for that same devotion from a man she could love in return. Her chin trembled again. 'But you think he's gone away, don't you? That – that he doesn't want to see me again?'

Her grandfather was silent for a moment before saying slowly, 'I'd like to know what that quarrel in the office was about. And where this "unexpected" windfall came from.'

'Miss Tate wouldn't say. I've no doubt she feared for her job if she divulged too much and I wouldn't have wanted to put that in jeopardy. I just wish—'

'He'd let you know himself,' Martha finished the sentence for her and Annabel nodded.

'Perhaps, my lovely, he wasn't able to,' Edward said soberly.

Annabel drew in a breath and gazed at him, wide-eyed with fear. 'You don't think something's happened to him?'

'No, no, I didn't mean that. I should have said, perhaps he wasn't *allowed* to get in touch with you.'

'You mean by Mr Smeeton?'

'No, I was thinking of your father.'

'Father!' Annabel knew only too well about her father's ambitions for her, that she should marry well and produce a grandson, who would one day inherit his company. That was why she'd feared he would not look kindly on a liaison between his daughter and one of his employees. If he had somehow found out about her meetings with Gilbert, then why hadn't he confronted her? She couldn't believe he would be so devious as to dismiss Gilbert and prevent him from even saying goodbye to her.

Again the two older people exchanged a glance, then

Edward went on, 'Annabel, your parents are both – though it grieves me to say it about my own daughter – ruthlessly ambitious and, now, perhaps not only for themselves.' He was speaking slowly, thoughtfully, as if only just coming to the realization himself. He sighed. 'Your granny and I married for love. She could have done so much better for herself than an impoverished farmer's son.'

'Tut, tut, Edward,' Martha frowned, but her merry eyes were twinkling, 'perish the thought.'

'And,' Edward went on, 'we wanted the same for our daughter and though it pained us that she took no interest in the farm and all that we had worked so hard to build up for her, we still wanted her to follow her heart's desire. We believed that that was your father, but –' he sighed heavily – 'I believe now that their union came about more because of a mutual desire for advancement in the world than because they were deeply in love.'

Annabel thought about her own life. How she had had governesses at home, how she had been sent to an expensive finishing school, how she was not allowed to cultivate friends of her own age unless they were from well-to-do families. And that didn't happen very often because those same families wanted nothing to do with 'new money' or 'trade'. It was very hard for anyone to climb up through the levels of a class-ridden society. But Ambrose Constantine would die trying.

'So you think,' Annabel whispered, 'that Father found out about Gilbert and had him dismissed and sent away.'

'It wouldn't surprise me, though we'll probably never be able to prove it.'

'And Gilbert? Surely he could have written to me?'

'Maybe he was – encouraged' – Edward hesitated to

43

use the word 'threatened'; he didn't want to turn the girl completely against her own father, although he did believe she should see him for exactly what he was – 'to go at once and not to contact you again.'

'Then he was rather weak, wasn't he?'

Edward touched her cheek in a fond gesture. 'Not everyone has your strength of character, my lovely. You are hurt now, but trust me, you will get over it.'

Annabel leaned her head against his broad chest. 'I wish I could stay here for ever.'

Edward stroked her hair tenderly. 'Your father would never allow it. But you're here now and whilst you are, I'm going to teach you everything about the farm that will one day be yours.'

Annabel raised her head and looked up into his face. 'Will you? Will you really? I'd love that, because whatever happens, I'll always have the farm. I'll never let it go, I promise you.'

Edward kissed her forehead in thankfulness. His lifetime of hard work – and Martha's too – had not been in vain after all.

Six

Over the next three weeks whilst Annabel stayed at Meadow View Farm, she spent her time immersed in learning even more about the farm. Edward showed her the diaries he had kept for years, each marking the activities on the farm – when to plough, to sow and to reap and all the statistics of crop yield that followed. He had noted when it was lambing time, when his cows calved and the subsequent milk quantities each animal produced.

'It's all here, Annabel. The good years and the bad are all noted. And you do get bad years, we all do, through inclement weather that spoils the crops or a disease that hits our animals. Farming is a precarious business and it's hard, grinding work that never ends, but it's a good life that has its own rewards.'

Edward had always had a head for figures and his one 'vice', as he always termed it, had been to gamble on the stock market. He had introduced Sarah to trading and, five years ago, he'd shown Annabel the ledgers he kept with his gains and losses again faithfully recorded. 'I have a stockbroker in town,' he'd confided, 'and each market day I visit him and we discuss what we should sell or buy. It's instinct as much as anything, Annabel. Here –' he'd pulled down a new ledger from the shelf above his head in the small room at the back of the farmhouse which he had as his farm office – 'I'll set you off with ten pounds and next week when we go into town, I'll introduce you to Mr Henry Parker and you can begin to trade on the stock exchange though, of course, at first all your dealings will have to be in my name.'

'But what if I lose your money, Gramps?' the young fifteen-year-old girl had worried.

Edward had chuckled. 'You won't. We'll help you.'

The following week Annabel had been introduced to the kindly middle-aged man who, with her grandfather, would guide her. Sitting with Edward in Mr Parker's office, she'd said, 'But once I have to go home, I won't be near enough to see Mr Parker regularly, will I?'

Henry Parker had smiled over his spectacles at her. 'You can follow the stock market prices in your father's newspaper and write your instructions to me, always making it clear at what price you want to buy or sell, just in case there should be a fluctuation before your letter reaches me. We do, of course, charge a commission on every transaction, you realize that?'

Annabel had nodded, excitement rising in her. Here was something she could have as an interest of which surely even her father would not disapprove. Her grandfather's next words dispelled any lingering doubt. 'I taught your mother when she was about your age. I don't know if she has kept it up.'

'Now I remember that,' Henry put in. 'She used to come here with you. I was a young office boy then, but I remember it clearly.' He beamed. 'And now it'll be my pleasure to help you, Miss Annabel.'

'I think maybe she still trades,' Annabel had said. 'I see her positively devouring Father's paper when he's done with it and she gets letters from a stockbroker quite frequently.'

'Then – hopefully – she will guide you too.'

To her surprise, both her mother and father had been delighted to learn of Annabel's new-found interest, though not so enamoured to hear of her love for the farm.

'It will be a good inheritance for you and your children. When the time comes, you can employ a bailiff but it is not the sort of thing a woman ought to involve herself with,' Ambrose had said firmly.

Annabel had said nothing; she had other ideas.

For the next five years, Annabel had played the part of a dutiful daughter and Ambrose had seen no reason to stop her frequent visits to her grandparents' home. He was confident of her complete obedience, until he heard about her secret meetings with Gilbert Radcliffe. That, he decided, must be stopped, though nothing was said between Ambrose and his daughter.

When Annabel arrived home again from her most recent visit to Meadow View Farm, her parents' plans for her to be presented at Court and take part in the coming London Season were well advanced.

'I have been in touch with Lady Carruthers and we are to visit her next week at her country home in Brocklesby Park.'

Sir William Carruthers had now retired from the business world and had entered parliament, securing a safe seat for the Tories. Though they still had a home in the countryside just west of Grimsby, the pair spent much of their time in a town house in London and it was there that Annabel would stay for most of the summer with her sponsor. No expense was to be spared and arrangements went ahead at an alarming rate as it dawned on Annabel that both her parents and Lady Carruthers had been planning this for some months.

'You have certainly grown into a beautiful young woman.' Lady Carruthers looked Annabel up and down. 'You will take London by storm, I am sure of it, but please don't set your sights too high on what kind of man you might ensnare. Your background goes against you, my dear.' At her side, Annabel felt her mother bristle at the insult, but, wisely, Sarah held her tongue. 'However,' Lady Carruthers went on, 'the dates for the Court Drawing Rooms held in Buckingham Palace have been announced and I have written to the Lord Chamberlain suggesting your name. He and Her Majesty go over the lists very carefully and only young women who have hitherto led a blameless life will qualify.' She eyed Annabel shrewdly. 'I presume that they will not find even the merest hint of scandal when looking into your background?'

'Certainly not,' Sarah said swiftly now, unable to bite back a sharp retort any longer. 'She has been brought up and educated to be a gentlewoman and has led a sheltered life.'

'Good. Then we must hope for a favourable reply.'

Lady Cynthia Carruthers was a petite woman in her late thirties, Annabel guessed. She had startling blue eyes – the colour of the sky on a summer's day – and her blonde hair was sleek and arranged in the latest fashion. She dressed in the finest silks and satins that her husband's money could buy. She was like a pretty, porcelain doll and yet behind the image was a steely determination and an intelligent mind. She had always been an asset to her husband in the business world and now she more than held her own in the political world. The great and good of the land clamoured to be invited to attend her soirées in London or her countryside shooting-party weekends in Lincolnshire. She had two children – both boys. The younger daughter of an earl, she had the title 'Lady Cynthia' in her own right. It was whispered that she saw very little of her own family now as they considered that she had married beneath her, even though plain William Carruthers had risen in the world and had been knighted for his services to industry. But Lady Cynthia had built her own, very respected, circle of friends and acquaintances. Ambrose had been helpful to Sir William more than once over the years they had known each other and if repayment came in the form of assisting them to achieve their dreams for their daughter, then Lady Cynthia was happy to oblige.

Years earlier, she had been presented at court and whilst she had attracted two proposals of marriage from noblemen, she had returned home to marry William Carruthers, whom she loved. The union had been much against her parents' wishes, but Cynthia was not a woman to be diverted from her own desires. Now, as she regarded Annabel, she wondered if the lovely young girl possessed that same rebellious spirit. At the moment the serene face in front of her seemed happy to comply, though the sharp-eyed Lady Cynthia was sure she detected sadness in those violet eyes. She wondered if the girl was hiding an unhappy love affair that the mother was unwilling to speak about. Or perhaps it had been a secret liaison of which the mother was not even aware.

Just before Easter, Lady Cynthia had sent word that the 'summons', as she called it, for Annabel to be presented had arrived.

We have three weeks to prepare, she wrote to Sarah,

but that is the usual time given. If you and your daughter could come to London and stay with us at our town house, we will begin at once . . .

The following weeks passed by in a flurry of planning for the big event and, much to Annabel's disappointment, she was only able to visit her grandparents once more before being swept off to London.

'Once it's all over,' she promised them, 'I'll be able to spend more time with you.'

'But what if you meet a handsome young duke who sweeps you off your feet?'

Annabel had laughed. 'Gramps, do you really think that's likely? They look for a bride amongst their own class.'

'Love can do strange things,' Martha murmured. 'And you are a beautiful and lovable girl.'

'Oh Gran!' Annabel laughed, 'You say the nicest things, but I don't think it's going to happen.'

Seven

'Now, we must have a full court dress especially made for you. For young women the bodice is cut low, with short sleeves and a train falling from the shoulders. Of course, it must be white and you should wear long white gloves and two white plumes in your hair with a veil. I'll take you to my own dressmaker. She knows all the dress regulations.'

'Regulations?' Annabel laughed. 'Are there rules as to what you can wear?'

'Very strict rules, my dear,' Cynthia said seriously. 'Just as there are definite rules about how you should conduct yourself and how the presentation takes place.' Then she smiled and waved her hand. 'Don't worry. By the time I have finished with you, you'll be perfect – every inch most suitable to captivate, at the very least, an earl.'

Annabel chuckled inwardly. She wanted to make some flippant, comical remark about ensnaring a duke, no less, but she realized that the whole process of 'coming out' was a serious business to Lady Cynthia. She had no wish to offend the lady, who was being so kind to her, so she bit back the retort and composed her face into sober, dutiful lines.

On the May afternoon when Annabel was to be presented, she was sitting in a queue of carriages on

The Mall with Lady Cynthia beside her. 'Now, can you remember everything I've told you?' Cynthia asked, seeming far more agitated than Annabel. The girl herself was serenely composed. Perhaps this was because she viewed the whole thing as rather a lark and not to be taken too seriously. The idea that she was to be paraded in some kind of marriage market amused rather than angered her. But at least, she thought ruefully, it's taking my mind off Gilbert. He had been a bitter disappointment to her. So she tried to listen attentively as Cynthia went through the procedure with her yet again.

'Once we get to the palace,' Cynthia said, fanning her face vigorously, 'and goodness knows when that's going to be – oh, do go away!' She broke off to wave angrily at the curious faces peering in through all the carriage windows to see the debutantes in their finery. 'Now, where was I? Oh yes. You'll wait in an ante-chamber with all the other girls. And I warn you, it can be dreadfully hot . . .' On and on she went until Annabel found herself not listening. Instead, she was fascinated by the crowds of people in The Mall, who were determined to be part of this special day.

Lady Cynthia had not exaggerated her warnings of the stuffiness of the room in which they had to wait.

'You'd think they'd at least give us a drink,' one girl, pressed up against Annabel, muttered. 'And my flowers are wilting already.'

Each girl carried a bouquet, a fan and a lace hand-kerchief. Annabel's posy was a small, neat arrangement, but the girl beside her had a large bouquet that she was finding difficult to manage. Annabel opened her mouth to offer to help, but at that moment she was called forward. Picking up her train and carrying it over her left arm, as Cynthia had instructed, she walked with her head held high and a slight smile on her lips out of the room, and she dropped her train to be spread out behind her by an official. Annabel was fortunate to be one of the first to be called shortly after three o'clock.

'Please remove your right glove,' the man murmured. Taking a deep breath, she walked forward into the drawing room and moved towards Queen Victoria. As she curtsied, her name was announced and she kissed the small wrinkled hand now resting in her own. She glanced up and met the eyes of the Queen and, suddenly, she understood the importance of the moment. To be received by the monarch in such glittering surroundings was indeed an honour. Annabel smiled as she rose and moved backwards with several more curtsies until she reached the door of the anteroom. So much preparation and practice had gone into what was over in a brief moment, and yet Annabel would not have missed it for the world.

'And now,' Cynthia said as their carriage headed back to her Mayfair town house, 'the Season starts in earnest. I have several invitations for you already, but tonight, we will dine quietly at home – we've both had enough excitement for one day. Tomorrow night, however, we will be attending your first three balls.'

'Three?' Annabel exclaimed. 'In one night? How do we manage that?'

Cynthia chuckled. 'It's usual to attend a dinner party and then go on to a ball. If there is more than one being held, the etiquette is to go from ball to ball, having spent about half an hour or so at each one and end up at the most prestigious. You'll see how it's done. And then,' Cynthia was not finished, 'the following day we are invited to a garden party in the late afternoon and then on Saturday night, I am hosting a dinner for you at home. I have already sent out the invitations.'

'Is there anything special I should know? I mean – regarding etiquette at all these events.' It was beginning to sound rather daunting.

Cynthia's laugh was infectious. 'My dear, for a little country mouse, you are doing remarkably well. I am very proud of you. Don't worry, I will be close at hand and keeping an eye on you. But you do realize, don't you,' her expression sobered, 'that your parents wish you to meet a suitable young man with a view to making a good marriage?'

'Oh, but –' Annabel began and then lapsed into silence. Gil was gone and she doubted he would come back. For whatever reason he had chosen not to say a proper 'goodbye' to her and for that she would never forgive him. He'd been a coward, unable to face her to end their romance, and, instead, had slunk away without a word. Annabel lifted her head with a new determination to put him out of her mind. He was not worth her tears. Whilst she wasn't yet ready to entertain thoughts of marriage, she told herself, a little fun and flirtation during the Season wouldn't hurt.

'Tomorrow morning, we are invited to breakfast at Lady Pilkington's; she lives close by. It will be a small, informal event and will introduce you nicely to what, my dear, is going to be a whirl of parties, balls and functions, so mind you get a good night's sleep whenever you can.'

Annabel was far too excited and when morning came, she felt she had hardly slept at all. But she had a strong constitution and no one would have guessed from the sparkle in her magnificent eyes that she lacked sleep as Cynthia led her into the room and introduced her to their hostess. Annabel followed Cynthia closely and copied whatever her mentor did, helping herself to eggs and muffins. There were several dishes laid out that Annabel didn't recognize, but there was one she did; pigeon set in jelly. Her grandmother made a similar dish and for a moment an acute feeling of homesickness overwhelmed her.

'Don't eat too much, my dear,' Cynthia whispered. 'We are due at Lady Mortimer's for luncheon.'

A few men were present at breakfast, but older, whiskered gentlemen, who were obviously not on Cynthia's list of possible suitors. Later, however, at the more formal luncheon timed for two o'clock, there were younger gentlemen present.

'Luncheons can be either a formal occasion – a sit-down meal served by their servants – or a buffet,' Cynthia explained. 'I think Lady Mortimer's will be the former. It usually is, but there still might not be many gentlemen present. They're often engaged in business or other duties.'

And yet, on arriving for luncheon, Cynthia seemed to be looking around the room for someone and when she didn't see whoever it was, she made a moue and murmured, 'I trust he will be at the ball tonight.'

'Who?' Annabel ventured to ask.

Cynthia waved her hand vaguely as if the absence of a particular man was of no consequence, 'Oh, just one of the young men I want to introduce you to. It doesn't matter.'

But Annabel had the distinct feeling that it mattered very much.

Eight

'Annabel, may I present James Lyndon, the Earl of Fairfield?'

The young man standing before her was undeniably handsome with brown hair and dark eyes. He was tall and slim, his head held proudly, his back straight, and he looked splendid in his smart uniform. He took the hand she extended to him and bowed over it. 'I am delighted to meet you, Miss Constantine. May I be permitted to claim a dance with you?'

After an afternoon of resting and a light dinner – just the two of them – Cynthia and Annabel had travelled to first one ball and then on to this one in a carriage, which had pulled up outside the grand, four-storey house overlooking St James's Park. Every window in the house blazed with light and the sound of music and laughter drifted down to them from a terrace at second-floor level. Annabel's dance card was almost full already, but at Cynthia's insistence, she had deliberately left a few lines unfilled. 'Just in case a young man comes along with whom you *ought* to dance.'

Receiving a slight nod of approval from her chaperone, Annabel inclined her head and began to write his name on her card.

'Perhaps I might claim the supper dance?'

Annabel's eyes widened. She believed that the supper dance, where the partners stayed together throughout the meal, was regarded as something special. It meant that the young man had serious intentions.

'I – I think we may be going on to another ball,' Annabel stammered, for the moment unsure of what was the correct thing to do. Smoothly, Cynthia stepped in as Annabel glanced at her for guidance.

'Perhaps Lord Fairfield is heading in the same direction.' She raised her well-shaped eyebrows and James Lyndon asked, 'To Lady Fortesque's?' Cynthia nodded and they smiled at each other before she turned to Annabel and advised, 'One dance here with his lordship and then he may claim the dance just before the buffet is served at Lady Fortesque's.'

James Lyndon proved to be an excellent dancer. He held her fingers lightly and guided her through the steps and when the music began for the next dance – a waltz – he put his arm around her waist and whirled her away before the gentleman, who should have been her partner for this dance, could claim her.

'We must take leave of our hostess,' Cynthia said, when the dance came to an end. 'It's time we were moving on.' She turned to James Lyndon. 'My lord, you may travel with us, if you so wish.'

James gave a little bow. 'It will be my pleasure.'

He was courtesy personified, Annabel thought, and found herself charmed not only by his handsome looks but also by his manners and his attentiveness to them both.

Lady Fortesque's ball was a far grander one than the first two they had attended that evening, but their hostess was charming and effervescent, seeming not to stand on ceremony. She was an older woman, in her late fifties, Annabel surmised, and no doubt the benefit of age allowed her to break the rules of strict etiquette if she so wished. She greeted both Cynthia and James with outstretched arms. 'My dears, how wonderful to see you both, and James, I was so very sorry to hear of your brother's untimely death. I haven't seen you since then, have I? Losing both your father and brother within two years must have put a great strain on all your family. And particularly on you, my dear boy, since you can't have expected ever to inherit the title and all the responsibilities that go with it. Will you be leaving the Army to run your estate now?'

James bowed low over the woman's hand and murmured a greeting, adding, 'Nothing has been decided yet, but I hope not. I love the Army life and I have a good bailiff to manage the estate. And, of course, my mother and my sister are always on hand.'

'Of course, and if you are blessed with good tenants, an estate almost runs itself.' Then she turned her attention to Annabel. 'And this must be your protégée, Cynthia. My dear, you are most welcome.' To Annabel's surprise Lady Fortesque kissed her on both cheeks and then linked her arm through hers. 'Now, let us see what eligible young men I can introduce you to.'

But it seemed that James Lyndon had other ideas about her meeting and dancing with other young men. When Lady Fortesque had finished parading her around the room and was called away to greet other guests arriving, she found the earl at her elbow.

'May I sign your card?' he murmured in her ear and when she handed it to him, he wrote his name across all the dances so that there were no spaces left for anyone else. Annabel looked around for Cynthia, but she was engaged in conversation with Lord Fortesque and Annabel didn't like to interrupt.

Oh well, she thought, what harm can it do, just this

once, and he was being very kind to her. And besides, she smiled to herself, he was the best-looking man in the room and she was the object of envious glances from other debutantes, who were also engaged in the rounds of parties and balls hoping to ensnare an eligible bachelor.

He guided her through the supper buffet and was courteous and attentive, as if there was no one else in the room who mattered. At the end of the evening when the carriages began to line up outside the door, James Lyndon bent over her hand, his lips brushing her fingers. 'May I be permitted to call on you tomorrow?'

Before Annabel had time to form a reply, Cynthia, hovering close by, said, 'We should be honoured, my lord.'

In the carriage on the way back home, Annabel noticed a small smile of satisfaction on her chaperone's lips.

The Earl of Fairfield was attentive and persistent. He was a guest at Cynthia's dinner held on the Saturday following Annabel's presentation at court and had been placed next to her.

'Do you ride?' he asked suddenly as the third of eight courses was being served.

'Oh yes,' Annabel replied enthusiastically. 'But I don't suppose there's much chance in the city.'

'That's where you're wrong. A favourite rendezvous during the Season is Hyde Park. You can ride on Rotten Row, or drive in a carriage or just take a stroll, meet with friends, and, no doubt, many a ball or luncheon or dinner is arranged. But it starts early. May I call for you on Monday morning?'

'But I haven't got a mount.'

James chuckled. 'Leave that to me. One does have connections being in the Army.'

Annabel would never have thought that Hyde Park could be so busy at nine o'clock on a Monday morning. Young women paraded in their finery, meeting and talking with young gentlemen, but still under the watchful eyes of a chaperone. This morning, however, Cynthia was not with her.

'I have the most dreadful headache, my dear, and if I am to be well enough to attend the party tonight, I must rest. My maid can come with you, for propriety's sake. Mind you ride up and down so that she can see you.' But once on horseback, Annabel forgot Cynthia's warning. It was wonderful to be out of doors and in the saddle once more.

'I wish we could gallop,' she said, lifting her face to the warmth of the sun.

James laughed, the sun glinting on his brown hair. 'Not possible, I'm afraid. We would likely trample someone.' His expression sobered as he looked at her seriously. 'But I would love to gallop with you in the countryside, see the wind blowing through your lovely hair and your fine eyes sparkling with excitement.'

Annabel was lost for words; she didn't know how to respond to his compliments so she merely smiled and urged her horse to go as fast as was both respectable and safe.

From that morning, James Lyndon, Earl of Fairfield, was a frequent visitor at Cynthia's home. Even Sir William, on the rare occasions when he joined them at a dinner engagement or a sporting occasion, made the young man welcome.

'I'm not one for parties and balls,' Sir William said to Annabel, explaining his absence from such events, 'but I do like my sport and of course an invitation to dine is not to be sniffed at.'

Annabel grew very fond of Sir William during the time she stayed in London. She had met him once before when he had paid a brief visit to the Constantines' home to visit her father. Several years older than his vivacious wife, he was a kindly, benevolent man who, rumour had it, was a great orator in the House of Commons. And so it was that the four of them – Sir William and his wife, Annabel and the Earl of Fairfield – were seen constantly together. They attended the annual cricket match between Eton and Harrow, where the Carruthers boys – pupils at Eton – were playing. Ascot and the Henley Regatta were two events that Sir William never missed, but even when he was absent – Sir William could not be persuaded to go to the theatre or the opera – James Lyndon seemed always to be present.

She wondered how he managed to get such a lot of leave from the Army, but she thought it would be impolite to ask. Normally, Annabel wouldn't have given a fig for what anyone thought about her, but she liked Cynthia and, despite her initial reluctance to be a debutante, she was enjoying the round of parties and dinners. Besides, she thought, it was taking her mind off Gil.

And the person doing that was James Lyndon, Earl of Fairfield.

'I have to return to my battalion briefly,' he told her one evening when they were returning home late after another ball, 'but I'll come back as soon as I can.' In the darkness of the carriage, he felt for her hand and raised it to his lips. 'May I hope that you might miss me?'

Annabel laughed. 'Of course I will,' she said coquettishly. Her reply had not been serious, but, to her surprise, she found that over the next week while James was away, she did indeed miss him. No one else matched his good looks or his charming manners and his handsome face disturbed her dreams.

Though she danced and flirted mildly with her numerous partners, she longed for James to return and she was sure that Cynthia appeared to be fending off any other would-be admirers. They were both, it seemed, waiting for James.

Nine

'Do you know,' she told him with innocent candour when he returned to London. 'I *have* missed you.'

James smiled and kissed her hand.

When the Season came to an end with the Goodwood Races in late July and Annabel was due to travel home, the Earl insisted on accompanying her to meet her parents – in particular, her father.

Lady Cynthia was not due to return to Lincolnshire until the following week, so one of her maids accompanied the couple – as they had come to be regarded – on the long train journey north. They sat side by side in a first-class carriage, while the maid sat discreetly in the far corner, within sight but out of earshot.

James leaned towards Annabel and took her hand in his. 'My dear, you must know how very fond I have become of you. Might I hope that you return my feelings?'

Annabel turned her head and looked into his eyes. He was indeed handsome and when he smiled, as he was doing now, his brown eyes softened. She had been unbelievably hurt by Gilbert's desertion, and James Lyndon's attentions and his admiration for her were a salve to her wounded heart. To her surprise, she had to admit that she could scarcely recall Gilbert's features. How strange, she thought, when she had believed herself in love with him.

Annabel smiled in return but could not bring herself

to answer the man sitting beside her. Although she had enjoyed his attentions in London, she had not thought for one moment that the flirtation would lead to anything more serious. But taking her silence as a 'yes', James leaned back in the seat with a small sigh of satisfaction, continuing to hold her hand until, after a tedious journey, they arrived at the station in Grimsby. He took charge of Annabel's luggage, calling a porter and seeing that everything was safely loaded onto the waiting carriage. And then, to Annabel's surprise, he climbed into the carriage beside her.

'Didn't your mother write to tell you?' he said with a smile as he saw her startled expression. 'Your parents have kindly invited me to stay for two days.'

Annabel gasped aloud. A lord – an earl, no less – staying at their house on Bargate? She couldn't believe it. She was by no means ashamed of her background – indeed, she hardly thought about it; she had never had reason – or the desire – to compare herself with others. She neither looked up to those classes of society regarded as being above her, nor down to those considered by some to be below her. She knew, though, that her parents had ambitions to climb the social ladder and now she was beginning to realize that she was expected to play her part.

They wanted her to marry well, to bring prestige to the family and be a credit to her parents' upbringing of their daughter. Suddenly, it all became clear to her. She was to be but a pawn in her father's ambitions. She knew that he had inveigled her presentation at court and her participation in the Season through his business contacts with Sir William. And now, she suspected, he had asked Lady Cynthia to single out a suitable young nobleman to pay court to his daughter.

But what, Annabel thought, of love? Had that no place in Ambrose's machinations? With a heavy, disillusioned heart she knew the answer was 'no'. And now, another dreadful thought entered her mind.

Had Ambrose caused Gilbert to be dismissed and sent away because he was not a suitable suitor for his daughter? Her grandfather had hinted as much. She shuddered and at once James said, 'My dear, are you cold?' Then he laughed and raised his left eyebrow sardonically. 'Or is it the thought of my visit to your home?'

Annabel turned her violet eyes to look into his brown ones. 'I have to admit,' she said huskily, 'that the news surprises me. I never thought that a person of your social standing would' – she smiled as she continued – 'grace us with their presence.'

He gave a short bark of laughter and muttered, 'Needs must.'

Annabel frowned; she didn't understand the meaning behind his words, but now the carriage was slowing and turning into the gateway of her home and conversation between them ceased.

Now that Annabel believed she understood the reasoning behind her father's manipulations, his obvious fawning over Lord Fairfield sickened her. She was amazed that the young man didn't seem to mind. Perhaps, she thought with amusement, he's used to it. Or perhaps . . .

Annabel was by no means a conceited girl. She was innocently unaware of her beauty – her clear skin, glossy black hair and the unusual colour of her lovely eyes. Her slim, shapely figure was the envy of other women and the cause of admiration in men. But now she was obliged to think that perhaps the earl was attracted to her and had, as he'd confessed, become fond of her. He was tolerating her father's flattery so that he could pay court to her.

As she took her leave of the earl and went to her room to change from her travelling clothes, to bathe and dress for dinner, Annabel was thoughtful. If James Lyndon was serious, then no doubt she could soon expect a proposal. And what would her answer be?

She didn't know.

The dinner was lavish; Ambrose was determined to impress his distinguished guest. Course after course came to the table and the earl delighted in every one, exclaiming over and praising every dish. Annabel was amused. His sycophancy was as blatant as her father's. Though keeping her eyes demurely downcast, she watched him discreetly. He was indeed handsome, courteous and charming, and over the weeks of the Season when he had been so obviously attentive, she had enjoyed his company. And she'd missed him when he'd been absent for several days. But was she falling in love with him? She'd thought herself in love with Gilbert Radcliffe, and yet now, when she tried to think of him, she couldn't remember his face or hear the sound of his voice. Annabel sighed. Was she really so fickle that she had forgotten him already? For now the only face that filled her waking hours and haunted her dreams was that of James Lyndon. And the thought that James would leave shortly and she might never see him again brought tears to her eyes and a pain to her heart. So, yes, she believed she was falling in love with him.

After luncheon – as her mother insisted the midday

meal should be called – on the second and last day of his visit, James led her into the garden behind the house and to the summer house at the end of the lawn. Annabel's heart beat a little faster; she guessed what was about to happen. What she didn't know was that her parents were watching anxiously from an upstairs window.

'Will she accept him, do you think?' Sarah asked.

'She'd better,' Ambrose muttered morosely. 'But she can be very stubborn.'

'Perhaps she needs a little more time.'

'Time? What does she need time for? Doesn't she realize how much it's cost me to bring this about?'

Sarah raised her eyebrows. 'I rather hope not. Our somewhat wayward daughter has strict codes of what she believes is moral behaviour and I don't think she'd approve of a suitor being—'

'I blame your parents for that. No ambition, that's your father's trouble. Just content to run his farm and live the life of a country yokel. Thank God you're different, Sarah.'

'You wouldn't have married me otherwise, would you?' Sarah remarked.

Ambrose turned to look at her. 'Nor you me, my dear.'

Sarah laughed drily. 'That's true enough.'

'But together we've climbed mountains, haven't we? And now –' He turned back to look out of the window. 'And now there's just one more summit to reach, if only . . .'

In the seclusion of the summer house, the young couple sat side by side gazing at the smooth lawn, the well-kept borders filled to overflowing with brightly coloured flowers.

James took her hand and turned to face her. 'I have spoken to your father and he has given me permission to propose to you. Annabel – dear Annabel – would you do me the great honour of becoming my wife?'

She looked into his eyes, trying to read his true feelings for her. She ran her tongue nervously around her lips. 'Shouldn't – shouldn't I meet your family first? I mean—'

'There's only my mother, my sister and her son and when I tell them how much I – I love you, they will understand. I want us to be married soon – very soon.'

'Why? What's the hurry?'

'I have to return to my regiment. I'm a soldier, Annabel, and I have been absent for a very long time – with special permission, of course.'

She frowned. 'You mean that, normally, you're away from home a lot?'

'Yes. Until May of last year I was in Singapore, but I'm based in Woolwich for now. But I may be sent abroad again at any time.'

'Oh!' This was startling news. 'I – I thought you would run your estate. I overheard what Lady Fortesque said to you – about – about losing your father and then your elder brother. She hinted that you might leave the Army. In fact, with all the time you've spent in London during the Season, I thought that perhaps you had already done so.'

'I'm no farmer. I leave that in the hands of my estate bailiff. The Army is my life, Annabel, you must understand that.'

'But what if there's a war? Would you have to go?'

'Of course.'

Annabel stared at him. She couldn't understand anyone wanting to leave their farmlands in the hands of someone else whilst they went off to fight in some far-off country. 'But – but don't you at least want us to be married from your home?' Although the custom was for marriages to take place from the bride's home, Annabel realized that amongst the aristocracy, grander weddings than her home could offer were expected.

But James was shaking his head. 'No, that won't be possible. My mother is still in mourning.'

Annabel's eyes widened. If there had been a recent bereavement in the family, she was surprised that James had taken part in the Season. 'Oh, I'm so sorry. Your father?'

'No, he died nearly three years ago. My elder brother, Albert, inherited the title, but he died very suddenly last December. It was a great shock to us all.'

'And so,' Annabel murmured, 'you've become the sixth earl, but you never expected to be.'

James nodded.

'And you don't want to give up being a soldier?'

'No,' he said simply and decidedly, 'I don't.'

'Not even,' she said quietly, 'to become a husband and father?'

As if sensing that perhaps her answer to his proposal depended on his reply now, James hesitated. 'Is that what you'd want me to do?'

Annabel gazed at him as she said slowly, 'I'd never ask a man to give up doing what he loved just to please me. And I suppose' – she was thinking aloud now – 'if you never expected to inherit the title and to have to run the estate, it's only natural that you would want to build your own career.' She saw the hope spring into his eyes, felt the gentle squeeze of his hand on hers. She took a deep breath. 'But if you're likely to be away for long periods, then there is just one thing I would ask.'

'Name it.'

'I would want to help run the estate when you're away; not to take over from your bailiff, but to work alongside him.'

'Oh, I don't know about that,' he began, but she hurried on. 'James, I cannot be idle. And besides, I love farming. I have learned a lot from my grandfather and—'

'But that is just one small farm, it is not an *estate*.'

Annabel laughed. 'The principles will be the same – just on a grander scale.'

Now she could see the doubt in his eyes. 'You think your bailiff won't like me interfering, as he might see it?'

James laughed. 'Jackson will do as he's told.'

'Your mother, then? Or your sister? Do they run things now in your absence?'

James shook his head. 'No, they don't involve themselves. They just run the house. At least, my sister does. Since the deaths of both my father and my brother, Mama seems to have given up and leaves everything to my sister, Dorothea.'

'Then what's the problem?'

'Well, I hope you'll be a mother very soon. You'd want to devote your time to our son, wouldn't you?'

'Or daughter,' Annabel murmured, but got no response. She sighed. 'Of course I would. I wasn't proposing that I should plough the fields myself, but that I should be involved with the overseeing, the planning and so on.'

James wrinkled his brow thoughtfully. 'There's only Home Farm which we are responsible for. The other three farms are tenanted.' His voice dropped as he added, 'Usually.' He was quiet and then he shrugged his shoulders. 'If that's what you really want . . .' His tone was grudging, as if he was unwilling to agree to her request, and yet felt obliged to do so.

'It is,' Annabel said firmly. 'And I wouldn't want to offend your sister by trying to take over the management of the house. I suppose we will have our own rooms? A wing of the house, maybe?'

He looked at her strangely for a moment before glancing away and merely nodding. After a moment's pause, he prompted, 'So, what is your answer? Will you marry me, Annabel?'

She hesitated a moment. There had been no ardent declaration of love, of adoration, but perhaps, being a soldier, he found sweet words difficult. And he had shown his affection for her in so many little acts of kindness and attention during her stay in London. He had become part of her life – a very important part.

'Yes, James, I will marry you,' she heard herself saying, almost without stopping to think.

He smiled and leaned forward to kiss her gently on the lips.

A little later, James entered Ambrose's study and closed the door behind him.

'Well?' Ambrose asked impatiently.

'She has accepted my proposal.'

Ambrose beamed and rubbed his hands. 'And the wedding?'

'At first, she didn't understand the reason for such haste, but when I explained that I have to rejoin my regiment as soon as possible because I have already taken a lot of leave—'

'She agreed?'

'Yes.'

'Good, good.' Ambrose picked up a small piece of paper from his desk and held it for a moment, saying, 'There is just one more thing. I presume you have family pictures hanging in Fairfield Hall?'

James was puzzled. 'Yes,' he said slowly. 'It has always been the custom to have a portrait done to celebrate a twenty-first birthday.'

'So – there's already one of you?'

James nodded. 'In the dining room.' Now he was beginning to understand.

'I intend to commission an artist from London to paint Annabel's likeness,' Ambrose went on. 'He is able to come at once so that it can be done in time for the wedding. I'd like to think that a portrait of the new Lady Fairfield will hang in a prominent place in the hall.' Ambrose raised his eyebrows in question.

James hesitated for a moment, but, glancing at the piece of paper still in Ambrose's grasp, he murmured, 'Of course.'

Now Ambrose smiled and held it out towards James. 'My cheque for ten thousand pounds.'

James took it and gazed down at it. 'You can't imagine what this means to me, Mr Constantine. The death duties for both my father and brother have crippled the estate. But this' – he tapped the cheque with his forefinger – 'will save Fairfield. It's a great deal of money and I can't thank you enough.'

'My dear fellow, it's a small price to pay for my daughter becoming Lady Fairfield.'

Ten

The only disappointment for Ambrose was that there was no time to plan a lavish wedding. Because of James's commitments to his regiment, the marriage took place just over three weeks later on the last Wednesday in August in the nearest church with only Annabel's parents, grandparents, Sir William and Lady Cynthia and a few other guests who attended at Ambrose's invitation, present. Not even James's mother or sister and nephew attended, which Annabel found strange and rather worrying. James dismissed their absence with a wave of his hand, reminding her that his family was still in mourning.

Ambrose had insisted that a wedding breakfast be held in the large dining room at their home, where he made a speech briefly welcoming his new son-in-law into the family but dwelling more on how proud he was that his daughter was to be Lady Fairfield and that her son would one day be the seventh earl. Sarah nodded her approval and smiled around the table. Only Annabel's grandfather shook his head in despair. As the newly-weds were about to depart, Edward took Annabel's hands in his and, as he kissed her forehead, he whispered, 'We're only a few miles from where you're going to be living – only the other side of Thorpe St Michael. Any problems, my lovely, come to us. Promise me, now.'

There were tears in her eyes and her voice was shaky as she said, 'I promise, Gramps.'

And then they were on their way in a flurry of good-byes and good wishes.

They stayed at a hotel for the night in Cleethorpes.

'Forty or so miles is too far to travel now,' James said. He was driving the brougham, which Annabel's father had lent them. 'We'd be so late arriving. Besides,' he smiled at her, 'we must make the most of the next two days. I'm afraid I must leave on Friday. I have a very understanding commanding officer, but even he cannot grant me indefinite leave.'

Annabel tried to smile. She'd understood that the life of an army wife would not be easy but even she hadn't realized that their time together at the start of their marriage would be so short.

The room was not lavish, but it was comfortable and a welcoming fire burned in the grate, though it was hardly necessary. The day had been fine and bright and its warmth still lingered into the evening. Dinner was served to them in their room, though Annabel kept her eyes averted from the huge bed. She was nervous about her wedding night. She knew the basic facts of life – she hadn't stayed on her grandfather's farm without learning them – but all her mother had said to her was, 'Do your duty by your husband,' which told her little and left her feeling naïve and rather foolish.

As they finished their meal, Annabel's appetite having almost deserted her, James stood up. 'I'll leave you for a while.' Then he turned and left the room. She stared at the door as it closed behind him. He hadn't kissed her, hadn't even smiled, but she was left in no doubt that she was now expected to prepare for bed.

A few minutes later, a manservant brought in a tin bath and two maids followed with hot water. When the man had departed, one of the maids asked, 'Would you like one of us to help you, m'lady? We see you're not travelling with a lady's maid.'

'That's kind of you, but I'll manage, though perhaps you could just unhook my dress, please.'

Jane was to follow two days later, bringing more of Annabel's luggage to Fairfield Hall. She was Ambrose's wedding gift to his daughter and the young girl was happy to go with her young mistress. 'I'll be nearer my folks, Miss Annabel.' Jane had not added that she would be more than happy to leave the Constantines' household; she loved Annabel, but she did not even like Ambrose and Sarah.

Jane Moffatt's family were farmers and their lands adjoined Edward Armstrong's farm, which lay to the north of the market town of Thorpe St Michael. Now Annabel had learned that the village of Fairfield and its estate lay to the south of that same town. She would be living only six or seven miles from Granny and Gramps; the thought comforted her as she nervously readied herself for bed on her wedding night.

She need not have worried; James was gentle and tender with her, but it was obvious – even to the inno-cent and naïve girl – that he was experienced in the art of lovemaking. Annabel wasn't sure whether to be grateful or sorry that her new husband had obviously had previous lovers.

*

The following morning was bright, but already there was a nip of autumn in the air and a cool breeze blew in from the sea. Solicitously, James wrapped a rug round her knees as she settled into the brougham. Annabel was eager to see her new home. Although it was not many miles from Meadow View Farm, strangely, she had never seen Fairfield Hall, had not even heard of it, although her grandfather had found time to say to her at the wedding reception, 'Their bailiff, Ben Jackson, is a good man. If you are to be left in charge of the estate, he will help you. And I'm not far away,' he'd reminded her yet again as she'd kissed him goodbye.

They stopped for an early luncheon at an inn on the way. After a brief rest, they set off again. As they travelled, James was quiet, breaking the silence at last to say, 'This is where my estate starts. These outlying farms are tenanted. Home Farm and the village of Fairfield are near the Hall.'

Annabel leaned forward, looking about her. Then she frowned. She was surprised to see that there was no livestock in the fields; no cows or sheep or even horses and, worse still, there was no sign of harvesting. The fields looked neglected and choked with weeds. Only one field seemed to have a crop of wheat, but it had not been cut. It lay in sorry ruins, flattened by wind and rain. She couldn't stop herself asking, 'Is this farm tenanted?'

'No – no.' His reply was hesitant. 'It was – but he – they – left.'

'And you haven't found a new tenant yet?'

'No.' His reply was clipped, as if cutting off any more questions.

They travelled on in silence, yet the mystery for Annabel deepened. The next farm they passed was clearly occupied and yet there still seemed a strange lack of activity. Again, there were no animals in sight and a pall of silence hung over the farmyard, though smoke drifted idly from one of the chimneys.

And then they were dipping down the gentle slope towards a village.

'This is Fairfield village,' James said.

They passed by a thatched cottage on the right-hand side of the road, standing a little apart from the rest of the houses that clustered side by side along the one village street. Then came the school, but there were no children playing in the schoolyard. Perhaps they were all at their lessons; the windows were too high up in the wall for Annabel to catch a glimpse of the inside. More likely, Annabel reminded herself, it was still the summer holidays. But there were no children playing in the street or the fields either. No sign of any youngsters anywhere. Next to the school was the church, beside which stood a substantial house; obviously, Annabel thought, the vicarage. They moved on, the brougham's wheels rattling loudly in the strangely silent street. They passed a line of small shops, but not one seemed to be open. The windows of two of the premises were boarded up. Annabel glanced about her. There was no one about; there were no women hanging out washing in the gardens behind the cottages or scrubbing their doorsteps.

'Does anyone live here?'

'Oh yes, though some of the houses are uninhabited just now.'

Even the village pub was obviously unoccupied, its windows boarded up and a sign – The Lyndon Arms – swinging forlornly in the light breeze.

The brougham turned and began to climb the gentle

slope of the hill. The ground levelled out on to the curving driveway leading to the house. How lovely it would be, Annabel thought, if this could be lined with trees, and then she looked up and saw Fairfield Hall overlooking the vale. It was a lovely house, she thought, the excitement rising in her, with roses climbing the walls and framing some of the windows. And yet, she felt the building somehow had a forlorn look.

As they drew near, James ignored the archway leading into a courtyard at the side of the house and brought the vehicle to a halt at the front steps. He helped Annabel to alight and led her in through the door, which had been opened as they'd drawn up.

'This is Searby, the butler.' The man, in his early fifties, Annabel guessed, was tall and thin with a sallow face. His short, fair hair was smoothed back and he wore a black morning coat, trousers and waistcoat with a white shirt and black tie. He looked very smart, but Annabel couldn't help noticing that his clothes, though clean and cared for, were nevertheless shabby and show-ing signs of wear.

'Welcome home, m'lord. M'lady.'

Annabel held out her hand. 'How do you do, Mr Searby? I'm pleased to meet you.'

The man seemed startled and glanced towards James, who shrugged and turned away. The manservant took her proffered hand and shook it briefly, giving a little bow as he did so and murmuring again, 'M'lady.'

'Where are my mother and sister, Searby?' James asked.

'In the morning room, m'lord.' John Searby hurried ahead to open doors for them and James marched into the room. Annabel smiled up at the butler and mur-mured, 'Thank you.'

As she stepped into the room, Annabel blinked, trying to accustom her eyes to the gloom. Heavy curtains blocked out much of the natural light. What a shame, she thought instantly. It was a lovely room, facing east to catch the morning light, and yet much of it was shut out. Her glance came to rest on the woman who was standing on the hearth in front of an empty grate; a tall, spare woman in her late twenties, Annabel guessed. She was dressed completely in black, her thick light brown hair swept up onto the top of her head. Her features were sharp, her eyes beady and her lips thin and pursed. Beside her was a young boy of about five years old. He, too, was thin, his face pale and pinched, his brown hair dull. Sitting in a chair at the side of the fireplace, was an older woman with a shawl around her shoulders and a blanket over her knees. A lace cap covered her white hair. Her face was wrinkled and her eyes, as she looked up, were watery. She looked, Annabel thought, as if at any moment she might start to weep.

'This is my mother,' James said, 'my sister, Lady Dorothea, and her son, Theodore Crowstone.'

Annabel stepped forward, her hand outstretched towards the older woman huddled in the chair. 'How do you do, Lady Fairfield? I'm so pleased to meet you.'

Elizabeth Lyndon, now the Dowager Countess of Fairfield, looked up and held out her winkled hand. 'We're so very grateful—'

'Mama,' Dorothea said warningly. Elizabeth glanced at her with frightened eyes and then seemed to shrink even further into her chair.

Annabel turned to greet the younger woman, who attempted to smile in return, but it was obviously forced. Then Lady Dorothea looked at her brother and now there was obvious eagerness in her tone. 'It is done?'

'I'll talk to you later,' he replied brusquely.

'But have you got it?'

'Later, Dorothea,' he snapped.

Annabel could feel the tension in the room so she turned to the solemn-faced little boy standing beside his mother. 'And how old are you, Theodore?'

He gazed at her with huge brown eyes, but before he could answer, Dorothea interrupted curtly, 'Your room has been prepared.'

'On the top floor as I instructed?' James asked.

'No, the rooms there are not suitable at present.' Annabel saw the glance that passed between the brother and sister. 'For the time being you'll have to make do with your usual room.'

Though James glared at her, he offered no argument. He put out his hand towards Annabel in a gesture that they should leave. As Annabel turned away, Dorothea said, 'I understand you are bringing your own maid with you?'

'Yes, she'll be arriving tomorrow with more of my belongings.'

'She'll have to share a bedroom with Taylor. She's our housemaid. There are other servants' bedrooms, but they're not – ready.'

Annabel – for once lost for words – merely nodded her agreement, though she doubted her acquiescence was being sought. She was not being asked; she was being instructed.

Turning left out of the morning room, James led her up the staircase and along a landing. He opened a door into a bedroom that was obviously a man's – and a soldier's – room. It was sparsely furnished with a thread-bare carpet on the floor and worn curtains at the window. Even the bed, which looked comfortable enough, was covered with a well-worn counterpane.

'I'm sorry this is not what I'm sure you're used to, but no doubt when you've been here a while, you can furnish a room to your own taste. There are plenty to choose from.' The last few words were spoken cynically, as if there was something he was not telling her.

'You mentioned the top floor. Is that where we're to have our rooms?'

'We'll have to see.' Again, she felt that he was prevaricating, but for the moment she let the matter drop.

'There's a bathroom across the landing. Perhaps you'd like to freshen up before dinner. We usually dine at seven. And now, I must see Jackson.'

'May I meet him?'

'Not just now. Time enough another day for that. I'm sure you're tired after the last few days.'

Annabel was not in the least tired; she was excited to see her new home and to learn about the estate, but for the moment she inclined her head in agreement. As her husband said, there was time enough for that.

Eleven

Annabel took trouble over dressing for her first dinner with James's family. She was wearing her favourite gown – dark blue satin with a low neckline, adorned only by the delicate necklace her grandparents had given her as a wedding gift. Just before seven, she found her way downstairs to the dining room. To her surprise, no fire burned in the grate in this room either, even though the evening was now cool. Lady Fairfield sat at one end of the table, the black shawl still around her shoulders.

'Good evening, Lady Fairfield,' Annabel greeted her. The woman, who must only be in her mid-fifties, Annabel calculated, but looked much older, glanced up and murmured an indistinct reply. Annabel opened her mouth to begin a conversation, but at that moment James and Dorothea entered the room. They seemed startled to see her already there, but courteously, James held out a chair for her to sit down at the table. He sat at the opposite end of the table to his mother and Dorothea seated herself opposite Annabel.

Annabel wished she could ask about Dorothea's husband, but since he had not appeared and neither had he even been mentioned, she presumed he had died and such a question would be insensitive. Instead she said, 'I take it your little boy doesn't dine with us? Is he in bed?'

'Yes,' was the curt reply, with no further explanation, and Dorothea glanced swiftly at her brother.

'Has he a nanny?'

Again Dorothea glanced at her brother before she answered, 'Not at the moment.'

They ate in silence. Any attempt Annabel made at conversation was met with an abrupt reply. Annabel wondered if she was breaking some unwritten code of etiquette. Perhaps it was not customary for conversation to take place over dinner when the household was in mourning. That was something she had not encountered during her instruction with Lady Cynthia.

The meal consisted of watery soup, followed by a joint of very tough beef, which Annabel found difficult to chew. She was obliged to swallow big lumps of it. The mashed potato lacked the addition of butter and the cauliflower was so black that Annabel had to force herself to swallow it out of politeness. She couldn't ever remember having had to eat such a disastrous meal and she questioned the culinary skills of the cook employed at Fairfield Hall, who had not even bothered to produce a pudding.

When the meal ended, the maid, Annie, was reaching across Annabel to remove her plate. Her hand shook and she dropped the plate splashing lumpy gravy onto Annabel's dress.

'Oh, I'm so sorry, m'lady.'

Annabel looked up swiftly to reassure the girl that it was an accident, but the words never left her lips for the maid was looking across the table at her mistress, Dorothea. When Annabel swivelled her gaze, Dorothea's eyes were downcast, but there was no mistaking the smirk on her face. At last, she raised her head and stared straight into Annabel's puzzled eyes. 'I do hope your lovely gown isn't ruined,' the woman said, but the tone was sarcastic, the words insincere.

'A girl shouldn't be serving in the dining room,' James said tersely and glared at John Searby as if it were his fault entirely. The butler, red faced, pursed his lips, looking, Annabel thought, as if he would dearly like to reply, but dared not do so. Instead, he inclined his head, acknowledging his lordship's comment.

'No harm done,' Annabel said, determined not to let them see that she was annoyed by the girl's clumsiness – or, as she suspected, deliberate act – and that she was also puzzled.

What kind of a household had she come to and, more importantly, what kind of a family had she married into?

Lady Fairfield stood up and bade everyone goodnight. James rose and accompanied his mother to the foot of the stairs. Left alone at the table for a brief moment with Dorothea, Annabel smiled and opened her mouth to start a conversation, but Dorothea got up at once and with a brief nod and a brusque 'Goodnight', she, too, left the room. With a small sigh, Annabel left the table and went up to the bedroom she was to share with her husband. She was sitting up in bed by the time James came into the room. Without a word he went to the bathroom and came back several minutes later dressed in his nightshirt. He blew out the candle on his bedside table and climbed into bed.

To Annabel's surprise no maid appeared with early morning tea and, by the time she awoke, James's side of the bed was empty. She washed and dressed and went downstairs, but the dining room was deserted. There was no sign of breakfast either on the table or the sideboard. She glanced at the clock and saw that it was already half past nine. Perhaps they took breakfast very early and everything had been cleared away. She bit her lip. They might have told her what the house rules were; already she was feeling decidedly unwelcome – at least by the rest of the family. She smiled as she remembered James's ardent lovemaking the previous night; there was no doubting that he loved her and wanted her here. She pulled the bell cord in the dining room and waited. After ten minutes when still no one had come, Annabel lifted her chin determinedly. If they wouldn't come to her, then she would find the kitchen and, if necessary, get her own breakfast.

She went out of the dining room and down the servants' stairs that led to the basement. A little way along the corridor, she heard sounds from behind a door and, opening it, she saw four members of the staff sitting around the kitchen table, cups of tea in front of them. She was tempted – very tempted – to ask haughtily what they thought they were doing when she was waiting for her breakfast, but the words never left her lips. There was something very strange happening here; four pairs of eyes were staring at her in surprise and, yes, there was no mistaking it, something akin to fear on their faces. Her glance took in the whole kitchen swiftly. There was no sign of the remnants of breakfast either from upstairs or here in the servants' quarters, though she couldn't see into the scullery from where she was standing. All that could be seen were the cups the staff were using and a teapot standing in the centre of the table.

The butler got to his feet. 'You shouldn't be down here, m'lady. You should ring if you need anything.'

'I did,' Annabel said softly, her tone gentle. 'From the dining room.'

'I'm sorry,' the man apologized. 'The bell no longer works in that room.' There was a pause before he added, reluctantly, Annabel thought, 'Would you like me to bring you some breakfast?' She saw the glances of the other three go to him and then back to her. They were all hanging on her reply as if it was of great importance.

'No. It's late now. I don't want to disrupt your routine. But a cup of tea would be nice.' She closed the door behind her, moved further into the room and pulled out a chair at the table.

Now their faces were shocked. 'Oh, m'lady—' the cook began whilst John Searby said, 'I'll bring it up for you—'

Annabel held up her hand to silence them both. 'I don't intend to interfere in any way with Lady Dorothea's running of the household, but I believe I am free to go where I please, speak to whom I please. And I would like to get to know you all.' She smiled round the table, but there were no answering smiles. They all looked ill at ease, as if they had been caught out doing something they should not. She glanced around the kitchen again. Not only was there no sign of breakfast, but there was also no sign of any food being prepared for luncheon. She sat down and looked into the cook's face. She was thin, her greying hair covered by a mob cap. Her clothes hung loosely on her and her apron looked far too big for her.

'Mr Searby,' Annabel said quietly to the butler, though her gaze never left the cook's troubled face. 'Will you please introduce me to everyone?'

Reluctantly, John Searby said, 'This is Mrs Nelly Parrish, the cook-cum-housekeeper. We – we don't have a housekeeper at the moment, m'lady. Annie Taylor, the maid, and Luke Metcalfe. He does everything else that needs doing. And it's just "Searby", m'lady, Taylor and Metcalf, though we all give Mrs Parrish her courtesy title.'

Annabel glanced at him, though for the moment she said nothing. She would make up her own mind about how she addressed the staff – and certainly she would never refer to them as 'servants', not even in her own mind.

Annie placed a cup of black tea in front of her and said moodily, 'There's no milk – or sugar.'

Annabel looked up at the girl and smiled brightly. 'Thank you, Annie.' The girl blinked at being addressed by her Christian name, glanced at the butler but said nothing. Annabel turned her attention back to the cook. 'Now,' she said firmly, 'will one of you please tell me what is going on here?'

The members of staff all glanced at each other again, furtively, fearfully. Now, as she looked around at them, Annabel could see that they were all thin and pasty-faced as if they were undernourished. Their clothes – just like John Searby's – were shabby and ill fitting, hanging loosely on them.

They look *hungry*, she thought with a shock. But how can that be, living in a grand house like Fairfield Hall and on a large estate? Surely . . .? Annabel's wandering thoughts were interrupted by the cook.

'It's not our place to say owt, m'lady,' Nelly Parrish said in a low voice. 'It's been difficult of late, but we've been told that things will get better very soon now.'

Annabel knew that servants knew as much about each member of the family as the family knew them-selves. Nothing was secret from them. And at this moment, they certainly knew more than she did.

'How do you mean, "difficult"?'

'We're all starving, that's what,' Luke burst out and even though John Searby put a warning hand on the lad's arm, Luke went on angrily, 'There's no food. Not for any of us. Not even for the mistress or the old lady, though they do try to feed the little lad.' His tone softened as if none of them begrudged food being given to Theodore, but it hardened again as he went on, 'His lordship brings a bit of food when he comes home' – his lip curled disdainfully – 'for them upstairs, but there's little or nowt left for us. Scraps, that's all we get and—'

'That's enough, Metcalf. More than enough. Remember your place.'

'Oh aye, my place. My place, all right, and there's no getting out of it. I ain't the strength to walk to find work and who'd employ a scarecrow like me, who looks as if they haven't had a decent meal in weeks. And I haven't. None of us have. And there's not a rabbit or a hare left on the estate to be caught. They've all been eaten by now, I reckon. And we daren't be caught shooting owt. *She'd* have the law on us for poachin'. And as for picking owt growing wild, it's all gone and the villagers even come up here at night and strip our orchard bare the minute anything's ripe enough. It's a wonder she hasn't had the law on them an' all—'

'Hold your tongue, Metcalfe,' John Searby snapped.

'Whatever—?' Annabel began, appalled at what the young man had said, but before she could say more they all heard a bell tinkle in the passageway and Annie got up.

'I'd better see what they want.'

Annabel watched her go – a thin girl with dull fair hair and hazel eyes that never smiled. Her dress was stained and torn at the shoulder and her apron looked fit only for the ragbag.

'Please, m'lady,' Nelly Parrish was almost in tears now. 'Don't ask us no more. You'll find out soon enough, but please – just don't ask us.'

Annabel felt obliged to respect the woman's request. Her questions were obviously distressing the cook. She sighed as she got up. 'Very well. But I mean to find out. Thank you for the tea.'

She turned and left the kitchen, only to meet Annie running down the stairs.

'Oh, m'lady, they're looking for you. They're in the morning room.' She grasped Annabel's arm. 'Please – don't tell 'em you've been down here talking to us. You'll get us all into trouble.'

'I won't,' Annabel promised. 'By the way, my own maid, Jane, arrives today. I believe she is to share your bedroom. Lady Dorothea's orders. I hope you don't mind.'

'Will she be staying?'

'Yes.'

Annie grimaced and muttered morosely, 'Another mouth to feed!' She released her grasp on Annabel's arm, turned and hurried on towards the kitchen.

Annabel found her way to the morning room and as soon as she opened the door, a voice greeted her. 'There you are! Where on earth have you been?' James was standing by the fireplace, resplendent in his army uniform. Without waiting for a reply he went on, 'I have to go into town to do a bit of business and then I shall be returning to my battalion. If there's anything you need, just ask my sister. And now' – he strode across the room – 'I must be going.' He kissed her lightly on the forehead. 'I'll be home again as soon as I can.'

'Oh but, James – I need to talk to you. There's something I don't understand—'

'I'm sorry, I must go.' Without another word, he left the room, crossed the hall, opened the front door himself without waiting for the butler, and was gone.

'And this is supposed to be our honeymoon,' Annabel murmured, as she closed the door quietly.

Twelve

Annabel returned to the bedroom. The bed had not yet been made, so she straightened it herself and then went to the window that looked out over the front of the house. The unkempt lawn stretched to where the hill sloped down towards the village. She narrowed her eyes to squint against the sunlight of a day that promised to be fine and bright. She could see no movement anywhere. No one – as far as she could see – was walking up and down the village street. Beyond the houses, on the sloping hill opposite, there was no sign of activity in the fields. There was no one about anywhere. It was all very strange. She would love to find out more, but today she must wait for Jane to arrive and help her to settle in.

Jane arrived mid-afternoon, brought by Ambrose's carriage with Billy driving it accompanied by another man, who would take back the brougham. It was impossible to say which one of the two young women was the more pleased to see the other.

'I'm so glad you asked me to come with you, Miss Annabel. I wouldn't have stayed there without you.'

'And I'm delighted you've come,' Annabel said, hugging her. No doubt it wasn't etiquette for a lady to hug her maid, but Annabel and Jane were more than mistress and servant. 'But I should warn you,' Annabel told her, lowering her voice, 'there's something very strange going on in this house and I want you to promise me that you'll tell me everything you find out. It will be in the strictest confidence, of course. I went down to the kitchen this morning and found that there seems to be very little food. And there are no fires in any of the rooms. James went off this morning back to his battalion and I haven't even seen his sister or his mother today.'

'Who lives here, then, miss?'

Annabel ticked off the names as far as she knew them, whilst Billy unloaded the trunks and boxes. 'There seems to be only four staff for a big house like this. And when I said you were coming, Annie said, "another mouth to feed". She didn't sound too pleased about it. She's the only maid here. How she copes with all the work, I don't know.'

'Have you eaten, miss?'

Annabel pulled a face. 'A cup of black tea for breakfast and a bowl of watery soup for luncheon with a piece of dry bread.'

'Oh miss, I'll go down to the village this minute and—' Jane knew nothing of the rules of etiquette now that her mistress was a countess, but Annabel was happy for the girl to continue to address her as she always had done.

Annabel was shaking her head in response to Jane's offer. 'No use. When we passed through the village on our way here, there were no shops open. Everywhere is closed up. There must be people living in the village, but I saw no one – not even children playing in the street.'

'To tell you the truth, miss, I didn't notice. I was

that excited about coming here, I was just looking up at the house. But if only I'd known, I could have brought some provisions with me. Whatever would your mother and father say if they knew?'

'I don't want them to know,' Annabel said swiftly. 'If I need help, I shall go to my grandparents. Their farm isn't far away. Now, let's go and find Annie.'

They went down to the kitchen to find Nelly Parrish standing at the range stirring a pan of soup on the hob. Annie, coming in from the scullery, looked Jane up and down with a surly expression.

'Would you show us where Jane is to sleep, please, Annie?' Annabel asked.

'I'll tek her up. No need for you to come, m'lady.'

'I want to see the room,' Annabel said in a firm tone that brooked no argument. The sullen frown deepened, but Annie said no more. She led the way out of the kitchen along the passage and up two flights of stairs until they came to the servants' quarters on the first floor. Annie opened a door into a small room over-looking the front of the house furnished with two single iron bedsteads, a washstand, a wardrobe and a small chest of drawers.

'She can have half the wardrobe and the two bottom drawers.'

'Thank you, Annie.' Annabel smiled sweetly at the girl, but was rewarded with a scowl. 'I'll leave you to settle in, Jane, and you can get to know each other.'

When the door was safely closed behind their mistress and they both heard her footsteps going along the passage back towards the stairs, Annie turned on Jane. 'That's your bed under the window. And don't think you'll get called "Jane" here. What's your surname?'

'Moffatt.'

'So that's what you'll be called. I'll have to go. Can you find your way back down to the kitchen?'

'Yes, thank you.' Jane smiled at the girl, trying to be friendly, but Annie turned on her heel and left.

Jane glanced around the room. It was clean enough, she supposed, but so shabby. The counterpane on the bed was worn – there were holes in it – and when she turned back the covers the sheets were grey with constant wear and washing. The room was cold and dreary and nothing like the room she'd had at the Constantines' home. Still, she comforted herself, she was with her beloved young mistress and she was nearer to her own folks too. She was sure she'd be allowed at least one day off a month to go to see them as she always had been. Jane unpacked her few belongings and stowed them away in the wardrobe and drawers that Annie had indicated and then found her way downstairs to the kitchen.

'Is there anything I can do to help you, Mrs Parrish?' she asked, approaching the woman, who was now sitting at the table. Nelly looked up, startled. Then she said bitterly, 'There's nowt to do, not unless you fancy dusting the morning room and lighting the fire in there for the old lady. She feels the cold, even in summer. That's if,' she added bitterly, 'you can find owt to light it with. There might be a few logs left since Luke last went scrounging in the woods, but I doubt it. Poor lad hardly has the strength to go now.'

'I'll do whatever I can to help you and Annie,' Jane said gently. Annabel was right in her assumption; there was something very strange in this household and very wrong too. And as Annabel had asked her, she'd do her best to find out what it was and tell her mistress. At that moment, John Searby appeared.

'Who's this?' he asked sharply, nodding towards Jane.

'The new Lady Fairfield's maid. And,' Nelly added with a note of bitterness, 'she's staying.'

The butler raised his eyebrows as the two of them exchanged a glance. 'Oh well, I expect things will be better very soon now. No doubt the master left instructions in the town this morning.'

Mystified, Jane glanced at the cook, but Nelly was avoiding her questioning gaze.

'So, you'd like me to clean the morning room, would you? Anywhere else?'

'You'd better speak to Annie. I don't want you treading on her toes and upsetting her.'

'Where is she?'

'Upstairs in Lady Elizabeth's bedroom helping her get ready to come downstairs for dinner.' Under her breath she added, 'If you can call it that.'

Jane bit her lip. Four o'clock in the afternoon seemed very early to be getting ready for dinner and there were certainly no food preparations going on in the kitchen. Only the large pan of soup sitting on the range.

'In that case, I'll go and find Miss Annabel.'

Jane left the kitchen, pleased to escape from the dour atmosphere. She found Annabel in her bedroom on the first floor. 'You're right, miss. There is something very odd here. I don't think your parents would like it if they knew.'

Annabel smiled wryly. 'I think my father would want me to stay no matter what – for the sake of the title "Lady Fairfield".'

'Well, your grandfather certainly wouldn't,' Jane said firmly. 'If things don't improve, we're going there.'

Annabel smiled at Jane's fierceness, but she was

heartened to feel that at least now she had someone on her side.

Dinner was the same watery soup that had been served at luncheon. There was no main course to follow but tonight there was a pudding of sorts – a selection of what looked like wild berries. Annabel recognized small strawberries, and blackberries that had been picked before they'd scarcely had time to ripen properly. The meal passed in total silence. Dorothea and Lady Fairfield hardly acknowledged Annabel's presence at their table and there was no attempt at any conversation, polite or otherwise.

The following afternoon, Annabel walked across the yard to the rooms above the archway where she had learned that the estate bailiff, Ben Jackson, lived. She knocked on the door, but there was no answer. Annabel bit her lip. She didn't know what to do. If only James were here or even if Dorothea would talk to her.

Instead of going back into the house, she crossed the courtyard and went through a gate on the left-hand side of the stables to the garden, hoping to find a kitchen plot, but the area that obviously once had been culti-vated was neglected and overgrown. Some beautiful and colourful flowers were doing their best to bloom, but were being choked by long grass and weeds.

Once again, the meagre dinner – the same as the previous day – passed in silence. The only time Dorothea addressed her was to say, 'Mama and I go to church in the morning. Please be ready at ten-thirty when Jackson will take us in the pony and trap.'

So, Annabel thought, at least they still have a pony and trap. She guessed that the villagers had worked together to feed the one animal that was so vital in a rural area. 'Very well,' she said and went on, 'Dorothea, might I have a word?' But the woman had turned away to help her mother up from her chair and out of the room towards the stairs. 'Goodnight,' was the only word she said. The elderly lady didn't speak at all.

'What did you all have to eat downstairs?' Annabel asked Jane later. The girl grimaced. 'Just the same weak soup you had, but no bread for us.'

'You must be starving. I know I am.'

'It's not half so bad for us as them poor folks down there. I don't reckon they've eaten properly for weeks.'

'What about a pudding?'

'Some bits of fruit which were small and hard. The best had been sent upstairs, but even that's all gone now.'

'What is going on here, Jane?'

The maid shook her head. 'I don't know, miss, and they won't say owt in front of me. They just keep saying they've been promised things'll get better very soon. Oh, and the butler thought the master would have left "instructions" in the town yesterday.'

'What sort of instructions and to whom?'

Jane shrugged. 'They didn't say.'

'Well, I intend to get to the bottom of all this. I don't expect I'll be able to do much tomorrow, being Sunday, but, first thing on Monday morning, we'll find out.'

But Annabel was to find out a great deal the following day.

Thirteen

Sunday morning dawned bright and clear. Jane woke her mistress with a cup of black tea and a piece of dry bread.

'There's just no food in the place, miss. Nothing. I've never seen anything like it. There's not even anything growing in the gardens. At least, nothing that's not been picked already.'

'I know. I went to look yesterday. You know, we've been lucky,' Annabel said soberly. 'I've been brought up in a wealthy household and you, living on a farm even before you came to us, have never gone short of something to eat.'

'My mam always kept a good table, even though we did go through some hard times. But this . . .' Jane shook her head as if she couldn't believe it. 'It's not what I expected in a place like this. I thought lords and ladies were rolling in it.'

'Obviously not,' Annabel said dryly as she got out of bed and began to wash and dress in readiness for going to church.

At ten-thirty, she and Jane were waiting in the hall with the butler when Dorothea and her mother joined them.

'Your maid will walk to church with the rest of the staff,' Dorothea said shortly, without even a greeting. 'There's barely room in the trap for the three of us as well as Jackson.'

Pointedly, Annabel said, 'Good morning, Dorothea – Lady Fairfield. Of course, that's no problem.'

Taking the hint, Jane dipped a curtsy and disappeared back to the kitchen as they heard the sound of a trap pulling up. John Searby opened the door and assisted the three women into the trap, which was driven by a stocky man, with fair hair, blue eyes and sideburns. He was dressed in a check jacket and trousers and Annabel judged him to be in his thirties. No introductions were made, but she assumed this must be Ben Jackson, the estate bailiff. He tipped his cap to them, murmuring a deferential greeting, and, when they were comfortable, he flicked the reins and the pony began to walk down the hill.

There was no one in the church when they arrived, so they settled themselves into the front pew to wait. A tall, pale man, with thinning fair hair and dressed in a surplice, appeared from the vestry and came down the steps towards them. After a courteous greeting to Lady Fairfield and Dorothea he turned to Annabel, his light blue eyes gazing into hers. 'And you must be Lord Fairfield's bride.' He held out his hand. 'I can't tell you what this will mean to all of us. Your coming will save—'

'That will do, Mr Webster,' Dorothea snapped and the poor man looked startled and flustered. 'I'm sorry, I thought—'

'Then you'd do best not to think too much, Mr Webster.'

He gave a little bow and turned away just as the organist began to play softly. The door at the back of the church opened and the villagers began to file in. Annabel was surprised to see so many people; where on earth had they all been hiding? Why had she seen no one before today? After some time, she saw, out of the corner of her eye, the servants from Fairfield Hall take their places in the pew directly behind where she was sitting. The service lasted about an hour and at the end, Lady Fairfield, Dorothea and Annabel rose and made their way down the aisle. As she passed the villagers, Annabel smiled to right and left. But there were no answering smiles, no little bows from the men or curtsies from the women. They stared back at her in stony silence, their faces glum and resentful.

The vicar was waiting at the door to shake hands with each of them. He bowed courteously once more and held Annabel's hand a little longer than was necessary. 'My lady,' he whispered, 'might I have a word with you?'

'Of course.' She turned to see Ben Jackson helping Lady Fairfield and Dorothea into the trap. Then he climbed up and, at Dorothea's instruction, flicked the reins. He glanced back towards her, apologetically, she thought, but then the trap moved away.

'Oh miss, they're going without you,' Jane cried and made as if to run after the trap to stop it, but Annabel put her hand on Jane's arm. 'No matter,' she murmured. 'I can walk.'

The villagers were filing out now, but no one spoke to her. They walked down the path and dispersed to their homes, walking slowly, their heads bent. A small, thin man emerged. He was hunched, yet she didn't think he was any older than about fifty. He was dressed in what were obviously his Sunday best clothes and yet they were ill fitting and shabby. He paused and glared at Annabel. Then quite deliberately he spat, the globule of spit landing on the hem of her dress. Annabel stared back at him in horror, but she said nothing.

'Oh my lady, I'm so sorry. Mr Fletcher,' the vicar turned to the man, 'how could you? It's the new Lady Fairfield who will be the salvation of us all.'

The man's eyes were filled with hatred. 'Aye, an' I'll believe that when I see it, an' all. She'll be just like them selfish buggers up the hill. Living in luxury whilst we all starve in the village. God – how I wish the old man were back. At least, he cared about his tenants.'

'Mr Fletcher – please . . .' Richard Webster said, but the man turned away and hobbled down the path. Lastly, the servants from Fairfield Hall appeared, Nelly Parrish leaning heavily on John Searby's arm. Behind them, Annie walked alongside Luke, her arm through his. Annabel was concerned to see that the cook looked white and ill. She moved towards her. 'Why don't you wait here and Luke can ask Mr Jackson to bring the trap back for you?'

'Oh no, m'lady. That would never do. I'll manage – with Mr Searby's help.'

Annabel frowned. The poor woman looked as if she could scarcely take another step, never mind climb the slope back to the house. The cook glanced around her and, seeing the trap disappearing along the street, added, 'Have they gone without you, m'lady?'

'Yes, they have,' Jane said indignantly before Annabel could answer.

Annabel touched her maid's arm. 'You go with the others, Jane. I want to speak to the vicar.'

'I'd rather stay with you, miss. I'll keep out the way if you and the vicar want to talk private, like. But please let me stay with you.' The girl glanced over her shoulders at the other servants making their way along the street and shuddered.

'Very well.' Annabel turned back to the vicar. 'Now,

Mr Webster, will you please tell me what is going on here? There's something very wrong in this village and I want to know what it is.'

He sighed heavily. 'I'll likely lose my living here if I do.'

She eyed him quizzically. 'From what I can see, that would be no bad thing.'

He shook his head and his glance followed the last few villagers walking slowly to their homes. 'I wouldn't leave all these folk. They need me. There's not much we can do, but my wife and I have been doing what we can. But even our resources,' the vicar went on sadly, 'are running out now. The villagers have been scouring the fields and hedgerows for anything edible, but I have been so afraid that someone – particularly a child – would eat something poisonous by mistake or in ignorance.' He shrugged and added, helplessly, 'And I'm sure there's been poaching going on, but what could I do to stop it? I can hardly blame them.' He was silent for a few moments, then he shook himself and said, 'Would you come to the vicarage, m'lady? You can meet my wife.' Mrs Webster, who had played the organ for the service, was a small, wiry woman, her dark hair streaked with grey. Her hazel eyes were filled with an unfathomable sadness. She'd paused only to glance at Annabel as she'd passed her when hurrying away as soon as the service had ended. 'We can at least make you a cup of tea this cold morning, but we've no milk.'

Annabel was shocked; the day was warm and bright, not cold to her at all. She nodded, accepting the vicar's invitation. She was anxious to learn more. They walked towards the vicarage, Annabel obliged to match her step to his slow pace. They'd only gone a short distance down the path before Mr Webster began to wheeze, his breathing laboured.

'Here, take my arm,' Annabel offered.

'Oh m'lady, that wouldn't be right.'

She looked up at him, her mouth a firm line. 'I seem to be getting told "that wouldn't do" or "that wouldn't be right" far too frequently. I don't care a jot about propriety or etiquette. You need an arm and I'm young and strong. Please – let me help you.'

Though the vicar was no longer young, he was not old either and Annabel was troubled by what she was seeing; the villagers – all of them – looked thin and ill and the sight of the few children, who had been at the church service looking pasty-faced and so solemn, had tugged at her heartstrings. None of the youngsters had raced out of church to play in the street. It was unnatural. As they passed out of the gate to walk the short distance to the vicarage – Jane hovering beside them – a man ran out from one of the cottages opposite.

'Vicar, Vicar, please –'

He crossed the street and reached them, panting, his eyes wide with terror. 'Please come. Babby's dying.'

Annabel's eyes widened and she gasped in shock, her hand flying to cover her mouth.

Mr Webster turned towards her. 'I'm sorry, m'lady, but I must go with Adam. They need me. His wife gave birth to a baby boy only three weeks ago, but the poor woman has no milk to feed him. Perhaps – if we could talk another time . . .?'

Annabel shook her head firmly. 'I'm coming with you.'

The four of them crossed the road and entered the cottage. It was dark and dismal inside and it took Annabel a few moments for her eyesight to adjust to the gloom. Then she saw a woman sitting by a fireless range, rocking a tiny baby in her arms and weeping. Behind her stood two older children – a boy of about nine or ten and a small girl of about three, Annabel guessed – but her attention was drawn back to the baby. Its breathing was rasping, its colour like alabaster.

'He's dying,' the child's mother burst out. 'He's starving to death because I've no milk.'

'What does she mean?' Annabel whispered to the vicar, for the poor woman didn't even seem to notice who had come into her home. Her whole attention was on her sick infant.

'They've no proper food. None of us have. We haven't had any for weeks and poor Betsy can no longer produce milk naturally to feed her child.'

Annabel stared down at the baby lying limply in his mother's arms for a moment, her mind working swiftly. 'I'll get them some food.'

'But you can't feed the whole village, m'lady,' Richard Webster said. 'We thought when you married his lordship, all would be well. We thought your dowry—'

Annabel turned to look at him. 'My what?'

'Oh dear, didn't you know?'

Annabel shook her head. She longed to ask him more, but this family needed her help this instant. 'We'll talk later, but for now I'm going to get help.' She turned to Jane. 'Run and get Mr Jackson to hitch up the trap again and ask him to come with us.'

The girl turned and ran out of the cottage.

'What do you need?' Annabel addressed the weeping woman, but it was her husband who answered. 'Milk for the baby. We're all starving, m'lady, but if baby Eddie doesn't get some sustenance very soon, we'll lose him.' He nodded towards the other two children, who were staring up at Annabel, pleading in their eyes. 'The rest of us are all right for the minute, but Emmot here –' he put his hand on the little girl's shoulders – 'she'll likely be the next – she's so weak now –' He gulped and stopped.

Annabel bent down and took the little girl's hands in hers. 'I'll get you something to eat, darling. I promise.'

'But, Lady Annabel, the whole village is starving,' the vicar whispered. 'If we single out one or two folks, it'll likely cause terrible resentment. You can't feed everyone.'

Annabel stood up and turned slowly to face him. Quietly she said, 'Just watch me, Mr Webster. Just watch me.'

At that moment, they heard the rattle of pony and trap outside and Annabel hurried out.

'Mr Jackson was on his way back to fetch us, m'lady, so we can go straight away,' Jane called out. 'Wherever that is.'

The bailiff was sitting in the front of the trap holding the reins. He looked mystified as Annabel smiled at him briefly. 'I'll explain as we drive. We're going to town first and then on to my grandfather's farm. Meadow View Farm. Do you know it?'

'Aye, I do, m'lady. I know Mester Armstrong well.'

Mr Webster, who had followed Annabel out of the cottage, helped her into the back of the trap. For a brief moment he held her hands and looked up into her eyes. His voice was husky as he said, 'God bless you, my lady, and God speed.'

Fourteen

'Mr Jackson, thank you for coming with us. We're going to need your help.'

'Just "Jackson", m'lady.'

Even in the seriousness of the moment, Annabel chuckled. 'That's what *Mr* Searby said, but I'm very much afraid you're going to find that I'm no lady, even if I do bear the title now.'

He glanced at her briefly and smiled, the laughter lines around his blue eyes crinkling. It was the first real smile anyone in the village had given her, she realized, as her mind focussed on the immediate problem. As they passed the vicarage, the church and then the school, Annabel saw a little cottage standing on its own at the edge of the village and set apart from the rest of the dwellings. In the garden she saw a young boy of about four playing with a ball. He glanced at the trap as it passed, but he did not smile or wave as she would have expected a child to do.

It was not until very much later that Annabel realized what had been strange about the child playing on his own in the garden. But now, she turned her attention back to Ben Jackson. 'Do you know where the doctor lives in Thorpe St Michael?' Annabel asked.

'I do, m'lady. But it's Sunday. He'll not be available.'

Grimly, Annabel declared, 'Oh yes, he will. There's a baby dying back there and he's coming out to see that little boy if I have to drag him there myself.'

She couldn't be sure, but she thought she heard Ben Jackson chuckle softly as he flicked the reins and urged the pony to go faster. They were lucky; the townsfolk were just leaving their own morning service at the church in the centre of the small market town.

'That's Dr Maybury. The young man over there with the pretty young woman on his arm. He's not been here long. I don't expect he even knows where Fairfield village is.'

'He very soon will,' Annabel said, as she jumped nimbly down from the trap and hurried towards the tall young man whom Ben had pointed out.

'Dr Maybury?' Annabel stood in front of him, panting slightly.

The young man removed his hat courteously, the sun glinting on his fair, curly hair. He was a handsome man with even features, a strong jawline and smiling blue eyes. 'Ma'am.'

'I am Annabel Lyndon, Lady Fairfield.' The doctor raised his eyebrows and one or two people nearby paused to eavesdrop. But Annabel hardly noticed. 'I know it's Sunday, Doctor, but there is a very sick baby in Fairfield village and I want you to come out now to see him. I – I think he's close to death.'

The young doctor's eyes darkened and beside him, his wife said, 'Oh Stephen, you must go.' The young couple exchanged a loving glance, but there was something more behind the look and as the woman turned back, she was smiling gently though her eyes were full of sympathy. 'We're expecting our first baby in the spring,' was all she needed to say for Annabel to understand her compassion.

Annabel turned to look at the doctor who said, 'Of course, I'll come at once. I would have done anyway.

107

That's what I'm here for – the Sabbath or not. Let me harness my own pony and trap and get my medical bag.'

'We're going on to my grandfather's farm to fetch food. There's something very wrong in Fairfield, Doctor. I shall want you to see each and every one of the inhabitants over the next few days. I don't know what's been happening, how it's come to this, but I intend to find out and try to put matters right. The cottage you need is the first on the left-hand side as you drive into the village. I don't know the family's name yet –' She glanced at Ben Jackson, who had followed her more slowly across the road.

'It's Cartwright, Doctor,' he said.

'I'll find them. Don't worry.'

As the young doctor hurried away, Ben helped Annabel to climb back into the trap. He pulled himself up, though it was an effort for him. But he took up the reins once more and they were on their way to Meadow View Farm, which lay only a couple of miles beyond the town. Edward was near the back door of the farmhouse when the trap pulled into the yard. Annabel almost tumbled out of the back in her haste to reach him.

'Oh my lovely, whatever's the matter?' He held his arms wide and she flew into them.

'The villagers are starving – there's a baby dying. Oh Gramps – please help us.'

Edward held her close and patted her back. Then he looked beyond her to see Jane coming towards them and Ben Jackson tethering the pony. 'Come along in, all of you. Hello, Jane, love. And Ben,' he held out his hand to the man, 'it's good to see you.'

A smile flitted briefly across Ben Jackson's face. 'I'm not sure you'll think so in a minute or two, Mr Armstrong.'

'Edward, please. We've known each other long enough.

Mind you, I haven't seen you at the market for months now. I was beginning to wonder if there was owt wrong. I asked around, but no one seemed to know. Anyway, come along in. The missis will get you all a hot drink and dinner is underway. You'll stay and—'

'We can't, Gramps. We must get back. But if you could let us have as much milk and bread as you can spare . . .'

Edward looked puzzled. 'Of course, you can have whatever we've got and you're welcome to it, but why? What's happened?'

'It's a long story, Edward,' Ben said as the farmer ushered them into the warm farm kitchen and Martha hurried forward to greet them. 'Come in, come in, you're all very welcome. Sit down, sit down. I've freshly baked scones.'

Although Ben eyed them hungrily, he said softly, 'Please may we take them back to the village, Mrs Armstrong? They'll likely save lives, not to put too fine a point on it.'

Martha laughed. 'My scones – save lives? Now, you're teasing me.' But her smile faded as she saw the serious expression on the man's face. And even worse, tears filled his eyes, though he brushed them away in embarrassment. She turned to glance at her husband and then at Annabel. 'Whatever's happened?'

'I don't know yet, Ma.' For many years, Edward had often called his wife Ma and she called him Pa – it was a term of endearment between them. 'But I mean to find out.'

'I don't know it all yet myself, Gramps,' Annabel said, 'all I know is we need to get food to the villagers – all of them. Even the Lyndons up at the house and their servants. It seems everyone is bordering on starvation. I'll be going into town first thing tomorrow and will order proper supplies, but now—'

Ben was shaking his head. 'M'lady, the shopkeepers in town won't supply you, not unless you settle all their bills.'

There was a stunned silence in the kitchen until Edward said quietly, 'You mean, they haven't been paid?'

'Not for months,' Ben said. 'They've refused to supply anyone in Fairfield, not even the big house. The vicar's been the only one who could get any food but even his funds have run out now.' Bitterly he added, 'Except for her in the cottage at the end of the street, of course.'

In her anxiety, Annabel did not pick up on his remark; her mind was still on the starving villagers and especially the tiny baby whose life was ebbing away for lack of nourishment.

'That explains a lot,' she heard Jane mutter.

Ben was staring at Annabel. 'His lordship was supposed to settle everything on Friday, but when I went into town yesterday morning, they all said the same thing; they still hadn't been paid. And now he's gone away.'

'I see – well, I don't, but never mind all that now. We must get some immediate help to the villagers. Gramps, what can you let me have?'

'All we've got, my lovely.' He patted his rotund stomach. 'Won't hurt us to go without for a day or two, will it, Ma? I've plenty of vegetables in the barn. You could make some nourishing soup with them. I don't think starving folk should eat too much too quickly, but the doctor will advise you on that. Go and see him.'

'He should be already on his way to the village. I've asked him to see a baby who's very sick. He might – he

110

might already be too late . . .' Tears flooded Annabel's eyes and her grandfather hugged her to him. 'There, there, we'll do whatever we can.'

'I baked on Friday,' Martha said, bustling between her large pantry and the main kitchen. 'So you can have bread and scones and there are two cakes, a meat pie and two apple pies. And you can take a ham . . .'

'We mustn't take all your food, Mrs Armstrong,' Ben began, but his objections were waved aside.

'I'll bake more bread again tomorrow,' Martha promised Annabel, 'and your grandfather can bring it to you. He'll bring more milk too. We'll do whatever we can to help. You just say the word.'

'I may need Gramps to come with me to the bank in town tomorrow. I'll need to transfer my account from home and perhaps he could come with me to see Mr Parker. I'll sell some of my shares, if I have to, but I'll need Gramps's signature as I'm still not yet quite twenty-one. I must pay all the shops in town and get them supplying the villagers again.' She hugged Martha swiftly. ''Bye, Granny. I'll see you soon. And thank you for everything.'

And then they were on their way back to the village, with Edward Armstrong following them in his farm cart loaded with three churns of milk, sacks of potatoes, carrots, two hams wrapped in cheesecloth and everything that Martha had baked two days earlier. He'd even thought to put two sacks of coal, wood and kindling onto the cart.

'You go ahead,' Edward had said, as he'd climbed onto the front of his cart. 'I won't be far behind you.'

Fifteen

When they arrived back in the village they saw the doctor's pony and trap standing outside the Cartwrights' home. Ben pulled the pony to a halt behind it. Annabel jumped down and hurried into the cottage, carrying the small can of milk Martha had suggested she should take with her. Although Edward was following with more supplies, perhaps every minute would count where the baby was concerned. She opened the door and tiptoed inside, standing a moment for her eyes to grow accustomed to the gloom. They were just as she'd left them; Betsy sitting with the baby on her lap, the two older children watching with round, solemn eyes, and Adam, hunger and the most terrible fear etched into his gaunt face, standing a little to one side. But now Dr Maybury was kneeling down in front of Betsy and gently examining the tiny form. Annabel stifled a gasp. Was she already too late? But then she breathed a sigh of relief as Dr Maybury said softly, 'He needs milk. Since you haven't any yourself, Mrs Cartwright, you need to warm some cow's milk and feed it to him drop by drop with a tiny spoon. And you'll need to do that every hour to start with.'

'We've no milk, Doctor, nor coal to heat it with,' Adam said heavily. 'We've nothing.'

'But we have,' Annabel said. 'I've milk here and my grandfather's following with more supplies. He's bringing coal and wood. We can soon light the fire and—'

They were all staring at her, unable to believe what she was saying – not daring to believe it.

'Oh, m'lady,' Betsy said, fresh tears welling in her eyes and spilling down her cheeks.

Annabel smiled. 'And there'll be food for all of you – very soon. Now' – she placed the can of precious milk on the table – 'I'm going to the vicarage to see if we can use the kitchen there to make soup for the whole village.' She turned to Adam. 'If you could come outside with me, we can get you some wood and coal the minute my grandfather arrives.' Then she turned to the doctor. 'Thank you so much for coming. Will you be able to come tomorrow to see the other villagers?'

'I'm staying now, Lady Fairfield.' He glanced down at the baby and his expression softened. 'I can't risk not seeing anyone else, who might need me urgently.' He picked up his medical bag and smiled at Betsy, adding softly, 'I'll call again before I leave.'

Outside the low door of the cottage, Ben and Jane were still standing near the pony and trap. All eyes now turned towards the road leading out of the village.

'Listen,' Ben said, 'is that cartwheels I hear?' They were all quiet, straining their ears.

'Yes, yes, it is. It's Grandfather.' With one accord they all moved forward as if they couldn't wait a moment longer for the cart to reach them.

'I'll go to the vicarage. Mr Jackson, will you direct Grandfather into their driveway as soon as you've taken whatever you need for this family off the cart?'

The man nodded and Annabel hurried away and was soon knocking on the heavy front door and ringing the bell at the same time. She couldn't bear to delay for another moment. Richard Webster opened the door himself, his face creased with concern. To him, in these dire times, such urgent knocking could only mean one thing. Someone needed his prayers.

'My grandfather is bringing some supplies – he's almost here,' Annabel said at once. 'Please may we use your kitchen to make soup for everyone?'

'Oh my dear lady, come in, come in,' he said, catching on at once and flinging the door wide open. 'Phoebe – come quickly.'

The vicar's wife was short in stature, but vigorous in her movements. Once she had been plump, but now the weeks of little food and of hard work in trying to help her husband's parishioners had taken their toll. Her smile was warm and when she heard what Annabel proposed, she led the way to her large kitchen where a young girl, who was the maid at the vicarage, was stoking the fire in the range.

' 'Tis the last of the coal, missis,' the girl said as they entered the kitchen.

'There's more on the way,' Annabel said, 'and there'll be even more tomorrow when I can get into town.'

Startled, the girl, Lizzie, looked up and her mouth formed a silent 'Oh!'

'Now,' Annabel went on briskly. 'If you could find a large pan' – she glanced around the kitchen shelves, where there were numerous copper pans of all sizes – 'we'll go and bring in the supplies. We'll soon have some good, thick soup going.'

At the sound of cartwheels pulling up in the vicarage yard outside the back door, they all hurried out.

'I thought it best to come round to the back, Mrs Webster,' Ben said as he and Edward began to unload and carry everything into the kitchen. Very soon, Ben looked exhausted and Annabel took his place.

'You shouldn't be doing that, m'lady,' poor Ben protested, but he was leaning against the wall, panting.

'I've been doing it on Grandfather's farm most of my life,' Annabel said cheerfully, tugging at a bag of carrots. 'Why should I stop now?'

'But it's not right—'

As she passed by him again, she patted him on the shoulder and murmured, 'Don't worry, Ben.' It seemed so natural for her to call him 'Ben', not even 'Mr Jackson'. 'Just let's get these poor folk fed.'

At last, all the supplies had been unloaded.

'Right, my lovely, what next?' Edward asked his granddaughter.

Annabel glanced around but no one else seemed to have the strength left to do anything. Even Richard Webster was now slumped in a chair, having helped to carry one or two sacks in. He sat gazing at the piles of vegetables and fuel as if he couldn't believe what he was seeing. His wife came to stand by his chair and put her hand on his shoulder. He clutched at her hand. ''Tis a miracle,' he murmured.

For the next two hours Annabel, Jane, Phoebe Webster and her maid, Lizzie Harness, peeled and chopped all the vegetables that Edward had brought. Soon the kitchen was filled with an appetizing aroma. Phoebe tested the soup every so often, adding a little more salt.

'Is it nearly ready?'

'Another five minutes.'

'How shall we do this?' Annabel asked. 'Can they

eat here or would it be better for them to bring containers from home?'

Phoebe shook her head. 'It'd be best for them to have it good and hot and since none of them have any coal left at home for warming it up, they'd better eat here. We can use this table and the one in the dining room and have several sittings. Children first.'

'What about using the school room?' her husband suggested.

'Hasn't been used for months. It'll be dusty,' Phoebe replied promptly.

It was another shock for Annabel. 'No school for months? Why?'

'The schoolmaster left when things started to get difficult,' Richard sighed, 'and we haven't been able to get anyone else. I did a little teaching at first, but . . .' His voice faded away.

'It got too much for him,' Phoebe said briskly. 'He was making himself ill, what with his church work and trying to look after the villagers. And with little food ourselves too.'

Annabel nodded understandingly. 'I'm sure it did.' She put her hand on his arm. 'We'll soon have everything back to normal.'

Richard pulled a face and murmured, 'If any one of us can remember what normal is.' He was thoughtful for a moment before saying slowly, 'Perhaps it would be best if I open the church again. We could get everyone to come there and then bring them in here as soon as there's room.'

'Whatever you think, Richard,' his wife said, 'but these two pans are ready now. Right, Lizzie, let's have those other two you've got ready across here to the hob.'

'Is there anyone else nearby who could make soup? There's a mountain of vegetables ready. We just need a range.'

'No one's got any coal, m'lady.'

'Grandfather's brought some.'

Phoebe's face brightened. 'Then any one of the nearby cottages would help out.'

'What about taking some up to the big house, miss?' Jane suggested. 'Mrs Parrish could make a lot of soup on her range.'

'That's a good idea, Jane. Mr Jackson could take some supplies up and—' Phoebe began, but she was interrupted by Lizzie muttering, 'They'd keep it all for themselves, that miserable lot up there.'

'Shush, Lizzie. That's enough,' Phoebe said.

Annabel looked questioningly at the maid, but Lizzie blushed and turned her face away. Something very strange had happened in this village to bring the whole community to the edge of starvation and Annabel was determined to find out exactly what it was. But, for the moment, there were far more urgent matters.

Annabel took charge. 'Jane, go to the nearest cottages and tell them we've fuel and vegetables and ask them if they can make soup for themselves and their neighbours. And then go up and down the street knocking on every door and tell them all to come down to the church. Everyone in the village must be fed.'

'Ask them to bring spoons and bowls,' Phoebe said. 'We haven't enough for everyone.'

'And don't forget the little cottage beyond the school—' Annabel began, but she was interrupted abruptly by both Phoebe and Lizzie saying together, 'No, not her.'

'But there's a little boy. I saw him in the garden.'

'They've no need of our help,' Phoebe said shortly, but she would not meet Annabel's gaze. Then she felt Ben touch her arm and say softly, 'Leave it for now, m'lady. I'll explain later.' Annabel frowned but did as he asked. It seemed that there was another mystery to solve.

Sixteen

'What about the outlying farms on the estate?' Annabel asked Ben as they stood watching the villagers begin to drift in ones and twos into the church. To her surprise, not one of them asked questions; they merely glanced at her as they passed. There were no smiles, no words of greeting, just a surly expression here and there; mostly there was hopelessness in their eyes.

'I'll go and tell them.'

'Not before you've had something to eat yourself.' Ben smiled.

When it seemed that all the villagers had gathered in the church and Jane was back in the vicarage helping Phoebe and Lizzie make yet more soup, Annabel stood on the steps leading up to the altar. She hesitated a moment, feeling suddenly vulnerable in the face of their belligerent stares. She glanced at the vicar and her grandfather who were standing to one side. Edward smiled and gave her a little nod of encouragement.

Annabel took a deep breath and opened her mouth to speak, but before she could do so, a man, sitting halfway down the aisle, said loudly, 'I suppose you've come to tell us we've all got to leave – to get out of our homes.' He paused and with sarcastic bitterness, added, '*My lady*.' Annabel recognized him as the man who had spat at her earlier that day. His name, she had learned, was Jabez Fletcher.

'Not a bit of it, Mr Fletcher,' Annabel said with asperity. 'My grandfather – Mr Armstrong from Meadow View Farm on the other side of town, whom some of you may know' – there was murmuring amongst a few – 'has brought supplies from his farm. We're making soup for you all. You're to go into the vicarage a few at a time and be served. The children should go first. Now, apart from the outlying farms, is everyone here? The Cartwrights aren't here, I know that, but they're being attended to.'

'Old Mrs Brown in the cottage near the pub is bedridden,' someone called out.

Annabel nodded. 'Then I will take her some.'

'T'ain't fit for a *lady* to go into her hovel,' Jabez Fletcher said scathingly.

This time, Annabel chose to ignore him. 'There's no one else missing?'

Jabez laughed, but there was no humour in the sound. 'Only the trollop at the end cottage.' A murmur ran around the congregation. 'You've no need to feed her and her bastard. They're well looked after.'

'Mr Fletcher, please . . .' Richard admonished, but Jabez just glared at him sourly.

As Annabel was about to start shepherding the first batch of hungry folk into the vicarage, Dr Maybury came into the church and walked down the aisle towards her. He glanced from side to side. 'So, here's where you all are.' He came to stand beside Annabel and turned to face the villagers. 'Now, I don't want to keep you from your hot soup any longer, but I must warn you all – especially those of you with children – you must not eat too much or too fast. I know it's tempting, but you've been some time without proper food and your digestive system will need time to adjust.

Please, heed what I say, or you'll make yourselves really ill.'

'Aye,' Jabez once again seemed to be spokesman for them all. 'An' we can't pay expensive doctor's bills.'

Dr Maybury met the cantankerous man's baleful stare. Quietly, he said, 'There'll be no doctor's bills for anyone in this village for a long time to come, I can assure you. I know desperate need when I see it and I'll be happy to help you all back to health.'

But Jabez was not to be thwarted. 'Oh aye, and can you feed us all, Doctor?' He spread his hands. 'We've no money. Only two men in the village have jobs in the town – me an' Josh – and we have to walk there and back every day. We've tried to help, but our meagre wages won't feed a whole village. And them buggers up the hill' – he jerked his thumb in the direction of Fairfield Hall – 'won't lift a finger to help us. They'd rather see us all in our graves from starvation.'

Annabel didn't trouble to tell them that the situation at the big house was almost as bad as here in the village. She doubted they'd believe her anyway and, besides, she had to admit that it wasn't. There had been meat of sorts on the nights that James had been at home and they'd still been eating watery soup and dry bread, un-appetizing though it had been. Instead, she turned to the doctor. 'Have you time to stay to—?' she began but he smiled and said, 'I'm staying a while longer and then tomorrow – as soon as I've finished morning surgery in the town – I'll be back.' He turned towards the villagers. 'Now, let's get the youngest children fed first. Come along.'

Clutching their bowls and spoons the smallest children formed a line in the aisle and followed the doctor out of the church towards the vicarage.

121

'And the mothers with babes in arms,' Annabel added. 'You go too.' She turned to Richard. 'I'll leave you to organize things here and I'll take some soup to Mrs Brown.'

'I'll go back home and see what else I can bring,' Edward said quietly. 'I left Ma baking more bread and pies. Mebbe there'll be summat ready to bring back. Tell you what, my lovely,' he added, as a sudden thought struck him. 'I'll get the shops in town stirred up, an' all, if they'll answer the door to me on a Sunday evening.'

'They'll want paying what they're owed afore they'll let us have owt,' Jabez said morosely. 'They're owed a lot of money by the big house and by us villagers. They supplied us for a while, but when they could see there was no money forthcoming, they stopped. They won't even let us have owt if we go in with money. They just take it off the debt.' He glared at Annabel. 'We all thought it'd be better when his lordship married this wealthy heiress, see, but, from what I hear, your dowry – *my lady* – has gone to save the house and the land. There's not enough left to save us. And soon enough, we reckon, we'll all be thrown out because we've not been able to pay rent for months.'

Annabel stared at him, her heart thumping. She still didn't understand everything he was saying, but now she caught the gist of it. Her mouth tightened. 'You'll be fed, Mr Fletcher. You and everyone else in the village, and you will not be turned out of your homes. I give you my word.'

The man's lip curled. 'Your word? And what's your word worth, may I ask, *my lady*? You're only a woman.'

*

122

Annabel walked down the one and only street in the village and stopped outside the low cottage standing next to the public house, The Lyndon Arms. There was an air of desolation about what was the largest building on the street, save for the church and perhaps the vicarage. Annabel imagined that once it had been a thriving business, filled each evening with farmers and their labourers slaking their thirst after a long day's toil in the fields. But now it was deserted. She wondered what had happened to the landlord. Was he still living here in the village or had he gone elsewhere where there was more profit to be made?

There was so much she had to find out and she vowed she would do so, but, for the moment, the old lady lying in her bed in this cottage needed to be fed. She went round to the back of the dwelling and pushed open the creaking door. 'Mrs Brown?' she called tentatively and then louder, 'Mrs Brown?'

A frail voice answered. 'In the front room.'

The cottage was dark inside and smelled stale. And it was cold, even on this late summer's day. No place for an elderly, bedridden woman. She pushed open the door into the front room to see the bed set against the far wall of the tiny, cramped room. Accustoming her eyes to the dim light, she could see the woman, dressed in a dirty nightdress and nightcap, sitting in bed resting against two pillows.

'Who are you?' the querulous voice asked.

'I'm Annabel Lyndon and I've brought you some hot soup.' She was glad she'd had the forethought to bring a bowl and spoon with her. She daren't think what state the poor woman's kitchen might be in.

She set the pot of soup on the table and ladled some out into the bowl and added some pieces of bread into the liquid. Then she sat on the side of the bed and fed the old woman, mouthful by mouthful. When the amount that the doctor had advised she take to Mrs Brown was all gone, the old lady leaned back against her pillows and closed her eyes.

'Ah've never tasted owt better than that, m'duck. I don't know who you are, but I thank you.'

'Do you live here alone, Mrs Brown?' Annabel asked gently.

'Aye,' the voice was fading now and Mrs Brown's eyes remained shut. Annabel realized that the woman was falling asleep. She rose quietly from the bed and put the empty pot, bowl and spoon back into her basket. She glanced once more towards the bed, but decided not to disturb her any more. She'd find out what she needed to know from the woman's neighbours.

Back at the church, she found that most of the villagers had gone home, replete for the moment with their unexpected meal. 'We've told them to come back later this evening. The doctor says they can have another helping then as long as it's not too much,' Phoebe Webster told her.

Annabel nodded. 'Is there anything else I can do now?'

'You've done more than enough already, m'lady,' Richard Webster said, clasping her hands.

'Oh Mr Webster, I've hardly started.' Annabel smiled, her eyes sparkling.

'Your grandfather's gone home. He said he'd be back either later tonight or first thing tomorrow.'

'And I'll be going into town myself early tomorrow morning. But now, I want to see Mr Jackson. Do you know where he is?'

'He's waiting in the vicarage to take you and Jane home.'

'Is there any soup left for us to take up to the house? The staff up there haven't eaten properly recently either' – she smiled wryly – 'despite what Mr Fletcher thinks.'

'And the rest of the village too. They all think the folk at the big house have been living in luxury whilst down here . . .' Richard's voice faded away and he sighed. 'Mr Jackson will tell you everything. He knows more than I do.'

'Has he had enough to eat?'

'For the moment.' Richard nodded.

Before they set off, Annabel said, 'Oh, I must just see how the baby is.' She picked up her skirts and hurried across the street to knock gently on the door of the Cartwrights' cottage. After a few moments, Adam opened it.

'I just wondered –' she began hesitantly as she searched his face for any tell-tale sign that the baby might be worse. 'How . . .?'

'Come in, m'lady. Doctor's just called back. He's with the missis and babby now.'

'I don't want to intrude . . .' But she stepped inside, eager to know what was happening to the sick child. As she entered the room, Stephen Maybury stood up and turned to face her. Annabel held her breath for an instant, but then she could see that he was smiling. 'I think we were just in time.' He turned back to Betsy. 'Now, you know what to do, don't you, Mrs Cartwright?'

Betsy, now smiling through her tears, nodded. 'God bless you, Doctor. And you, m'lady. But for you . . .'

She dropped her head and they saw tears fall onto her baby's head. But they were tears of relief; now she had hope.

Seventeen

Bidding the family goodnight, Annabel and the doctor walked out of the cottage together. Across the road, Ben and Jane still waited.

'I'll be on my way,' Stephen Maybury said, 'but I'll be back in the morning. I want to make sure everyone in the village eats sensibly. Too much, too quickly, and they could make themselves really ill. Especially the youngsters.'

'Thank you for what you've done, Dr Maybury. I'll see you tomorrow and by the way, although it was kind of you to offer your services for nothing, please send your bills directly to me. I'll see that they are paid although I would ask you not to let that fact be known amongst the villagers.'

He stared down at her for a few moments before saying, soberly, 'You really don't know what's been going on here, do you?'

Annabel shook her head. 'No, but I intend to find out.'

A look of sympathy flitted briefly in his eyes. He seemed about to say more but then changed his mind, gave her a small, courteous bow and climbed into his own pony and trap.

'How's the babby?' was Jane's first question.

'I think little Eddie's going to be all right,' Annabel replied, smiling.

When they arrived back in the courtyard, Annabel

said, 'Take the soup and bread into the house, Jane. I'd like a word with Mr Jackson. If you're not too weary, Ben, I would like a few moments of your time.'

'Of course, m'lady.'

They climbed the steps to Ben Jackson's living quarters above the archway leading into the courtyard of Fairfield Hall. The rooms were clean and tidy, but there was no fire in the small sitting room into which he showed her.

'Please sit down, m'lady. I'm sorry I've nothing to offer you . . .'

Annabel waved his apologies aside. 'Now, Ben, I want you to tell me everything that has led to the villagers being in this dreadful state. And things are not much better up here either,' she nodded her head in the direction of Fairfield Hall, 'as I expect you know. So, please tell me.'

He sat down opposite her with a heavy sigh. 'It'll sound so disloyal, m'lady.'

'Whatever you tell me will go no further than this room, I promise you. But I need to know everything if I'm to do anything about it.'

He passed his hand wearily across his brow in a gesture of utter despair. 'I don't think there's anything you can do. It's all gone too far.'

'Please tell me,' she pressed him gently.

'I'll need to start way back with a bit of family history. It – it might take some time.'

'I'm listening.'

'I don't know how the Lyndon family came to be given an earldom and this estate. They've always been a soldiering family, so I'm guessing it had something to do with service to their country. You know the sort of thing?'

Annabel nodded, but did not interrupt him. The time for questions would be later.

'In the early years, so I understand, they prospered. The estate was well run, their tenants were granted sensible rents both for the farms and the cottages in the village. Most of the villagers worked on either Home Farm, run by the estate, or for the other tenant farmers. A grocer opened up, a butcher, a small general store and a smithy-cum-wheelwright. And at that time a carrier would visit once or twice a week from the town bringing goods that couldn't be obtained locally. The third earl built the public house and the school to add to the church. So, at that time it was a prosperous, happy little village.' He paused. 'This continued until the fourth earl's time. At first Charles Lyndon – that's your husband's father, m'lady – ran it well. I came to work for him as a young boy nearly twenty years ago. All was well then, but it was when his eldest son, Albert, reached maturity that things first started to go wrong. At eighteen, he was a wild young man. He lived the high life, spending most of his time in London. He drank heavily and he was a womanizer and a spendthrift. He refused to further his education and took no interest in learning how to run the estate. He even refused to go into the military, which had always been a strong tradition in the family. In each generation, there'd been a son who'd joined the army, though not always the eldest son. Albert brought further disgrace to the family by seducing one of the maids here in Fairfield Hall and she bore him a child. That's the young woman to whom Jabez Fletcher was referring.'

Annabel gasped and now she could not stop herself from interrupting briefly. 'The child in the cottage at the end of the village? He – he's Albert Lyndon's son?'

Ben pursed his lips as he nodded. 'At first the villagers were reasonably sympathetic. She's not the first young maid brought down by a son of the household where she worked and, sadly, she won't be the last. Albert Lyndon did one thing for her – he gave her that cottage – but there's been no other kind of support from the big house. At first, she and her mother made a living by dressmaking, but when times got hard, Nancy took to having a couple of – er – gentlemen callers from the town. Now, the villagers shun her because of that and also, more recently, because she's the only one who's been able to feed her child.' He smiled grimly. 'She tried to help others, but they'd sooner starve than accept charity from the likes of her, as they put it.'

Now Annabel realized what had puzzled her about the little boy in the garden; he was not thin and sickly like the other children in the village. He was well fed.

'They'd even see their own children suffer because of – of pride?'

Ben nodded, his face grim. 'It seems so.'

'Go on.'

'Where was I? Oh yes – Albert Lyndon. Well, he almost bled his poor father dry. Instead of making the foolish young man stand on his own feet, the old man – Charles – bailed him out time after time and after he died –' he wrinkled his brow, trying to remember – 'that'd be about three years ago now, well, Albert soon ran through the rest of his inheritance. He took out a loan against the house and the estate and put all the rents up so high that the farmers could no longer make a living or pay their labourers. The whole estate was on a slippery slope and still, Albert continued to drink and party. I'm not really sure how he lost his fortune. Maybe he made some bad investments, but he was forever in debt, that I do know. And, of course, there'd been death duties when his father died and then, when Albert died suddenly last December, the taxes were crippling. So things have been going steadily downhill for over three years. Farmers couldn't afford to pay their labourers and because all the estate workers lived in the village, soon they had no money to spend in the local shops, so they closed.'

Annabel was frowning. 'I still can't understand why everyone is in the same terrible state all at the same time. I mean, surely the farmers kept their animals for a while and there'd be something growing in the fields?'

Ben gave a heavy sigh. 'I'll say one thing for the folk here, everyone shared what they had. No one was fed whilst others starved, but of course that's why they're all so hungry now – all at once. Cattle were slaughtered to feed the whole village, fields were stripped of anything edible, and as for the local wildlife . . .' he gave a humourless laugh – 'it's almost non-existent. It's a fool-hardy rabbit or hare that comes anywhere near Fairfield now. We've fed on rooks, pigeons – and even hedgehogs, which were baked in clay.'

Annabel stared at him in horror. Now she was beginning to understand and her thoughts came back to the man who had caused all this hardship.

'What did Albert die of?'

'Liver failure, I shouldn't wonder,' Ben said sarcastically. 'But I never did get to know the official verdict. The family closed ranks and wouldn't say. He died in London and I reckon there might have been a bit of scandal, though it was all hushed up. But he was brought back here to be buried in the family plot as if he was some sort of hero. More money spent on a man who didn't deserve it.'

'And my husband?' Annabel asked in a small voice. She was beginning to realize that she had fallen for the charms of a young man she hardly knew anything about. There had certainly been no hint of anything like this in his family background; he had kept that very well hidden.

'I haven't got to know him very well, m'lady, I have to say,' Ben said carefully. 'As a boy and a young man growing up, he was certainly nothing like his wayward brother. He did well at school, as far as I know, though he was away at boarding school.'

'Another expense the family could ill afford,' Annabel murmured.

Ben shrugged, but made no comment on her remark. Instead, he continued with his story. 'As soon as he left school, he went straight into the army, so since about the age of twelve, he's never been at home much.'

'But what's happened since his brother died and my husband became the sixth earl? Hasn't he tried to put matters right here?'

Ben shook his head. 'He's an army man. He has no interest in farming or the estate. He's left it to me and I'm afraid I've failed to pull it round. Lord Fairfield told me to see his sister about matters I couldn't handle, but she flatly refuses to release any money to help the estate. They – the family, that is – need it, she says and I suppose in a way she's right. The big house is crumbling around their ears. But she has no thought for all the folk in the village. *Their* village.'

'What do you mean? "Release any money"? I thought you said there was none left?'

Now Ben was ill at ease. He shifted uncomfortably in his chair.

'The only thing the master could do was to marry

131

into money, m'lady.' Annabel gasped and her eyes widened, but she said nothing as Ben continued. 'We all thought your dowry would be the saving of us all, but it seems it's not to be.'

'Ah yes, my dowry?' This was the second time it had been mentioned. 'Tell me about it.'

He blinked at her. 'Don't you know, m'lady?'

Annabel shook her head.

'I shouldn't be telling you all this,' Ben murmured worriedly.

Annabel recovered enough to say, 'I won't let you down, Ben, but I would like to know everything.'

He sighed and went on, albeit reluctantly. 'It seems a mutual acquaintance of your father's and the Lyndon family – a Lady Carruthers – introduced James Lyndon to you. She knew that he was in desperate straits and needed to marry an heiress and she also knew that your father –' he paused briefly before taking a deep breath, for he was finding this deeply worrying – 'was anxious for you to marry into the nobility. He wanted you to have a title and for his future grandson one day to become a lord and a wealthy landowner. The rumours say that your father was prepared to give his lordship ten thousand pounds upon his marriage to you.'

'I see,' Annabel said quietly – and she did. Her quick mind was leaping from one thing to another and soon she had pieced it all together. How naïve and gullible she had been. Hurt by Gilbert's desertion, she had been vulnerable to James's undoubted charms and blind to her father's schemes. She wondered again, briefly, if Ambrose had been instrumental in Gilbert's disappearance too. And now – after everything that Ben was telling her – nothing would surprise or shock her.

Ben had fallen silent and sat with his head bowed.

Annabel felt sorry for the man and tried to put him at his ease. 'I will keep my promise to you, Ben. No one will hear from me what you have told me, but I am going to need your help.'

Slowly, he raised his head. 'My help, m'lady? How can I help you?'

'Because, Ben, you and I are going to revive the fortunes of this estate, the village and everyone in it.'

'I don't see how you can. If what I've heard is true, that money has been used to pay a substantial amount off the loan on Fairfield Hall and the estate. I heard a whisper that the bank was about to foreclose and the Lyndons were going to be –' he ran his tongue around his lips in embarrassment – 'evicted.'

'But you see, Ben, I have money of my own. My grandfather taught me to buy and sell shares, which I still do. I seem to have an intuitive sense of what will make money and what will lose. I have built up a rather nice little nest egg for myself and have been able to invest some of that money in secure stocks, which give me a steady income.' She smiled. 'I still like the thrill of playing the stock market, but I certainly don't ever risk a huge amount at any one time.'

'But why should you spend your money on folks who are nothing to do with you and who probably won't appreciate it anyway?'

'Whether they like it or not, Ben – in fact, whether I like it or not – they are now *my* people. And, as you rightly say, if I am blessed with a son, he will one day inherit.'

Ben began to smile slowly, but then his face clouded. 'Then beware of your new sister-in-law, m'lady. She is adamant that her son, Master Theodore, will one day inherit. She didn't want James to marry you – or anyone else, for that matter. But she had no choice. The way things were going there would have been nothing to pass on to the lad anyway – except perhaps a worthless title. She was forced to give in – and she did – but certainly not gracefully.'

'That explains a lot,' Annabel murmured as she got up. 'I'll let you rest now, Ben. You've had a busy day. But I would like to go into the town first thing tomorrow morning.'

He rose too. 'I'll take you, m'lady.'

Annabel shook her head. 'No; if you harness the trap, I'll drive myself, because I'd like you to stay and help my grandfather when he returns. And now,' she said with an ironic grimace, 'I'd better go and face the lioness in her den.'

Eighteen

When Annabel entered the house by the side door and went down to the basement kitchen, Jane ran to her at once, tears flooding down her face.

'Oh miss, thank goodness you've come.'

'Whatever's the matter? What's happened?' She glanced beyond Jane to see the grim faces of John Searby and Nelly Parrish. Even Annie and Luke seemed subdued.

'We don't want a thief in our midst, m'lady,' Nelly said.

'A thief?' Annabel was shocked, even though, since Ben's revelations, she'd thought that nothing could surprise her again. 'Whatever are you talking about?'

'Her!' Nelly Parrish pointed an accusing finger at Jane. 'Where's she got soup and bread from, I'd like to know?'

'She's pinched 'em, that's where,' Annie said spitefully. 'Taken 'em from folks who're already starving, I'll be bound.'

'You may certainly know, Mrs Parrish. Please sit down – all of you – and I'll explain.'

'I tried to tell them, miss, but they wouldn't listen.' Jane was still sobbing. 'They wouldn't believe me.'

'Wait till Lady Dorothea hears about this. You'll be out on your ear, girl.' Nelly was still vitriolic, but the four servants sat down grudgingly at the table to listen to what Annabel had to say.

135

'The food has all come from my grandfather's farm
. . .' Annabel began, and she went on to explain the
events that had taken place down in the village since
all those from Fairfield Hall had gone home after church.

'And he will be back again tomorrow with more
supplies and, first thing in the morning, I am taking the
trap into town. I shall visit all the tradesmen and get
them to start delivering not only to this house, but to
all the villagers too.'

'They'll not do that, m'lady.' John shook his head.
'They'll all want paying before they'll supply any more
goods to anyone in Fairfield and that includes us.'

'Then they'll be paid,' Annabel said promptly.

'What with?' Annie smirked. 'Fresh air? 'Cos that's
all we've got.'

'I shall pay them.'

'How?' Nelly asked. 'Your dowry's been swallowed
up rescuing this place.' She cast her eyes to the ceiling.
'You'll not be able to touch it.'

Annabel thought quickly, anxious not to let Ben
down. She had given him her solemn promise. But she
was on safe ground for the moment. It seemed they all
believed she knew about the dowry that had come with
her marriage to Lord Lyndon.

Airily, she said, 'I have some money of my own I
intend to use.'

'Then you'd best not let Lady Dorothea hear about
it,' Nelly warned. 'She doesn't think the dowry was
enough anyway. If she hears you've got more – she'll
want it. She dun't care about the villagers. All that
matters to her is her precious son's inheritance; this
house and the estate.'

Annabel rose. 'Then I think it's high time I had a
conversation with my sister-in-law. In the meantime,

please use the food which Jane brought. It has been obtained honestly, I promise you.'

Without another word, Annabel turned and left the room. She hoped the servants would have the grace to apologize to Jane, but she doubted it. They were a surly lot and no mistake. But, the kindly young woman told herself, they had good reason to be after the hardships they had endured recently.

Annabel found Dorothea alone in the morning room, crouched in front of a dying fire, a thick shawl round her shoulders. She looked up malevolently as Annabel entered. 'What do you want?'

Annabel crossed the room and sat down in a chair on the opposite side of the hearth to her sister-in-law, suppressing a shiver as she did so; the room was undeniably cold for the time of year.

'I want to talk to you, Dorothea. There's something very strange going on here and I want to know what it is.'

'It's none of your business.'

'I think it is,' Annabel said softly, but there was a hint of steel in her tone. Dorothea must have noticed it, for she looked up and met Annabel's steady gaze.

'You'd do best to go back to your folks,' she snapped and then added grudgingly, 'at least until James comes home again.'

'My place is here now and I intend to stay, but I also intend to help you and your son, and your mother and the villagers.'

Dorothea's thin mouth curled in a sneer. 'And how do you propose to do that? Unless you're a millionairess, you won't be able to do anything.' She gazed into the sorry fire that glowed, but gave out little warmth. 'We had logs to burn for a while, but none of the men have the strength to cut down any more trees now.' Her tone hardened. 'Though I expect those idle beggars in the village could, if they wanted to. Still, they'll all be gone soon. We'll get new tenants who can pay their rent and work the land again.'

'And how are you going to do that?' Annabel asked, copying Dorothea's own wording. She kept her voice level and calm, though inside she was seething at the woman's callousness.

Dorothea's eyes narrowed. 'Jackson should already have given them all notice.' She held Annabel's gaze but the latter said nothing in response. She rather thought that Ben Jackson had not carried out those orders; if he had done so, Annabel would have heard about it today. She smothered a smile. Jabez Fletcher would have been the first to say something, she was sure.

'Your dowry,' Dorothea's tone was scathing, 'such as it was – has helped us secure the bank loan on this house and the estate, but it wasn't enough' – her tone became accusatory now – 'to cover the rents that haven't been paid for months.' She sniffed. 'Still, my son's inheritance is secure for the moment and, once we get some new tenants, things should improve.'

Annabel, with her head on one side and being careful not to give too much away, eyed the woman. 'What do you mean – your son's inheritance?'

'Theodore will inherit after James.'

Annabel frowned. James had told her he wanted a son of his own. He had been adamant about it. And their wedding night – and her first night at Fairfield – had seemed to bear out that fact. For the moment Annabel decided to hold her tongue; she would ask no questions. It seemed, however, that Dorothea could not keep silent. She wanted to plunge the knife into Annabel; she was determined to be rid of James's unwanted bride. The family had her money now; that was all any of them had needed or wanted.

Dorothea's eyes gleamed with spite as she said, 'James may have told you he wants a son, but he has promised me that *my* son will be his heir. He swore he would not consummate his marriage to you and – after an appropriate interval – he will have the marriage annulled on those grounds.'

Annabel was appalled and, even though she had quelled her anger thus far, now she could not suppress a shocked gasp. She bit her lip, deliberately holding back any retort. She was not even going to try to score points against this manipulative woman. Only time would prove that already James had broken his promise to his sister. With great dignity, Annabel rose and looked down at the woman still kneeling in front of the fire.

'Despite what you obviously feel about me and your plans for me, Dorothea, I am not a vindictive person. Everyone in this house – including you and your son – need my help. And you shall have it.'

Before the woman could make any further comment, Annabel turned away with a swish of her skirts and left the room.

Annabel spent a restless night and awoke early the following morning. She dressed quickly and crept down the stairs to the kitchen where she helped herself to a drink of milk before letting herself quietly out of the side door. Ben was near the stables, just finishing harnessing the pony into the shafts of the trap.

''Morning, m'lady. Are you sure you don't want me to come with you?'

'I'll be fine, Ben, really. I'd sooner you were here to help my grandfather.'

For a moment, Ben leaned against the side of the trap. He looked weak. Annabel sighed inwardly, but decided to say nothing. She climbed into the back and, as Ben moved away, she picked up the reins and urged the animal forward, calling out, 'I don't know when I'll be back, but don't worry about me. I'll be fine. Give Grandfather my love – and thanks.'

Ben nodded and raised his hand as she pulled away. She drove at a steady pace down the slope, through the village and past the lonely cottage on the outskirts. Once more the solemn-faced little boy was alone in the front garden, kicking a ball. Annabel waved and smiled at him, but there was no response. He just stood very still and stared after her until she rounded a corner and disappeared from his sight. It was the first time anyone from the village had even acknowledged his existence.

The pony picked up speed of his own accord and soon they were bowling along the country lanes. Annabel lifted her face to the early morning sun. Ahead of her she saw the figures of two men walking towards the town. One she recognized as Jabez Fletcher and the other one, though she did not know his name, had been in church sitting beside Jabez. As she drew level with them, she pulled on the reins and the pony slowed its pace.

'Good morning, Mr Fletcher. Are you both going into the town? May I take you there?'

Jabez stopped and squinted up at her against the early morning sun. 'Now, why should you want to do a thing like that, *my lady*?'

The man beside him stopped, too, and after a quick glance at Annabel he sank down onto the grass verge and dropped his head into his hands.

'Why wouldn't I, Mr Fletcher? Five miles is a long way for anyone to walk twice a day.' She nodded towards the other man. 'Your companion looks in need of a ride in my trap. Please' – she moved a little to make room for them both – 'climb in.'

After a moment's hesitation, Jabez looked down at the other man, who was much younger than him, but who looked even more exhausted. Jabez sighed and offered his hand to help him up. He almost lifted him into the trap and then climbed in himself.

'This is Josh Parrish, Nelly Parrish's nephew. He's not well this morning, m'lady, but since we're the only two in the village who have work in the town, we have to try to get there.' He glanced at Annabel and seemed to have to force the words as he added reluctantly, 'We're grateful for the ride.'

'Shouldn't you be at home if you're not well?' Annabel said to the young man. 'Dr Maybury will be visiting again today and—'

'There's nowt wrong with him that a good, square meal won't put right.'

'In that case, we'll soon have you fit again, Mr Parrish. I'm on my way into town now to have supplies sent to the village. By tonight – with my grandfather's help as well – there should be enough for everyone, even though you'll all have to take it steadily at first like the doctor advised.'

'They'll want paying first,' Jabez grunted, 'afore they'll give you a crumb.'

'Then they'll be paid, Mr Fletcher.'

He stared at her, dumbfounded for once. 'Why?' he

said at last. 'Why are you doing this for folks you don't even know?'

Annabel smiled. 'I don't know you yet, but I soon will. You're my people now and I intend to help you.'

'Jackson told me that he's supposed to have given us all notice 'cos none of us have paid any rent for months.'

'Well, if he does – and I sincerely hope he doesn't – then just ignore the notices. You're staying – all of you – though there is one thing you could do for me, Mr Fletcher.'

'Aye, I thought there'd be a catch.'

Annabel smiled. 'No catch, I promise, but I just want you to give me a chance. That's all I ask. You seem to be the – um – spokesman for the villagers and I'd like you on my side. Do you think you could do that?'

Josh nudged the older man and muttered, 'She's the only chance we've got, Jabez. And she's already saved Adam's little babby's life. Only another few hours and –' He bit his lip and Annabel saw tears well in the young man's eyes.

Jabez stared at her for a long moment and then slowly his wrinkled face, as if it was unused to it, began to smile. 'Aye, m'lady. I'll give it a try, but I'll be watching . . .'

'That's fair enough.' Annabel smiled and flicked the reins to make the pony trot a little faster.

Nineteen

Annabel left the two men outside their place of work – the town's smithy. As she drew away she was thoughtful. She wondered what the background of the two men was and she made a mental note to ask Ben. But then her mind turned to what she had to do today. Her first call was at the stockbroker's.

It was lucky – very lucky – that this was the same town where her grandfather banked and where his stockbroker had his office. Through Edward Armstrong, she knew both the stockbroker, Mr Parker, and the bank manager, Mr Hoyles. Both men would receive her courteously, though whether they would be helpful was another matter.

Mr Parker greeted her as an old friend. He'd watched her grow from a young girl, when Edward had first brought her to meet him, into the beautiful and poised young woman she was now. As she was shown into his office and sat down in front of his desk, she smiled at him. But now, he regarded her solemnly over the top of his steel-framed spectacles. 'I understand you are to be congratulated on your marriage, Lady Fairfield?'

It didn't sound as though he were actually congratulating her but Annabel smiled anyway and thanked him prettily. Then he sighed as he said heavily, 'I take it you've come to transfer your holdings into your husband's name?'

'Certainly not!' Annabel replied firmly. 'Thanks to the Married Women's Property Act I can now manage my own affairs and I intend to do so, though I believe you'll need my grandfather's signature until I reach twenty-one?'

Mr Parker's expression lightened a little, but his eyes were still wary. 'Then I take it you're here merely to alter your name on all the documentation.'

'Partly – but I need to sell some shares to raise some capital quickly.'

Mr Parker raised his eyebrows. 'I – see,' he said slowly and Annabel could see that he was dying to ask why, but was far too circumspect to do so. He managed and advised Annabel on her stock holding, but it was not his business to ask why she wanted to sell some of her shares and at the present time, Annabel was not prepared to confide in him. It wasn't that she didn't trust him – he was a fine stockbroker – but she feared he might try to persuade her not to spend her money in the way she intended.

Mr Hoyles was a different matter. When, over an hour later, she entered his office, the large, ebullient bank manager greeted her with outstretched arms and a kiss on both cheeks.

'I don't greet all my customers like that,' he laughed, his double chin wobbling. 'But you are rather a special young lady to me – have been ever since your grandfather first brought you to this bank to open an account for you on your tenth birthday. And your account has grown steadily over the years and more rapidly recently, with your clever stock market deals.' He gestured towards the chair in front of his desk, inviting her to sit down, then took his place behind the desk, dropping heavily into a chair that squeaked protestingly. He leaned back and linked his fingers across his rotund stomach and smiled benignly at her. 'And what can I do for you today, my dear? I presume you wish to change your name on your accounts in view of your recent marriage.'

'That and other things, Mr Hoyles,' Annabel said, drawing off her gloves. Now here was a man in whom she was happy to confide completely. Indeed, she was obliged to do so for she needed his help.

'I don't know whether you know or not,' she began, for this was not her father's bank, 'that upon my recent marriage, my father paid my husband a substantial dowry. I understand that it was supposed to rescue the ailing Fairfield Estate.' She spoke calmly and rationally even though deep inside her was a burning resentment against the two men who had treated her so callously for their own ends. But for the moment, her mind was not on herself but on the starving villagers. 'It seems, however,' she went on, 'that that money has been used solely to safeguard Fairfield Hall and the estate.'

Mr Hoyles's expression was now very serious. He leaned forward and rested his forearms on his desk as he said quietly, 'You know I cannot discuss your husband's affairs with you, even though this is where he banks. But, go on.' They stared at each other across the broad expanse of his desk and, shrewdly, Annabel guessed his intention. He could not tell her anything, but if she were to say what she believed to be the facts and he did not deny them, then she would be able to glean most of the truth.

'I presume that the ten thousand pounds has paid all or part of a loan or whatever it is on the house and land.' She paused and Mr Hoyles said nothing. 'But – if I'm right – it has not left anything with which to revitalize the estate.' Still he remained silent. 'I have been

145

told by my sister-in-law that –' here Annabel paused. She did not intend to tell him everything that Dorothea had said. Choosing her words carefully, she went on, 'Mr Jackson has been instructed to give everyone on the estate – and that includes the tenant farmers and all the dwellings in the village – notice. It is hoped that new tenants will be found to pay what I'm guessing will be extortionate rents. Personally, I doubt the sense in that anyway since no one in their right mind is going to take on tenancies with exorbitant rents, especially considering the dilapidated state of the farms and cottages.'

'I agree,' Mr Hoyles said briefly, able for once to make a comment.

'So, I intend to help the tenant farmers and the villagers get back on their feet and see that they are charged affordable rents when they are able to start paying them again.'

'Your husband has agreed to this?'

'He knows nothing about it. He's away playing soldiers.' Immediately, she regretted her sarcasm and the hint of censure against her husband her words held. And yet, she was angry with him for not noticing that his people were in dire need.

'And the dowager countess? Does she approve?'

'It's of no consequence. She takes no interest in the running of the estate and my sister-in-law has no empathy with the villagers.'

'I must warn you that whatever you spend, my lady, you are unlikely to recoup it.'

Annabel shrugged. 'I realize that. But it's only money and there are people's lives at stake here.' She leaned forward to emphasize her point. 'The villagers are starving, Mr Hoyles. We have to act swiftly.'

146

He nodded. 'I had heard that there was suffering amongst the villagers. What can I do to help you?'

'I have this morning asked Mr Parker to sell some of my shares and my grandfather will have to counter-sign my instructions. This may take a few days for the money to come through. In the meantime, could you advance me a loan so that I can pay the town's tradesmen whatever they are owed and buy more supplies for the villagers?'

'Your deposit account already has a healthy sum in it and I'll arrange a transfer of that to your current account so that you may make cheques out immediately, which I will ensure are honoured. And we'll arrange a temporary loan too,' Mr Hoyles agreed readily and smiled as he rang a bell to summon his chief cashier. 'But of course I, too, will need to see your grandfather.'

'I'll make sure he calls in to the bank. Will tomorrow morning be soon enough?'

'Certainly. Any cheques you make out today probably won't be presented immediately, so as long as everything is in place by tomorrow that will be fine.' He paused and added, with a note of caution in his tone, 'You're a very astute businesswoman, Lady Annabel, for one so young, but I wonder if you realize just what a consid-erable amount of money it is going to take to restore the estate?'

Annabel treated him to her most winning smile. 'I had been wondering what to do with the money I have made – and am still making. Rather than just buying more and more shares, this seems like a very worthwhile investment.' Mr Hoyles still didn't look convinced, but Annabel went on, 'The Fairfield Estate is now my future and – if I'm blessed with children – it's their future too. And in the meantime, I'll be helping the tenants get back their livelihood. They've been treated rather shabbily, I fear, though that is just between you and me, Mr Hoyles.'

'Of course,' he murmured, his gaze still on her lovely face that had not only beauty but also a steely determination. He took a deep breath as he said, 'I will make sure the bank supports you in your worthy endeavours, my lady.'

An hour later, armed with her chequebook and the promise of ample funds to be available in her current account to meet any cheques she needed to make out, Annabel stepped out into the market town's main street. She made her way at once to the grocer's shop. As she entered, there were three customers and the proprietor behind his counter. All four heads turned to look at her, but she took her place in the queue behind the other women. When they'd all left, whispering to one another, Annabel approached the counter.

'Good morning. I am Annabel Lyndon and—'

'I know full well who you are and I'm sorry to say it, but you're not welcome in my shop.' The man stood tall and rotund behind his counter, a white apron stretched around his middle.

'Then would you be kind enough to tell me the amount that is owed to you by both Fairfield Hall and everyone in Fairfield village too? I will pay you in full and then find another supplier. I'm sure there must be another grocer in the town, or I could travel to Lincoln, of course. It's not so many miles away.'

'Ah well, now, m'lady, there's no need to be hasty. You'll not find another establishment within easy reach to compare with my shop. And if you've come to pay up, then—'

Annabel's eyes gleamed. 'I have and I have also come

to buy a quantity of supplies which I intend to pay for at once.'

'It'll take me a few moments to add everything up that's owed.'

'Then I'll go next door to the butcher's whilst you do.' With that, she turned on her heel and left the shop with the man staring after her, his mouth half open.

More or less the same words were exchanged in the butcher's shop further along the street. He was reluctant at first to serve her but then the shopkeeper almost fell over himself in his eagerness to retain her custom. When she returned to the grocer's, he was waiting for her with an itemized bill in his hand. Annabel glanced at the total and was not surprised that the man had refused to serve her. For a small businessman, he was owed a great deal of money by Fairfield Hall and the villagers. She glanced up at him. 'I promise you this will not happen again. And now, if you will make up this order as soon as you can and add it to this account, I will settle at once. You will take a cheque?'

For a brief moment the man looked uncertain again. He hesitated and bit his lip.

'Mr Hoyles is my bank manager. If you wish to check with him first, I am happy to wait.'

The man relaxed and nodded. 'That'll be all right, m'lady. It's where I bank too.'

'There is just one more thing. Are you able to deliver to Fairfield? I won't be able to get everything in my trap.'

'Of course.'

'If there's a charge for delivery then please add it to the bill.'

'Since you're settling everything, I'll not charge on

this occasion, though in normal circumstances, I do make a small charge to come out to Fairfield.'

Annabel nodded as she left his shop to make similar arrangements with the butcher. The goods were promised for delivery later in the day.

As she climbed into the trap once more and turned for home, another thought struck her and she pulled to a halt outside the smithy's where Jabez and Josh worked. She climbed down and went into the yard and to the doorway, but hesitated to interrupt the two men who were working at the glowing forge. She waited until another man came up and asked what she wanted.

'Is it ya pony, missis?' He jerked his head towards the animal standing patiently just outside the gate.

'No, no, I just wanted to speak to Josh or Jabez, but I didn't want to interrupt them.'

'That was thoughtful of you, missis. You'd be surprised how many folk just walk in here and disturb them without realizing how dangerous this work is. Can I give them a message?'

'If you would, I'd be grateful. What time do they finish work tonight?'

'About six.'

'Then please tell them I'll arrange for Mr Jackson to fetch them in the trap.'

The man's eyes widened in surprise, but he nodded. 'I'll be sure to tell them. They'll be glad to hear it. Young Josh don't look too well today.'

Annabel made no comment but merely smiled and bade him good day. Then she climbed back into the trap, anxious now to get home.

Twenty

When her pony trotted into the village, Annabel saw her grandfather's farm cart standing outside the vicarage gate. Edward, Ben and the vicar were carrying goods into the house. When they saw her, they stopped what they were doing and came to her. Further down the street, she could see the doctor's pony and trap and guessed he had arrived already to continue his examination of all the villagers as she had asked.

'Grandfather,' she greeted him and kissed his cheek.

'Ben told us where you'd gone, but we were starting to worry. You've been a long time.'

Her eyes sparkling at the success of her morning's work, she said, 'Let's go inside. Perhaps Mrs Webster can find us a cup of tea and I'll tell you everything.'

'Oh, miss, I've been that worried.' Jane hurried towards her as they entered the kitchen. 'When I found you gone, I – I thought – well, I didn't know what to think and Lady Dorothea said you'd likely gone home – back to your folks. But I – I didn't think you'd have gone without me, miss.'

'Of course I wouldn't have, Jane.' Annabel smiled as she sat down and drew off her gloves. 'Besides, this is our home now. Whatever anyone else says, we're here to stay.'

Jane couldn't stop herself grimacing, but she said softly, 'Whatever you say, miss.'

'Don't worry.' Annabel patted the girl's hand. 'Things will soon be better.' And, as Phoebe Webster poured out tea for them all, she told them everything that she'd done that morning. 'You'll have to call in at both Mr Parker's and the bank, Gramps, to sign some papers, but they said there was no immediate hurry.' When at last she fell silent, they were all gaping at her – all except her grandfather, who was smiling with pride. 'That's my girl,' he murmured.

It was the vicar who said what they were all thinking. 'You shouldn't have to spend your own money. Your dowry was supposed to –' He stopped in embarrassment, wondering if he had said too much. Gently, Annabel reassured him, but she was careful not to let Ben down in any way. 'I know about my dowry and, yes, it should have solved everything, but it didn't. My sister-in-law wasted no time in telling me that the sum of money my father paid my husband – a large sum of money, I might add – was not nearly enough. It has only secured Fairfield Hall and the land, and, I suspect, only for the time being, seeing as there is no income from the estate at the present time.' Now she glanced at Ben. 'She also told me that you had been instructed to give notice to the tenant farmers and to all the villagers. I do hope you haven't done anything about that yet.'

Ben glanced uncomfortably around the gathering before saying, stiltingly, 'No, m'lady, I haven't. I was hoping – like you've just said – that the money his lordship had been promised on your marriage to him would . . .' He spread his hands in a helpless gesture and didn't finish his sentence, but everyone there knew exactly what he meant. Instead, he went on flatly, 'But if, as you say, it's all been used to save the house and estate, then' – he sighed heavily – 'I suppose now I have no choice but to carry out those orders. But who'll want to take on the farms in their present state?'

'You'll do no such thing,' Annabel said swiftly, but her smile took the sting out of her demand. 'Everyone will be staying. Between us, we'll get this village – and the estate – back on its feet. Oh, and by the way, Ben, please would you take the pony and trap into town to be at the smithy's in town by six o'clock. Jabez and Josh need a ride home.'

A slow grin spread across Ben's face. 'Indeed I will, m'lady. And – thank you.' His deep voice was suddenly husky with emotion and Annabel knew he was thanking her for a good deal more than her thoughtfulness for the two working men.

Hands on her hips, Phoebe was looking at the goods stacked around her kitchen. 'And you say there's more coming from the town later today, m'lady? Whatever are we going to do with it all?'

'Ah, now I need to talk to Dr Maybury and ask him the best way to distribute everything. I don't want anyone to make themselves ill with over-indulgence.'

'Shall I go and find him, miss?' Jane offered. 'He's down the street.'

Annabel nodded. 'Yes, please. Then we can organize how it's to be done. In the meantime,' she added, as her maid hurried out, 'I want to be sure that the woman and her child in the cottage on the outskirts of the village will be included when the provisions are given out.'

There was an uncomfortable silence around the table and no one would meet her questioning gaze. Beside her, a puzzled frown furrowed her grandfather's brow. After several minutes, it was Lizzie who burst out,

'Begging your pardon, ma'am' – she glanced at her mistress – 'but it has to be said. That woman is a whore.'

Now there were startled gasps and the vicar said sternly, 'Lizzie, curb your tongue. I will not have such language in my house.'

Unfazed, Annabel said softly, 'Then tell me about her, Lizzie, if you please.' Even though she knew the story, she was anxious yet again not to let Ben down. He was sitting across the table from her, his head bowed. But now, Lizzie too seemed uncertain. She glanced at her mistress, who shrugged and said flatly, 'You'd better finish what you started, Lizzie, but mind what you say.'

'She had a bairn out of wedlock. The boy you see playing in the garden. It wasn't so bad at first. She lived with her mam and they were dressmakers, but when times got hard and there was no work coming in, Nancy had no means of supporting her child so she turned to –' again Lizzie hesitated before whispering, 'entertaining a couple of men from the town. They come nearly every Friday night. Mrs Banks couldn't stand the shame so she – she left.'

'So – Nancy's regarded as a fallen woman and her child is treated as an outcast? Is that it?'

'He's a bastard, m'lady, he—'

'Lizzie!' Richard Webster thundered.

'Sorry, sir, but he is. And the rest of the village will have nowt to do wi' her – or him.'

'You mean she is shunned by everyone? And the little boy has no playmates?'

Lizzie shook her head.

'She's a lost sheep,' Richard murmured sadly.

Annabel turned to look at him, her jaw set deter-

154

minedly. 'Then, Mr Webster, it's high time she and her child were brought back into the fold.'

He shook his head. 'Not whilst she still – um – entertains.'

'That will be stopped. She'll have no need to earn her living outside the village.'

He gazed at her for a moment before saying. 'No one in the village or on the estate will employ her. They could forgive her bearing an illegitimate child, but not what she's doing now.'

'Maybe not, Vicar, but I can and I will find gainful employment for her in due course. In the meantime' – Annabel pushed back her chair and stood up – 'she and her child are to be fed along with the rest of the villagers. Now, that sounds like Jane returning with the doctor. Come along, we have work to do.'

For the rest of the day, until dusk fell, they worked as a team. When the supplies arrived from the town, they doled out the food to each household, under advice from Stephen Maybury with regard to how many adults and children lived in each dwelling.

'Give them what we've given them today for the next three or four days and then they should be all right to eat more or less what they want, though,' he laughed, 'there may still be one or two cases of indigestion, but it'll no longer be harmful. I think most people have taken notice of what I've told them, particularly where their children are concerned. Country folk understand nature – even human nature – better than most. I'm confident now that they'll all be sensible. It was just for the first few days when they were so desperately hungry that I was fearful they would over-indulge.'

As the doctor was about to leave, Annabel held out her hand. 'I don't know how to thank you, Doctor, for everything you've done. You will send your bill to me, won't you?' But he waved her plea aside.

'I've been glad to help. And don't hesitate to call on me any time. I mean it.' He took her hand in his warm grasp and looked down into her beautiful eyes, losing himself for a brief moment in their depths. 'You are a most remarkable woman, Lady Fairfield. It is a privilege to know you.'

Without waiting for her to reply, he turned and climbed up into his pony and trap and as he drew away, Annabel found she was blushing.

By the time Ben returned with Jabez and Josh, it was almost dark, but there was just one more thing Annabel wanted to find out before she went home. She was waiting for them outside the vicarage when the trap rattled into the village street. Seeing her, Ben pulled the pony to a halt and his two passengers stepped down.

'Thank 'ee, m'lady. That were kind of you,' Jabez said.

'Provisions have been left at your home, Mr Fletcher. I understand Josh lodges with you?'

'He does, m'lady. He came to live with me and the missis as my apprentice lad at the forge. My wife died some while back and he stayed on.' He put his hand on the younger man's shoulder. 'He's like a son to me. He's no family of his own, except for Nelly Parrish and her old mother, but, of course, she's not here now.' He lapsed into a sad silence.

'What forge would that be, then?'

Jabez sighed heavily. 'My old forge, m'lady. Here in

the village, but when things got so hard, I had to close it down. We was lucky to get work in the town, me and the lad here. We was the only ones who could. We've shared what we've earned, but it's not nearly enough.' He drew the back of his hand across his eyes that were suddenly suspiciously wet. 'We've lost two of the old folk in the last month. They were just too frail to survive the hunger. Two or three families left to go to relatives, but most of us either haven't got anywhere to go or – or we're too proud to ask.'

Annabel touched his arm, but for the moment she could promise nothing, so she kept her counsel and merely bade them 'goodnight', promising them that Ben would drive them into town the following morning.

'Let me help you into the trap, m'lady,' Ben offered. 'You've had a long day. You must be tired.'

She hadn't felt it at all until this moment, but suddenly the weariness washed over her and she accepted his offer gratefully.

Twenty-One

'Take me round to the side door, Ben. I don't want to bring Mr Searby to the front door. Poor man's exhausted. They all are.'

'I will, m'lady, but may I offer you a little piece of advice?'

'Of course.'

'They *expect* you to use the front entrance. The Countess of Fairfield does *not* enter her home via the servants' entrance.'

Despite her tiredness, Annabel giggled. 'Ben, you know and I know that I am no lady.'

'I didn't mean to imply for one moment—'

'I know you didn't, but the fact remains. I realize now that the earl has married me for my money – or rather my father's money. Seeing how things are, in a way I can't blame him for that. The person I do blame is my father. He is fixated on having a grandson with a title and his obsession has led him to – to *sell* his own daughter. That I find hard to forgive. But here I am, Ben, and now I have another purpose in my life beyond producing a male heir. I mean to rejuvenate this estate and if I am to do so, people will have to accept me as I am – lady or no lady.'

Dutifully, Ben drove the pony and trap into the court-yard. As he drew to a halt he turned to her and said huskily, 'M'lady, you are more of a true lady in your little finger than many a one born to the position. I only wanted to save you their –' he paused as if searching for the right word – 'comments.'

She guessed he had been about to say 'censure' or even 'ridicule' but had settled for a kinder word. She put her hand on his arm. 'I appreciate your concern for me, Ben, truly I do. Now, you go home and have a good rest yourself and I'll see you in the morning. And don't forget to take Jabez and Josh to their work, will you?'

'I won't, m'lady,' he promised as he helped her down from the trap.

The four members of the staff, John Searby, Nelly Parish, Annie and Luke, were sitting around the kitchen table when Annabel let herself in through the side door and went down to the basement. Jane was there too. In front of them, spread out on the table, were the supplies of food, which Annabel had ordered to be delivered to the house. For a brief moment they stared at her as if they had seen a ghost. A fire burned brightly in the grate of the range and the coal scuttle standing beside it was full. Then they pushed themselves to their feet, their chairs scraping on the floor.

'Oh m'lady,' Nelly began, her voice wobbling with emotion. Annie burst into loud tears and even John and Luke looked suspiciously wet-eyed.

Moving towards them, Annabel put her arm round the maid. 'There's no need to cry.'

'But – but what about all the folk in the village? We can't eat all this if – if—' Again, she dissolved into noisy sobs.

'All the villagers have been fed too. There's no need for anyone to feel guilty.'

'But how did you manage it?' Nelly was wide-eyed with disbelief. 'How did you get the townsfolk to supply you?'

'I paid them what they were owed.' She laughed. 'Then they were falling over themselves for new orders.'

'How did you pay them?' Nelly asked.

'That's hardly our business, Mrs Parrish,' John Searby said swiftly before Annabel could reply. 'Let's just be grateful that Lady Fairfield has at least provided us with some food for the moment.'

'It won't be just for the moment, Mr Searby. I mean to get this estate back on its feet.' She was still standing with her arms around the weeping Annie's shoulders. She gave the girl a little squeeze. 'But I'm going to need help. From all of you.'

Annie sobbed all the harder. 'Oh m'lady, I'm so sorry. Please – forgive me.'

'Whatever for?' Annabel said, pretending innocence.

'For spilling gravy on your dress. I – I did it deliberately, because Lady Dorothea told me—'

'Annie!' the butler said warningly and the girl shot him an anxious look.

'Think no more about it,' Annabel said. 'Now, Mrs Parrish, have my mother-in-law and Lady Dorothea had dinner?'

The cook, still mesmerized by the mound of food she now had at her disposal, shook her head.

'Then something simple for all of us tonight. Luke, could you carry coal up to the morning room and Annie, would you see that the fire is still alight in there, please? And tomorrow, I shall want you to light fires in all the rooms.'

Galvanized into action by her requests, the two younger ones hurried to obey.

160

'And Jane, will you please help Mrs Parrish prepare dinner? In the meantime, I'd better have a word with my sister-in-law.'

She found Dorothea as she had found her the previous evening; in the morning room bending towards the dismal fire. But the coal scuttle was now empty.

Annabel sat down in the same chair she had sat in previously. What a lot had happened since then, she thought.

Dorothea didn't even bother to look up as she said, 'What do you want now?'

'Luke and Annie are bringing coal up for the fire and dinner will be served in about an hour.'

She watched as the woman turned her head slowly to look up at her. But her eyes were still filled with bitter resentment; there was not even the tiniest flicker of gratitude. 'What on earth are you talking about? We've no coal, no food, nothing!'

Annabel smiled. 'We have now. The tradespeople have all been paid and new orders placed and a great deal of goods have already been delivered to us all – with more to follow.'

Slowly Dorothea straightened up. 'What have you done?' Her tone was harsh with accusation. 'The money? Have you interfered with the money that was paid to James? Surely Mr Hoyles hasn't allowed you to divert any of the—?'

'Of course he hasn't,' Annabel interrupted. 'I have spent my own money. Money over which I have complete control.'

Dorothea's eyes gleamed. 'You have more money?'

Aware of the grasping woman's thoughts, Annabel said swiftly, 'I have, but not to spend on paying off the loan on this house. Fairfield Hall is safe for the moment, but what I do intend to do is to make the estate a paying concern again.'

Dorothea's lip curled disdainfully. 'Then you'll need to find new tenants to replace that idle lot we've got. Why on earth my brother didn't give them all notice months ago when he knew how badly things were going, I don't know. But of course,' she added with a sneer, 'he was too busy finding himself an heiress to marry.'

Annabel ignored the barb. Instead, she felt a sudden spark of hope. Maybe her new husband wasn't quite so heartless after all, if he had held off giving notice to his tenants just because they could no longer pay rent.

Annabel got to her feet. 'No one will be given notice. No one is going anywhere.'

'Then you'll soon run out of money however much you've got supporting that feckless lot.'

'I would like to see your mother.'

'You can't. She's not well.'

Annabel turned away determined to ask no more. She was anxious about the dowager countess; she looked weak and ill as if all the spirit had drained out of her, making her look much older than her fifty or so years. Annie, she thought. Annie will tell me where she is.

'She's in her room, m'lady,' the maid told her a few moments later when Annabel met her coming to mend the morning-room fire. 'She's in bed. She's not well. In fact, she hasn't been herself for a few days.'

'Has the doctor been called?'

'They can't afford his fee.'

Annabel clicked her tongue in exasperation. 'Where is her bedroom?'

Moments later, Annie was opening the door of Elizabeth Lyndon's bedroom on the first floor at the back of the house and ushering Annabel inside. It was the biggest bedroom in the house with a four-poster bed. A single candle burned on the bedside table. In the dimness of the room, Annabel could see the elderly lady lying in bed, the covers pulled up to her chin. There was no fire in the grate and the room was cold and had a musty dampness to it.

'Lady Fairfield,' she said softly.

Lady Elizabeth opened her eyes and stared at her, but she did not speak. She tried to pull herself up but as she did so, she began to cough, a harsh, rasping sound that wracked her thin frame.

'Annie,' Annabel said. 'Please light a fire in here at once and ask Mrs Parrish to prepare some nourishing broth.' As the girl turned to hurry away, Annabel added, 'Ask Luke to find Mr Jackson and tell him, when he goes into town tomorrow morning, to ask Dr Maybury to come as soon as possible to see Lady Fairfield. Tell him, it's urgent.'

Annie scuttled away, but Annabel fetched more pillows and blankets from her own bed. She raised Elizabeth into a sitting position against the pillows and wrapped a shawl around her shoulders. Her breathing was laboured and her cough tight and painful.

A little time later, when Annie had got a warm fire blazing in the grate, Jane came into the room carrying a tray with two bowls of thick soup and crusty new bread. 'I brought yours an' all, miss. You must be hungry. Luke's been across to see Mr Jackson like you asked and given him the message.' She grinned. 'They're all down there now eating like they've not eaten for weeks.'

Annabel smiled thinly. 'I don't think they have, Jane, not properly. Thank you. Now you go back down and get yours. I'll be fine.'

163

'If you're sure, miss?'

'I'm sure. I'll ring if I need you.'

Annabel took a few spoonfuls of her own soup and then turned her attention to Elizabeth. Gently she spooned the warm liquid between her mother-in-law's lips, but progress was slow, for bouts of coughing interrupted her. When the bowl was only half empty, Elizabeth fell back against her pillows and shook her head.

'Just a little more,' Annabel coaxed, but Elizabeth's eyes were closed. With a sigh she sat back to finish her own soup and then set the tray on the dressing table. The room was warmer now and Elizabeth had fallen asleep. Annabel dozed by the warm fire and when she was roused by the sound of the bedroom door opening softly, she was unaware of how long she had slept. She looked up to see Dr Maybury standing there.

'Oh, I didn't mean for you to come out again tonight.'

'Mr Jackson said it was urgent and I guessed it was the dowager countess, even though' – he smiled briefly – 'he only said "Lady Fairfield".'

'She does seem very poorly, so I am relieved you've come. Would you like me to fetch her daughter?'

'No need, as long as you don't mind staying while I examine her.'

When he was done, Stephen said soberly, 'I'm sorry to say, she has pneumonia.'

'Oh dear.' Annabel knew how serious this was especially in someone of Elizabeth's age and weakened state of health.

'Now, I do need to see her daughter.'

Dorothea took the news surprisingly calmly; Annabel would have said 'callously'. She was still sitting in front of the now roaring fire in the morning room and made no effort to go at once to her mother.

'Perhaps I ought to send for my brother,' Dorothea murmured, but there was a strange note of reluctance in her tone.

'It might be wise. She is frail through lack of nourishment and warmth, though those two things are being rectified.'

Dorothea arched her eyebrow and glanced at Annabel. 'Oh, because of Lady Bountiful here, you mean?'

Stephen frowned, but Annabel, despite her concern for James's mother, smiled. At Dorothea's next words, however, even Annabel's smile faded. 'I won't deny that her money is welcome, though why on earth she wants to waste it on those idlers in the village, I don't know. Still, it's her money, though I think James will have something to say about it all when he comes home.'

Twenty-Two

The next morning, Annabel rose early once more and caught Ben in the courtyard just as he was setting out to take the two men from the village to their place of work.

'While you're in town, Ben, I need you to send a telegram to Lord Fairfield. This is the address and I've written the message.'

Ben glanced over the words. *Your mother ill. Pneumonia. Please come home asap. Annabel.*

'I presume they'd deliver any reply?' she asked.

Ben nodded as he climbed into the trap and set off at once.

It was too early to start calling on the people in the village she intended to see that day, so Annabel went back inside. On entering the dining room she found Theodore sitting at the table eating his breakfast. Annabel helped herself to bacon, sausage and scrambled egg from the sideboard and sat down opposite him. The boy was eating milky porridge, but he eyed her plateful hungrily.

'I'm pleased to see you again, Theo.' The boy merely stared at her sullenly for a moment and then carried on eating as if she wasn't there.

'Your grandmother's rather poorly. Did you know?' Annabel was determined to make him speak to her somehow.

He nodded, still eating.

'Are you feeling quite well?'

Again, just a nod.

She began to eat too.

'Do you go to school?'

He shook his head, but volunteered no information. He finished his meal and set down his spoon neatly in the empty dish. Then he folded his arms and sat back in his chair and stared unblinkingly at her. He had the 'Lyndon colouring', Annabel mused. James, Dorothea and her son all had brown hair and brown eyes. And she remembered the portrait on the landing of Charles Lyndon; he had the same-coloured hair and eyes too.

Theo was undoubtedly a rude, sullen little boy of about five years old, but Annabel's overriding feeling for him was one of sympathy. It couldn't be much fun being shut away in this great house with his bad-tempered mother and a frail grandmother. Visits from his uncle James would be infrequent and fleeting. And recently, he can't have had much to eat either; no one had.

'Would you like to go to school or have a tutor here?'

Now he blinked in surprise and at last he spoke. 'Mama teaches me.'

'Do you enjoy your lessons?'

He shrugged. 'She's teaching me to read and write and do arithmetic. And about my ancestors. She says that's all I'll need to know.'

'Oh, and why is that?' Annabel asked, although she rather thought she knew the answer already.

'For when I inherit the title and the estate from my uncle. It's my destiny.'

The last words were straight out of Dorothea's mouth. The idea had been drilled into him all his young life and it was all he knew. She didn't blame the young boy; she blamed his mother.

She gazed at him across the table. If he had been older, she would have told him that he would not inherit anything if she had a male child, but she thought he was too young to understand the laws of hereditary titles.

'Your uncle will no doubt be home very soon. We have sent word that your grandmother is ill.'

'He won't come home just for that.'

Annabel stared at him in surprise. 'Of course he will. It's what they call compassionate leave in the Army, isn't it?'

The boy seemed lost for a moment. Perhaps because he was so young, Annabel thought, he didn't understand the seriousness of Elizabeth's condition. But his next words shocked her, especially coming from one so young. 'He'll come home for her funeral, if she dies. It'd look bad if he didn't.'

As he pushed back his chair and left the table, Annabel stared after him, the fork she was holding half-way between the plate and her mouth, suspended in mid-air.

After she had finished her own breakfast, she went in search of Dorothea and was heartened to find her with her mother. 'I'll be out most of the day,' Annabel told her. 'Is there anything you need before I go?'

Grudgingly, as if it pained her to do so, Dorothea said, 'No, but I must thank you for sending for the doctor.'

'He'll come again today and I've organized a telegram to be sent to James. He'll be home soon.'

'I don't think so,' Dorothea said flatly. 'Not unless
. . .' Her words were left hanging between them, but
now Annabel understood their meaning.

As she turned away to begin what was to be another
busy day, she shook her head in disbelief. There was
so much about this family she had yet to learn and, so
far, she didn't like what she was finding out.

Annabel went first to the vicarage. A smiling Richard
Webster opened the door. After an exchange of greetings
with him and his wife, Annabel said, 'Now, let's get
down to business. Today, I shall be asking Mr Jackson
to take me to visit the farms. He, I understand, runs
Home Farm on behalf of the Lyndon family, but the
other three farms are tenanted. Is that correct?'

Richard and Phoebe Webster glanced at each other
before the vicar cleared his throat and said, 'Two of
the three tenanted farms are vacant and the third is
likely to be so very shortly. Mr Jackson will fill you in.'
He seemed reluctant to say more.

Annabel was puzzled but she nodded and accepted
the offer of a cup of tea before going in search of Ben.

'I've just got back from town,' he greeted her when
she met him in the street. 'And I've sent the telegram.
If there's a reply, they'll deliver it to the big house.'

Annabel raised her eyebrows. 'You think there might
not be?'

He shrugged. 'No knowing where his lordship might
be. The Army's a law unto itself.'

'Quite. But surely they'd see he got the news somehow? Ah well, we've done our best.'

'How is Lady Fairfield?'

'Poorly. Very poorly, but she's warm and nourished

now and the doctor has promised to call again today. How is everyone in the village? The Cartwrights' baby?'

Now Ben smiled. 'Thriving – thanks to you.'

Annabel flapped her hand, brushing away his compliments, and changed the subject swiftly. 'I'd like to visit the tenant farmers today, but Mr Webster tells me there's only one farm occupied. Why is that?'

Ben took a deep breath. 'The Chadwicks are at Blackbird Farm.' He paused briefly to explain. 'All the farms have bird names, m'lady – except, of course, Home Farm.'

'Go on.'

'They've just given notice that they're leaving.'

'Where are they going?'

Ben's voice was heavy as he said, 'Same place where the Broughtons from Chaffinch Farm have gone.'

'To another estate, you mean?'

Sadly, Ben shook his head. 'No, m'lady. The Broughtons are in the town workhouse and the Chadwicks'll be following them any day now.'

Twenty-Three

Annabel stared at Ben in shocked dismay. Huskily, she whispered, 'No, oh no! You mean that my husband has allowed his tenants to sink to such depths that there's nowhere else for them to go but the – the *workhouse*?'

'I doubt he knows. Since his brother died last year and Master James inherited the title – and the estate – he's hardly been here. His mother's too frail to take on the responsibility and as for his sister –' he hesitated and Annabel prompted gently.

'Go on. Whatever you say will go no further, I promise you.'

Ben nodded, sure now that whatever he told her would not be repeated. She had proved that already. He'd watched how she manipulated conversations so that she gave nothing away.

'You've probably seen it for yourself by now. Lady Dorothea's only interest is in the house and her son's inheritance.'

'Yes, I have, but what I don't understand is that if she's so concerned about her son inheriting, why is she not anxious that the estate should be profitable?'

He sighed. 'Things have got so bad that I don't think she can handle it. No doubt she does want the estate for him, if possible, but her main ambition is to see him as Lord Fairfield in a grand house.'

'But she can hardly have one without the other. Where would his income come from?'

To this, Ben had no answer.

'And the third farm?'

'Sparrow Farm. Now, they did go away to relatives, I believe. Certainly, they're not in the workhouse.'

Annabel shuddered. 'And nor will anyone else from here be in such a place for much longer.' She stood up quickly. 'Come, we'll go to see the Chadwicks. Tell them they needn't leave.'

Ben was smiling as he stood up. He liked this feisty young woman. She had given him real hope.

When they drew into the farmyard at Blackbird Farm, the place seemed deserted already.

'Whom am I about to meet, Ben?'

'There's only Jim Chadwick and his wife, Mary, now. They had two daughters but they both married and moved away.'

'And they've been running the farm between them?'

'They employed men from the village, but, of course, they haven't been able to pay them any wages recently, so—'

'Couldn't they have gone to one of their daughters instead of – instead of . . .?' Annabel couldn't bring herself to stay the dreaded word.

'Too proud to ask.' He smiled. 'Jim is a grand fellow – big, burly and always cheerful – but he has a saying and he lives by it.' Ben lapsed into the local dialect as he quoted the farmer. ' "Ya dorn't see the chicks scratching for the owd hen".'

Annabel was smiling as she climbed down from the trap, but when Jim Chadwick appeared at the back door, her smile faded. The man standing there bore no resemblance to the farmer whom Ben had described.

He was tall, but now he stooped a little and, yet again, as she had seen so often, his well-worn clothes hung loosely on his thin frame.

'Come to see us off, 'ave ya, Ben? That's decent of you.' His eyes went to Annabel and his murmured greeting to her was stiff and formal and bore none of the friendly tone that had been in his voice when he'd spoken to the estate bailiff. 'M'lady.'

Annabel remembered now that she had seen this man sitting in church with a thin, nervous little woman at his side. She moved forward and held out her hand. 'Mr Chadwick. I'm pleased to meet you. May we come in?'

He hesitated a moment and then stood aside for her to pass into the kitchen. Annabel glanced around swiftly at the empty grate, her eyes coming at last to Mary Chadwick, standing at the table. She was tying up a bundle of their belongings. Tears were flooding down her cheeks and she turned her head away from Annabel's gaze.

'We'll be gone in a few minutes, m'lady,' Jim said heavily. 'We're not taking owt wi' us. Just a few personal bits. We won't be needing owt where we're going.'

Mary pressed her hand to her mouth, but sobs escaped her.

'No, you won't be taking anything,' Annabel said, adding firmly, 'because you're not going anywhere. This is your home and you're staying here.' She moved forward to put her arms around Mary's shoulders and lead her to the Windsor chair near the hearth. The woman sat down but clung to Annabel's arms, looking up at her beseechingly.

'We can't stay, m'lady. We can't pay the rent because we can't run the farm no more.'

Annabel patted her hand and then glanced over her

shoulder towards Jim. 'Come and sit down, Mr Chadwick, and I'll explain.'

The man moved slowly towards the chair on the opposite side of the hearth and sat down heavily.

'We'll get your farm back on its feet. It'll take a while, I realize that, but in the meantime, you'll pay no rent.'

'But we've no money to buy even food for oursens, let alone tek on farm labourers and, with the best will in the world, I can't run this place on me own.'

'Food will be provided and the men you need will be paid.'

'How?'

Annabel licked her lips. This was a proud man she was dealing with. He wouldn't accept charity happily. 'By me, Mr Chadwick, but,' she added swiftly, as he opened his mouth to protest, as she'd guessed he would, 'it can be a loan. If you wish, you can keep a ledger of every penny spent on you and your farm and one day – when the farm is paying its way again – you can pay me it all back. In instalments, of course.'

He gaped at her and then rubbed the back of his gnarled hand across his eyes. 'I must be dreaming. Am I dreaming, Ma?' Annabel felt tears start in her own eyes to hear the man address his wife as her grandfather addressed her grandmother.

Mary was smiling through her tears and still clinging to Annabel's hand. 'If you are, Pa, then I'm in the same dream and I don't want to wake up.'

'No dream, I promise,' Annabel laughed. 'Now, unpack your belongings and get a fire lit in the range and cook yourselves a meal.'

Jim and Mary glanced at each other. 'We've no coal, m'lady.'

'Nor any food left. We had the last bits yesterday, that's why – that's why' – Mary's head dropped in shame – 'we were on our way this morning.'

'Then we've come at just the right moment.' Annabel turned to Ben. 'Mr Jackson will organize for some coal to be delivered to you and some food, too. More supplies will be coming sometime today.'

'But we can't pay you.'

'Please accept these first few items as a gift.' Her eyes twinkled with mischief as she added, 'Then you can start keeping an account.'

Jim was staring at her. 'D'you know, I nivver believed in prayers being answered, but I do now. You're the answer to all our prayers.' And now, quite unashamedly, he wiped the tears from his eyes. 'God bless you, m'lady. May God bless you.'

Annabel was embarrassed and didn't know how to respond as she felt the blush creeping up her face, so she smiled and nodded and turned her attention back to more practical matters. She looked at Ben. 'Now, where next? The workhouse in town to fetch the Broughtons home?'

'We could.' There was doubt in his voice. 'But their house will be cold and possibly damp. It's been unlived in for some weeks.'

'Then we'll go there and see what needs doing, but I don't want them staying in that place any longer than they really have to.'

'We could help clean it up, m'lady.' Already there was a new strength and vigour in Jim's voice.

'That's kind of you and I'd be glad of your help, of course, but you and Mrs Chadwick must get yourselves well and strong first.'

'Be warned, m'lady,' Jim said seriously, 'Dan

Broughton is an awkward old cuss. He was very bitter about having to leave.'

'I don't blame him.'

'And he'll not tek owt he sees as a handout.'

'Were you on good terms with him, Mr Chadwick?'

Jim chuckled and Annabel caught a glimpse of the man whom Ben had described before life had weighed him down and killed his jovial nature. 'Before all this happened, we got along fine.'

'Then it sounds as if I'll need your help.'

Mary was already unfolding the bundle and placing her precious family photographs back on the mantelpiece.

'Are those your daughters?' Annabel asked.

'Aye, and them's our grandbairns.' She pointed to a picture of three children; two boys and a girl.

'You must be very proud of them.'

'We are,' she said and her face fell for a moment. 'And I hope they'll soon have reason to be proud of us again.'

'I'm sure they've never stopped being proud of you. None of it has been your fault, I know that, but now we must all pull together. I'd be glad of your support.'

'You have it, m'lady,' Jim said. 'Be sure of that. If there's owt we can do, though it bain't much at the moment, be sure to ask us.'

'There is perhaps one thing you could advise me about.' She glanced between Ben and Jim. 'Both of you. The farm that's empty – Sparrow Farm – is there anyone in the village who might be capable of taking it on?'

The two men exchanged a look before Jim said slowly, 'Well, if Ben agrees with me, the only man I can think of would be Adam Cartwright. He worked for me from being a young lad.'

Mary paused in dusting her photographs. 'The farm'd be a grand place for their bairns to grow up and their eldest boy, Simon, is old enough to help out. Country children learn to do whatever little jobs they can from quite an early age and he'll soon be past school age anyway.' She paused and nodded, smiling now. 'We heard about his babby and what you did, m'lady.'

Annabel nodded, avoiding yet more compliments neatly by saying, 'Do you agree, Ben?'

'Aye, aye, I think I do. With a bit of help and support from us' – he included Jim – 'I think he could make a go of it.'

'That's settled then. We'll see him later, but first we'll go and take a look at Chaffinch Farm.'

'How many are there in the Broughton family?' Annabel asked Ben when they had climbed back into the trap and were heading out of the yard and turning towards the neighbouring farm.

'Dan, his wife, Lily, and their sixteen-year-old, William.'

Ben had the keys for Chaffinch Farm and when he opened the back door and they went inside, Annabel was appalled at the filthy state of the house.

'How long did you say it has been since they left?' she asked, looking around her. It was going to take a while longer than she had anticipated to get the place habitable again.

'Just over two months. I'm sorry, m'lady. It looks as if they haven't been keeping it right for some time. I heard tell that Dan got very depressed and just sat by the fire all day leaving the work to Lily and young William.' He paused and his expression was anxious as he asked reluctantly, 'Would you rather we found some new tenants?'

'Heavens, no! Don't ever think that, Ben. They'll just need more help, that's all.'

Ben's face brightened. 'William's a good lad – a hard worker – though his dad never appreciated him. With a bit of guidance, though . . .'

Annabel chuckled. 'It seems there are going to be several needing "a bit of help and guidance". We're going to be busy, Ben. Right, I've seen enough here – more than enough. Now, let's take a look at Sparrow Farm.'

Ben took his watch out of his waistcoat pocket. 'Do you want to stop for lunch, m'lady?'

'Is it that time already? Are you hungry?'

'Well, a bit, m'lady.'

'Sorry, that was a silly question. You must be hungry all the time. All of you. We'll go back to the vicarage. I'm sure Mrs Webster can find us something. Then we'll carry on. That's if you're not too tired.'

Ben smiled, his blue eyes twinkling. 'Not any more, m'lady. Not now. You've given us all hope and there's nowt like hope to put life back into us.'

Phoebe was standing at her kitchen table, red faced from the heat of her kitchen, carving the biggest joint of beef that Annabel could remember ever having seen. Villagers were already queuing at her back door.

'They're all cooking their own vegetables,' she explained as Annabel and Ben walked in, 'but I've cooked this in my big oven this morning. It was easier that way. Now, sit down at the end of the table and I'll cut some for you both. Lizzie, are the vegetables ready?'

'Coming, ma'am.'

Richard joined them and they all sat down at the kitchen table to eat. When they had finished, Ben leaned back in his chair. 'I can't remember when I last enjoyed a meal so much. And that beef! I reckon it's the best I've ever tasted.'

'Now,' Annabel began, rising from the table, but she was interrupted by a knock at the back door. Annie opened it to Edward.

'Now, my lovely,' he smiled, opening his arms to Annabel, 'your gran and I thought I should just come over and see how you are.'

'We're getting things sorted out gradually, though Lady Fairfield has pneumonia. Dr Maybury has promised to come every day and we've sent word to James.'

'I'm sorry to hear that,' Edward said. 'That's serious in someone so frail.'

'I must go up and see how she is,' Richard put in, rising from his seat.

'And we'll be bringing the Broughtons home from the workhouse as soon as we can, but their farmhouse is in a dreadful state. We'll need to get it cleaned and aired. I'd ask Jane to help, but she's helping out at the house. There are plenty of women in the village who I know would help, but they're weak from lack of food. I don't like to—'

'I'll do it,' Lizzie said at once. 'If Mrs Webster doesn't mind.'

'Thank you, Lizzie, but you can't do it on your own. It's a daunting task, I don't mind telling you.'

'The workhouse,' Edward said. 'You mean to tell me that Dan Broughton and his family are in the workhouse?' He shook his head sadly. 'I wish I'd known that, Annabel. I'd've done summat about that 'afore now. Tell you what, my lovely,' his face brightened. 'I'll ask my workers if their wives'd help out. They can come over in the cart.'

'That would be wonderful, Gramps. And now we're on our way to Sparrow Farm. It's been empty for some time.'

'I'll come with you. Your gran isn't expecting me back till tea time.'

Strangely, though it had been deserted for some months, Sparrow Farm was not in as bad a state as the Broughtons' farm.

'Just a good clean, that's all it needs,' Edward said looking around. 'And there are implements in the barns. All that's missing is folk to run it and a couple of horses.'

'We've being thinking that Adam Cartwright might like to take on the tenancy. Do you know him, Gramps?'

Edward wrinkled his brow for a moment, before his face cleared and he said, 'The one who's baby was so poorly? Oh aye, I know who you mean. He used to work for Jim Chadwick. Nice young feller.'

'That's him,' Ben said. 'Jim thinks he'd do all right, with a bit of guidance.'

Edward nodded. 'Be grand for his young family. How's the babby doing now?'

'We'll call when we get back to the village.'

As the three of them climbed back into the trap, Annabel sighed as she looked about her. 'Isn't it a sad sight, Gramps? Deserted, neglected fields; no crops, no livestock. It breaks your heart.'

Edward put his arm around her shoulders. 'You're doing a grand job, my lovely. Now, 'tis time I was on my way home and you can go back to the village and give Adam the good news.'

Twenty-Four

'Come in, m'lady,' Adam greeted Annabel and Ben. 'I don't know how to thank you for what you've done . . .'

Annabel smiled. 'I wanted to see how little Eddie is, of course, but we've come about something else too.'

'Oh.' The young man's face clouded. 'You – you want us to leave because we haven't paid the rent?'

Annabel shook her head, 'No – nothing like that. Hello, Betsy. How are you?'

'Fine, m'lady. And babby's doing grand. The doctor still calls in every day.'

'Good.' Now Annabel turned to Adam. 'You know that Sparrow Farm has been empty for some time, don't you?'

He nodded.

'We wondered if you would like to take on the tenancy?'

Adam's mouth dropped open and he stared at her. 'Me?'

'Yes, you. Mr Chadwick – and Ben here – think that with a little help, you'd be the ideal person. And the farm would be a good place for your family to grow up. I understand that your eldest boy will be able to help out a little and, when he's a little older, there'll be permanent work for him.'

Adam sat down suddenly in a nearby chair as if his legs had given way beneath him. 'Oh m'lady, do you really mean it?'

'Of course I do, Adam.' She chuckled. 'You'll find that I never say anything I don't mean. Now, what do you think?'

Adam turned to look at Betsy, who was staring at her husband, her hand to her mouth, her eyes filling with tears of joy.

'D'you think we could do it, love? It'd be a lot of hard work and a big responsibility.'

'We'll give you all the help and support you need, Adam,' Annabel said softly. 'I promise.' She could see that the young man longed to say yes – she could see it in his eyes – but that the prospect was daunting.

Betsy put her arms around her husband and leaned down to put her cheek against his hair. 'It'd be wonderful,' she whispered.

Slowly, Adam stood up and held out his hand, his voice husky as he said, 'I'm honoured at your trust in me, m'lady, and I'd like to accept your kind offer.'

Annabel put her small hand into his work-worn paw and smiled up at him. 'You won't be paying any rent until the farm starts to prosper, Adam, so don't worry about that. Mr Jackson will draw up the tenancy agreement and you can move in as soon as you can, though the house does need a little cleaning.' She turned to Betsy. 'And don't you go overtiring yourself doing that. We'll get you some help.'

With a sudden movement, Betsy flung her arms around a startled Annabel and sobbed against her shoulder, but now she wept tears of joy.

'Oh m'lady, how can we ever thank you?'

'Seeing the baby – and all of you – thriving at Sparrow

Farm, will be thanks enough,' Annabel said, patting Betsy's shoulder.

'Now, there's one happy family,' Ben said as they left the Cartwrights' small cottage and walked down the street together. 'What now, m'lady?'

They came to a stop in front of the three empty shops and, beside them, was the building that had once been the village smithy and wheelwright's business. All were closed and shuttered. Annabel stood in the middle of the road with her hands on her hips. 'Tell me about these premises, Ben.'

Ben pointed to each of them in turn. 'They're all tenanted properties, just like all the houses. That was the grocer's run by Ozzy Greenwood. He took it over from his father. Made a good job of it an' all, but when folks stopped buying, there was no point in trying to carry on. He was losing more money than he was making. He's still in the village. He never married and he lives with his widowed mother in the first cottage this side of the church. The rooms over the shop were occupied by the dressmaker –' He hesitated before adding, 'That was Nancy Banks and her mother before Albert Lyndon gave them the cottage. I don't know whether you know, m'lady – I don't think I said before – but Mrs Banks used to be the housekeeper up at the big house and Nancy was a housemaid. When the – um – trouble happened, they left and came to live here for a while. Nancy had the babby here, but then when things started to go wrong for the whole estate, the dressmaking business failed. It was then Albert gave her the cottage. At least they had a roof over their heads, but nothing else. And – well – you know the rest.' He cleared his throat and went on, 'So this shop premises is completely empty. The next one was the butcher's. Percy Hammond and his wife still live above the shop.'

'No children?'

Ben shook his head. 'All grown up and left home.'

'And the one next to that?'

'The general store. Sells anything and everything – or, rather, it used to.'

Annabel moved closer to peer through part of the window that wasn't shuttered. 'I can't see much, but there still looks to be some stock in there.' She stepped backwards and glanced up at the windows above to meet the eyes of a man staring down at her. Ben followed the line of her gaze. 'That's Eli Merriman. He lives above his shop an' all. Once he was a happy-go-lucky bloke with a smile and a bit of banter for everyone. Just like his name implies, but not any more.'

'And that, I suppose,' Annabel went on, turning her attention to the final business premises, 'used to be the smithy and wheelwright's?'

'Run by Jabez Fletcher and his apprentice, Josh Parrish. He closed it down and they both found work in the town.'

'That reminds me, don't be late meeting them from work.'

'Jabez said this morning they'd walk home,' Ben began, but Annabel shook her head firmly. 'No, you fetch them. That poor lad isn't fit enough yet to walk all that way. A couple of meals won't have got him back to full strength yet.'

'Very good, m'lady.'

She stood a moment longer, eyeing the shops and the smithy. 'Do you think they'd be prepared to open them up again?'

'I'm sure they'd be delighted, but how? I mean,

what with? They used to get a lot of their supplies from the local farms.' He didn't need to explain further; Annabel knew full well that there was nothing coming from the farms just now, nor would there be for several months. 'And most of Jabez's work came from the farms too.'

'I'll talk to Gramps. There might be a way.' As they moved away, Annabel avoided meeting the gaze of the forlorn man at the window; she didn't want to give him false hope.

'I ought to go home and see how things are at the house and it'll soon be time for you to set off to town. Thank you, Ben, for all your help. I'll see you tomorrow.'

Ben tipped his cap politely and, as she walked away from him and began to climb the slope towards the house, his gaze followed her.

'There's been a telegram come, m'lady,' John informed her when, as she had been advised, Annabel rang the front door bell. 'But it was addressed to Lady Dorothea.'

'Thank you, Mr Searby. Where is she?'

'In the sitting room on the first floor.' He smiled. 'It's a lovely room, now we can afford a fire in there again. And please, m'lady, won't you call me just "Searby"?'

'I can't, I really can't. If Mrs Parrish is "Mrs", then your position within the house deserves the title "Mr". Besides, I really can't bring myself to address anyone by their surname only. The younger ones, I'll call by their Christian names, but the older and more senior staff – well, I just can't. I'm sorry if it offends your sense of propriety, but there it is.' She smiled up at him. 'You're just going to have to put up with me being exactly what I am. No "lady".'

John was chuckling as he preceded her upstairs and opened the door of the sitting room for her.

'What on earth do you think you're doing?' Dorothea was on her feet the moment Annabel entered the room. 'Interfering in the business of the estate. You have no right.'

'I have every right,' Annabel said calmly, moving towards her. 'In James's absence, he agreed I could help with the running of the estate.'

Dorothea gasped. 'He did no such thing. You're lying.'

'Dorothea, I may be many things, but I am no liar.'

'Well, we shall see.' Dorothea waved a piece of paper in her face. 'He's coming home, so we'll see what he has to say about your interference.'

'Good. I'm glad he's coming to see his mother.'

The other woman's lip curled. 'Oh, it's not because of her. I sent a telegram of my own and told him about your meddling and that if he wanted to save his estate, he should come home at once. He'll be here tomorrow.'

'Good,' Annabel said again. 'And now I'll go up and see your mother.'

'She doesn't want to be disturbed.'

'Who's looking after her?'

Dorothea shrugged. 'The maids, I suppose.'

Annabel was appalled by the woman's callous attitude towards her own sick mother. She had already been disappointed – though not surprised – that Theodore was rarely seen. She knew that children were kept in a nursery or schoolroom for most of the time. And yet there was no nanny or governess that she knew of. His brief appearance at the breakfast table no doubt was because there were not enough members of staff to take his meals upstairs to him. Though she said nothing,

186

Annabel resolved to find out more about how the boy was living. For the moment, though, Lady Fairfield was her main concern.

She left the sitting room and crossed the landing to enter the master bedroom opposite. Elizabeth was alone, propped up against the pillows, her eyes closed. Her breathing was still rasping and it seemed as if every breath she pulled in was painful. At least the fire was being kept built up and the room was much warmer. A glass of water stood on the bedside table, though Annabel doubted Elizabeth had the strength to reach out and lift it to her lips. She didn't want to wake her so she sat down beside the bed until the dowager countess should stir. A coughing fit roused her and Annabel held the glass of water for Elizabeth to drink. Then the sick lady sank back exhausted against the pillows.

'How are you feeling?' Annabel asked gently. Elizabeth opened her eyes but could only shake her head.

Annabel watched her for a few moments more and listened to her breathing. Then she glanced around her. Three doors led out of the bedroom. One opened on to the landing, but Annabel didn't know what lay behind the other two. Dorothea's room was through the one to the right, Annabel discovered, and the other led into what she guessed had been a gentleman's dressing room. Thoughtfully, Annabel sought out Dorothea once more.

'She's still very poorly. I think we should get a nurse to live in for a week or so until she improves.' Without waiting for Dorothea's agreement, Annabel went on, 'I'll see Dr Maybury first thing in the morning and arrange it.'

'And who do you suppose is going to pay for the luxury of having a live-in nurse?'

Annabel shrugged. 'If you can't afford it, then I will pay.'

'And why should you concern yourself in keeping an old woman alive?'

Annabel shook her head in wonderment; she'd never met anyone like Dorothea before and wondered briefly if the woman was quite right in the head. 'I don't want to see anyone suffering. She needs expert nursing. And besides, she's not old. She's just ill and frail. And whilst we're on the subject of your family, what about your son?'

Dorothea's interest sharpened. She frowned. 'What about him?'

'I understand he doesn't go to school.'

'What – with those urchins in the village? He'll go to boarding school when he's eight. James promised me that.'

'And in the meantime, you teach him. Is that right? Are you content with that arrangement?'

Slowly and with deliberate emphasis, Dorothea said, 'We – can't – afford – a tutor.'

'We could now,' Annabel said mildly, 'if you'd like one. Give it some thought, Dorothea, and let me know.'

Without waiting for another word, Annabel left the room.

Twenty-Five

Edward had been as good as his word. The following morning, when she walked down to the vicarage, it was to find that three women – the wives of his farm workers – had already arrived in a horse and cart, armed with all the cleaning materials they would need.

''Morning, m'lady. Where do you want us to start?'

'How good of you all to come. I'm so grateful.'

'Your grandfather explained,' the oldest of the three said. 'We'll do all we can to help. Poor folks – if only we'd known earlier.' The other two nodded their agreement.

'You're here now and that's what matters. Could we start at Chaffinch Farm, please? The family are in the workhouse and I want to get them out and back home as soon as we can. The other farm – Sparrow Farm – is to be taken on by a young man in the village. The place isn't as bad as Chaffinch Farm, but it will need some work and Betsy Cartwright isn't strong. She's not long had a baby and they're all weak from lack of food.'

'We heard.' The spokeswoman was grim-faced. 'But we'll help. And before we start, m'lady, there's one thing we must settle. Don't you go offering us payment, else you'll offend us. We're glad to help these poor folks who've been suffering so and we didn't know.'

Annabel held out both her hands to the woman, who took them into her own, which were wrinkled and care-worn. 'Then I won't – but thank you.'

'My name's Rebecca Clifton. And this 'ere's Tilly Abbott and Rosie Hall. Now, if you'll tell us where to be, m'lady, we'll get going.'

The three women worked in the farmhouse at Chaffinch Farm like beavers and Annabel knew she could safely leave it to them.

'We'll likely be a couple of days here and then we'll do Sparrow Farm, an' all,' Rebecca told her. 'I'll go and see Mrs Cartwright first, of course, afore we start there.'

James, accompanied by a young soldier, arrived at midday. Annabel saw the hired pony and trap coming along the street as she was about to go up the hill from the village towards the house. James drew the trap to a halt beside her and the young soldier leapt down to help her into the trap.

'Were you watching for us?' James smiled.

'Yes – and no.'

James arched his eyebrows as she added, 'I've so much to tell you.'

'This is Private Jenkins. He's my batman.'

Annabel smiled and nodded. 'Pleased to meet you, Private Jenkins.'

He was a stocky man, with strong, broad shoulders and a face that looked as if he had done a lot of boxing in the army. But he had kind, hazel eyes. 'Just "Jenkins", m'lady.'

'How is my mother?' James asked.

'Rather poorly, I fear. Dr Maybury visits every day and I've sent word to him this morning that I'd like him to find us a nurse to live in for a week or so. She needs expert care that neither Dorothea nor I can give.'

'A live-in nurse will be expensive,' he murmured.

'That will all be taken care of.'

No more was said for the moment, but as they entered by the front door held open by the butler, Dorothea came forward to greet him.

'James, I am sorry to bring you home, but your wife has been interfering in matters which don't concern her.' She turned briefly to the butler. 'Searby, bring refreshment for his lordship and tell Mrs Parrish we'll have luncheon in the dining room in half an hour. And take his lordship's man with you.' She looked the soldier up and down with obvious distaste, silently indicating that such a person should not have entered by the front door.

'Why's *he* here?' she asked her brother before the man was out of earshot.

'He had some leave due and as it's too far for him to go to his own home, I invited him to come with me. Surely, one more mouth won't stretch our finances too far. I've brought some provisions with me as usual.'

Dorothea shot a look at Annabel and pursed her lips but said no more. Instead, she led the way to the morning room. At the door, she turned to face them. 'Not you.' She nodded towards Annabel. 'I wish to speak to my brother alone.'

'I'm sure there's nothing that Annabel can't hear. She seems most concerned about Mama.'

'It's not about Mama,' Dorothea snapped. 'It's about *her*.' She jabbed her forefinger towards Annabel.

James raised his eyebrows. 'Then she certainly ought to be present. Come along in, my dear.'

He brushed past his sister and opened the door. On the threshold to the room, he paused. 'Good heavens! What's this? A fire? Now, that is a welcome sight. Early September can be chilly.'

He moved towards it, held out his hands briefly to warm them, then turned and stood on the hearth with his back to the fire, smiling with contentment. 'Now, Dorothea, what is it you want to say to me?'

'She's been interfering in the running of the estate. It's no concern of hers. And she's been spending all her time down in the village, most of it in the company of *Jackson*.' She almost spat out his name as if it was abhorrent to her.

'And your point is?'

'It's not seemly for Lady Fairfield to be occupying herself with matters of the estate nor to be keeping company with your bailiff.'

James glance swivelled to Annabel, but she could not read his expression. 'May I ask what *exactly* you have been doing?'

Annabel took a deep breath. 'I understand that the money paid to you by my father upon our marriage has been enough to secure the estate for the time being, but it has not been sufficient to help the villagers. Your farms and their tenants – indeed all your tenants – are suffering.'

'They've all been given notice and we plan to get new tenants who will start paying rent,' Dorothea interrupted, but James held up his hand to silence her.

'Go on,' he said to Annabel.

'I have some money of my own—'

'That should belong to James now.' Dorothea was not to be kept silent for long, but Annabel was gratified to see that James was shaking his head. 'No, Dorothea, you're wrong there. Married women now have the right to keep – and manage – their own money.' He nodded towards Annabel inviting her to continue.

'I've sold some of my shares to raise more capital

192

and I plan to use it to help the estate become a thriving concern once more. Your tenants were starving, James. A baby almost died—'

'She's exaggerating.' Dorothea was incensed. 'They're nothing of the kind. They're just idle layabouts, who think the estate will always bail them out and unfortunately your meddling wife has proved them right.'

He turned slowly to look at his sister. 'In my absence, you were placed in charge of the estate to work with Jackson. I knew things were difficult, but I had no idea they'd got so bad. Why was I not told? And why, might I ask, have you thought fit to summon me home because of what my wife is doing, rather than because my mother is very ill?'

'Mama's old. She's bound to get sick now and again. Do you want to be summoned every time she has a head cold?'

'Pneumonia is hardly a cold.'

'The estate is what matters,' Dorothea persisted. 'It's my son's inheritance.'

The brother and sister now stared at each other in a battle of wills. But when James said quietly, 'Or *my* son's,' she gave a strangled sob, turned and rushed from the room, slamming the door behind her.

Annabel went at once to stand in front of James. She put her hands on his chest and looked up into his dark brown eyes. 'James, I have no wish to come between you and your sister, but I had to do something. Two farms are already empty and at Blackbird Farm, Mr and Mrs Chadwick were about to give up and go into the workhouse in the town.' She shuddered. 'I understand the Broughton family are already there. I have arranged for their farmhouse to be cleaned and I intend to bring them home as soon as it is ready. Everyone in the village

193

was hungry. The shops here are closed down and the town's tradesmen had stopped supplying the village and even this house. My grandfather helped out at first, but I've paid what was owed and supplies are now coming into the village again. James, I wouldn't have done it without your knowledge, but there was just no time to write to you to ask for your approval. People were ill with hunger. If you don't believe me, ask Mr Jackson – ask the vicar.'

'I do believe you, Annabel, and I'm grateful to you for what you've done. I knew things had got difficult, but I didn't realize they were quite so serious. I know I should be here running the estate myself, but my life has been the Army. I was never trained to manage the estate. That' – his face clouded – 'was supposed to have been my brother's job. But he squandered his inheritance and left us with a mountain of debts.' His dark gaze searched her face. 'But you – you seem to know what you're doing. How come?'

Swiftly, Annabel told him about the many happy holidays she had spent on her grandfather's farm, how one day he had promised it would be hers. And how, too, he had instructed her in the intricacies of the stock market and how, happily, she seemed to have a sixth sense for trading and was able to make more money than she ever lost.

'Trading on the stock market is always a precarious business and over the last few years it has been even more difficult, though things seem to be improving a little now. Under my grandfather's guidance, I have invested most of my money in the larger, reputable railway companies.'

'How unfortunate that my late brother didn't have your foresight,' James murmured dryly. 'I understand he lost a lot of money speculating on doomed ventures.'

'So,' she asked him at last, 'have I your approval to carry on with my plans?'

'Of course, but don't spend too much time with Jackson, will you? I don't want him falling in love with my beautiful wife.'

As he bent to kiss her, Annabel felt a thrill of pleasure. There had been a warning note in her husband's voice that she believed to be the delicious sound of jealousy. Perhaps, after all, she thought as she wound her arms around his neck, he really does love me.

Twenty-Six

The following morning, after a night of passion that left Annabel tired but exhilarated, she took James's arm happily as they left the house together. She was sure now that he loved her; surely no man could make love to a woman as ardently as he had and not be in love with her. Private Harry Jenkins followed at a discreet distance behind them.

'I thought I'd bring Jenkins along. He's a great chap and always likes to be busy. He might be able to help.'

Annabel turned briefly and smiled at the young soldier.

'Now, now,' James patted her hand. 'No flirting with my batman.'

Annabel chuckled. 'I wasn't. I only smiled at him.'

'Well, some young men take that as an invitation, Annabel. I did myself at the ball where we first met.' He raised her gloved hand to his lips and kissed it.

'James, I'm a married woman now. I wouldn't dream of flirting with anyone – except you, of course.'

'Mind you don't.' The words were said jocularly and yet there was a hint of steel about them – a scarcely hidden warning. You're mine, his tone said, and the thought thrilled her.

From his windows above the archway, Ben Jackson must have noticed them leaving for he hurried to catch up with them and touched his cap politely. 'Good morning, m'lord – m'lady.'

'My wife has been telling me all that the two of you have been doing, Jackson.'

Did Annabel imagine it, or was there a veiled threat in the seemingly innocent words?

'It's mainly her ladyship, m'lord. She's doing a wonderful job. But for her—'

James nodded swiftly and interrupted, saying, 'We're on our way to have a look at the shops first and then the farms.'

'I'll fetch the trap, m'lord. The pony's harnessed and ready.'

'You walk with us. Jenkins will fetch the trap.'

After James had given instructions to his batman, the three of them walked down the hill and along the street until they reached the three empty shops and the smithy. After a few moments, Eli Merriman appeared down the narrow passage at the side of his shop. He was scowling and made no move to touch his cap in greeting.

'Come to give me notice, have ya, *your lordship*?' His tone was heavy with sarcasm. 'And where d'you think I'll end up? The workhouse, I suppose? But do you care? Nah.'

He spat on the ground, his spittle landing inches from James's shoes. At least, Annabel thought, this time it had not hit her dress.

His tirade was not finished. 'Saved your grand house, ain't she, but she'll not save my shop and my livelihood, will she? From what I hear, we're all to be turned out. But who do you reckon will come to take our place, eh? No one in their right senses.'

Before James could answer him, Annabel said, 'Mr Merriman, it seems you're rather behind with the latest news. No one is to be given notice and we're here this

197

morning to see what can be done about these shops and the smithy.' She turned and looked up at her husband, anxious not to be seen to be taking the lead and belittling him. A wary expression came into Eli Merriman's eyes and he met James's gaze.

'Merriman, I'll be honest with you. I'm no farmer nor have I experience in estate management. That was supposed to be my brother's place in life.'

Eli's frown deepened as he growled, 'And a fine mess he made of it, an' all. He's brought us all to ruin. You included, because unless you get this estate paying its way again, or your fine lady here has a bottomless pit of money, you're going to lose it all eventually.'

'Like I say, I've no experience in such matters and my life is dedicated to the Army. I want no other, but,' he went on swiftly as the other man opened his mouth to speak, 'we are fortunate in that my wife does have the experience needed and, even more importantly, she is willing to spend her own money – over which she has complete control – to help us all.'

Eli's eyebrows rose in surprise, but still he muttered, 'Aye, an' I'll believe it when I see it.'

'I'll bid you "good day" for the moment, Merriman.'

James turned away, pulling Annabel with him as he strode towards the trap that Private Jenkins had brought. However, at that moment, they heard the rattle of another pony and trap and turned to see Dr Maybury driving down the street. Beside him sat a middle-aged woman dressed in a nurse's uniform.

'Ah, I'd better have a word,' James said.

The doctor pulled his vehicle to a halt and climbed down to shake James's hand. After an exchange of greetings, Stephen Maybury said, 'This is Nurse Newton. She has come to live in at Fairfield Hall to care for your mother for a week or so. We'll then reassess the situation.'

James nodded to the woman and turned back to the doctor. 'I've seen my mother this morning. She seems to be wandering in her mind. She thought I was Albert, my brother. He was always her favourite.' He smiled wryly. 'Reprobate that he was. But she seems very poorly to me. Is there any hope of her recovery?'

'Good heavens, yes. But she is undernourished and weak because of it. But your wife—'

'Yes, yes, I know what my wife has been doing.' Suddenly, James seemed irritated by the compliments being heaped on Annabel's head. No doubt he felt it reflected badly on him, she supposed. 'We're on our way to inspect the farms now, but I'd like to know what you think of my mother today.'

'I'll be in the village for the rest of the morning.'

'Very well. I'll see you when we get back.'

Ben Jackson took the reins from Private Jenkins and the four of them squeezed into the trap. As they left the village, they passed the lonely cottage and Annabel glanced into the front garden. The boy was there again, but this time his mother was standing beside him, her gaze following the occupants of the trap, and Annabel fancied that the young woman's gaze was fixed on her husband, James, but he was staring straight ahead and didn't even seem to see the two people standing in the garden.

There was one other, however, who most certainly did. Even after the trap had passed by, Private Jenkins was craning his neck to stare back at them.

Rebecca Clifton and her helpers had worked hard. A fire burned in a shining black-leaded range in the kitchen at Chaffinch Farm. The walls had been dusted down, cobwebs removed from the ceiling, the floors scrubbed and all the shelves in the pantry had been washed. In the best parlour, the dust had been banged out of the old sofa and chairs and the curtains had been washed and rehung. Upstairs, the beds had been made up with freshly laundered linen and the windows cleaned and flung open to air the rooms.

'You've all done a marvellous job,' Annabel enthused. 'Thank you.'

'We're about finished here, m'lady. We're off across to Sparrow Farm now.'

Outside again, James asked, 'Why are you so effusive with your thanks? They're being paid.'

'Actually, James, they're not. They wouldn't take payment.'

'How very philanthropic!' he murmured, but Annabel chose to ignore his sarcasm.

Adam was already at Sparrow Farm, sorting out the rusty machinery in the barns. He doffed his cap as he emerged into the yard at the sound of the trap.

'Your lordship.' For a moment, his tone was wary, as if he feared that James might rescind what his wife and Ben Jackson had agreed. But James sprang out of the back of the trap and held out his hand to the startled young man 'Cartwright – I'm glad you've agreed to have a go at this place. Let her ladyship know if there's anything you need to set you on your way.'

Annabel smiled, but said nothing, glad that James now seemed to be approving of what had been done. He could very well have moodily countermanded everything she had set in motion, but he had not.

'We're very grateful, m'lord. We'll work that hard and Jim Chadwick's promised his support. I used to work for him, y'know.'

James looked blank for a moment, seeming as if he didn't even know who Jim Chadwick was, never mind that Adam had worked on Blackbird Farm. Perhaps he didn't, Annabel thought, seeing as he'd had little interest in the estate. But James was nothing if not adroit at covering his ignorance. He smiled and nodded.

'Mrs Clifton and her friends are on their way over to give Betsy a hand in the house, Adam,' Annabel said, feeling that this would not undermine her husband's authority. Cleaning, after all, was a woman's domain.

'I'm grateful, m'lady,' Adam said again. 'Betsy's in there now. She's made a start, but she soon gets tired. Their help'll be a godsend.' For a moment his eyes clouded. 'I can't pay them, though, m'lady.'

'No need, Adam. They're doing it out of the goodness of their hearts.'

They drove back to Fairfield Hall.

'Sir,' Jenkins asked, as they climbed out of the trap in the courtyard, 'would you mind if I took a look around the village?'

'Help yourself.' James chuckled and was still smiling as Jenkins turned and began to walk through the archway and back down the hill. 'Don't be too late back, though. We must leave at four.'

'What are you laughing at?' Annabel wanted to know.

'It hasn't taken Jenkins long to find out exactly who and what Nancy Banks is.'

'*What!*'

He was still smiling. 'You know about Nancy, don't you?'

Grimly, Annabel nodded. 'Enough, but I mean to put a stop to all that. Call him back, James. I won't have it.'

But James only glanced after the figure of his batman

marching determinedly in the direction of the isolated cottage and shrugged. 'I've no intention of stopping him, my dear. A man has his needs.'

Dismayed, Annabel stared after Jenkins. There was nothing she could do, but her heart went out to the solemn, lonely little boy who was witnessing such goings on. She berated herself for not having seen Nancy earlier. She could have stopped it before now, but she had been so concerned with other, more urgent, matters.

'Come along, Annabel. The doctor's trap is standing outside the front door. I need to see him.'

Annabel followed him, her mind taken over with sudden anxiety over her mother-in-law. Why was the doctor still there? Was she worse? Fear rose in her throat as she hurried to catch up with her husband's long strides.

As it turned out, she need not have worried unduly; although Elizabeth was still very poorly, Stephen Maybury assured both her and James that there was a slight sign of improvement. He had installed the nurse, had attended one or two patients in the village and had returned to Fairfield Hall briefly before going back to town to hold his surgery.

'Nurse Newton will be sleeping in the dressing room next door to Lady Fairfield's room. She's an excellent nurse. Your mother is in good hands.'

At luncheon there were the two of them and Dorothea.

'I thought you had two days' leave,' Dorothea remarked and Annabel thought she detected a sly note in her voice.

'I have,' James replied easily, 'but now that I see Mama is in good hands, I have business to attend to in London before returning to barracks.'

'Business, indeed,' Dorothea murmured, smirking as she exchanged a knowing look with her brother and leaving Annabel feeling excluded from their shared secrets.

Twenty-Seven

Annabel was sorry to see James leave later that afternoon as she stood on the steps to wave him off. She nodded briefly to Private Jenkins, her lips pursed in disapproval, but when she looked at him more closely, she decided that the young man didn't look at all happy, certainly not like a man who had just had 'his needs', as James had called them, satisfied.

Annabel promised herself that she would visit Nancy as soon as she could. A 'house of ill-repute' was not wanted in the village and she was concerned for the little boy's welfare.

As the trap disappeared down the hill, Annabel went down to the kitchen.

'Mrs Parrish, can you spare me a moment?'

'Of course, m'lady.'

How different was her reception in the kitchen to what it had been at first, Annabel mused. 'I expect you know that the Broughtons of Chaffinch Farm are sadly in the workhouse and—'

Nelly's face crumpled suddenly and she sat down heavily in a chair.

'Whatever's the matter?' Concerned, Annabel bent over her. 'Didn't you know?'

'M'lady' – John Searby was at her side – 'I think I know what has caused Mrs Parrish's distress.' Now Nelly was sobbing, covering her face with her white apron and rocking backwards and forwards. 'It was you mentioning the workhouse.'

Annabel blinked up at him. 'Why? Oh' – a sudden though struck her – 'was she afraid that she might end up there? Oh, Mrs Parrish, I'd never let that happen.' She put her hand on the cook's shoulder but the woman still shook with distress.

'It's not that, m'lady,' John said quietly. 'It's her mother. She's in there.'

Annabel stared up at him, dumbstruck for a moment. 'Her mother?' she repeated stupidly. 'How? I thought she used to be cook here – before Mrs Parrish.'

'She did.'

'Then—' Now Annabel was angry. How could the Lyndon family let someone who had served them loyally end up in the workhouse? She was appalled and not for the first time since her arrival here.

'She lived in the village in a grace and favour house near the smithy. Old Lord Fairfield always used to look after his servants when they retired, but –' John hesitated and fell silent.

'I see,' Annabel said grimly. And she did – only too well.

She turned back to the cook and put her arm around her shoulders. 'I'll bring her home, Mrs Parrish. Get Annie to clean that spare bedroom in the staff quarters and make up a bed. She can stay here until we can get her back into her own cottage.'

Nelly lowered her apron to stare up into Annabel's face. 'You'd do that?' she whispered. 'For me? After—'

'Now, now, that's all forgotten. Dry your tears because I want you to help me organize some food for the Broughtons when I get them home. Is there anyone else from the village who is in the workhouse?'

Nelly and John exchanged a glance. 'There is one,' he said hesitantly.

'Who?'

When he still seemed reluctant to say more, Annabel glanced at Nelly.

'Tell her, Mr Searby. She'll hear anyway.'

'Mrs Banks.'

Annabel frowned for a moment and then said, 'Do you mean Nancy's mother?'

John nodded, still looking uncomfortable.

'Why on earth is she in there? I thought – well – that they were all right because of –' She stopped and shrugged her shoulders expressively. 'You know. Lizzie, the Websters' maid, told me that Mrs Banks had moved away.'

'It was the shame, m'lady,' Nelly said. 'Agnes Banks was devastated when Nancy got pregnant, but she stood by her then.' She glanced at John. 'That wasn't alto-gether the young girl's fault. We were all a bit to blame – we should have protected her more.'

'She was a maid here, wasn't she?' Again, Annabel was careful not to reveal that she'd already heard all this from Ben.

Nelly nodded. 'Yes, and her mother was the house-keeper. Mrs Banks came here after she lost her husband. Her and my mam were good friends and I was under-cook then to my mam. It fair broke our hearts to see what Nancy's downfall did to her mother. They left here, of course, and went first to the rooms above Ozzy Greenwood's shop and later they moved to the little cottage on the outskirts of the village.'

'Yes, I've seen it and I've seen her little boy in the garden. He looks a lonely little chap.'

'He is. None of the folks in the village will let their children play with him.'

Annabel's tender heart twisted for the child; whatever his mother was, none of it was his fault.

'At first, they was all right. The villagers didn't shun them – they knew full well what was what, if you get my meaning.'

Annabel nodded grimly. She understood how the young girl had been seduced by James's elder brother.

'Nancy and her mother set up as dressmakers. Nancy was a good little needlewoman – I'll give her that – but when things started to get tough and the work dried up, they had no other income. That was when she – well, you can guess the rest, m'lady.'

'Thank you for telling me, Mrs Parrish. I wanted to go and see Nancy and now I have an excuse.'

Nelly's eyes were suddenly wide. 'Oh m'lady, I don't think you should go there.'

Annabel chuckled. 'Then all the more reason why I should.'

'His lordship wouldn't like it.'

'His lordship isn't here.'

'But he'll hear about it, m'lady. Mark my words, he'll hear about it.'

Nelly did not need to say who the teller of tales would be. Annabel could guess: Dorothea.

The boy was not in the garden when Annabel opened the gate and walked up the path to the front door. She glanced around her. The garden was well tended – the grass cut short, the borders neat though the summer flowers were dying now. The front door and the windows were freshly painted and Annabel wondered if one of Nancy's 'gentleman callers' had done the work.

She took a deep breath and knocked on the door. It

was a while before it opened tentatively and a young, fair-haired woman's face peered out. Her blue eyes were wide with fear.

Annabel smiled. 'You must be Nancy. May I come in?'

The young woman gasped in surprise, but opened the door wide enough for Annabel to step inside. Then she led her through to a small, neat front parlour.

'M'lady,' she said in a low, sweet voice. 'You shouldn't be here. There'll be such talk.'

Annabel shrugged. 'So?'

'Well . . .' Nancy was lost for words.

'May I sit down?'

'Oh – of course. I'm sorry. Would – would you like a cup of tea?'

'No, thank you. Where's your little boy?'

'He's playing in the back garden. I – I don't let him go into the front much. He – he gets called rude names.'

'I'm sorry to hear that.' Annabel paused and then went on, 'Nancy, it has to stop, you know.'

Nancy's face flooded with colour and she sank into a chair. 'You know?'

Annabel nodded. 'And I also know that a young soldier came to see you yesterday.'

'I didn't let him in, m'lady. I swear. Yes, I admit I have two – friends – from town who come to see me, but I'm not – not a whore, though I know that's what the villagers call me.' She hung her head in shame.

'Then it must stop. Right now.'

Nancy raised her head slowly, tears in her eyes. 'I want that more than anything, but how am I to feed Bertie if – if . . .'

'I'll support you until we can find you some work.'

Nancy shook her head. 'No one around here will

have anything to do with either of us. They'll certainly not employ me.'

'I do have an idea, but it may take some time to organize. Will you trust me?'

Nancy raised her head and looked into Annabel's eyes. 'Yes,' she whispered. 'I will.'

'Then the first thing we need to do is get your mother home.'

Nancy drew in a sharp breath and stared, wide-eyed at her. 'From the workhouse? Oh m'lady, that's so good of you, but she won't come.'

'She will. You've a room here for her, haven't you?'

'Yes, yes. It's just as she left it.' Fresh tears welled in Nancy's eyes as she remembered the acrimonious parting with her mother and the guilt she'd felt ever since. 'But she won't come,' she said sadly again. 'She can't forgive me.'

Twenty-Eight

'Are we ready, Ben?' Annabel asked as she crossed the courtyard early the following morning.

'I think so, m'lady. The Broughtons' farmhouse is spick and span and there's food waiting for them.'

'We'll get the three of them in the trap, but we might have to have a second trip for the other two.'

'The other two?' Ben was mystified.

'Mrs Parrish and Mrs Banks.'

Ben gaped at her. 'Mrs Parrish I can understand, but Mrs Banks . . .' He grinned suddenly. How he admired this young woman's courage and determination. 'That'll cause a stir, but I don't think she'll come back here.'

'That's what Nancy said.'

'Nancy? You've been to see her?' This surprised him, even though he had watched her over the last few days and seen her iron resolve improve things.

'Of course,' Annabel said calmly. 'I had to make sure that there was somewhere for Mrs Banks to come home to.'

Ben shook his head. 'She won't go back there, not while Nancy—'

'Ah, but you see, Nancy won't be – um – plying her trade' – Annabel smiled impishly – 'any more. You and I, Ben, are going to put a stop to it.'

'Me! Oh now, I don't want to get involved.'

'I'm afraid you might have to be because I shall need

210

one or two men to be with me when I confront her – um – callers the next time they are due to visit, which I understand is Friday night – tonight, in fact. I'm sure Adam will help and perhaps the vicar will too.'

'The vicar! You can't ask him, surely.'

'I thought vicars were supposed to gather up lost sheep.'

Ben fell silent, confounded by her reasoning; he couldn't think of an answer!

'Let's be on our way. The sooner we get there, the sooner we can get these poor folks home again.'

Ben flicked the reins, wondering exactly what the day had in store for them.

The workhouse was a large, grim building situated on the outskirts of Thorpe St Michael. As they turned in at the huge gates, Annabel shuddered. She could only imagine the dreadful feeling of helplessness and despair that must engulf each and every person who was forced into such a place.

A thin woman in a shabby striped dress and grey apron showed them into the master's office. They saw one or two more inmates who wore a similar uniform.

Mr Pinkerton was a rotund, florid man with light brown hair and whiskery sideburns. He was dressed in a black suit with a flamboyant waistcoat. The matron of the workhouse – his wife – stood beside him as Annabel faced them both across his desk.

'You want to take out five people?' Mr Pinkerton – Annabel never learned his Christian name – was surprised. 'All at once?'

'Yes.'

'Do they know about this?'

'Not until you – or I – tell them.'

'I don't think I can allow them to be discharged so swiftly. I mean, there's paperwork to fill out. I have to be sure they have a means of supporting themselves. And there'll be a discharge fee of seven shillings and sixpence per head.'

Annabel raised her eyebrows and met his gaze squarely. 'I hadn't heard of a charge being levied for their release, but so be it and *I* will be supporting them once they are home. They will be well taken care of in the community to which they belong.'

'Obviously, they weren't supported very well by their community before they came in here,' he said sarcastically, leaning back in his chair and lacing his fingers across his ample stomach.

'I wasn't there then,' Annabel retorted sharply. She had introduced herself as Annabel Lyndon, omitting to give her title.

Ben, standing beside her, cleared his throat and said quietly, 'This is the new Lady Fairfield.'

The man's expression changed at once and he stood up, flustered and now anxious to please. 'My lady, why didn't you say? Please, sit down. I'll have the – er – inmates brought here at once. And, of course, there will be no charge to you.'

Annabel smiled inwardly. It never ceased to amaze her how people's attitudes altered as soon as they knew who or what you were. She had seen it before. Attitudes changed towards her father whenever someone had realized just how wealthy he was or how he could help them. Now, it was the title that impressed; just as Ambrose Constantine had known it would. She wondered now how the master was able to bypass the regulations so easily – if indeed the charge for release

212

was a regulation. Maybe, she thought, it went straight into his pocket and she resolved to have a word with her friend Mr Hoyles, the bank manager, whom she knew was on the board of the town workhouse.

'Is there a room where we might talk privately to them? I don't think they know anything about this and it might be rather a surprise. A pleasant one, I trust, but nevertheless . . .'

'Of course, you may use this office.' The man was almost bowing to her. 'My wife will find them and bring them here.' He turned to the woman, who had been standing quietly all the time the conversation had been taking place. 'My dear, perhaps you would fetch the Broughton family here first and then the other two. They can wait in the outer office until her ladyship is ready to interview them. Don't tell them the reason they are being summoned.' He turned a fawning smile on Annabel. 'We can leave that pleasure to her ladyship.'

Already, Annabel disliked the man intensely but she needed to keep on his right side until she had her people, as she thought of them, safely on the outside. She didn't trust him not to turn awkward and to find reasons why he could not let them leave. She wanted no more delays; the poor folk had been here long enough. So, she smiled politely, inclined her head and said graciously as befitted her status, 'I would be most grateful.'

After some while, Mr and Mrs Broughton and their sixteen-year-old son, William, were ushered into the office. Annabel rose to greet them, holding out her hand, but the surly man in front of her ignored it, stared at her for a moment and then glanced beyond her. Seeing someone he recognized, he muttered, 'Mr Jackson, what brings you here?'

Annabel was appalled by their appearance. Their work-house uniforms hung loosely on their thin frames, but it was the hopeless, defeated look on each of their faces that distressed her. She wanted to gather them to her and whisk them away as quickly as possible, but she kept quiet and let Ben explain. 'This is the new Lady Fairfield.'

'Oh aye. I've heard rumours – even in here,' Dan Broughton said bitterly, 'that his lordship had married a wealthy woman and that her dowry was saving his grand house. But there'll be nowt left for the rest of us, I expect.'

'That's partly true,' Ben was obliged to admit, 'but since Lady Fairfield has found out about the poor condition of the estate, she is using her own funds to help us. The Chadwicks were about to join you here in the workhouse, but she has prevented that. She has also installed Adam Cartwright in Sparrow Farm and your own farmhouse has been cleaned from top to bottom. Dan, my old friend, she has come to take you home.'

There was a moment's stunned silence before Lily Broughton fell on her knees in front of Annabel and kissed the hem of her dress. Annabel reached down at once and helped her to her feet. 'Oh, don't do that, Mrs Broughton, please don't.' Then she put her arms about the woman, who was now weeping tears of gratitude and relief.

'We can be together,' Lily Broughton wept. 'We can be a family again. We've been separated in here, m'lady. I've only seen my husband and my boy once a week.'

Annabel hugged her even closer, murmuring, 'There, there, you're going home now.'

But Dan Broughton's face was still angry and resentful. 'Oh aye, an' what sort of rent are we expected to find?'

'None, Mr Broughton,' Annabel said, over his wife's head, 'until your farm is paying its way.'

'An' how am I to restock and plant crops with not a penny to me name?'

'All that will be provided—'

'I won't accept charity,' he spat. ''Twas bad enough having to come in here and be a burden on the parish, to know that I couldn't look after me own wife and son, but to take money from a woman. No, never!'

Lily Broughton turned on her husband with a sudden vigour that surprised both Annabel and Ben. 'Dan, how can you be so ungrateful? Think of William – please. Even if you don't want to get out, at least let him go.'

'You're *all* coming home,' Annabel said firmly, 'and it won't be charity, Mr Broughton. Jim Chadwick said exactly the same. Careful records will be kept of all the money spent to get your farm up and running again and then, over time, you can pay me back.'

'Aye, with a crippling interest we can't afford.'

Annabel laughed – a merry sound that wasn't often heard within those walls. 'Do you know, I hadn't even thought of charging interest, Mr Broughton. I'll have to give that some thought.' Then, seeing the poor man couldn't understand her sense of humour, she touched his hand. 'There'll be no interest added on, Mr Broughton, I promise you. And once we get you a herd of cows, you'll soon have some sort of income.'

'I'll have lost me customers by now. They'll all be getting their milk elsewhere.'

For some reason the man was being obtuse, putting obstacles in the way of everything she suggested. She glanced at Ben for an explanation but he just shrugged, as mystified as she was. It seemed to both of them that Dan Broughton didn't want to leave the workhouse. It

215

was the boy who, speaking for the first time, gave a hint of the reason for his father's strange attitude.

'Dad's got very depressed, m'lady. It was a dreadful day when we had to leave the farm and come in here. And now he's lost all hope. I know I'm too young to take on the tenancy, but I'm not too young to work and I'll work day and night for you, if you'll give me the chance. And I'll look after me mam and me dad, an' all. Mr Chadwick was always a good friend. He'll advise me – and Mr Jackson here –' he nodded towards Ben – 'he'll help me.'

'We'll all help you, William,' Annabel promised. 'Now, get your things together and we'll take you home.'

'What? Now?'

'Right now, William.'

Taking an arm each, Lily Broughton and her son almost dragged Dan from the room. When the door closed behind them, Annabel couldn't stop her laughter, though she was careful to keep it low so that the family outside wouldn't hear. 'I don't think that poor man has much choice in the matter now, do you?'

'It's strange,' Ben murmured, staring at the closed door. 'Dan never used to be like that. He was a jolly, optimistic sort of a chap.'

'Having to come into the workhouse must have devastated him.'

'I wonder what sort of a reception we'll get from old Mrs Parrish and Mrs Banks.'

They didn't have to wait many minutes to find out. The matron ushered the two women into the room together.

The older of the two women, whom Annabel judged to be the cook's mother, was leaning heavily on the other woman's arm and she also used a stick in her right hand.

'Please sit down, Mrs Parrish,' Annabel said, after Ben had introduced her as the new Lady Fairfield. The older woman eyed her but said nothing. She was very bent, her thin shoulders hunched. The other woman – Mrs Banks – stood beside her friend and looked expectantly towards Annabel.

'We've come to take you home,' Annabel said gently. 'There's a room for you at Fairfield Hall, Mrs Parrish, until we can get you back to your little cottage, and your daughter, Mrs Banks, has kept your room ready for you. We're going to take the Broughton family home first – to their farm – and then we'll come back for you.'

Grace Parrish said nothing. Annabel thought she looked very frail and rather ill. She didn't seem to understand what was being said, but Agnes Banks spoke up. 'I'm sure Mrs Parrish will gladly go with you, m'lady, but I can't go back there. I thank you for your kind thought, but I shall stay here.'

Annabel stared at her for a moment, unsure how best to persuade the woman. 'I've talked to your daughter, Mrs Banks, and everything will be different from now on. Her "friends" from the town will no longer be welcome and I have plans to help Nancy find employment.'

'Are you a miracle worker, then, m'lady, because that's what it'll take for anyone in that village to give her work?'

Annabel laughed. 'We'll see, but for the moment, won't you come back home? Your daughter and your grandson need you.'

The woman's face crumpled. 'Poor little chap. None of it is his fault. Not even his birth.' She sighed heavily and then murmured, 'But I can't come back. I really can't.'

Annabel smiled sadly and touched the woman's arm. 'Very well, we'll leave it for today, but I'm not giving up on you, Mrs Banks. I'll keep coming back and back until you're so sick of the sight of me, you'll give in.'

Agnes Banks smiled weakly and avoided looking into Annabel's brilliant eyes. She knew that if she did, her resolve would crumble in the face of this determined young woman.

Twenty-Nine

An hour later, they left the workhouse with the Broughton family squeezed into the trap. 'Oh m'lady, I can't wait to get back to me own home, me own kitchen.'

'And what d'you think you're going to start cooking with, woman?' Dan said roughly. 'There'll be no coal, no food – nothing. We're going back to a cold, empty house. We'd've been better off staying where we was. At least we had three meals a day.'

'Huh! You call that rubbish we were fed in there proper meals – watery gruel and hardly ever the sight of a decent piece of meat?' Lily snapped back. 'If you're so ungrateful to her ladyship, you can go right back there, but me and William – we're going home.'

Dan growled but said no more.

When they drew into the yard at Chaffinch Farm, Dan refused even to look about him. He sat hunched in the back of the trap, his head down, looking at the floor of the vehicle. But William leapt out, helped his mother down and then ran around the yard, peering into the buildings.

'Everything's still here – just as we left it. The machinery's here. All we need is horses.'

Dan roused himself enough to mutter, 'And where d'you think you're going to get shire horses from? We'll need at least two and they cost money – a lot of money.'

Lily was already hurrying to the back door, anxious to see her kitchen. She disappeared inside but after only a couple of minutes, she reappeared calling, 'Dan – William – oh, do come and look. Hurry!'

William ran to the house whilst Annabel held out her hand to Dan, who was still sitting in the back of the trap. 'Come along, Mr Broughton. At least come inside and have a look. If you're adamant you want to go back to the workhouse, then we'll take you, but by the look of it, you'll be going on your own.'

Slowly, he raised his eyes to look into her violet gaze. 'Why?' he asked huskily. 'Why are you doing all this to help the likes of us?'

'Give me one good reason why I shouldn't.'

'We let you down. We couldn't run the farm well enough to make it pay.'

Annabel shook her head decisively. 'None of it was your fault, Mr Broughton. The rents were raised beyond reason. The whole estate failed, not just you. Remember that. Now, do I have to climb back into the trap to *push* you out?'

He stared at her for a long moment before saying slowly, 'Aye, an' I reckon you would, an' all. You're a determined young woman, aren't you? Do you always get your own way?'

Annabel stared back at him. His words had touched a raw nerve as she realized that until now, she had never had her own way in life. Her 'way' had always been ruled by her father or her mother, even to determining the man she should marry. Somehow, her father had engineered for Gil to leave without a word of good-bye to her and then he had arranged for her 'coming out', the Season and meeting James; James, with a title, whom her father had bought for her.

'Not always, Mr Broughton,' she said a little shakily, 'but I mean to in this.'

'Come on, Dan.' Ben came up behind her at that moment. 'At least come and have a look.'

He was still reluctant, refusing to get down until there came an excited call from his son, 'Dad, Dad, you must come. Everything's here just as we left it. In fact, it's better than we left it.' He disappeared again, but now Dan gave a deep sigh and moved stiffly to get out of the trap. He walked slowly across the yard towards the back door, his shoulders hunched, his eyes downcast. Inside the house, he still did not look around him but went straight to his Windsor chair by the fire in the range and sat down in it, gazing into the flames.

'He'll be all right in a bit, m'lady,' Lily said. 'It's all been a bit of a shock for him. A wonderful surprise, but a shock nevertheless.' Her face clouded. 'We all thought we was in there for good.' She glanced at her son. 'We didn't mind for ourselves, but it wasn't right that William should be in there.'

William was like a caged bird that had suddenly been allowed to fly freely. 'M'lady,' he said a little shyly. 'What do we do first?'

'What did you *used* to do, William?'

The boy glanced at his father for guidance, but Dan was still staring into the fire as if his mind was far away from the farm. William turned back to Annabel. 'We had a herd of about twenty cows, m'lady, and we used to supply the shops in the village as well as one or two of the shops in town. We teamed up with Mr Chadwick and the folks at Sparrow Farm too. And I think Home Farm did, an' all.' He glanced at Ben as if asking the question. Ben nodded.

'Yes, that's right. The estate had a very good milk business, m'lady.'

221

'The cattle market in town is on a Wednesday, isn't it? We'll go next week, Ben. You, me, Jim Chadwick and William here – and his father, if he'll come. And ask Adam if he'd like to come too. We must get everyone stocked up. And if Grandfather visits again before then, we'll ask him to join us.'

'He always used to go regularly, m'lady. He'll probably be there anyway.'

'But now, we must get back to town to fetch Mrs Parrish. I do hope Mrs Banks has changed her mind and is waiting for us too.'

But Agnes Banks had not changed her mind; she was nowhere to be found when they arrived back at the workhouse to find Grace Parrish with her few possessions tied up in a bundle. She had changed out of her workhouse uniform and was dressed in the clothes Annabel presumed she had been wearing on the day she'd been admitted. What a dreadful day that must have been. Annabel shuddered at the thought.

As Ben helped Grace into the back of the trap, she said, 'I don't know how to thank you, m'lady. This is the happiest day of me life.'

'There's a room waiting for you at Fairfield Hall and then, as soon as we can, Mrs Parrish, we'll have your cottage made ready for you in the village.'

'Where's Josh now? Me nephew? Well, me great-nephew. He's not been to see me all the time I've been in there. Ashamed, I expect.'

'Josh has been working very hard, Mrs Parrish,' Annabel said gently. 'He got a job alongside Mr Fletcher at the smithy in town, but they had to walk there and back every day. They both look exhausted. I'm sure he

222

would have come to see you if he could have done.'

Grace eyed her sceptically, but didn't disagree.

'I was sorry not to see Mrs Banks waiting with you,' Annabel said, tactfully changing the subject.

Grace sighed. 'Poor woman. Now *she* has got summat to be ashamed of. She just can't face all the pointing fingers and whispering tongues.'

Annabel frowned. She was still debating how she was going to deal with the problem of Nancy Banks.

And today was Friday.

Thirty

There were tears of joy when Grace Parrish walked into the basement kitchen at Fairfield Hall and into the waiting arms of her daughter. They wept on each other's shoulder and then Nelly turned wet eyes to Annabel. 'Oh m'lady, how can we ever thank you?'

'It's thanks enough to see you both happy and to know that your mother will soon be back in her own cottage.'

'I can help in the kitchen, m'lady,' Grace said. 'I can help Nelly. I know you're short of staff.'

'But your legs, Mam—' Nelly began and though Grace tried to 'shush' her, Annabel's sharp ears hadn't missed the words.

She glanced from one to the other and then said, 'Let's all sit down at the table and have a cup of tea. Where's Annie?'

'Upstairs helping the nurse with Lady Fairfield.'

'Oh dear, she's not worse, is she?'

'No, no, it's just that the sheets needed changing and Annie's just helping, that's all.'

'That's a relief! You had me worried for a moment.'

'I'll make the tea,' Jane, who had overheard the conversation, offered. 'You all sit down.'

As they sat around the kitchen table, Annabel said, 'Now, tell me about yourselves and then maybe we can work something out.'

'I used to be the cook here, m'lady, in the old earl's

day, but when me legs got bad, Nelly here took over. I taught her all I know.' She glanced at her daughter with pride. 'And I have to say she's a better cook than I ever was.'

'Aw, Mam, go on with you.' Nelly flushed with embarrassment, but Annabel could see that her mother's praise had delighted her.

'At first, when I retired, Lord Fairfield let me live in the cottage next door to Ozzy Greenwood and his mother rent free, and even paid me a small pension, but after he died and his son took over – that's Albert, m'lady, not your husband – well, they stopped the pension and then he wanted the cottage back. He said he could get a paying tenant. Josh lived with me then, but he was only on an apprentice's wages. He couldn't pay the rent the master set and feed us both.' Her eyes were haunted by the memory. 'So there was nowt else we could do. Nelly couldn't help, because he'd cut the wages of all the staff here at the house an' all – those that were left, that is, 'cos he got rid of a lot, didn't he, Nelly? Oh, he were a bad 'un, that Albert. And then, of course, there was poor Nancy and her mam, but I expect you know all about that.'

'Sort of,' Annabel said, 'but I'd like to know everything. I'm hoping I can help sort things out, but to do so, it'd be better if I knew all the facts.'

Grace and Nelly glanced at each other. Between them, they told Annabel the whole sorry tale.

'Mrs Banks came as housekeeper and her young daughter as housemaid just before the old earl died. She was a good housekeeper,' Grace began. 'Strict, but fair, and she and Mr Searby between them ran the house perfectly. We all knew our place and what was expected of us.'

'And she didn't show favouritism to her own daughter, either,' Nelly put in. 'I'd been promoted from kitchen maid to under-cook when Nancy came.'

'But after his lordship died and Albert inherited the title and the estate, it all changed. He'd been a problem to his parents before that – drinking and womanizing. His father had paid off a lot of his debts and rumour had it there were other girls he'd got pregnant that had to be paid off to be kept quiet,' Grace said.

'But then he started his shenanigans closer to home. He seduced poor Nancy. She was only just sixteen, m'lady,' Nelly added.

'Didn't anyone know what was going on? Her mother?'

Both Grace and Nelly shook their heads sadly. 'Nobody knew until she started being sick of a morning and putting on weight. He was careful to keep it very quiet even though it was going on under this roof,' Grace told her. 'I suppose, in his way, Albert did try to look after her. He gave her the cottage on the outskirts of the village – had it put in her name – everything. And, for a time, he gave her money.'

'But she had to earn it,' Nelly said grimly. 'He kept visiting her down there – if you know what I mean.'

'Then – after he died suddenly – and the estate was plunged into even more debt, the money being paid to her stopped.' Grace looked up swiftly at Annabel. 'Your husband wasn't involved, m'lady, so he had no reason to keep paying her. He couldn't take back the cottage – that had all been done legally and binding – but Nancy had no means of income. So then –' Grace paused.

'She started entertaining men from the town,' Nelly finished for her.

'Only two – and always the same two, Nelly.'

'And that makes it better, Mam?'

Grace dipped her head and did not reply.

'And what about Mrs Banks when all this was going on? Where was she?' Annabel asked.

'When it all came out that his lordship had got her daughter pregnant, she resigned her post here. She could hardly carry on in a position of authority over the rest of the staff, now could she?' Grace replied.

'At first she went to live with Nancy. She didn't like his lordship visiting, but there wasn't much she could do about it since they both depended on him,' Nelly said.

'And the little boy?'

Despite their disapproval of his mother, both Grace and Nelly softened when they spoke about the child. 'Bertie? Aw, you have to feel sorry for the little chap. He's no friends – doesn't go to school,' Grace said.

'He's hardly old enough yet, but then the school's closed anyway.'

'Yes, that's something else I'll have to look into,' Annabel murmured, 'The school, I mean.' But her thoughts were drawn back to the immediate problem of Agnes Banks. 'So how did Mrs Banks end up in the workhouse?'

'After Albert died and they had no income at all, Nancy took up with the two men who still visit every Friday. It was all she could think of to do to feed her child, her mother and herself,' Grace continued.

'But her mother couldn't stand the shame any longer. Just think about it – a well-respected housekeeper for what had once been a good family to come down to that.'

'For a while – after they first left here – Agnes and Nancy set up as dressmakers,' Nelly said.

'In the premises above the grocer's?'

'That's right.' Nelly nodded. 'But then when the estate started to go downhill, the last thing women were spending their money on was clothes. Even the mending service she offered dried up; women did it themselves, however bad a job they made of it.'

'Now that's a thought,' Annabel said, thinking aloud. 'Maybe if I offer her those premises again, that might prise her out of the workhouse.'

The two women stared at her. 'But there'd be no work. No one can afford a dressmaker now, any more than they could then,' Nelly reasoned.

'Not at the moment, no,' Annabel was forced to agree, 'but soon . . .'

Nelly was intrigued, even excited by the idea. 'Nancy's a good little needlewoman too. Her mother taught her. She used to do a lot of the mending when she was here as a kitchen maid. It wasn't part of her duties, of course, but she wanted to better herself in time. Poor girl never got the chance because of that brute. He ruined her life – and her mother's.'

'Well, that's all going to change, I hope, starting tonight.'

They both stared at her and even Jane, busy sorting out the vegetables for the evening meal, turned to look at her.

'I'm afraid Nancy's two gentlemen callers are going to be met with more than they bargained for when they arrive tonight.'

'Oh m'lady, whatever are you going to do? Do be careful.'

'I'm going to meet them and tell them that they are no longer welcome in Fairfield village.'

'Not on your own, surely?'

'No, I shall ask Ben and probably Jim Chadwick and Adam to be with me.'

'Take young Luke, an' all. He's handy with his fists,' Nelly said. 'Well, he used to be before we started having to go without food.'

'I hope it won't come to a fisticuffs, but, yes, I'll take him along.'

Thirty-One

That evening, as dusk fell, five shadowy figures walked along the street towards the solitary cottage on the outskirts of the village. Annabel had not asked the vicar to go with them. On reflection, she had felt that it would put him in a difficult position.

'Are you sure Nancy is going to agree with this?' Jim whispered through the gloom.

'I've talked to her. It's what she wants more than anything – to have her mother home and be accepted back into the community once more.'

Adam laughed ironically. 'You're asking a lot there, m'lady. I don't think the villagers will want to have owt to do with her.'

Annabel smiled grimly. 'We'll see,' she murmured.

When they arrived at the cottage, Nancy opened the door before they had even knocked. Shyly, she ushered them into the small living room. Her face was bright red and she could not meet the eyes of the four men who were with Annabel.

'Where's your little boy, Nancy? I don't want him involved in any of this.'

'He's in his bedroom. He won't come down.'

'Well trained, is he?' Jim Chadwick muttered and Nancy's colour deepened.

'What time are they due?'

'Any time now, m'lady.'

'Then we'll sit down to wait, if we may?'

'Oh, I'm sorry, I—' Whatever Nancy had been going to say was cut short by a soft knock at the back door.

Before Nancy could make any move, Annabel went to open it.

'Well, well, well, what have we here? Another pretty girl to entertain us?' A man's deep voice came out of the darkness.

'Hardly,' Annabel said crisply, as the four men accompanying her ranged themselves protectively behind her. 'I'm sorry to disappoint you, gentlemen, but your visits here are to stop.'

'Now, look 'ere, we've paid Nancy good money over the years. She owes us—'

'She owes you nothing.'

'Who the hell do you think you are?' A second man stepped out of the shadows and thrust his face close to Annabel's.

'I know who I am,' she said quietly, unmoved by his threatening action, even though her insides were churning. 'But, more to the point, do *you* know who I am?'

'Another little whore who wants to cash in on Nancy's business.'

'Oh, a business, is it? And do you keep records of all the transactions? I'd love to see the entry in your ledgers.'

'What are you talking about, you stupid bitch?'

At her shoulder, Ben moved closer. 'That's enough. You've heard what Lady Fairfield has said. Now, be on your way and we don't want to see you back in this village.'

'Oh aye, an' who are you? You're his lordship, I suppose.'

'No, and we don't want to get his lordship involved – unless it becomes necessary.'

The stranger shook his fist in Ben's face. 'You ain't heard the last of this. We'll be back. You can't stand guard outside her house morning, noon and night.'

'That's true,' Annabel admitted quietly. 'But if you do come back, I shall find out exactly who you are and where you come from and I shall pay a visit to town. Where do your wives think you are? In the local pub having an innocent drink with your mates?'

'You wouldn't dare.'

'Oh, but I would.' The threat was no idle one and the two men realized it.

'Come away, Sid. Leave it. There's plenty more trollops who'd be only too pleased to oblige us.'

'Mebbe. But they're not like Nancy. She's—'

'That's enough.' Jim now stepped forward, afraid of what filth was going to come out of the man's mouth. 'Be on your way.'

'And don't come back,' Ben added.

By the time they had closed the door on the two men, Nancy was shaking and in tears. 'They'll come back, I know they will.'

'Don't open the door to them,' Annabel told her. 'And keep Bertie inside in the evenings – just in case.'

'I don't think they'd hurt him. They're not *bad* men. Just . . .' She bit her lip and avoided Annabel's eyes.

'We've spoilt their fun and they're angry,' Jim said. 'Begging your pardon, m'lady.'

'Quite,' Annabel said tartly, but had to struggle to hide her smile.

'You go home, m'lady,' Jim offered. 'Me and Adam'll stay with Nancy a while until we're sure they're not going to come back. Mr Jackson and Luke can see you safely home.'

'If you're sure . . .' she murmured, not sure what their two wives would think about the arrangement. She turned to Nancy. 'I'll go back to the workhouse tomorrow and explain to your mother what has happened. Maybe that will help her change her mind.'

As they walked out into the darkness, back the way they had come, Ben said softly, 'It might change her mam's mind, but I doubt it'll change the villagers' feelings towards her. They don't forgive or forget easy, m'lady.'

'Mm. I've been thinking about that. Maybe they will when I've had my say in church after the service on Sunday.'

Though she couldn't see him through the gloom, Ben's mouth dropped open and he gaped at her. Whatever would this amazing woman do next?

The following morning, Annabel took the trap, driving herself, and went back to the workhouse. Again she faced the master over his desk. 'I have come to take Mrs Banks home.'

'I understand she doesn't want to go.'

'Things have changed now. I would like to talk to her again, if you please.' Annabel gave him the full benefit of her dazzling smile, her violet eyes sparkling as she added, 'You'd be doing me a great favour if you'd allow me to see her again.'

The man stood up and gave a little bow. 'How can I possibly refuse you, Lady Fairfield? Please be seated and I'll send for some tea and – for you – I'll go and find the dear lady myself.'

As he left the room, Annabel was chuckling to herself. She doubted the master had ever before had cause to refer to one of the inmates as a 'dear lady'.

A maid brought in a tray set with two cups and saucers, a pot of tea and milk and sugar and, a few moments later, the master ushered an obviously reluctant Agnes Banks into the room and then closed the door quietly, leaving the two women alone.

'I'm not coming home, m'lady,' she said, before she'd hardly got into the room.

'Sit down, Mrs Banks, and we'll have some tea. I'll pour, shall I? How do you like it? Milk? Sugar?'

The woman nodded in answer to each question and sat down on the edge of the chair opposite. 'It's a long time since I had a decent cup of tea. I expect it's too expensive for us to be given it in here.'

'Now,' Annabel said, handing her the tea. 'A lot has happened since I last saw you. With the help of some of the menfolk from the village, I went to Nancy's cottage last night and we were waiting for her friends when they arrived. They left in no doubt that they are no longer welcome, either at Nancy's home or in the village. Nancy and your grandson, Mrs Banks, want you to go home. *I* want you to go home. Things are going to be very different.'

'How can they be?' the woman whispered. 'We'll still be outcasts in the village. How can I ever hold my head up again?'

'I'm very much hoping that when I've spoken to the villagers after the service in the church tomorrow, they'll be prepared to help you both have a fresh start.'

Agnes shook her head sadly. 'They won't.'

'If that's the case, then I'll help you both to move somewhere else. I'll buy the cottage from Nancy and that will give you some money to start somewhere else.'

Agnes gaped at her. 'Why? Why are you doing this? Why are you trying to help us?'

'Because I want to revive the fortunes of the Fairfield Estate and everyone on it. And that includes you and Nancy.'

'Even if we stayed, what could we do? How could we earn money?'

Annabel smiled and said gently, 'The rooms you and Nancy once occupied above the grocer's shop as dressmakers are still empty. Perhaps . . .'

There was a sudden spark of interest, of hope even, in the woman's eyes. But it was gone almost as quickly as it had come. 'The locals'd never patronize us in a million years. And besides, not one of them has the money to be spending at a dressmaker's.'

'Not immediately, no. I understand that, but given time . . .'

Mrs Banks considered Annabel's suggestions for several minutes before placing her empty cup and saucer back on the tray.

'First, m'lady, let me say how very grateful I am for everything you're trying to do.'

Annabel's heart sank, believing that the woman was still adamant she wasn't going home, but Agnes's next words surprised her. 'So I'll tell you what I'll do. If you can come back to me on Monday morning and tell me that the villagers are prepared to give Nancy – and me – another chance, then, yes, I'll go home. And I'll try what you suggest. We'll set up as dressmakers once again, though where we'll find the work, I don't know, but we'll try.'

Annabel beamed and held out her hands to the

woman, clasping them in hers. 'That's wonderful. Nancy will be thrilled.'

'No, m'lady, please don't tell her. Not yet. See how things go tomorrow, eh?'

'Perhaps you're right,' Annabel said, realizing suddenly just what an enormous task she had set herself.

Thirty-Two

On the Saturday afternoon, Richard sat in his study pondering how to write his sermon for the following day. He knew exactly what he wanted to say – what he needed to say. He reached for the appropriate lectionary sitting on the shelf above his desk and turned to the page that would tell him what the readings set for that date were. Slowly, he smiled. One of the choices was just perfect.

During the morning service, at the end of the hymn preceding the Gospel reading, the congregation remained standing as Richard Webster took the Bible down the chancel steps and stood amongst his parishioners as they all turned to face him.

'The holy Gospel is written in the seventh chapter of the Gospel according to Saint Matthew beginning at the first verse.'

The congregation responded with the words 'Glory be to thee, O Lord.'

Richard cleared his throat and began to read, ' "Judge not, that ye be not judged. For with what judgment ye judge, ye shall be judged . . ." ' and ended with the words, ' "Therefore all things whatsoever ye would that men should do to you, do ye even so to them: for this is the law and the prophets." This is the Gospel of the Lord.'

And everyone responded, 'Praise be to thee, O Christ.'

Richard moved to the pulpit, said a short prayer and the congregation sat down, turning their gaze up to him as he began his sermon inspired by the words he had just read.

When, at the end of the service, the vicar announced that Lady Fairfield wished to address them all, there was shuffling and murmuring amongst the villagers.

Today, neither the dowager countess nor Lady Dorothea were present and for that at least Annabel was thankful. But everyone else seemed to be there except for Dan Broughton. Even Nancy and her son had crept into the back pew just as the service was starting. One or two saw them arrive and raised their eyebrows at each other. No doubt word had already gone around the village about what had happened at her cottage on Friday night and now they were curious. Richard Webster, knowing what Annabel intended to do, had already played his part by the content of his sermon.

As Annabel stood in front of them all and waited for silence, she suddenly realized how nervous she was. Her insides were quaking, her hands actually trembling. But she lifted her head and smiled around at them putting on a display of bravery that she wasn't feeling inside. 'I have a favour to ask of you all.'

'Aye, I thought there'd be a catch to all this philanthropy,' Jabez said loudly, but Annabel noticed that he was smiling as he said it and he was 'shushed' by those near him.

'No, Mr Fletcher, this isn't emotional blackmail. Nothing will change in what I plan to do for the estate, even if you all say "no". I'm not bargaining with you.' Her glance fell on Nancy, who had gone red in the face and had dropped her head. Only her little boy sitting beside her stared at Annabel, his face solemn, his eyes so sad.

Annabel drew in a deep breath. 'I'm sure most of you have heard by now what happened at Nancy's cottage on Friday night.'

Whispering broke out once more and heads leaned towards each other. Annabel raised her voice. 'Things are going to be very different now. Mrs Banks will be coming home and she and Nancy will be resuming their dressmaking business. I'm asking you to forgive and forget and give Nancy a fresh start. I know her story and – let's be quite honest here – it wasn't her fault at the outset. She's not the first maid in a big house to be seduced by the master or the master's son, now is she? And sadly, she probably won't be the last.' She paused, glancing around her.

A woman sitting halfway down the aisle got to her feet slowly and hesitantly. Annabel saw that it was Betsy Cartwright. In her gentle voice, Betsy said, 'M'lady, you say it won't make any difference to what you're still going to do for us all, whatever we say?'

'That's right, it won't.'

'But you know how grateful we all are for what you've done already. How can we refuse you?'

Annabel shook her head. 'I don't want that sort of gratitude, Betsy. All I want is for you all to be well and happy and thriving and the estate to be as it once was. You have a perfect right to refuse if you all feel you can't forgive what has happened. I know I'm asking a great deal of you to accept Nancy and her family back into the community and to treat her as you treat all your other neighbours. But if you can find it in your hearts . . .' She paused, hoping that Richard's earlier sermon had found its mark.

'And if we don't agree?' Another woman from the back, sitting not far from Nancy and Bertie, spoke up. 'What then?'

'I shall help Nancy and her family – including her mother, whom I want more than anything to get out of the workhouse – to move away and make a fresh start somewhere else.'

Mrs Broughton now got up. 'Begging your pardon, m'lady.' She glanced around at her fellow villagers. 'Mebbe I haven't the right to say owt, since we've been away for a while, but life in that place is a living hell. You all knew my Dan – what a good, jovial feller he was and a hard worker. And now look at him after a few weeks in there. He's a broken man. I don't' – her voice trembled and she pressed a handkerchief to her mouth – 'know if he'll ever be the same again.'

There was more murmuring. There were no secrets on this estate and the village grapevine had been hard at work over the past couple of days.

Slowly, Jabez Fletcher, whom Annabel believed many looked upon as the village elder and their spokesman, rose to his feet. He was frowning now and Annabel held her breath. She was sure that whatever Jabez had to say would determine the reaction of the rest. As both Betsy and Lily Broughton sat down, Jabez stared at Annabel. She met his gaze steadily but her heartbeat quickened. The next few minutes would determine the future of Nancy, her son and her mother.

Jabez cleared his throat and began to speak slowly and deliberately. 'M'lady, what has befallen this village, this estate, was none of our making. We were *all* hard-working, honest folk like Dan Broughton, but when that – that bugger up the hill – begging your pardon, m'lady – inherited it all, then we was done for. And he was the same bugger who shamed a nice little lass and brought her low. We all understood that and – at first – we stood by her, overlooked it, you might say. But it was what she did when things got tough that we find hard to excuse.' He paused and Annabel's heart sank. There was a movement at the back of the church and she glanced up to see that Nancy had risen and was hurrying out, dragging her son with her. Jabez carried on speaking as if nothing had happened. 'But if we're honest – and I hope we are still all honest, despite what has happened to us – might not any one of us have turned to such desperate measures to feed our little ones?' He glanced around the congregation, searching the faces of all the women there. 'Wouldn't you' – he pointed his finger – 'and you and you have done the same, if you'd had the chance, rather than see your children starve?' One or two of the women began to cry and several of the men looked shamefaced. 'Aye,' Jabez nodded. 'We've come close to starvation. We all – every one of us – knows what it's like to feel a gnawing hunger in our bellies and to have to listen to the bairns crying to be fed and we've nowt to give 'em.' He nodded, embracing them all in what he was saying. 'Aye, I've seen you all with that desperation in your eyes. That same desperation that young Nancy must have felt. She'd no man to lean on and her mam took herself off to the workhouse because she couldn't bear the shame of what her daughter became. But she became a whore to feed her boy; a boy who, let me remind you, if he hadn't been born on the wrong side of the blanket, would be our future lord and master. He is, as we all know, Albert Lyndon's son and by the law of nature he should have inherited on his father's death. But because of *man's* laws, he's a bastard and he can never inherit the title and the estate.'

'So, what are you saying, Jabez,' Jim Chadwick called out, 'that we should give Nancy another chance?'

'I am, Jim, yes.'

'And is that because that's what you genuinely feel we should do or because, despite what she says, it's Lady Fairfield who's asking?'

Jabez turned slowly to look at Annabel. 'No,' he said slowly at last, 'it's not because it's her who's asking. I believe what she says. She'll still do her best for us no matter what we decide, but I reckon she would be very disappointed in us all if we say "no". And I reckon she'd have a right to be.'

A stillness descended, each one of them was lost in their own thoughts, making up their own minds without influence from anyone else. Jabez sat down and leaned back in his seat, waiting as Annabel and the vicar were waiting too.

At last, when whispering began and grew like a breeze rippling through the church, Richard stepped forward and cleared his throat. 'How do you want to do this? Would the easiest way be to take a vote?'

'Aye, Vicar, I reckon that's a good idea.'

'Very well. So those in favour of giving Nancy a second chance, of treating her with kindness and under-standing, of accepting her and her son back into the community in *every* way – and that will include allowing your children to play with Bertie, agreeing that he should attend school alongside them, patronizing her dress-making business as and when you can afford it, sharing anything we have with her until times improve – with no more censure, no more disapproval, no more making her and her family feel like outcasts—'

'What if she falls back into those ways again?' a voice from the back asked.

Before Richard could answer, Annabel spoke up. 'Then she will leave the village.'

'Could you make her do that, m'lady? She owns that cottage.'

'Oh, I think I could find a way,' Annabel said quietly, 'but I don't think for a moment that will happen. Nancy wants – more than anything – to change her life.'

'So,' Richard said again, 'will those in favour please raise their hands?'

Jabez was the first to put up his right arm, swiftly followed by Betsy and Adam Cartwright, Lily Broughton and her son, William, and Josh Parrish. All the staff from Fairfield Hall followed suit and, as Annabel glanced round, slowly, one by one, the whole congregation raised their hands in the air.

Annabel felt the tears start in her eyes as she clasped her hands together. 'Thank you, oh thank you.'

Thirty-Three

The next morning, Annabel brought Agnes Banks home from the workhouse. She had been overjoyed when Annabel gave her the news.

'Nancy left the church yesterday before she heard the decision, but I went straight to her cottage afterwards and told her what had happened.' Annabel omitted to tell Agnes that the young woman had wept tears of thankfulness against Annabel's shoulder.

'How can I ever thank you, m'lady?' Nancy had said.

'By keeping your promise to me, Nancy, that nothing like that will ever happen again. If you need help, you come to me.'

'I swear it on Bertie's life, m'lady.'

Annabel hadn't expected such a dramatic reply, but now she knew Nancy would keep her word. She just hoped the villagers would keep their side of the agreement. But as she drove down the village street with Mrs Banks sitting beside her, she was heartened by the number of folk who came out of their cottages to wave and shout a greeting. When they reached Nancy's cottage, they found Betsy and Lily there. Betsy had made a stew and Lily had baked an apple pie. Even Grace Parrish had come down from the big house to welcome her friend home.

After a moment's hesitation – as if she could hardly believe it was true – Nancy fell weeping into her mother's arms. 'There, there, it's going to be all right,' Agnes murmured, but the tears were running down her face too.

'We'll leave you to settle in,' Lily Broughton said. 'Now, Nancy, you know where to come, love, if you need help. You've only got to ask.' Both Betsy and Grace Parrish nodded their agreement.

As they stepped outside and closed the door behind them, Lily sighed. 'I hope they're going to be all right. That poor little lad looked as if he didn't know what on earth was happening.'

Annabel said nothing, but Bertie's solemn face had touched her heart and she promised silently that she would keep her eye on him. After all, as Jabez had said, he was by rights a Lyndon, though she doubted Dorothea or even her own husband would see it that way.

Two days later, on the Wednesday, Annabel, accompanied by Ben, Jim Chadwick, Adam Cartwright and William Broughton, drove into the town to attend the cattle market.

'I couldn't get me dad to come,' William told them. 'He just sits in his chair by the fire all day. Me mam says it'll take a rocket up his –' The youth stopped and turned red at what he'd been going to say. 'Sorry, m'lady,' he mumbled.

Annabel hid her smile. 'Maybe the sight of cows in his fields once more will get him out of his chair, William.'

'We'll have him up and about again, don't you fret, lad,' Jim said. 'And in the meantime, we'll all pull together. We'll help you.'

'We'll need shires. How many do you think?' Annabel asked the men squeezed in beside her as the trap rattled towards town.

They glanced at each other and then Ben said, 'We've been having a chat about that, m'lady. To start with, we reckon we could manage with four between us.'

'For four farms? Do you really? There's a lot of ploughing to be done.'

'If there are some decent ones on sale today, we could get them and see how it goes.'

'Very well. And how many head of cattle do you want each?'

'Chaffinch Farm was mainly cattle,' William said. 'We had twenty cows at one time. Not that I expect you to buy me that many, m'lady,' he added swiftly. 'But we haven't a lot of arable land. It's mainly pasture for the cattle. And Mam would run the dairy. She's a dab hand at making butter and cheese.'

'And I'm more arable than cattle,' Jim put in. 'Though I had a small herd of about six milkers.'

'Home Farm's was a good mix,' Ben told her. 'A little bit of everything. A few cows for both milk and beef – we had Lincoln Reds for beef. . .' There was a wistful note in Ben's tone and, hearing it, Jim put his hand on the younger man's shoulder, as if to say, It'll be all right, Ben, though he didn't say the words aloud. 'A few sheep, hens, ducks,' Ben continued, 'turkeys for Christmas and fields of wheat, barley or oats and root crops too, of course.'

'What about you, Adam?' Annabel asked. 'It seems you can choose. I haven't had time yet to take a good look at Sparrow Farm, but you can do whatever you want.'

As they arrived near the centre of the town, Adam

was gazing wide-eyed around him at the bustling marketplace as if he'd landed in a magical land. 'What d'you advise, Mr Jackson? I always liked working with Mr Chadwick's cows.'

'Aye, you were a good stockman, Adam,' Ben said. 'I reckon you'd do well to concentrate on a dairy herd or mix of both. The chap who had Sparrow Farm before you kept both and he had a lot of pigs too, so between us all we supplied the local butcher. I don't think Percy Hammond needed to go off the estate much at all for his meat supplies. There's a slaughterhouse behind his shop, m'lady. I don't know if you've seen it, but Mr Hammond used to do all his own slaughtering.'

'I don't want to tread on William's toes,' Adam said worriedly.

'You won't do,' Annabel said firmly. 'How's Betsy with dairy work? Once she's well enough, of course.'

Adam laughed. 'She's like a new woman already. You should see her cooking and baking and cleaning. And she can't wait to have a few hens to look after.'

'Tell her not to overdo it. We don't want her ill again. It's not long since she had the baby, but do you think she'd like to learn dairy work?'

'Afore we were married she used to work for Mrs Broughton in her dairy. Do you remember, William?'

William furrowed his brow. 'Vaguely, but I wasn't very old then. But if she learned under me mam, she'll know what's what. Me mam's a stickler for things being done right.'

'Here we are.' Annabel drew the trap into the back-yard of the pub where all the farmers gathered on market day. 'And there's Grandfather waiting for us.'

Before the sales began, Annabel made sure that each farmer from the estate would bid for his own stock, leaving Ben to buy four shires that would be shared amongst them all for a while until they saw what was needed.

'Grandfather,' she whispered, as they found their places near the railings of the first pen of animals to be auctioned. 'Stand near William and give him a bit of advice if he needs it. I wouldn't want to belittle him.'

Edward looked down at her. 'Of course I will, my lovely.' He frowned. 'But why do you think you'd belittle the lad?'

'Oh Gramps! A woman telling him what to bid for! What do you think? I want him to take his place amongst the local farmers and today is a good chance to start, but I don't want him bidding for rubbish.'

Edward chuckled. 'You think of everything, lass, don't you? And just so's no one else feels belittled, as you put it, lunch at the pub after the market is on me. And I won't have any arguments.'

Annabel squeezed his arm in silent thanks.

The morning went well. There was pen after pen of cattle, both dairy and beef, and all looked sturdy, healthy animals. The auctioneer was assuring his audience that all the dairy cattle – ten in all – were in calf.

'Gramps, why are they being sold if they're in calf?' Annabel whispered, frowning. She was puzzled. 'I'd have thought the farmer would want to keep them.'

'They've all come from old Sam Bennett's place,' Edward whispered back. 'He's just died suddenly and his son doesn't want to come back here. He has a city job. So, the farm's being sold. They're all right, my lovely.' He chuckled. 'I've made enquiries and had a good look at them myself. They're due to calve again about next May. You'll be getting milk straight away, of course, but the only trouble is they might all have their two months' drying-off period at the same time. Still, that'll not happen until next March, April time. We've time to think about that before then.'

William was pink with delight when the hammer fell on six of the dairy cows for him. Next, it was Jim's turn to buy the remaining four milkers. 'And I'd like some pigs, m'lady, if that's all right.'

They were able to buy four gilts for Blackbird Farm.

'They look healthy,' Jim murmured. 'What d'you think, Edward?'

'How old are they?'

'Six months.'

Edward wrinkled his brow. 'That's about right. Need a bit of fattening up before they'll be ready for the boar. About the end of November, I reckon.'

Jim nodded. 'Let's see, they'd farrow in March.'

'Three months, three weeks, three days,' William piped up and they all laughed at the young man airing his knowledge.

Ben bought livestock for Home Farm and Adam, too, obtained three in-calf cows, two sows and six ewes. 'I like sheep, m'lady. I'd love to build up a nice-sized flock.'

'I always loved lambing time, if I could wangle a visit to my grandparents' farm at the right time,' Annabel told him, smiling at the happy memories of seeing ewes safely delivered of their young or helping to rear an orphaned lamb in Martha's warm kitchen.

'You can have loan of my ram,' Edward offered. 'You'll be needing him early October. We'll sort it out between us, Adam. And my neighbour, Joe Moffatt – you know, Annabel, your Jane's dad, who has Glebe Farm next to mine – he keeps a boar he hires out. There's no need for you to buy them – at least, not yet.

Now, my lovely, we'd best have a look at those shires over there. Four, do you say?'

'That's what they've decided between them,' Annabel said, 'though I don't know if it's enough for four farms.'

'Ben can always fetch mine for a few days, if I'm not using them.'

Four beautiful shires – black and white heavy horses – were knocked down to Ben. The excited expressions on the faces of all the men were reward enough for Annabel, whose bank balance was being eroded steadily. But she didn't mind; there were more shares she could sell and it would be so good to see livestock in the fields once more.

'Good strong workhorses, they are, Ben.' Edward nodded his approval. 'They're from Sam Bennett's place, an' all. There's a farm sale on site on Friday. It might be worth your while to take a look, but I think he thought he'd get a better price for some of his dad's livestock in the town market.'

'You go, Ben,' Annabel urged him. 'See what there is. In fact, you can all go. I might not come as there's still so much to do in the village.'

'Would you come with us, Mr Armstrong?' Ben asked. 'We appreciate your advice.'

Edward eyed him, wondering why the man was asking him. Ben had already been a bailiff for a few years and had run Home Farm and the estate efficiently before things had got tough. Why, Edward wondered, was he seeking his help and advice? Perhaps, the older man thought shrewdly, if Annabel wasn't there, he'd need advice on how much he could spend of her money. So, Edward smiled and nodded. 'I'd be glad to.'

They bought ducks, geese, chickens and a proud, strutting cockerel for each farmyard.

'Mam will love them,' William said happily. 'She'll take on the poultry.'

Over lunch, which Edward insisted on paying for, they discussed what else they needed. 'I don't like the look of the rest of the sheep for sale today. I reckon we got the best of what's here,' Ben said as he tucked into steak pie with a glass of ale at his elbow.

'There might be more back at Sam's place when you go on Friday. And have a good look around at what machinery you've got and what you might need – and tools, too. He ran his farm well, did Sam, poor old feller. There'll be all sorts at the sale on Friday and it'll be in good condition,' Edward reminded him. 'You could pick up a lot of stuff quite cheaply.'

The chatter continued between the men and Annabel listened, joining in now and again but for the most part she ate in silence, enjoying hearing the talk. Several local farmers came up and patted Ben's shoulder, or Jim's, and one or two were even bold enough to ask William how his dad was doing.

Then their curious glances lingered on Annabel's face and she knew the word was spreading around the district about the new Lady Fairfield. She smiled and greeted them and was introduced to so many people that her head whirled. 'I'll never remember all their names,' she laughed. 'I've enough to remember with everyone in the village.'

They returned to Fairfield, tired but happy with their purchases and full of hope for the future. But what awaited Annabel at Fairfield Hall spoiled her day.

Thirty-Four

'What's all this I've been hearing?' Dorothea's thunderous face greeted her. 'Just who do you think you are?'

'What have you heard, Dorothea?' Annabel was tired after the day's events and yet elated by what had been achieved. The last thing she wanted was to engage in a quarrel with her sister-in-law. But it seemed she had no choice; Dorothea was spoiling for a fight. Annabel was determined not to let the other woman gain the upper hand. Whatever it was could wait until she had washed and changed her clothes. And there was something even more important she had to do first. 'I must see your mother. I'll see you at dinner, Dorothea.'

'You'll listen to me now,' the woman almost shouted. 'And you won't disturb my mother. She's sleeping.'

'How is she?'

Grudgingly, it seemed, Dorothea was obliged to admit, 'She's improving slowly.'

'I'm glad. And is the nurse proving satisfactory?'

Again there was reluctance, but she said shortly, 'Yes.'

'Then what is so important that it can't wait until I've had a cup of tea and changed my clothes?'

'You're bringing shame and disgrace on this family. Wait until my brother hears about what you've been doing.'

Annabel raised her eyebrows, but Dorothea's tirade

continued. 'Bringing folks out of the workhouse back to the estate – folks who rightly belong there because they couldn't manage their farms. Reinstating a common whore into the village. Wasn't it bad enough we couldn't get rid of her because my stupid oaf of a brother *gave* her the cottage?'

'And who made her into a whore?' Annabel said quietly.

Dorothea face was purple with anger. 'How dare you? How dare you speak ill of my family like that?'

'It's the truth, though, isn't it? If your older brother hadn't seduced her and sired her child, Nancy would have continued quite happily, I'm sure, as a maid.'

Dorothea couldn't deny it. Instead, she shook her fist in Annabel's face and shouted, 'James will hear about it. About all of it and he'll send you packing. Sham marriage or no sham marriage, you'll be out on your ear.'

Annabel met the woman's furious gaze and her tone was deceptively soft as she said slowly, 'Oh, it's no sham marriage, Dorothea, I assure you.'

With that she turned, picked up her skirts and ran lightly up the stairs without looking back to see how her words had affected her sister-in-law.

When she went into the dining room as John Searby sounded the gong for dinner, Annabel was surprised to see not only Dorothea there, but also Theodore.

'Annie is sitting with my mother whilst the nurse has an hour or two off. Theodore will be eating with us this evening.'

Annabel smiled down at the boy. 'That will be nice. I've been wanting to get to know you, Theo.'

'It's Theodore,' Dorothea said shortly. 'He's named after my grandfather, the third earl. It'll be most appropriate when he becomes the seventh earl.'

Annabel decided not to rise to the woman's goading. For all any of them knew at the moment, Theodore might very well become the next earl after James. If she and James were to have no children, or only girls, then he would inherit the title and all the estate.

Annabel smiled at him as they sat down and after Dorothea had said grace, she asked, 'How old are you, Theodore?'

The boy glanced up at his mother as if seeking permission to answer. Receiving a curt nod, he said, 'I was five in June.'

'I understand you have lessons with your mother. What is your favourite subject?'

Again, there was a swift glance for approval before he said, 'I like learning all about the estate.'

'That's wonderful. Then perhaps – if your mother agrees – we could go out for a drive one day and you could show me around. I've seen a lot of it already, but not everything.'

'I don't think—' his mother began, but the boy interrupted excitedly. 'Oh please, may I, Mama?' It was the first time he'd shown any enthusiasm, the first time he'd responded to Annabel's attempts to be friendly. Though no doubt instructed by his mother to have nothing to do with the unwelcome newcomer in their midst, the child could not curb his excitement at the thought of an outing. Poor little boy, Annabel thought. I don't expect there's been much fun in his life. 'I'd like to show Aunt Annabel everything: the farms, the woodland, even the river that runs through the estate.'

Annabel smiled. She liked being called 'Aunt Annabel'.

'I'd take good care of him, Dorothea, but you could come too, if you wish.' She could see by the expression on Dorothea's face that the woman was struggling with conflicting emotions.

'Please, Mama.' Theodore's thin little face and big brown eyes were appealing. Surely she can't refuse him, Annabel thought, but she kept silent.

'Very well,' Dorothea said at last, but there was still doubt and reluctance in her tone.

Annabel met her gaze and said softly, 'And please give some thought to what I said about a governess or tutor. I meant it.'

In silence, they ate the meal that now deserved the name 'dinner'. Out of the corner of her eye, Annabel watched the little boy devour every morsel, clearing each plate of food that was placed in front of him. It was good to see and already his cheeks were pinker, his hair brighter.

'And now bed for you, young man,' Dorothea said as she rose from the table.

'Goodnight, Aunt Annabel,' Theodore said as he skipped towards the door.

Dorothea made to follow him, but then hesitated and turned back towards Annabel. Haltingly, she said, 'I didn't want James to marry. Not anyone. You know why. It's nothing against you personally, but I have to thank you for what you've done for us here in the house. For my mother, for Theodore. You needn't have done anything, I know that. You needn't have stayed here at all whilst James is away. And he will be away a lot. But you should know that whilst part of me is grateful, I will never give up my intention that Theodore will inherit.'

'I understand how you feel, Dorothea, truly I do.

But only time will tell on that matter. In the meantime, if we can't be real friends, perhaps we could at least try to get along together.'

The woman bit her lower lip. 'I still intend to write to James and tell him what you're doing on the estate, because I don't think he'll agree with it.'

Annabel shrugged. 'Please do, but I shall be telling him everything myself when I write.'

Dorothea gave a curt nod and turned away. Annabel watched her go with a sigh. It was the nearest she was going to get to a truce, she supposed. But she was glad about one thing; she wanted to get to know her nephew a lot better and now it appeared that she might be given the chance.

Thirty-Five

The following morning, Annabel went first to the vicarage. She sat at the kitchen table with Richard and Phoebe for a while, drinking tea and chatting whilst she recounted all that had happened the previous day at the market.

'So,' she said happily, 'there'll soon be livestock in the fields once again. And we bought horses too, so the ploughing can start. A little later than normal perhaps, but not too late, I hope.'

The vicar shook his head in disbelief. 'Cows, horses and sheep,' he murmured, 'after all this time.'

Annabel smiled but then, in a businesslike tone, she went on, 'And now, we need to move on to the next stage. First, Mr Webster, about the school . . .'

'The master left at Easter and the school hasn't been open since.'

'So, the children haven't been learning anything during that time?'

'Richard took classes for a while, but it got too much for him,' Phoebe said, putting her hand on her husband's arm. 'I took the girls for needlework and sewing and a little bit of cooking, but soon there was no food to cook and no money to buy materials of any sort. Though the children still had slates, we had no chalk left for them to write with.'

'How do we go about engaging a new teacher? Is

there a board of managers – or whatever they're called – for the school?'

Richard Webster grimaced. 'There used to be. It's a Board School and as the name implies, it's managed by an elected school board. I was an ex officio member because of my position in the community. Lord Fairfield – whoever held the title – was always the chairman, but Albert never attended and recently, of course, your husband just hasn't been here.'

'Who else was on it?'

'Anyone of standing in the community. The shop-keepers, the farmers – that sort of person made up the numbers. Mr Broughton was very active. He used to do a lot for the school. Mr Chadwick, too and, of course' – he smiled – 'Jabez Fletcher.'

Annabel laughed aloud. 'Why am I not surprised by that?'

'And we co-opted Ben Jackson to the board. That's all we had latterly, though maybe we should have more. I'll write some letters to see what I can find out and seek advice.'

'So, what do we do? Call a meeting of the board members?'

'It'd be for the best, but I doubt Mr Broughton will come.'

'It might be just the thing to prise him out of his depression. We'll try anyway. And may I attend?'

'I expect we could probably co-opt you to stand in for your husband,' Richard said.

'The sooner the better. We must get these children back to school – by after Christmas, if we can. Now,' she added, as she rose from the table. 'I must seek out the butcher, the baker and the candlestick maker.'

Richard looked up at her and blinked. Annabel

chuckled. 'Not really, I just meant I want to see if we can get the village shops open again.'

Richard, too, rose. 'Would you like me to come with you? You might meet with some bitterness.'

'I'd be very glad to have your company, Mr Webster. This isn't quite Mr Jackson's territory.'

They called first on Ozzy Greenwood, who lived in a cottage near the church with his elderly mother. A middle-aged man with thinning ginger hair and a freckled complexion opened the door tentatively. When he saw who was standing there, his eyes widened.

'Oh my lady, please come in. And you too, Vicar. Do you mind coming into the kitchen? There's no fire in the front room and Mother likes to sit near the range.'

As they moved into the room and Annabel took a seat on the opposite side of the range to where the old lady was sitting, she smiled and greeted her. The seventy-nine-year-old woman was hunched towards the fire, a warm shawl around her shoulders and a blanket over her knees.

'Mother feels the cold,' Ozzy explained. 'Mother,' he raised his voice, 'Her ladyship and Mr Webster have come to see us.' He turned back to them. 'She's a little deaf.'

Annabel leaned forward. 'How are you, Mrs Greenwood?'

The woman raised watery, faded blue eyes to look at her. 'Nicely, thank you,' she quavered and then went back to staring into the fire.

Annabel turned to Ozzy. 'Have you plenty of fuel and food?'

'Yes, m'lady, we have now, thanks to you.'

'We were wondering how you would feel about opening up your shop again?'

If eyes could truly be said to light up, then Ozzy Greenwood's certainly did. 'Oh, m'lady, do you think I could?'

'Of course. We're restocking the farms and soon there'll be milk, butter and cheese available locally. Where did you used to get your other supplies from before you had to close?'

'From the same people who supply the town shops, but my account with them will have lapsed by now and I don't know if they'd . . .' His voice trailed away and he avoided meeting her steady gaze.

Gently, Annabel asked, 'Do you still owe any of them money?'

Ozzy sighed heavily. 'One or two, I'm afraid, yes.'

'Then we'll have their accounts settled and I've no doubt they'll be happy to supply you again. If you give me a list, I'll see they are paid.'

'Oh, but my lady, I couldn't let you do that.'

'It'd be a loan, Mr Greenwood. We'll keep a careful note of what you owe me and once your business is thriving again, you can repay me.'

'What – what about the interest rate, m'lady?'

Here was a true businessman, Annabel thought with amusement. 'It'll be an interest-free loan, Mr Greenwood. Please allow me to do that at least.'

'I'd be very grateful and I'd repay every penny as soon as I could.'

'No rush for that.' She stood up. 'But let me have the list of debtors as soon as you can and we'll get things moving.'

'By tonight and – and will it be all right to start cleaning the shop out? I wasn't sure how things stood now. I mean, I haven't been paying any rent for the premises since it closed nor for this cottage.'

'All rents are suspended until the village is back on its feet, so don't worry about that. But what about your mother? Is there someone who can help look after her?'

'My sister and her family live further down the street. She'll look in on her.'

'What does her husband do?'

'He used to work on the land, m'lady. He was employed up at Sparrow Farm, but after the tenants there left . . .' Ozzy's voice dropped away.

'Adam Cartwright is taking over that tenancy. Tell your brother-in-law to go and have a talk with him. He'll be needing some help, I'm sure.'

'Thank you, m'lady. And –' He hesitated and Annabel prompted gently, 'Go on.'

'Is it true that Grace Parrish is home? I've seen two young girls going in and out of the cottage next door where she used to live. I just wondered . . .?'

Annabel smiled. 'Yes, she's home and the two girls were Annie from the Hall and my maid, Jane. They've been cleaning the cottage ready for Mrs Parrish to move back in.'

'That's wonderful news. And she'll be company for Mother. They were great friends before she – when she lived here.'

Again, there was the light of hope in the man's eyes and as Annabel and Richard Webster left, Ozzy was effusive in this thanks. When they were out of earshot, Richard chuckled. 'I don't think you'll get that sort of gratitude from Mr Merriman. You've won over Jabez Fletcher, but Eli Merriman might be an even harder nut to crack.'

Annabel laughed with him. 'I almost prefer it. Their gratitude is embarrassing.'

'Don't snub them, m'lady. Let them show their appreciation. You're saving lives and livelihoods here. And they know it.'

'We'll see Mr Hammond next,' Annabel said, changing the subject. 'And leave Mr Merriman until last. And I'll have to catch Mr Fletcher when he comes home from work tonight.'

'I think we'll have to go round the back,' Richard suggested. 'Mr Hammond might not hear us knocking on the shop door.'

'Is that the slaughterhouse?' Annabel asked, nodding towards some buildings across the yard from the back door of Percy Hammond's premises.

Richard nodded and might have said more but at that moment the door opened and Percy Hammond – a small, thickset man in his fifties, Annabel guessed – invited them to step inside.

'We'll go upstairs,' he said. ''Tis cold in the shop.'

'Actually, I wouldn't mind seeing the shop,' Annabel said on a sudden impulse.

Percy turned slowly to look at her, his eyes anxious. 'Are you thinking of taking it on, m'lady? Turning me out? I couldn't blame you if you did, 'cos I haven't paid rent for several months.'

'Far from it, Mr Hammond,' Annabel said, as she followed him into the front of the shop. The counter and the once white slabs were thick with dust, the windows smeared and grimy. There was a lot of work to be done before this shop would be clean enough to sell meat. 'I'm hoping you would like to open up your shop again.' She went on to tell him all that had happened in the last few days, how the farms would soon be up and running. 'But until they can supply you with meat once again, I'm sure we could buy supplies from town for you. You might not be able to make much profit at first, but it would be a start.'

'Do you mean it?' The man was flabbergasted; there was no other word to describe the incredulous look on his face.

'Of course I do, Mr Hammond.'

'Oh, my lady,' and now there were tears in his eyes, 'how can I ever thank you?'

'By running the best butcher's shop this side of Lincoln,' she teased him.

What was now becoming the usual conversation about loans and repayments followed, but Annabel and Richard emerged smiling from the butcher's shop.

'What a nice man,' she murmured.

'I don't think you'll be able to say that about the next one,' Richard said, and he grimaced as, once again, they went round to the back door. When it was opened and they faced Eli Merriman, even Annabel's resolve wavered. But she plastered a smile on her face and held out her hand. 'Good morning, Mr Merriman.'

He looked down at her hand with distaste and did not take it. 'What d'you want?' he said gruffly. There was no invitation to step inside. Instead, he just glared belligerently at her.

Annabel took a deep breath. 'We've come to see if you would like to reopen your shop.'

For a moment, the man looked startled as if this was the last thing he had been expecting. Then a suspicious look settled on his face. 'And how am I supposed to do that?'

'With a little help in the first place.' And pre-empting his next question, she added, 'And an interest-free loan to buy stock to be repaid when the shop is making a profit once more.'

'And how long do you reckon that's going to take? Folks round here have no money.'

'Not at the moment, but they soon will have.'

'How come?'

'All the farms on the estate will be operating very soon. The villagers will be re-employed and earning a wage again.'

He narrowed his eyes and regarded her with his head on one side. Annabel found she was holding her breath. Then with a sudden movement that made her jump, he pulled the door open wider. 'Come in, take a look, and if you've any clever suggestions on how I should start again, I'll be interested to hear them.'

They walked through the back room, which was used as a storeroom. Various objects and boxes cluttered the space. Then Eli led them through into the front of the shop. Like the other shops, the shelves were thick with dust and months of neglect. More boxes lay higgledy-piggledy on the floor. There was no order and it irritated Annabel's tidy nature. She liked a place for everything and everything in its place. But here, she doubted he even knew what stock he had left.

'First of all, you need an inventory of all the stock you have with its cost price and approximate selling price. You still have the invoices from when you bought the goods, I presume?'

Eli shrugged.

'My wife used to see to all the paperwork. I'm no good at that side of things. I can sell owt – coal to Newcastle, as they say, but paperwork – I don't understand it.'

'So, your wife would handle that again, would she?'

His face was stormy as he growled, 'My wife left me months ago when things started to go downhill.'

'I'm very sorry to hear that,' Annabel said quietly. 'Is there any chance—?'

'No,' he interrupted harshly. 'Even if she came crawling on her hands and knees, I wouldn't have her back. She took my lad with her and I can't forgive her for that. He'll be thirteen now but I ain't seen him for over a year.'

Annabel was shocked; she loved children and longed to have a child of her own. She couldn't imagine how heartbreaking it would be to be separated from one's own child. She drew in a deep breath. 'Then maybe I can help you with that to start with and then – if you agree – you could employ someone from the village to do the paperwork for you.'

He gave a humourless bark of laughter. 'And who do you think in this village can read and write and do bookkeeping? My wife was an educated woman.' He paused and then muttered. 'More's the pity. Mebbe if . . .' But there he stopped, lost for a moment in his own thoughts.

Annabel stepped closer to him and looked up into his face. Softly, she said, 'We'll get your shop running again, Mr Merriman, I promise.'

Slowly, he raised his head and stared into her eyes. 'I'll believe it when I see it.' With a long, deliberate pause, he added at last, 'My lady.'

Annabel took luncheon with the Websters and stayed in the village making plans. But when the sun sank in the western sky in glorious red-gold streaks, she walked back along the street towards the smithy. She smiled to see that already Ozzy Greenwood and Percy Hammond were hard at work cleaning and scrubbing out their respective shops, but now she wanted to see Jabez Fletcher.

She had been waiting outside the smithy for about ten minutes when she heard the rattle of a trap's wheels and turned to see Ben driving up the street with Jabez and Josh beside him. She was glad that he was still taking them to and from their work in the town.

'My lady,' Jabez greeted her as he climbed stiffly down from the back of the trap. 'Is owt wrong?'

Josh jumped down nimbly and Annabel thought he looked a little fitter already even after only a few days of proper meals.

'No, nothing, I just wanted a quick word before I go home. I'll not keep you long. I just wondered how you felt about reopening your smithy? We have horses back in the village now and—' She stopped. She had not expected this reaction from the bluff, no-nonsense man who had been so rude to her when she'd first arrived. He covered his mouth with a shaking hand and tears streamed down his face as he stared at her, disbelief in his eyes.

'I know four horses and the one we have at the Hall at the moment won't keep the smithy running full time,' Annabel said, rushing on, 'but we plan to get more very soon.' She was gabbling; his emotional response had unnerved her. 'And I'm sure there'll be plenty of other work for you and Josh. The vicar was telling me this morning that you doubled as a wheelwright and carpenter, too.'

Jabez nodded, still unable to speak. Suddenly, he stepped forward and clasped her hand, raising it to his lips and kissing her fingers.

Annabel laughed nervously. 'I'll take that as a "yes", then, shall I?'

Still, he couldn't speak so it was a grinning Josh, standing beside him with his hand on the older man's shoulder, who said, 'It is, my lady. It'll be a dream come true for him. And for me, an' all. And there's others in the village who might like to apply for our jobs in town when we give in our notice, so it'll help more than just us.'

Gently, Annabel gave Jabez's hand a tiny squeeze and then released her hand from his grasp as she said, 'And now I must go. I want to read a bedtime story to my nephew, and I mustn't be late.'

As she climbed into the trap beside Ben and they turned to go up the hill, she glanced down the street to the cottage at the very end of the road where another little boy to whom she would also very much like to read stories lived; a little boy who should, except for an accident of birth, be living in the big house at the top of the hill.

Thirty-Six

'Dorothea,' Annabel asked as they sat down to dinner that evening, 'do you read bedtime stories to Theo – Theodore?' Tonight, the little boy was not with them.

'When I've time. But I have to sit with Mama tonight. The nurse must have some time off duty.'

'Of course. I'd be willing to do that, too, if it would help you, but I'd really like to get to know Theodore. Would you allow me to read a bedtime story to him, if you're busy?'

For a moment, Dorothea eyed her suspiciously. 'Why would you want to do that?'

'Because I'd like to get to know my nephew.'

Dorothea blinked and then frowned. She was still trying to work out what possible ulterior motive Annabel might have. She couldn't possibly believe that there wasn't one.

'Very well,' she said at last, grudgingly, 'but his light must go out at half past seven. Not a minute later.'

When they'd finished dinner, Annabel ran lightly up the stairs and found her way to the nursery on the second floor. She knocked on Theo's bedroom door and, when his boyish voice said an uncertain, 'Come in,' she entered the room. He was standing by his bed, leafing through a book of nursery rhymes. His eyes widened when he saw her.

'I've come to read to you, if you'd like me to. Mama

is busy looking after your grandmother tonight.' She crossed the room towards him. 'Will that be all right, Theo?'

For a brief moment the boy hesitated. 'Has – has Mama said so?'

'Yes, she knows I'm here and she says you have to go to sleep at half past seven. But we've at least twenty minutes, so – what would you like me to read?'

He shut the book he'd been looking at, ran across the room and into the neighbouring nursery to a small bookcase to replace the book he carried and pull out another. '*Aesop's Fables*,' he said, carrying it back to her. 'The story about the fox and the crow.'

Theo settled into his bed and Annabel sat down beside him. For the next half an hour, she read from the book. At twenty to eight, she said, 'We must stop now or we'll both be in trouble. Snuggle down and I'll put the book back on your bookcase. There now, do you have a teddy in bed with you?'

The boy was suddenly solemn-faced again. 'No, Mama says only babies have cuddly toys. She's given them all away.'

Annabel felt the prickle of tears in her throat. The little boy was only just five. She went to the side of the bed and bent down to kiss his forehead. Suddenly, his arms were around her neck and he planted a kiss on her cheek. 'Thank you for reading to me, Aunt Annabel.'

'I've enjoyed it,' she said, her voice not quite steady. 'I'll read to you again when Mama is busy.'

'Mama only ever reads one story. You read three,' he whispered, as if it should be a secret between them. And it would be, Annabel thought.

'Night, night, sleep tight,' she said as she tiptoed out of the door.

On the landing she stood for a moment. What a sad, lonely little boy he was. If only, she thought, he could meet his cousin. Perhaps they could be friends. She sighed. But that was something Dorothea would never allow.

Reading a story to her nephew at his bedtime became a regular occurrence and one which Annabel looked forward to each day. Her restoration of the estate and the village continued. Progress was slow and yet already there were definite signs of improvement. Fields were being ploughed and winter wheat set – a little later than usual, but at least it was being done now.

Over the next few weeks, more livestock arrived at the farms, thanks to Annabel's grandfather. Edward was well known – and well liked – in the district and word soon spread about the hard times the folk of Fairfield were suffering. More cattle arrived through Edward's shrewd bargaining and sometimes by just appealing to his generous fellow farmers. Now, the four farms had six cows each and Ben had six Lincoln Reds too.

'Now it's my turn to embarrass you, m'lady,' he told her with a chuckle, 'by saying a heartfelt thank you. You couldn't have bought me a finer present.'

A further flock of twenty ewes arrived for Adam, and Edward's ram was brought in during the first week in October.

'I've put the red ochre on his chest for you,' Edward told Adam when he delivered the animal.

When Adam looked mystified, Edward chuckled. 'It's a trick I've learned. You'll see.' And three weeks later, Adam understood. All the ewes now had red marks on their hindquarters, indicating that the ram had serviced them.

'I've got you some more sows, six in all,' Edward announced in November. 'They've already been serviced by Joe Moffatt's boar, so I know they'll be of good, strong stock. And Joe's bringing his boar here next week – free of charge this time, he said. He wants to do his bit to help. Now, my lovely, who's to have them?'

'My goodness, Gramps! However did you manage that?'

Edward laughed and tapped the side of his nose. 'It's not always what you know, it's who you know – and a bit of smart negotiating. You don't always need to go to market to find a bargain.'

'It'd be nice if all four farms could have one each, I think, and then maybe an extra one for Jim and for Dan and William too. A couple of pigs might be just the thing to prise Dan out of his armchair.'

The livestock thrived and soon, a little money began to trickle back into the pockets of the farmers, but not enough yet to repay Annabel, whose bank accounts and share holdings were being sorely depleted.

'Don't you spend all your money,' her grandfather warned. 'I've a little put by. Let me help.'

'No, Gramps,' Annabel said firmly. 'You've done enough already.' She smiled and hugged him. 'But thank you for the offer. You're a dear.'

'Just promise me that if you need help, you know where to come. I don't expect there's any more money on offer from your father, now that he has what he wants.'

When speaking of Ambrose Constantine, Edward's voice always hardened. He hadn't approved of Annabel's marriage, believing – quite rightly – that it was Ambrose's machinations that had brought it about. Still, he comforted himself, she seemed happy enough and she wasn't far away from him now if she wanted help. Though, he smiled to himself, she really didn't seem to need it. How safe his farm would be in her capable hands, he thought, even if she still had the estate to manage too.

Annabel had been dutiful in writing to her parents each week, but she kept the letters light and was careful not to mention the true state of affairs on the estate. And certainly she didn't tell them that she was spending her own money on its restoration. Nor was she particularly anxious to see them; their devious manipulation in bringing about her marriage to a nobleman had sickened her. So she was thrown into consternation when a letter from her mother said that she would be visiting. It was not a request or a suggestion; it was a statement. Annabel felt a moment's panic until she read the next few lines:

I shall be staying with your grandparents at
Meadow View Farm for two nights just before
Christmas. No doubt your grandfather will
drive me over to see you.

She breathed a sigh of relief. Her mother needn't see the dilapidated state of the whole house, nor know the extent of the neglect on the farms. Two of the village shops were now open – only Eli Merriman's remained firmly closed. He was still refusing to budge. But today, Annabel had other matters on her mind. The school and its continued closure concerned her. The village children – healthier now that better food and more of

272

it was available – were running wild. It was time something was done and there seemed to be one person standing in the way of the management board taking steps to appoint a teacher: Daniel Broughton.

Annabel folded her mother's letter and tucked it away in the drawer of her dressing table. She would reply to it tonight once she had finished reading Theo his bedtime story; that time was now sacrosanct. And Dorothea seemed quite happy to hand over the task to her, but Annabel didn't see it as a chore; she cherished the time she spent with the little boy. She put on her coat and hat and wrapped a warm scarf around her neck against the raw November day to walk to Chaffinch Farm. She didn't want to take up Ben's time by asking him to take her there; he now had so much to do with revitalizing Home Farm as well as keeping an eye on the progress of all the tenant farmers. She really must get a pony and trap for the use of those at the Hall. Luke would care for the animal, she decided, alongside the one which Ben used. In the courtyard there were empty stables and coach houses just waiting to be used again. As she walked, she glanced about her, gratified to see the livestock grazing in the fields. Already there was a feeling that the farms were slowly coming back to life. In an arable field close to the farmyard she saw William struggling to control two heavy shires pulling a plough across the field. She paused to watch him for a few moments. The first few furrows were crooked, but the last two he had ploughed looked much better. Annabel smiled ruefully. Poor William; he was learning the hard way.

When Lily opened the back door in answer to her knock, Annabel stepped into the warmth of the kitchen with its appetizing smell of freshly baked bread. A pan of stew simmered on the newly black-leaded range and

Lily bustled about her kitchen, chattering all the time, covering, Annabel thought, for the silent man, who still occupied the chair near the fire. He didn't even look up when she sat down in the chair opposite him and accepted Lily's offer of a cup of tea and a newly baked scone with jam and cream.

'I can't tell you what a joy it is to have the dairy up and running again, m'lady,' Lily enthused. 'And William's doing very nicely with the ploughing, though he's finding it hard on his own.' She glanced swiftly at her husband but then looked away again. Annabel could see at once that Lily resented her husband's idleness whilst their son struggled to cope. But, today, Annabel was determined to try another tack.

'Mr Broughton, I need your help.'

She waited until the man slowly raised his head. 'Mine?' He sounded incredulous.

'We need to get the school open again and I under-stand you were on the board. The vicar has arranged a meeting for tomorrow night and we need you there. James is away and I shall attend – if everyone is agree-able – in his place, but my presence won't be official. So, Mr Webster says, we need you there.'

'Is Fletcher going?'

'Yes.' Mentally, Annabel crossed her fingers; actually, she didn't know. Richard Webster had said he would see both Jabez and Jim Chadwick.

'It's the least you can do, Dan,' Lily, who had been listening to every word, put in. 'After all her ladyship has done for us all.'

Annabel stood up. 'I'll ask Ben to pick you up in the pony and trap, shall I? About seven?'

She turned, nodded her farewells to Lily, and walked out of the room without waiting for an answer.

'I aren't going,' Daniel growled once Annabel was out of earshot.

Lily said no more; she knew better than to badger her husband. He was more likely to go if the matter wasn't mentioned again and his own conscience was left to do the nagging. But it was William who unwittingly caused his father to have a change of heart. He came in at teatime, fuming with indignation. 'It's high time they opened the school again. I've had four little buggers – sorry, Mam – following me all day throwing clods of earth at the horses. I've enough trouble handling them shires without them being pelted by hooligans. If I knew who they were, I'd tell their dads. They should be in school – that's where they should be – not running wild around the village.'

Lily dished up their meal and sat down at the table, taking care to keep her glance away from Dan. She said nothing, but later she told William about Annabel's visit. 'Don't say owt, but I can see he's thinking about it now.' She patted his arm. 'You did well, son, to tell us when you did.'

'It'll do no good,' William muttered. 'Nowt'll get him out of that chair.'

But William was wrong, for the very next evening, Dan appeared downstairs dressed in his best suit. True, the suit had seen better days, but there was no money to spend on new clothes and at least he had made the effort.

'What time did her ladyship say Ben'd come for me?'

'Seven,' Lily said, sitting down near the range and taking up her mending. She lowered her head to hide her smile.

'I'll walk out an' watch for him coming, then.'

'Aye, good idea, and while you're out there, have a

look at how William's getting on with the ploughing.'
She said no more. If Daniel had even a tiny spark of
pride left, he wouldn't want to see the furrows in his
fields all higgledy-piggledy. Maybe . . . Lily dared to
hope.

Thirty-Seven

The meeting went well. Richard Webster took the chair and the five members of the previous board who were present co-opted Annabel onto the board. Out of deference to her position, Richard suggested they should appoint her as chairman, but Annabel demurred.

'I can't possibly act as chairman when I know so little about the position. Please, if the others are happy, you should continue as chairman, Mr Webster.'

'His lordship was always the chairman,' Jabez said, 'that were the old man, of course. Lord Albert never attended a meeting at all, and your husband – well, he's not here, is he? That's different.'

Annabel smiled, though she was rather afraid that even if he had been here, James might not have taken up his duties either. She was glad when the topic of conversation moved on to how they could appoint a suitable teacher quickly.

'I was talking to the vicar of St Michael's Church in town,' Richard told them. 'And he said that they've recently appointed a new headmaster for the school there. They had several very good applicants and the decision was difficult and came down to a close-run thing between two. They finally agreed on one, but he wondered if we'd like to consider the other one. Evidently, he was a very good candidate.'

'Mr Chairman,' Jabez spoke up. 'Do we have to advertise the post?'

'I'm not sure, I'll make further enquiries, but because there is a matter of urgency perhaps we could make a temporary appointment and then advertise it if we have to. This man could then apply for the permanent post, if he wished.'

'But surely he won't leave his present post for a temporary one with no guarantee of it being made permanent,' Dan said, speaking for the first time since the meeting had begun.

'That's a very good point, Mr Broughton,' Richard said and scanned down the page of neat handwriting in front of him. 'It seems,' he said slowly, 'that Mr Porter has lost his wife recently. He has two young children and has come to live in Thorpe St Michael to be near his wife's parents, who are to help him care for the children.'

There were murmurings of sympathy around the table for the unknown man.

'So,' Richard asked them, 'what do you think?'

They glanced at each other before Jim Chadwick ventured, 'I say give him a trial. Can't hurt as long as we have a get-out clause in place. That is, if his appointment is temporary.'

'Then may I have a seconder for Jim's proposal?'

Dan nodded and then Richard asked, 'Are we all in favour?' When there was a chorus of 'ayes' around the table, Richard noted it down. He was also acting as unofficial clerk for the meeting and would write up his notes later in the official minute book.

'Then I will write to Mr Porter and invite him to come to see us.' A suggested date was agreed upon and they moved on to the next item on the agenda, which Richard had prepared.

*

'How did it go?' Lily asked when Dan arrived home, sat down in his chair and bent to unlace his boots.

'Fine,' Dan answered, and he recounted all that had happened in the meeting. When he had finished, he glanced around. 'Where's William?'

'Gone to bed. He's shattered, poor lad.'

Dan grunted. 'He's trying hard, I can see that, but his ploughing's not up to much. Reckon I'd better show him how it's done tomorrow.'

Lily hid her smile and sent up a silent prayer of thankfulness, remembering to thank the Good Lord for the arrival of the new Lady Fairfield in their midst.

Eli Merriman remained obstinate and Annabel decided to leave things as they were for the time being, but there was still one household in the village she had not visited since the day she had brought Agnes Banks home from the workhouse and it was now the first week in December. On the Friday morning, it rained but the afternoon was fine so Annabel decided to visit Nancy and her family. She walked down the village street while it was still daylight so that all the villagers should see exactly where she was going. She knocked on the front door of the cottage and smiled when a wide-eyed and flustered Nancy opened the door.

'May I come in?'

'Oh – er – your ladyship. Yes, yes, of course.'

Annabel stepped inside. 'How is your mother?'

'She's well. She's in here.' Nancy opened the door to the front parlour where Agnes sat near the window, embroidering a large linen tablecloth, with huge butter-flies in each corner. When she saw Annabel she began to get up, but Annabel waved her to sit down again.

'Please don't disturb yourself. My, what fine work, Mrs Banks. How clever you are.' Annabel laughed. 'Despite my mother's best efforts to have me instructed in all the creative arts that a woman is supposed to possess, I can't sew or knit or even paint a passable watercolour. And as for playing the piano, my poor music teacher despaired.' She sat down in a nearby chair and came straight to the point of her visit. 'Have you thought any more about starting up again as dressmakers?'

Agnes looked up quickly at her daughter. 'We've thought of nothing else, m'lady, but I don't see how we can.' She dropped her gaze as she murmured, 'Who'd bring their patronage to the likes of us?'

'Now, now, Mrs Banks, that's all behind us now. The villagers are courteous to you, aren't they?'

'They serve us in the shops, if that's what you mean. And some of them are quite friendly in the street.'

'But they ignore us when we go to church,' Nancy said softly. 'I'm sure they don't think I should set foot in there.'

'Give it time,' Annabel said gently. 'Hopefully, the school will be open again soon and Bertie will be able to go to school. If he—' She stopped, startled by the look of fear that flitted across Nancy's face. 'What is it?'

'He can't go there. He'd be bullied, taunted. Called all sorts of – of horrible names.' She blushed furiously and hung her head. 'And worse still, they'd be true.'

'No one will call him names or mistreat him,' Annabel said firmly. 'I'll see to that.'

Nancy smiled wistfully. 'I know you mean well, m'lady, and I'm – we're so grateful for what you've done for us already.' She moved to her mother's side and placed her hand on the older woman's shoulder.

'You don't know what it means to have my mother back with us and – and to know that she has forgiven me for bringing shame—'

'Now, now, no more talk of that. We're interviewing a teacher for the school and if he takes up the post, I'll have a word with him – ask him to watch out for Bertie. Where is Bertie, by the way? I'd like to see him.'

'He's playing in the back garden.'

'Still on his own?'

Nancy nodded and bit her lip.

'He'll make friends when he goes to school,' Annabel said with a confidence in her tone that she wasn't feeling inside. These villagers had long memories and their youngsters would have overheard the gossip.

A few moments later, Nancy ushered Bertie into the room. Shyly, he came to stand in front of Annabel and, obviously coached by his mother, he said, in a clear, piping voice, 'Good afternoon, Lady Fairfield.'

'Hello, Bertie. I've brought you some books. Would you like me to read a story to you?'

The boy blinked and, above his head, Annabel saw Nancy and her mother exchange a startled glance. Bertie put his thumb in his mouth and nodded, sidling a little closer to Annabel. As she opened one of the books she had brought, he leaned against her knee, following her finger moving along the line of printing as she read and looking at the pictures in the illustrated book. When she closed the last page, she looked down into his upturned face and found herself staring into his huge soft brown eyes. She smoothed the flick of dark brown hair back from his forehead. There was no doubting whose family this boy belonged to; he was a Lyndon and no mistake.

'I'll come another day and read to you again,' she

said softly as, with an impetuous gesture, she dropped a kiss on his forehead. 'But now I must be going. It's getting dusk.' She didn't add that she was hurrying home to read to his cousin.

As she left the cottage, Annabel didn't notice two men lurking behind the hedgerow of the field opposite.

'That's 'er,' whispered Sid. 'That's me fine lady what spoilt our Friday evening's bit o' fun. What I wouldn't like to do to 'er . . .'

'Too dangerous, Sid. We'd best take our revenge on Nancy and her brat. Villagers won't miss them, I can tell ya.'

'Aye, mebbe you're right. We'll think about it, plan it careful, like. But tomorrow night, we'll be back. They won't be expecting us on a Saturday night, now will they?'

As the darkness closed in around them, the two men crept away.

Thirty-Eight

'James! How lovely!'

When Annabel arrived back at the house, it was to find James striding up and down the hall, a deep frown on his face. Private Jenkins was standing to one side watching his superior officer, whilst Dorothea was standing in the doorway into the dining room, a satisfied smirk on her face.

Annabel ran towards her husband, her arms wide, decorum forgotten in her pleasure at seeing him. But instead of enfolding her in his embrace, he caught her by the shoulders and held her fast, glaring down into her face.

'Where have you been until this hour?' he demanded harshly.

Annabel gasped. 'James, you're hurting me.'

He released her quickly, almost throwing her off-balance by the sudden movement. She resisted the urge to rub her arms where his strong fingers had bruised her flesh. She faced him calmly, but defiantly. 'I've been down in the village,' she began, but then stopped. She didn't think James would be pleased to hear where she'd been for most of the afternoon and she certainly didn't want Dorothea to know.

'On your own?'

'Why, yes. Oh James, you should see how things are taking shape. We have livestock back on the farms, the

283

fields are being ploughed and two of the shops are open again. Even Jabez Fletcher has given his notice in at the place he works in town and is to reopen his smithy. There's only . . .' She had been about to say that there was only Eli Merriman to come round and everything would soon be as it once had been, but James was still glowering.

'If you still insist on involving yourself in running the estate, you will oblige me by taking your maid with you everywhere you go. Everywhere, do you understand? A *lady* would never dream of going anywhere without her maid and she certainly wouldn't be seen in the company of the estate bailiff without a chaperone.'

Annabel was about to burst into laughter at the veiled suggestion that lay beneath his words. It was a preposterous notion, but she could see that her husband was deadly serious. She stared up at him as she said softly, 'I will do as you ask, James, because I respect your wishes, but I promise you, you can trust me implicitly. And Jane has been busy helping care for your mother.'

His expression seemed to soften a little. 'I am thinking of your reputation, my dear.'

Annabel inclined her head and said, 'Of course,' even though she didn't think that was the case at all. James was unaccountably possessive, but, strangely, the thought that he cared enough about her to be jealous warmed her.

'And besides,' he went on, 'Mama is much improved now. And I –' he hesitated before saying stiffly as if words of thanks did not come easily to him, 'I do realize that we have you to thank for that.'

'Please,' Annabel smiled up at him and linked her arm through his, 'don't let's mention it again. I have so much to tell you. Will you come up with me while I change for dinner?'

'Of course.' As they moved towards the staircase, James glanced back over his shoulder. 'I won't be needing you again tonight, Jenkins. I'm sure you can find something to amuse you, though I'm sorry the pub hasn't reopened yet.' He smiled mockingly. 'Obviously, it is not one of my wife's priorities.'

Annabel glanced back too, an anxious frown on her face. She couldn't say anything, but she fervently hoped that Private Jenkins would not go to Nancy's cottage. Once in the privacy of their bedroom, however, all thoughts of the soldier and even of Nancy were driven from Annabel's mind as her husband lifted her into his arms and carried her to the bed.

'And now, how about a proper welcome home for your husband?'

There had been no time left for her to relate everything that had taken place since he had last been home before it was time to dress hurriedly for dinner. And at the table, Annabel had no intention of talking about estate matters in front of Dorothea, but it seemed that Theo had other ideas. He had been allowed to dine with the grown-ups as a special treat because his uncle was home and also because it was the first time his grand-mother had come downstairs since her illness. But the child did not know that Annabel had had a hand in all the improvements; he only knew the changes he had seen.

'Uncle James, we've got horses in the fields and cows and sheep. And Aunt Annabel says they've got pigs at the farms and hens. Oh, all sorts! Isn't it wonderful?

And the farmers are ploughing their fields. Next year, Aunt Annabel says, there'll be all sorts of crops growing.'

James raised his eyebrows and glanced at his wife as the boy continued excitedly, 'And yesterday, we went out in the new pony and trap. Luke took us and we drove all around the estate. Aunt Annabel pointed out all the farms. I know all their names and who lives there now.'

'Then you know more than me, Theodore. But a new pony and trap, you say? How has that come about, then?'

There was silence around the table until Dorothea was obliged to say, grudgingly, 'Annabel bought it for the household to use. It will save having to use Jackson's.'

'I'm delighted to hear it,' he murmured and Annabel knew at once that he was pleased because she would not be calling on Ben any more to take her wherever she needed to go.

'And,' Dorothea went on, taking a deep breath, 'your wife has offered to employ a tutor for Theodore until he is old enough to go to boarding school. The school both you and Albert went to, of course.'

James turned his head slowly to look at his sister. 'I think you should get in touch with your errant husband to ask him to support his son's education. It shouldn't fall to either me or my generous wife.'

Annabel kept her eyes firmly on the plate in front of her but the revelation had startled her. She had assumed – obviously incorrectly – that Dorothea was a widow. She glanced at the woman beneath her eyelashes, to see that Dorothea had blushed scarlet.

'James,' Dorothea hissed, 'how could you? Not in front of the boy, please.'

James shrugged, unfazed by her anger. 'He's got to know the truth one day. The younger he is, the better he will deal with it.'

'Nonsense,' she whispered so that Theodore, sitting further down the table near his grandmother, could not hear. Though Annabel's sharp hearing could pick up the gist of what was being said, she was careful to give no sign that she was aware of what they were saying.

'There's no need for him ever to know,' Dorothea went on sotto voce. 'Henry Crowstone is out of our lives and I want it to stay that way.'

James smirked. 'You know, I can't help feeling rather sorry for Crowstone. You used him, Dorothea, to get what you wanted, a son and possible heir for Fairfield, and then you made the poor fellow's life such a misery that he found solace elsewhere. One can hardly blame him.'

'Oh, in just the same way as you have used your *wife*, you mean? You've got what you wanted out of her, haven't you? Her money!' James face darkened. Dorothea was treading on dangerous ground, but she carried on heedlessly, picking up on what was dearest to her heart. 'And what do you mean a *possible* heir? Theodore is your heir. You promised me.'

'If I don't have children of my own – or if I only have daughters – he will certainly be my heir. But if I do have a son –'

Two bright pink spots still burned in Dorothea's cheeks. 'But you promised. You swore to me that your marriage would be in name only.'

James gave a wry laugh. 'I grant you that, originally, that was my intention, but I had reckoned without the delectable young woman I have married.'

They were carrying on the quarrel in such low voices,

confident that Annabel could not hear what was being said, but as their anger grew, they both became unguarded and now Annabel could hear every word quite plainly, though still she gave no sign and pretended to involve herself in Theo's chatter with his grandmother.

'So, what about your marriage vows? What about the "forsaking all others" bit? Have you given up your amour in London?'

Annabel could detect that her remark angered James. 'That, my dear sister, is none of your business.'

Now it was Dorothea who, feeling she had the upper hand, leaned back in her chair with a smug smile. 'It is, if I choose to make it so, *my dear brother.*'

But James was to have the last word. As he rose from the table he said, nonchalantly, 'There'll be no need for Theodore to have a tutor here. Until he's ready to go to boarding school – which I will agree to – he can attend the village school.'

With that, he turned and left the room, leaving Dorothea gaping after him.

Thirty-Nine

The next day, Private Jenkins was sporting a blackening eye and a bruised nose.

'What happened to you?' James asked as he passed him in the hallway on his way to breakfast.

'Village louts,' the man muttered morosely. James roared with laughter. 'Protecting their village whore, were they?'

Unobserved, Annabel came up behind them. This time she did not hide the fact that she had overheard their conversation. 'If you mean Nancy, she has changed her ways. There will be no more visits from gentlemen callers unless, of course, their intentions are honourable.'

James opened his mouth, but it was Jenkins who said quickly, 'My intentions are honourable, m'lady. I know what she is – or rather was – but I still like the look of her. I'm no angel but I'd like to court her proper-like, though no one would listen to me.'

'Was that your intention last time you tried to visit?'

The man hung his head and mumbled, 'Well, no, m'lady, it weren't, but' – he lifted his head – 'it is now, I swear.'

Annabel looked into his hazel eyes. 'I believe you,' she said quietly. 'I'll talk to Nancy and see what she says. The only thing is, you'll have to be chaperoned at all times – at least to start with. She's making a great effort to be accepted back into the village, but if the villagers see a man visiting her cottage, they won't believe her.'

Later that afternoon, as dusk gathered, James and Annabel, wrapped up against the winter's chill, walked down to the village.

'I need to see for myself what's happening,' James said. 'Jenkins, you come too. We'll let the villagers know you meant no harm.'

They came to a halt in front of the two shops that were now open when Jabez appeared from the smithy. He touched his cap to James and murmured, 'M'lord.' His tone was deferential, but there was a coolness and a wary look in his eyes. His expression softened as he turned towards Annabel. 'My lady.' Then his glance went to the soldier standing a pace or two behind. 'Bit o' trouble last night, then, was there, young feller? Well, I'll say one thing, you look to have come out of it better than the other two.' He jerked his thumb over his shoulder. 'Young Josh is battered black and blue and they say Adam Cartwright ain't much better.' The old man chuckled. ''Spect you know a few more moves than they do, what with you bein' a soldier and learnin' to fight.'

'Jenkins got the message,' James said curtly.

'Good,' Jabez said. 'We're trying to help that lass and her young 'un be accepted back into the community and it dun't help if fellers still think they can – use her.' His eyes hardened. ''Twas that what brought her down in the first place.'

James met the older man's steadfast glare and it was his lordship who looked away first with a brief, 'Quite.' There was an uncomfortable pause until James cleared his throat and changed the subject abruptly. 'I understand you're reopening the smithy.'

'Aye, m'lord. If you remember – but p'raps you won't as you were only a young 'un then – my father ran the smithy and joinery business here.' He jerked his thumb over his shoulder towards the buildings behind him.

James frowned. 'Vaguely. He was a wheelwright too, wasn't he?'

'That's right.'

'And you aim to do the same?'

'I do, m'lord. God willing.' His glance went once more to Annabel and a slow smile spread across his mouth. 'And with her ladyship's help.'

James's mouth hardened and he seemed about to retort, but Annabel squeezed his arm and, reading his thoughts, said quickly, 'Mr Fletcher – and everyone else – is keeping careful accounts.'

'Oh aye,' Jabez said, catching on. 'Every penny she lends us will be repaid. You need have no fear of that. Once we're on our feet.'

'Mm,' was all James said, but there was doubt in the sound.

'Any development with Mr Merriman?' Annabel knew that his neighbours were doing their best to encourage the man to reopen his shop.

Grimly, Jabez shook his head. 'A'kward old cuss. Begging ya pardon, m'lady, but he is.'

'Perhaps if he was told he'll be given notice if he doesn't buck his ideas up – that might spur him into action,' James said, with deceptive mildness.

Annabel bit her lip. She would have liked to have denied such an action, but realized that it would be belittling her husband in front of his tenants.

291

Immediately, Jabez's tone was hard once more. 'Would you like me to relay that message to him?'

James shrugged and said ironically, 'I'm sure her ladyship will bring him round eventually. She seems to have the rest of you wrapped around her little finger.'

For a moment, Jabez stared at him and then chuckled, 'You're right there, m'lord. We'd do owt for her ladyship.'

Annabel blushed prettily, but her husband was far from pleased by the compliment. Instead, he nodded curtly and turned away, forcing Annabel, who still had her arm tucked in his, to do the same. She glanced back over her shoulder and gave Jabez one of her dazzling smiles. Her action did not go unnoticed by her husband and his frown deepened. 'It's getting dark,' he said, 'we should go back.'

The three of them were about to turn and retrace their steps, when a flash of light at the end of the road caught Annabel's eye. 'Wait! What was that?'

They stood a moment, watching as the light turned into flames licking the night sky.

'My God! It's a thatched roof on fire,' James muttered and, wrenching himself free of Annabel, began to run towards the blaze.

'It's Nancy's,' Jenkins exclaimed and ran after James. Then he shouted back, 'Get help. Get all the villagers to come and help.'

Galvanized into action, Annabel picked up her skirts and ran the few paces back towards the smithy. 'Mr Fletcher! Mr Fletcher! Come quickly. Nancy's cottage is on fire.'

Jabez was still in his backyard. Hurrying out of the gate, he glanced just once down the road and saw what was happening. 'I'll get Josh. We'll bring buckets. Get the others.'

Quickly, she banged on the neighbouring doors, bringing both the grocer and the butcher out of their shops. Word spread down the village street as quickly as the fire on Nancy's roof and soon most of the men were running towards the burning cottage carrying whatever they'd been able to find that would hold water to douse the flames. Annabel ran to the vicarage, the nearest house to the cottage. Swiftly, she explained that they needed water and soon a chain of villagers had formed from the back door of the vicarage passing heavy buckets from hand to hand.

'We can't get up to the roof,' James said, taking his place in the line. Annabel stood beside him, making one more pair of hands. 'If only—'

'Will this help, m'lord?'

James and Annabel turned with one accord to see Eli Merriman standing behind them, carrying a long ladder.

'Good man,' James said and reached out to take one end of the ladder. Together they began to carry it towards the blazing cottage.

'James – do be careful,' Annabel cried. 'Where's Private Jenkins? Let him help you.'

James turned briefly. 'He's gone into the cottage to get them out.'

'Oh my God – are they still in there? Don't they know?'

At that moment, Ben appeared at her side. He had run all the way from the Hall and was panting hard. 'What happened?' he asked, taking the place in the line vacated by James.

'We don't know. We just saw the flames. Oh Ben, they're still inside.'

'What?' He passed her the full bucket of water he

was holding and dashed forward, just as a dark shadow appeared in the doorway of the cottage. Private Jenkins staggered out with Bertie in his arms and Agnes clinging to his arm, but there was no sign of Nancy.

Passing the full bucket of water she was holding, Annabel now left the line and hurried forward to take the boy from Jenkins's arms. Bertie was crying and struggling to free himself. 'Mamma, Mamma!'

'I'll get her,' Jenkins said, and he turned and dashed back into the flames that were now engulfing the whole cottage.

'Oh, save her, please!' Agnes gasped, but then a fit of coughing overwhelmed her and she sank to the ground, doubling over as she fought to breathe.

As Jenkins entered the cottage again, Annabel saw Ben climbing the ladder onto the roof. James followed him whilst Josh Parrish stood at the bottom and passed up buckets of water. But they were all fighting a losing battle. The fire had taken such hold that although everyone worked as hard as they could the flames were too fierce for them.

James came down from the ladder and shouted up to Ben. 'Come down, man. Save yourself. There's nothing more we can do.'

With one last despairing look at the burning roof above him, Ben slid down the ladder. 'Where's Jenkins? He's not still in there, is he?'

They both ran towards the door. 'Jenkins! Jenkins!' James roared, but there was no reply. Ben made as if to enter the house, but James gripped his arm. 'No, man, no. It's certain death. The roof's going to collapse inwards any minute.'

'But if there's a chance . . .'

'James, James!' Annabel was running towards them.

'Get back,' the two men cried in unison.

'Look, look. They're safe. They must have gone out the back way.'

James and Ben turned to see Jenkins staggering round the corner of the cottage, carrying Nancy in his arms. He carried her well away from the building just as, with a crash and the sound of splintering wood, the roof caved in sending a fresh burst of flames skywards. Now that they knew the occupants of the cottage had all been brought out, the line of water bearers put down their buckets. 'There's nowt more we can do for the cottage now we've got 'em all out,' Jabez said wisely. Luckily, the dwelling was set apart from any others and the fire would not spread to other buildings.

But none of them knew yet if Nancy had survived. Tenderly, Harry Jenkins laid her on the ground and bent over her. 'She's breathing, but it's shallow.' He looked up. 'Is there a doctor here?'

'I'll go,' Ben volunteered, though his face was black from the smoke. 'I'll fetch him.' But he got no further for at that moment Nancy began to cough and open her eyes. She struggled to sit up. 'Bertie,' she gasped hoarsely. 'Mam!'

'They're safe. They're both safe,' Annabel reassured her, kneeling on the grass beside her, but it was Harry Jenkins who cradled her in his arms.

'You're safe,' he murmured gruffly. 'You're all safe.'

Without thinking, Annabel turned to say, 'Ben, fetch the trap. We'll take them up to the house.'

'Couldn't they stay at the vicarage?' James muttered. 'I don't think—'

'They need someone with medical knowledge. Nurse Newton was preparing to leave now that your mother is on the mend, but she's still with us at the moment.'

James knew himself defeated as his wife issued the orders. 'Mr Fletcher, can you organize a watch to be kept until it's burnt itself out? Mr Webster,' she added, seeing the vicar who'd been helping in the line of water carriers, 'please could you make sure everyone's all right – that no one's got injured. I must go home and make sure we have beds ready for our guests.'

James watched in amazement as everyone hurried to do his wife's bidding. Slowly, he began to realize just what a remarkable woman he had married and just how much she was doing to rescue his estate. But there was one thing that still rankled and, as she took his arm once more to walk home, it was his unreasonable jealousy that surfaced, causing him to say softly, 'Ben, is it? I can see I shall have to watch that bailiff of mine.'

But Annabel, her head still full of what needed to be done, hardly heard his words and certainly, their underlying meaning did not register.

Forty

'I'm not having that woman and her little bastard under the same roof as my son,' Dorothea stormed when the trap pulled up at the front door of Fairfield Hall. Annabel and James had arrived home just ahead of it and had swiftly explained the reason for their dishevelled appearance and forewarned the household of the imminent arrival of unexpected guests.

'It seems, my dear sister,' James drawled, 'that we have no choice. Annabel has organized it and here they are. Make the best of it, Dorothea, as I will have to.'

Annabel was already issuing orders to Annie and Jane to make ready a room for Nancy, her mother and son.

'There are only the guest bedrooms on the top floor, m'lady. Mrs Parrish senior is still in the spare one in the servants' quarters.' Annie, catching the excitement of the moment, suggested, 'But they only need use one room. The two women can share the double and the little boy can sleep on a truckle bed. Jane, go and get the warming pan ready while I find clean sheets. Oh my!' she added, as she caught sight of the bedraggled trio being brought in through the front door. Harry was carrying Nancy and Ben carried Bertie, with Agnes leaning heavily on his arm. 'Looks like they could do with a hot bath, an' all.'

'Thank you, Annie. And would you ask Mrs Parrish if she can find food and drink for them? And please, would you tell Nurse Newton she is needed?'

'I'll see to it all, m'lady.'

The household was suddenly a beehive of activity as everyone rallied round the homeless family. Dinner was put back until James and Annabel, whose clothes were covered with smuts, had had time to wash and change. Amidst the bustle, Theo appeared at the top of the stairs. 'Mama, what is happening? Grandmama wants to know what all the noise is about.'

Dorothea whirled round to look up at him. 'Go back to your room this instant and don't you dare come out again until I say you can.'

Theo's face crumpled but he turned and disappeared, running back up the stairs to the nursery and his bedroom. But, at the turn in the staircase where no one could see him from below, he paused to listen. His mother was not finished yet. She turned on James as he began to mount the stairs. 'Isn't it enough that you humiliate me by threatening that Theo will have to attend the village school?' She spat out the last two words, the very sound of them abhorrent to her. 'But now I have to endure the disgrace of having – of having these people in the house as *guests*?'

James, suddenly overwhelmed with weariness, leaned on the banister. 'Dorothea, I don't like it any more than you do, but I'm sure Annabel would remind you – whether you like it or not – that, but for an unfortunate accident of birth, the boy is your son's cousin.'

Dorothea put her hand to her throat as she pulled in a sharp breath. James, tired of all the arguments, turned away and continued to climb the stairs. And Theo crept quietly up to the top floor and the safety of his bedroom.

*

At breakfast, Dorothea was still angry. She had hardly slept, her wrath keeping her awake far into the night. 'How long do you intend them to stay here?'

'As long as it takes,' Annabel replied calmly, helping herself to breakfast from the dishes set out on the sideboard. They were alone in the dining room. 'And aren't you forgetting to enquire how they all are this morning?'

'No, I'm not forgetting. I have no interest whatsoever in how they are. It would have been better if they'd all perished in the flames.'

Annabel whirled around on her sister-in-law. 'Dorothea, that's a wicked thing to say.'

The woman's face twisted. 'Oh, I'll be even more wicked and add "and you along with them" since you seem to put such creatures ahead of your husband's wishes.' Her eyes narrowed spitefully. 'You think you're so clever, don't you? Playing "Lady Bountiful". Spending your own money on the estate, buying the tenants' affection, even buying James's gratitude. Well, let me tell you something, he'll never love you.'

As Annabel sat down at the table, Dorothea leaned across it and hissed in her face. 'His marriage to you was just a marriage of convenience. The woman he loves lives in London. She's his mistress and he has no intention of giving her up, not even now he's married to you.'

Annabel kept her hands hidden beneath the table as she clasped them together to stop them trembling. Surely it wasn't true? Dorothea was just being vindictive; trying to make her leave Fairfield Hall. The words were like a knife through Annabel's heart and yet as she slowly raised her head to look into Dorothea's eyes and saw the hatred and resentment there, her resolve hardened. She'd known from the start that she and her sister-in-law would never be real friends, but she had begun to hope that they could rub along together. But in that moment, Annabel knew that Dorothea was showing her true colours; she was her bitter enemy. From now on, she realized, she would have to be on her guard.

On the Monday afternoon, Theo sat alone in the nursery, surrounded by his books and toys, which had been collected in an earlier age before the family had fallen on hard times. He read the same books his father and uncle had read, played with their toys, but he had no companion with whom to play toy soldiers or engage in rough and tumble; he had no idea what it was to have a playmate of a similar age.

But now he knew there was another little boy in the house – on this same floor and just down the corridor. The main house was quiet; his mother had gone into town in the pony and trap and his grandmother was taking her afternoon rest after luncheon. Aunt Annabel was down in the village and his uncle and the soldier, who'd rescued the little boy from the fire in their home, were out too.

Quietly, Theo tiptoed out of the nursery and along the corridor. Now he could hear the piping voice of the boy and a softer tone – a woman's voice – answering him coming from inside one of the guest bedrooms. He knocked softly and heard the scrape of a chair. The door opened and Theo stared up at the pretty woman standing there, a startled look on her face.

'Oh, Master Theo. You shouldn't be here. Is – is there something wrong?'

Theo shook his head and craned his neck to look

around her. 'I've come to see the boy – to see if he'd like to play.'

'Play!' The woman, whom Theo guessed was the boy's mother, was shocked but Theo nodded firmly. He was to be the next earl of Fairfield and one day this would be his house. Surely, he could say what went on in it even now. 'Yes, I want to play with him.'

'Oh, well, I don't know,' Nancy still hesitated, but stood aside and held the door wider so that he might enter. 'I don't think your mother would—'

'She's out,' Theo said matter-of-factly. 'And Grand-mama is resting. No one can hear us up here.' He marched purposefully into the room and stood in front of the other boy. 'What's your name?'

The little boy, his eyes wide, stood up slowly. 'B-bertie,' he stuttered and glanced at his mother for reassurance. Nancy gave a wan smile and a slight nod of encouragement. Now Theo turned to speak to the woman.

'May Bertie come to my room? It's only just down the corridor. He won't be far away. You can come and see, if you like.' He glanced around the room that was devoid of toys. He knew about the fire, knew that whatever the little boy had owned had been lost. The only thing Bertie seemed to have left was the battered knitted soft toy he was clutching. 'I've lots of toys,' Theo went on. 'He can have some of them to keep, if he likes.'

'That's very kind of you, Master Theodore, but it wouldn't be right.'

Theodore was only six months older than Bertie, but he acted and spoke with far more confidence than the younger boy. Theo had grown up with his mother's undivided attention. Not only was he advanced in his learning, but he was also mature for his age. Dorothea, ever mindful of the position her son would one day hold, had schooled him for that very role.

'No one will know,' Theo said and suddenly there was an unexpected mischievous twinkle in his eyes that was rarely seen. Under his mother's strict guidance, 'fun' was not part of her curriculum. She never played with him; that was left to the nursery maid, but there had not been a nursery maid for months now. His Uncle James played occasionally with the young boy, but his visits home were fleeting. Theo was lonely. He hungered for a playmate. On his rare trips out, he had seen boys playing in the road, kicking a tin can, or girls skipping, and he'd yearned to join in. He'd even seen, and recognized, the loneliness of the little boy who lived in the cottage at the end of the village and, though he was too young to put into words the feeling he'd had, he had empathized with him. And now that same boy was here in his house and Theo was determined not to miss such an opportunity.

'Well . . .' The woman was wavering. 'As long as he comes back in here the moment your mother comes home.'

Theo nodded, his eyes shining. 'I promise.' He held out his hand to the younger boy. 'Come on. I've got some toy soldiers. We can play going to war, like Uncle James does.'

Nancy gasped and her eyes widened. Her fingers covered her mouth. Did the boy know? But then she relaxed. No, of course he couldn't know, she tried to reassure herself. Theo was referring to the earl as his own uncle. A five-year-old boy could not possibly realize that the little chap he was leading towards his own room and a mountain of toys shared the very same

302

relationship to the present earl, for James Lyndon was not only Theo's uncle but Bertie's too. Could he?

Nancy was wrong. Theo did have an inkling that Bertie was somehow connected to the family; crouching on the stairs, he'd overheard his mother's conversation with Uncle James on the night of the fire. He was too young to understand the full significance of their words, but all Theo wanted was a playmate. Now, he showed Bertie the lines of lead toy soldiers. 'You can be Napoleon Bonaparte at the head of his army and I'll be the Duke of Wellington.'

Bertie had no idea who either of the men were, but he followed Theo's instructions and the two young boys played happily together until Theo heard his mother's voice on the landing below. 'Quick,' Theo said, scrambling up from the floor and holding out his hand to Bertie to drag him towards the door. 'Run!' And Bertie ran.

Alone once more in the nursery, Theo set the soldiers that had been scattered by Bertie's hasty flight upright as Dorothea came into the room.

'I trust you haven't been playing all afternoon, Theodore. I left you some reading to do. Have you done it?'

'Yes, Mama,' Theo said, not looking up. It was the first time he could ever remember deliberately lying to his mother, but he would not be caught out. He'd read that particular book before and he had a good memory. If she questioned him about the story, he would be able to answer perfectly.

The Banks family stayed three nights until Annabel was able to arrange for them to move into the rooms above the grocer's shop which they had occupied once before.

'Back to where we started,' Agnes murmured as Annabel led them into the upstairs rooms, which the village women had spent the last three days cleaning. They had all brought bits of furniture and household goods to make the three people, who'd lost everything they owned, feel welcome. Agnes wiped the tears of gratitude from her eyes as she looked around her. Annabel put her arms around the woman's shaking shoulders. 'There, doesn't that prove they want to accept you back into the community?'

'I – hope so,' Agnes said. 'Oh, I do hope so.'

'When you've got settled in, we'll buy you all the materials you'll need to start up your dressmaking business again. You can start by making new clothes for yourselves.' Her glance went to Bertie, still holding Nancy's hand as he gazed around the rooms that were to be his home from now on. Under his arm he carried a large box wrapped in brown paper. It was so big it looked almost too heavy for him to carry, but it seemed he would not be separated from it. 'And toys. We must get some toys and books for Bertie.'

Bertie looked up at her. 'I've got one toy; a rabbit called Hoppy that Granny knitted for me when I was born. I was holding him when Mr Jenkins rescued me. And now I've got another. A train set. Theo gave it to me.'

'Theo?' Annabel was startled. She hadn't realized that the two boys had even met; Dorothea had been careful to see to that. But Bertie was grinning. It was the first time Annabel had seen the solemn-faced little boy smile since the dreadful fire that could have cost them their lives.

'It was when you were all out the other day. He came

304

to find me and took me back to his room. We played for ages until we heard his mother come back.' Now Bertie frowned. 'He's frightened of his mama, isn't he? Is she cruel to him?'

Annabel bit her lip, not knowing quite how to answer. She couldn't possibly tell the little boy exactly why Lady Dorothea didn't want her son playing with him. 'Not cruel, no,' she said carefully, 'but she's very strict.'

'He says he's going to come to the village school when it opens again after Christmas. We could be real friends then.'

'Would you like that?'

The young boy was thoughtful before he said, with a poignancy that struck at Annabel's heart, 'I've never had a friend before.'

With a catch in her voice Annabel said, 'I think you'll make lots of friends when you go to school.'

'But I'd really like Theo to be my friend. And he would too. He said so.'

Poor little boys, Annabel thought, as her heart went out to both of them. They'd both led such a solitary life, but for very different reasons. Well, she vowed silently, if I can, I'll change that.

Forty-One

The fire had been reported to the police in Thorpe St Michael, but the culprits – believed to be Nancy's former Friday-night visitors – had suddenly declared to their families that they had found more lucrative work 'up north' and had disappeared, leaving no forwarding address. Not even their wives knew where they had gone. But all that mattered to Annabel was that Nancy, Bertie and Agnes were safe and miraculously unharmed.

Bertie had not been the only one to make a friend following the fire. The next morning, when the homeless family were waking up on the top floor, Private Harry Jenkins approached John Searby. 'Mester Searby, I'd like to see Nancy, but I don't want to cause more gossip and speculation about the lass.'

John Searby had eyed him suspiciously. He knew what soldiers were like. Even his own master had a mistress in London, if the rumours were to be believed. 'You'd better talk to Mrs Parrish. She's in charge of the women-folk in this household at the moment. She'll tell you what's best.' But Nelly Parrish had shrugged her shoulders. ''Tis nowt to do wi' me. I'm just carrying out her ladyship's orders. Though I'd be careful, young feller, while they're in this house.' She dropped her voice. 'Lady Dorothea's in a temper about it all now, so—'

'I want it to be all above board, ma'am. I've spoken to her ladyship – Lady Annabel, that is – and she said she'd speak to Miss Banks, but then the fire happened and – well – I don't rightly know what to do now and we're going back to camp in a couple of days. I don't want to go without speaking to Nancy.'

'Is it just speaking you want or summat more?' Nelly asked bluntly and, hardy soldier though he was, the colour flooded Harry's face.

'I just want to talk to her, ma'am. I promise you that's all.'

Nelly regarded him for a moment and then suddenly seemed to make up her own mind about him. She gave a brief nod. 'I tell you what,' she said. 'You help me this morning – if it's not beneath you. With all these extra folks about the place, I don't know if I'm on me head or me heels, and when she comes down, you can have a little chat with her right here in my kitchen.' She wagged her finger at him. 'I rule the roost in here and don't let anyone else tell you different.'

Harry grinned at her. 'I wouldn't dare, ma'am. You're far more frightening than any drill sergeant. Now, what do you want me to do?'

'Them potatoes need peelin' if we're to eat today and there's no need to call me "ma'am". I'm Mrs Parrish.'

Harry laughed. 'Right you are, Mrs Parrish, and I'm a dab hand at peeling spuds. In the Army, it's a punishment and I've done a fair few in me time.'

'It's not a punishment today, lad, but,' her eyes twinkled, 'it could earn you a reward.'

Harry set to work in the scullery but he kept glancing out of the doorway to see if Nancy might be there. Nelly chuckled to herself. 'Eh, what it is to be young.'

A little later, Nancy came downstairs, slipping shyly into the kitchen unsure of her welcome amongst the staff.

'There you are, Nancy,' Nelly greeted her, raising her voice so that Harry could hear. He appeared in the doorway leading from the scullery into the kitchen, a half-peeled potato in one hand, a small knife in the other and dripping water onto the floor.

'Don't mek a mess on my kitchen floor,' Nelly remonstrated, but she could hardly hide her laughter. 'Ya can leave that now and come and help Nancy get breakfast for her little boy and her mam.' She turned back to Nancy. 'Are they coming down?'

'I – we didn't know quite what we should do.'

'Well, lass, you nip back upstairs and tell them to come down here and you can all sit at my kitchen table to have your breakfast.' Her glance went to Harry and, unseen by Nancy, Nelly winked at him. 'And I expect you'd like a plate of bacon and eggs, wouldn't you, young feller?'

'Never say no to that, Mrs Parrish. Ta.' And as Nancy turned away with a faint pink tinge in her cheeks, he returned Nelly's wink.

The friendship between the soldier and Nancy Banks blossomed, but under the watchful eye of Agnes Banks or Nelly Parrish and her mother, who was still living at Fairfield Hall, helping out with whatever little jobs she could do. Restoring her cottage was taking longer than expected and there was far more pressing work to be done in the village. There must be no more scandal, the three older women had decided between them.

'He's a good 'un to even think of teking her on,' Agnes sighed.

'Put it all behind you, Agnes, and move on,' Nelly

advised. 'Lady Annabel will help you get resettled and, if I'm not mistaken, the villagers will forgive in time.'

And now Agnes, Nancy and Bertie were standing in their new home surrounded by the gifts from the villagers; gifts they could barely afford to give and yet they had wanted the family to know that they were ready to welcome them back into the close-knit community. They knew it was what the new Lady Fairfield wanted and in their gratitude for her help, they were prepared to extend a forgiving hand.

Harry Jenkins carried up the last of the boxes and set it down. 'You'll be all right here,' he said, smiling at Nancy. 'I've got to go now, but I'll come and see you next time I come home with his lordship.' Suddenly the young soldier was tentative. 'Will – that be all right?' His gaze was on Nancy's pretty face, but his question was addressed to both Nancy and her mother. Agnes was the first to answer. 'It's fine by me, if it's what Nancy wants.'

Shyly, Nancy nodded.

'I'll say "goodbye", then, and let you get settled in.'

'Right,' Agnes said, rolling up her sleeves. 'Let's get this place ship-shape. I don't want Lady Annabel visiting and finding us still in a mess.'

But Lady Annabel was at that moment saying a fond farewell to her husband. They lay together in the huge bed, both of them reluctant to leave it. 'I'd better make a move. Jenkins will be waiting.'

Annabel chuckled and snuggled closer to James. 'I doubt it. I think he's saying his own farewells to Nancy.'

'I hope his intentions are honourable!' James laughed.

'From what I hear, they're anything but, but I think

he's being made to toe the line by her mother and – of all people – Nelly Parrish. And no doubt they'll be under the watchful eye of the whole village.'

With a sigh, James heaved himself out of her arms and rolled out of bed. 'I must say "goodbye" to Mama and my dear sister and then I'd better be on my way.' He turned and looked over his shoulder. 'And just you mind you behave yourself while I'm away. There's no need for you to spend so much time with Ben Jackson now. You've got the villagers back on their feet. They can fend for themselves. If you need something to occupy your time, you could concentrate on getting this house back in order. It's all but falling to pieces.'

Annabel stared at him, but said nothing. She was amazed and appalled at how the man she had married seemed to be two people. Last night he had been loving and tender but all that had been spoilt by a few brusque words. But instead of retaliating, she murmured, 'I'll see what I can do.' Inwardly, she was seething and she had no intention of staying away from either the village or from Ben Jackson.

James and Harry Jenkins had left with promises that they'd get home again as soon as they could, though they doubted that it would be for Christmas, which was less than three weeks away. Annabel breakfasted leisurely, even though she wanted to visit both the village and the outlying farms to see how things were progressing, and she steeled herself to linger. She didn't want Dorothea writing to James to tell him that the moment his back was turned, she had sought the company of Ben Jackson.

'So, he's gone again, has he?' Dorothea joined her

at the breakfast table, helping herself to generous portions of the food that was now available.

'Mm, back to barracks, I presume.'

Dorothea smirked. 'If you believe that, then you're more naïve than I thought.'

Annabel raised her eyebrows but said nothing, knowing that Dorothea would not be able to contain herself. 'He's not due back at camp until tomorrow. He'll spend the night in London –' she paused for effect before adding maliciously, 'with his mistress.'

Annabel forced herself to reply calmly. 'So you keep saying. I presume you know who the lady is.'

Dorothea's eyes narrowed. 'Oh yes, I know. I know her quite well.' She leaned forward. 'And so do you.'

Now Annabel was startled. 'Me? How could I possibly—?' she began, but then stopped as realization came slowly and she understood even before Dorothea added, triumphantly, 'James's mistress is Lady Cynthia Carruthers – the woman who introduced him to you.'

Forty-Two

It was a bitter pill to swallow, but with magnificent control of her features, Annabel managed not to let Dorothea see how much her words had affected her. Foolishly, she'd believed that James's ardent lovemaking – and passionate it had certainly been – had been genuine; that he really did love her. But in her world a man who truly loved his wife did not keep a mistress. Perhaps it was different in the aristocratic world, perhaps it was accepted, even expected. It seemed it was if Lady Carruthers, who was supposed to have married for love, could also be unfaithful to her husband. But it was not what Annabel wanted. In the privacy of her bedroom, she allowed the tears to fall as all hope of her love for him being returned finally faded. Resolutely, Annabel lifted her head and vowed that she would continue as she had begun. She would bring this estate back to its former glory whether James would love her for it or not. At least she would have affection and respect from the grateful villagers. And perhaps even Dorothea's attitude would thaw a little if Annabel's money refurbished Fairfield Hall.

Annabel jumped to her feet. She would begin that project right now, just as her husband had instructed. Once begun, she could write to him truthfully telling him of the progress of the renovations on the house and omitting any mention of her ongoing restoration of the wider estate. Though she was sure he would hear of it, for Dorothea would make sure he knew.

With renewed vigour, Annabel went along the corridor to the dowager countess's bedroom. She tapped on the door, and it was opened by Nurse Newton.

'Good morning, my lady. Her ladyship is in good spirits this morning. I'm sure she'd be happy to see you. Do come in. She's so much better now, m'lady. Although it's taken a long time for her to recover, she really doesn't need me any longer. I shall be leaving tomorrow.'

Annabel approached the window where Lady Fairfield was sitting, gazing out across the expanse of neglected lawn behind the house.

'I can't quite see my garden from here,' Elizabeth murmured. She did look much better. There was colour in her cheeks but her voice still quavered. Annabel sat down near her and asked gently. 'Your garden? Where is that?'

Elizabeth Lyndon waved a bony, wrinkled hand. 'Behind the stables. My husband built me a walled garden as a wedding present where I could sit, sheltered from the east winds. It used to be so beautiful in summer, with all kinds of flowers. I loved the roses especially. Have you seen it? Is it still there?'

'I don't know, but I'll find out.' Annabel had had little time to look at the gardens; the estate had been her priority, but now she promised that she would explore the grounds belonging to the house.

Elizabeth's voice trembled as she said, 'I'd so like to see it again but I expect it's overgrown. Dorothea says we haven't a gardener now. Only young Luke, and he can't cope with all the outside work on his own.' She lapsed into silence, her head drooped forward, and she slept.

Quietly, Annabel stood up and moved away saying softly to the nurse. 'I'll come back later.'

'Just before dinner is the best time.' Nurse Newton smiled. 'She dozes on and off throughout the day, but in the early evening, the thought of a good meal seems to revive her.'

Annabel went down to the kitchen, deep in thought. As she entered, Nelly Parrish seemed flustered. 'Oh m'lady, Lady Dorothea's been down to talk about the menus. I hope that's all right.' The woman was suddenly anxious and Annabel was swift to reassure her. 'That's quite all right. I'm happy for Lady Dorothea to run the household as she always has done.'

Nelly could not stifle a chuckle. 'We're all hoping it won't be run as in the recent past, but please don't tell her I said so.'

Annabel smiled, but did not want to get into a conversation with a member of staff that belittled her sister-in-law in any way. Although she treated the servants as equals and always would, Annabel understood it was not the protocol observed in a noble household. Instead, she changed the subject. 'I came to find either Mr Searby or Luke.'

'Mr Searby's in the butler's pantry along the passageway, m'lady, and Luke'll be outside somewhere. Best you speak to Mr Searby first though.' Nelly raised her voice. 'Annie, come here, girl.'

Annie appeared from the scullery wiping her red hands on a cloth. When she saw Annabel she bobbed a curtsy.

'Fetch Mr Searby. Her ladyship would like a word.' Nelly turned back to Annabel. 'Would you like a cup of tea?'

'Thank you. Make one for all of us – Annie too. We

can talk about the extra staff we need.' Annabel sat down at the table and was soon joined by Nelly, John Searby and Annie.

'I really came to ask you what you thought about outside staff. Lady Fairfield has been telling me about the walled garden she seemed to be so fond of. I presume it's still there, but I expect it's neglected.'

'Oh m'lady, she loved that garden. Used to spend hours there with a book or her embroidery.'

'But it's badly overgrown now. No one's been near it for months – years, I suspect,' John said.

'And after her husband died, she lost heart for going there and then, when things got difficult and the number of staff dwindled,' Nelly put in, 'there just weren't enough hands to keep everything right.'

'And that brings us back to discussing just how many more staff we need in the house too.'

'You've been so good to us, m'lady,' John began, 'that the house is gradually getting back to what it used to be, but because it is, the work is getting too much for the staff we have.'

'Then tell me what you need, so I have an idea how many we're talking about, but I'd like you to talk this over with Lady Dorothea. Let the suggestions come from her. I don't want her to feel I'm undermining her household management.'

'It'd be nice to have a proper housekeeper again. I've enough to do with the cooking. I don't suppose,' Nelly added wistfully, 'Agnes would come back, would she?'

'I can ask her, but I think she'd rather stay with Nancy and Bertie now. They're going to start dress-making again.'

Nelly blinked. 'Will there be enough business for them?'

Annabel laughed. 'If we're getting new staff, there'll be uniforms to make and I don't think you'd say no to some new outfits, would you?'

The butler eyed his well-worn cuffs ruefully. 'I've done my best with this suit, but it's about falling to pieces on my back.' He paused and then went on, 'When Mrs Banks was housekeeper here she used the room at the side of the hall as a bedsitting room, but I believe you're planning to turn that into the estate office, m'lady, aren't you?'

'Only if it's not needed for anything else, but if you think we need a housekeeper . . .'

John and Nelly glanced at each other. 'We don't really, m'lady. To be honest, I think Lady Dorothea likes to hold the reins herself.'

'So,' Annabel said. 'Who else do we need?'

'We don't need a footman – it's not necessary with his lordship only coming home now and again – and he brings his batman with him, so no. A parlour maid would be a help, though. She can do a lot of the work a footman would do, and yet be able to help out in other ways.'

'I really could do with a kitchen maid,' Nelly said tentatively. 'Poor Annie's run off her feet with trying to do a housemaid's work and look after the Dowager Countess and Lady Dorothea. Your Jane's been a godsend, but she's looking very weary these days. Between them they've been trying to clean the whole house, but it's too much.'

'And Luke – he was originally employed as a boot boy, but he's now looking after the new pony and trap as well as Mr Jackson's, keeping up with cleaning boots and shoes and trimming all the lamps every day.'

'Oh my goodness, you're making me feel tired just

listening to you,' Annabel groaned comically. 'Right, so we need a young boy to come as a boot boy and to promote Luke. Is that what you're saying?'

John nodded. 'And we could do with at least one more housemaid.'

'I think one would be enough, Mr Searby,' Nelly said, 'especially if you're to have a parlour maid to help you. And they needn't live in, m'lady, except perhaps the boot boy. You could employ lasses from the village to come in daily.'

'What about the laundry? Who does that?'

'Annie's had to do it all on her own, but if we get more maids, they'd manage it between them.'

Annabel nodded her agreement and went on, 'Now, Mr Searby, if you can somehow bring the topic up with Lady Dorothea and get her approval – *without* mentioning me – then we can get things moving.'

As Annabel rose to go, Nelly, with tears in her eyes, touched her hand. 'We can't thank you enough for what you're doing, m'lady.'

Annabel felt a lump in her throat and all she could do was nod a reply. Their gratitude was overwhelming. She just prayed the estate would soon start to pay its way. She returned upstairs to fetch her coat and hat. Jane was nowhere to be seen, but she suspected she was helping out by undertaking more housemaid duties. Annabel went up to the nursery where she found Dorothea giving Theo his morning lessons.

'I wondered if Theo would like to come for a walk with me. I'm going down to the village.'

'Oh please, Mama,' Theo said at once, but his mother shook her head. 'Mornings are your lesson times.' She looked at her son's crestfallen face and relented enough to say, 'Perhaps you may go with your aunt one afternoon.'

He looked towards Annabel eagerly and she smiled and nodded. 'Of course. This afternoon about two-thirty, when you've had a little rest after luncheon. How would that be?'

'Thank you, Aunt Annabel,' the little boy said politely, but his eyes were shining with joy.

As she closed the door of the nursery quietly, she heard Dorothea's strident voice say, 'Now, back to your lessons.'

As Annabel left the house and walked along the driveway and down the slope to the village, she was unaware of Dorothea watching her with narrowed eyes from an upstairs window.

Soon she was standing outside the row of village shops. At the end of the row, the smithy was already open for business and she could hear the healthy sound of Jabez's clanging hammer. The door to the butcher's shop stood open and joints of meat lay on the cool slab in the window. She could see Percy Hammond serving two customers, his face beaming with happiness. Next door, Ozzy Greenwood's grocer's shop was also open. All the produce in the two shops had been supplied at Edward's instigation by the farmers in the neighbourhood. And to add to her delight, Annabel could see that Ozzy appeared to be showing Nancy Banks around the shop. As she stepped in through the door, he turned to greet her.

'Your ladyship. Nancy and her mam and little boy are settling in nicely upstairs and Nancy is going to help me out in the shop. I know her and her mam are going to start up their dressmaking business again, but I could do with a few hours' help a week 'specially when I go into town for supplies. I need someone to hold the fort.'

'That's wonderful, Mr Greenwood. How is your mother now?'

'Doing nicely, thank'ee, but her legs are bad. She can do a bit of housework at home and get meals ready, but she can't stand behind this counter no more.'

Only Eli Merriman's shop door remained closed, but as Annabel stepped closer to the window she could see Eli moving about inside. She tapped on the glass and saw him glance up. Reluctantly, he opened the door, which scraped on the floor. For a moment they stared at each other.

'I'm not ready to open quite yet, but another day or so and I will be.'

Annabel beamed at him. 'That's wonderful news, Mr Merriman. Is there anything I can do to help?'

'No,' he snapped. And with that, he shut the door in her face.

So, Annabel thought as she turned away, she hadn't won over everyone in the village. Not yet.

Forty-Three

Two weeks before Christmas, Sarah Constantine arrived at her parents' farm and word was sent to Annabel that she wished to see her. Luke harnessed the new pony and trap and Annabel drove herself over.

Her mother came out into the yard to greet her. 'Surely you have servants to drive you? You shouldn't be driving yourself, nor using a thing like that!' Sarah glanced disparagingly at the pony and trap. 'Where is your carriage?'

'Oh, I'm far too busy to bother with such things,' Annabel laughed airily. 'And I like to be independent. How are you, Mother? And how's Father?' Adroitly, she tried to steer her mother's conversation away from herself.

'Well, but he's busy. He's sorry he couldn't come this time. Perhaps in the New Year . . .'

'Of course,' Annabel murmured. Secretly, she was pleased her father had not come. No doubt he would have been far more inquisitive than her mother, but at Sarah's next words, her heart sank. 'However, I hope you're going to take me to Fairfield whilst I'm here. I want to meet the Lyndon family.'

'James won't be home until the New Year now, Mother, and Lady Fairfield has been ill—'

'I trust you are referring to the *Dowager* Lady Fairfield? *You* are Lady Fairfield now.'

Annabel shrugged. 'That's not how I think of myself.'

'Then you should. I hope you are behaving like a lady and not—'

For a moment, Annabel was in danger of losing her temper and said more than she meant to. 'I am behaving as is necessary. The people on the estate needed help and I hope I am giving it.' She bit her lip, immediately regretting her hasty words.

'The estate had become rather run down,' Edward put in mildly, trying to make light of the true condition of the Fairfield Estate and, at the same time, smoothing what he thought could become very troubled waters.

'I know that,' Sarah snapped. 'How else do you think Lord Fairfield would have been willing to marry someone of Annabel's birth? He was desperate to get his hands on Ambrose's money.'

Edward's face was thunderous, but it was Annabel who said quietly, 'So, it was all a business deal, was it? My father's money to save his estate and James to give me a title? And were we supposed to fall in love with each other?'

Sarah viewed her daughter through narrowed eyes. 'Such romantic nonsense has nothing to do with it. Achievement and success are all that matters. Besides, you'll have a far better life than you would have done married to an office under-manager.' Annabel gasped as Sarah continued, cruelly now, 'Oh yes, we knew all about your assignations with Gilbert Radcliffe, so your father got rid of him.'

The colour drained from Annabel's face and she put her hand to her forehead, feeling suddenly dizzy. So it was true. Her voice trembled as she asked, 'How – how did Father threaten him?'

Her mother laughed, but the sound was humourless.

'Radcliffe didn't need *threatening*. He was only too happy to take the five hundred pounds your father offered him to make a new start in another country. I believe he chose America.'

Edward moved to his granddaughter's side and put a supporting arm about her waist as he said, 'I never thought I'd hear myself say such a thing, but you disgust me, Sarah. I knew both you and Ambrose were ambitious, but to use your daughter like a – like a pawn in your power struggles – well – it beggars belief. Now, we'd better go in. Your mother has dinner ready and I don't want any of this talked about in front of her. You hear me?'

For a moment Sarah glared at him, but then she backed down. Even she had enough respect for her own father to obey him. All she said now was, 'Well, I still want to visit Fairfield Hall.'

The visit was awkward. Dorothea was civil to Sarah, but only just, and Elizabeth Lyndon seemed too frightened to say much. Every time she spoke, she glanced at her daughter as if seeking permission. Theodore did not appear at all. But the luncheon that Mrs Parrish had prepared was a banquet in comparison to the meals which Annabel had been served on her arrival. And when John Searby hovered attentively at Sarah's elbow and Annie bobbed a curtsy every time she encountered her, Sarah seemed to thaw in her attitude. Annie was dressed in a smart new maid's uniform, which had been Annabel's first order to Nancy and her mother. Indeed, she had placed orders for new uniforms for all the staff at Fairfield Hall. 'And there'll be more to come. I believe Lady Dorothea is planning to appoint additional staff,' she told them.

Luke was to drive Sarah back to Meadow View Farm, and as she left, she said to her daughter, 'There is no reason why you should not be happy here. It's a lovely house,' she cast her eyes around the hallway, 'though sadly in need of redecoration. Perhaps your father may be persuaded to part with a little more to help you refurnish it to your taste. And, of course, should you need any advice in that direction, I'd be only too happy to help.'

'Thank you, Mother,' Annabel said with steely politeness. 'I'll bear that in mind.'

As the front door closed behind her and Annabel heaved a sigh of relief, Dorothea stepped into the hall from the foot of the stairs. It seemed to be one of her favourite places to stand, listening and watching. 'Well, if your mother thinks she can have a say in the restoration of this house, she can think again.'

'Don't worry, Dorothea. That's one thing we are agreed upon – neither my mother nor my father will have any say in the refurbishment of the house. Besides,' she added craftily, 'I shall consult both you and Lady Fairfield in such matters. And now' – she smiled, her good humour restored at the thought – 'may I take Theodore out for a walk? I want to inspect this walled garden I've been hearing about and it sounds just the sort of adventure a small boy would love.'

Though she would no doubt have liked to have refused, Dorothea could find no excuse. In fact, when Theo and Annabel arrived back downstairs deliberately dressed in old clothes, Dorothea was waiting for them, dressed in her outdoor garments.

'May I come?' she asked, with a strange hesitancy. 'It was a place we three loved as children. And I know my mother would be thrilled if it could be restored.'

Annabel smiled, delighted that, for once, Dorothea seemed reasonably friendly. 'Of course you may,' she agreed readily, though when she glanced at Theo it was to see that his sunny smile at the thought of rampaging through an overgrown garden had disappeared.

When Annabel pushed open the gate into the garden that had been untouched for years, Dorothea stood looking about her. To her surprise, Annabel saw tears in the woman's eyes and she was moved to put her arm through Dorothea's. For once, her sister-in-law didn't object.

'It used to be so beautiful,' Dorothea whispered with a catch in her voice. 'Herbaceous borders full of flowers of every colour and fruit trees that kept the house supplied with fruit through the late summer and autumn and now look at it. Whenever I see it I feel sad. It would be wonderful for Mama if it could be restored to its former glory.'

'We'll get it put right. You can advise on how it used to be and then next summer, we'll be able to bring your mother here.'

'She'd love that though I don't know if she could walk this far now.'

'Then we'll get a bath chair for her.' Annabel was not to be defeated, especially now that she seemed to have found something on which she and her sister-in-law could work together. Dorothea was a strange mixture, Annabel mused. She could be vitriolic and almost cruel, even to her own son, and yet today Annabel was seeing a softer side. Maybe the restoration of the house and gardens was the way to reach her sister-in-law, even if she was aware all the time that Dorothea's motive was purely selfish; she wanted Fairfield Hall to be renovated for her son's inheritance.

Aloud Annabel said, 'Did you employ anyone from the village as gardeners?'

Dorothea nodded. 'Yes, Thomas Salt. He lived somewhere near The Lyndon Arms – I expect he still does.'

'Perhaps you'd see if he'd like to come back here.'

Slowly, Dorothea turned to look at her, their faces close together. 'If you'd like me to, yes, I will.'

'And would you also give some thought to what additional indoor staff you'd like to employ? It's high time we got some more help for Mr Searby, Mrs Parrish and the others. Don't you agree?'

'You – you'd leave that to me? Even when their wages will come out of your money?'

'I'd be happy to, Dorothea.'

'Actually, Searby has mentioned the matter, but I didn't know . . .'

'Anything you arrange with Mr Searby will be fine with me,' Annabel reassured her.

They turned back to watch Theo happily thrashing his way with a stick through the overgrown lawn.

'And think about a tutor for Theodore or whether you might feel able to let him attend the village school until he's old enough to go to boarding school. I'm sure it would be good for him to mix with other children in readiness for that.'

But to this, Dorothea did not reply.

Forty-Four

During the week before Christmas, three things happened. The portrait of Annabel, painted by a London artist at her father's request, was delivered to Fairfield Hall with instructions that it should be placed in the dining room on the opposite side of the fireplace to the one of the earl.

Dorothea was incensed, but there was nothing she could do about it.

'I'm sorry,' Annabel said to her, 'it was not my idea.'

Tight-lipped, Dorothea nodded. 'James told me about it. Your father wouldn't hand over the cheque until he'd agreed to it.' Grudgingly, she added, 'But it's a small price to pay, I suppose, for rescuing my son's inheritance.'

The second event was that The Lyndon Arms reopened. The public house in the village now had a new tenant, the son of a publican from Thorpe St Michael who, with his father's guidance, had been keen to take on the derelict building. He opened the snug for business whilst the rest of the property underwent restoration. Soon, the pub would be a thriving business once more.

The third – and in Annabel's estimation by far the most important of the three – was that Eli Merriman reopened his small general store. He was, Annabel discovered, an astute businessman. Although he knew that the villagers would not have much money to spend on Christmas goods, he reckoned – quite rightly, as it turned out – on them wanting to make merry as much as funds would allow. They had all been through such a hard time and they wanted to give thanks in the only way they knew how: by enjoying themselves.

Annabel asked Ben to organize a Christmas tree to be erected in the schoolyard. 'I'm hoping it will ease the children into going back to school in the New Year. And can you get me a tree suitable for the drawing room at Fairfield Hall?'

'Of course. I'll see to it. Have they appointed a new teacher, then?'

'He's coming for an interview tomorrow.'

Mr Porter arrived ten minutes before the appointed time and rang the bell at the vicarage.

'We'd have held this meeting in the school, but we haven't had time to get it ready,' Richard Webster told him as he ushered the candidate into the dining room where the members of the school board were ranged round three sides of the table. 'Please sit down here where we can all see you. I hope we don't look too daunting, Mr Porter,' Richard smiled as he took his seat on the opposite side and in the centre as chairman.

Douglas Porter sat down. He was tall and thin and fair-haired. There was sadness in his pale blue eyes, but that was probably because of his recent loss. He looked a little nervous, Annabel thought, and no wonder, with Dan Broughton staring solemn-faced at him and Jabez Fletcher frowning. And no doubt it was important to him to secure this job for the sake of his motherless children. Annabel smiled at him with what she hoped was encouragement. Douglas blinked and stared at her, mesmerized for a moment by her beautiful eyes and her dazzling smile.

Richard cleared his throat, rustled some papers and the interview began.

'So, what do you think?' Richard said, as the interview ended and he'd shown Mr Porter out to wait in the hall whilst they discussed his merits.

'He'll do,' Jabez said. 'If we're only offering him a temporary place, we can see how he shapes up.'

'I agree.' Richard nodded and a chorus of 'ayes' sounded round the table. 'Shall I call him back in, then?'

Ben rose. 'I'll do it, Vicar.'

Moments later, Douglas Porter was being offered the post of teacher at the school in a temporary capacity at first. 'You understand,' Richard explained to him, 'that if you prove satisfactory, there's no reason why your appointment should not be made permanent.'

'Better the devil you know,' Jabez muttered.

'Thank you,' Douglas said, and Annabel could hear the heartfelt sentiment in his tone. 'I'll not let you down. I love teaching and I will do my very best for your children.'

'As we explained, they've had no schooling for the last few months and may take some settling back into a classroom routine,' Richard explained.

'There's a meadow behind the school where the children used to play sport,' Ben said and glanced at Annabel. 'Will it be all right to use it again?'

'Of course,' she agreed as Richard stood up.

'If you'd like to come with me, Mr Porter, I'll show you the school, though please be assured that by the time you come in January to start the new term, it'll be in a lot better shape than it looks at present. We'll get it cleaned up and any repairs done.'

'I'd like to come over before then and help,' Douglas Porter offered. 'If – if that would be acceptable. There aren't many days left before term starts.'

'We'd be glad of your help and we'll all make sure it's ready in time,' Richard said.

'Well, you're not afraid to get your hands mucky then, young feller,' Dan said, shaking Douglas's hand firmly. 'I like that.'

'Anything that will get the children back to school as soon as possible,' the new headmaster said.

There were murmurs of agreement and nods of approval as they all left the dining room and moved out of the vicarage to take a look at the school.

The rooms were cold and damp, dusty and neglected. 'Now everyone is feeling better,' Richard said, 'I'm sure all the villagers will lend a hand.'

'I'll repair the gate and the fencing,' Jabez said.

'William and me'll paint the walls in the classrooms,' Dan said, and the offers of help went on.

As they parted they all shook Douglas's hand, wishing him well in his new post. Annabel was the last to say 'goodbye'. 'What about your own children, Mr Porter? Are they of school age?'

'The eldest one is, yes, but he will go to the school in the town. We are living with my late wife's mother and father and they are quite happy to look after them. Their care won't encroach on my duties here.'

'Oh, that's not what I meant, Mr Porter. Please don't think it was. I just wondered if you'd be bringing them here to school.'

Douglas shook his head. 'I'm not comfortable with a teacher's children being in the same school. I know it can't be helped sometimes, but when there is an alternative, I believe it's the best for all concerned.'

'I see,' Annabel conceded and once more bowled the young man over with her dazzling smile.

There was a definite feeling of optimism and a quiet joy pervading the church on Christmas morning. Lady Fairfield, Dorothea and Theodore attended the service, sitting in the family pew with Annabel alongside them. Annabel was amused to see Theo swivelling in his seat to catch Bertie's eye. She saw the two boys grin at each other and hid her own smile, hoping that Dorothea wouldn't notice.

At Annabel's request, Richard did not include gushing thanks in his sermon directed at her for all that she had done for the Fairfield Estate and its people, though to one of the prayers he added his own wording: 'We have come through a time of great suffering and hardship and we give thanks for that deliverance', and a fervent 'Amen' rippled through the congregation. Annabel kept her head down and her eyes firmly closed as she sent up her own silent prayer of thankfulness that she had been able to restore the estate and its people to what would soon be a thriving community once more. As the Lyndon family left the church, the villagers now stood in respectful silence. One or two women even dropped a curtsy, though each time their gaze was upon Annabel as they did so. It was obvious to everyone – including Dorothea – where their gratitude lay.

But it seemed that the Christmas spirit touched even Dorothea and she unbent a little to join in parlour games with Annabel and Theo after the superb luncheon, which Mrs Parrish had cooked and John Searby had served. Four new members of household staff had been appointed just before Christmas – a kitchen maid, a parlour maid to help the butler, a second housemaid and a boot boy. Two gardeners were also to start work in the New Year. Thomas Salt had gladly accepted the post and had also recommended Eli Merriman's thirteen-year-old son be given a trial as his under-gardener.

'Gregory's coming back to live with his dad though, sadly, Mester Merriman's wife is not. The lad's very interested in the land, m'lady, though he'd prefer gardening to working on a farm. He wants to grow fruit and vegetables – and flowers – he says. He's been working away, but I reckon his coming home will be the making of his dad.'

'He sounds ideal to work alongside you,' Annabel smiled, happy to think that perhaps the return of his son would lift Eli's spirits too, 'let's give him a try,' and she remembered to add tactfully, 'if Lady Dorothea's agreeable.'

The house was running smoothly now, with all the staff well fed and eager to please the new Lady Fairfield. After the family had eaten, the servants enjoyed their own Christmas dinner in the servants' hall and, unbeknown to her, they all raised a glass to their benefactor and gave thanks for Annabel's arrival in their midst.

If only James could have come home for Christmas, Annabel thought as she played a new board game called Snakes and Ladders with Theo, and if Bertie could have joined them too, the day would have been perfect.

Forty-Five

It was just after Christmas that Annabel began to feel unwell. It was nothing, she told herself, just a faint feeling of nausea first thing in the morning that usually disappeared by the time she'd had breakfast.

'I haven't time to be ill,' she told herself as she hurried to her office on the ground floor to the left of the front door. From here she conducted the running of the estate with Ben's help. He came most mornings and they talked about what needed to be done on Home Farm and also discussed the progress of the other three farms on the estate.

'Everything's going very well – thanks to you,' he told her. 'January's the time for mending fences and hedges – all the tasks we don't get time to do once spring is upon us.' He smiled at Annabel. 'But why am I telling you all this? You know the farming year as well as I do.'

She returned his smile as she added, 'When do you expect lambing to start?'

'Early March. But, another year, it'd be nice to have some a bit earlier, say mid-February.'

'Ah,' Annabel murmured. 'Early lambs to get the best prices at market.'

'That's right, m'lady.' He gazed at her, unable for a brief moment to take his eyes off her lovely face. How knowledgeable she was as well as being undeniably beautiful.

'Oh, and one more thing, Ben. What time of year is the best to plant trees?'

'Trees, m'lady?'

'Yes, if his lordship and his sister are agreeable, I was thinking how nice it would be to have the driveway lined with trees. Limes, perhaps. What do you think?'

'I'll – er – find out.'

'Good. In the meantime, I'll write to his lordship and seek his approval.'

In due course, a reply came back from James. 'Whatever Mama would like. She's the gardening expert.' So, to Elizabeth's joy, Annabel arranged with Ben that at the appropriate time of year, lime trees should be planted to border the drive.

The school had opened at the beginning of January. The classroom was now clean, warm and freshly painted. The children would take a little time to settle down. Douglas Porter was firm, but understanding. Dorothea was still dithering as to whether she should send Theodore to the village school, whilst the boy himself daily pleaded with his mother to be allowed to go.

Annabel kept silent on the matter, but there was one little boy she could perhaps help. Walking down to the village on the morning after the school term had begun, she knocked on the door leading to the rooms above the grocer's shop. She had an excuse to visit. It was Bertie's fifth birthday and she was carrying a bag full of toys and books. When he had opened the parcels and exclaimed delightedly over them all, Annabel asked, 'Would Bertie come for a walk with me? I thought I might take him down to the school. It's high time he

met some of the other children and there might even
be a place for him. He's a bright child. I'll talk to Mr
Porter, if you like.'

'Oh, I – er – I don't know whether . . .' Nancy began,
flushing with embarrassment.

'It'll be all right,' Annabel said gently. 'I promise.'

'Aren't you going to read these new books to me,
Aunt Annabel?' She was amused to hear his adoption
of her as an aunt – which indeed she was. She liked to
feel that he thought of her in that way, even though he
was probably unaware of his true relationship to the
Lyndon family. Perhaps, she mused, one day when he
is older he might question why his name is Albert
Lyndon Banks. 'Not today, Bertie, we're going for a
walk down to the school.'

At once, his face clouded. 'I don't want to. The other
children call me nasty names.'

'They won't any more,' Annabel told him firmly.
She held out her hand. 'Come along.' Reluctantly, he
took it and together they walked along the village
street; past the cottages and beyond the church until
they came to the school gates. Just beyond the school
lay the blackened ruins of his former home. Annabel
noticed that the boy kept his glance averted from the
sight. He scuffed the toes of his shoes and hung his
head and when the children clustered near the fence
surrounding the playground, he tried to hide behind
Annabel's skirts.

'Good morning, children.' Annabel smiled at them.
'I've brought Bertie Banks to meet you.' She glanced
around the inquisitive faces and recognized Simon
Cartwright, Adam's eldest son. No doubt he would
consider himself too old at ten to befriend a five-year-
old, but Annabel had reckoned without the gratitude

of the Cartwright family. Simon stepped forward. 'Is he starting school, m'lady, 'cos if he is, we'll look after him, won't we, lads?' He turned and fixed his classmates with a look that brooked no argument.

'That's kind of you, Simon, and if Mr Porter says there's a place for him, then he will be coming.'

'He can come an' play with us anyway, missis,' a younger boy piped up and was quickly nudged.

'It's her ladyship,' Simon hissed. 'You call her "m'lady".'

Annabel laughed. 'It's all right, Simon. I haven't got used to the title yet, either. You can all call me Miss Annabel, if you like. It's much more friendly, don't you think?'

Several heads nodded enthusiastically and one of the boys opened the gate for them to step into the playground. 'We'll look after him while you speak to Mester Porter. Come on, Bertie, we'll play football. Mester Porter has given us a real football to play with.'

When Annabel was satisfied that the children really were playing with him in a friendly manner, she entered the school and sought out the teacher.

'He'd be one of the youngest,' Mr Porter said, when they'd greeted each other and Annabel had explained the purpose of her visit, 'but if you think he'd benefit from being with other children . . .' They glanced out of the window to see that Bertie was the centre of attention; the children clustered around him, encouraging him to kick the ball. He was not being teased or called names now.

'I do, and there's someone else who would too. My sister-in-law's son, Theodore Crowstone. He's five and a half now and really ought to be having proper tuition, though whether I will ever be able to persuade his mother to allow him to attend the village school, I don't know.'

'Perhaps she doubts my suitability to educate the future earl,' he said, an edge of sarcasm to his tone.

'Possibly, but I think it has more to do with him mixing with the village ruffians.'

Mr Porter glanced at the clock above the blackboard. 'Time I blew the whistle for the end of break. Look, perhaps you'd like to leave Bertie here for the rest of the morning and we'll see how he copes and if I think he's ready.'

Whilst Bertie stayed at the school, Annabel walked back along the village street to report to Nancy. 'Simon Cartwright's keeping an eye on him and the other children seem to follow his lead.'

Nancy nodded. 'Simon's a good lad and the Cartwrights have been kind to us. In fact,' she added, with a note of surprise in her tone, 'everybody has. Thanks to you, m'lady.'

Annabel patted her hand and took her leave before Nancy could say any more.

Towards the end of January, Annabel realized just what was wrong with her and she ran her hand over her stomach, imagining that she could already feel the new life she was sure was growing within her. She should see Dr Maybury, she decided.

On the morning she had Luke harness the trap, it was snowing lightly, but Annabel wrapped up against the cold.

'I should drive you, m'lady,' the young man said. 'Or is Mester Jackson taking you?'

Annabel blinked. Oh dear, she thought, is it becoming

common knowledge that I am in Ben's company a lot? James would not be pleased.

'No, no, not today. I'll be fine, Luke.'

As she passed through the village, several folk waved to her. She wondered what their reaction would be if they knew the purpose of her journey.

When Stephen Maybury had questioned her closely and examined her, he smiled and said, 'I think you might well prepare for a happy event. How pleased his lordship will be.'

Will he? Annabel wondered. She hoped so, but there was one person who would most definitely not be pleased. In fact, she would be extremely angry.

Dorothea.

Forty-Six

Annabel hadn't wanted to tell Dorothea – or anyone else – before she had had time to write to James and for him to be the first to hear the news. But at breakfast the morning after her visit to Dr Maybury, she felt so nauseous that she had to leave the table. Luckily, Dorothea had breakfasted earlier and had left the room. Jane, who was helping to serve breakfast, came to her side at once and helped her upstairs to lie down. She hurried down to the kitchen to fetch a cup of weak tea and a piece of dry toast for Annabel, but she could not keep the smile from her face.

'What's got into you? All smiles this time in a morning,' Nelly Parrish laughed.

'Miss Annabel' – Jane still found it hard to use her mistress's new title – 'is feeling sick this morning. Just tea and toast – and no butter.'

Nelly's mouth dropped open and she stared wide-eyed at the girl. 'Well, I never,' she murmured. 'This'll put the cat among the pigeons and no mistake.'

Annie, who had overheard the conversation, sidled out of the kitchen unseen by the other two. She found Dorothea alone in the dining room. A warm fire now glowed in the grate, the shutters were opened and the curtains drawn back to let in the morning light. Outside, Thomas Salt and Gregory Merriman had begun their assault on the overgrown garden.

'M'lady,' the girl whispered. 'Before you came down, Lady Fairfield was feeling ill. She's gone upstairs to lie down and Jane's fetching her tea and toast. *Dry* toast,' she added with a knowing smirk.

Dorothea, reading the morning paper, didn't seem to pay much attention. She merely murmured, 'I didn't know my mother had started to come down for breakfast. I thought you were still taking it up to her in bed.'

'I am. I didn't mean your mother, m'lady, I meant Lady Annabel.'

There was a moment's silence before Dorothea raised her head very slowly and met the maid's gaze. '*What* did you say?'

'I said, it wasn't your mother, it was—'

'No, no, before that. About her being ill.'

'I'd say she's got morning sickness, m'lady. I've seen it enough times when me mam was having another babby.' Annie was enjoying herself, eager to impart a bit of information to her mistress and air her own knowledge on the subject. 'An' I should know, she had six more after me.'

Dorothea was very still and, for a brief moment, Annie felt a flicker of fear. She knew only too well that Dorothea was adamant that her son should inherit the title and the Fairfield Estate. If Lady Annabel had a son, that would not happen. Annie trembled, wishing she had kept silent. She'd seen Dorothea in a temper more than once and she didn't want to be the one who'd made her angry.

Slowly, Dorothea rose from the table, her mind working furiously. She would have to play this very carefully. With extreme control, she said, 'I'd better go and see her for myself, but not a word about this to anyone else, you hear me?'

Annie nodded and bobbed a little curtsy as her mistress swept from the room, outrage in every movement.

'It's a bit late for that,' Annie muttered as soon as Dorothea was out of earshot. 'They'll all know soon enough downstairs now.'

Dorothea entered the bedroom Annabel shared with James on his brief visits home without knocking. She approached the bed and stood looking down at her sister-in-law.

With great forbearance, she managed to say mildly, 'Annie tells me you were unwell at breakfast. I trust it's nothing serious. Perhaps it's something you ate. I was a little suspicious myself of the fish we had for dinner last night.'

Annabel sat up slowly and reached for the cup of tea, which Jane had placed on the bedside table. 'I don't think it's anything serious at all. In fact, I believe it's perfectly natural in my condition.'

She heard Dorothea pull in a sharp breath. 'What – what do you mean?'

'I am with child, Dorothea.'

'You're *what*!'

'I'm expecting a child.' For a brief moment Annabel felt afraid. She really thought for one fleeting second that the woman was going to attack her. Dorothea's eyes bulged. The colour drained from her face and then flooded back until she was almost puce. She staggered briefly and reached out to grasp the post at the end of the bed.

'How – how can you be?'

Annabel frowned. What on earth did the woman

340

mean? But at Dorothea's next words, it became clear. 'He swore he wouldn't touch you. Promised me that it was to be a marriage in name only. He's got that Carruthers woman for – for *that* sort of thing. He doesn't need you at all. Only your money.' She was glaring at Annabel as if she was wholly to blame and then, suddenly, she seemed to calm down. 'Oh, I understand now. I see it all. It's not his, is it? It's not James's child. It's someone else's. It's – it's Jackson's, I'll be bound.'

Now it was Annabel's turn to be incensed. 'How dare you? How dare you suggest such a thing – even think it!'

Now Dorothea was in control of herself again. 'Oh, I dare and I'll make sure my brother knows he's been cuckolded.'

Annabel turned her head away, feeling a sickness that now had nothing to do with her pregnancy. 'You're mad,' she muttered. 'Quite mad.' She swung her legs over the side of the bed and stood up. The tea and toast had worked and she felt much better. 'Please leave my room.'

'Gladly. I no longer wish to be in the presence of a whore! No wonder you were so keen to help Nancy Banks. You're two of a kind.'

'Just go, Dorothea.'

With an angry swish of her skirts, Dorothea left the room. Moments later, Jane came back into the room, her eyes swimming with tears. 'Oh miss, it's all my fault. I was that happy for you when I went down to get your breakfast, I couldn't keep the smile off my face and Mrs Parrish guessed. Annie must have overheard and gone running to tell Lady Dorothea. Even after all you've done for them, miss, they still seem to think of her as their mistress.'

'It's all right, Jane.' Annabel touched her hand. 'They'd all have known soon, but now I must write to my husband. I'll go down to the office.'

'Do you think you ought to stay here, miss? I could bring your writing things up.'

'No, no, I'm feeling much better now. Just stay with me whilst I go downstairs.'

Reaching the office and reassuring Jane that she was fine, Annabel sat down at her desk and picked up her pen. She would write to James at once to tell him the wonderful news and she would see that it was in the post before his dear sister could write to him. An hour later, safe in Luke's hands, her letter was on its way to the town. But, unbeknown to her, so was one from Dorothea. Luke, carrying out the instructions of both women, was ignorant of the dynamite the letters held.

Forty-Seven

When the pony and trap bringing James and Harry Jenkins from the station in town drew up outside the front steps, Annabel stood in the doorway to greet her husband. James had not been able to get leave for Christmas, but on explaining to his commanding officer that his wife had written to say that she was with child, special compassionate leave had been granted. He said nothing, however, about the letter he had received from his sister.

James bounded up the steps, but instead of taking her in his arms, he glared down at Annabel. 'Is it true? Are you expecting a child?'

'Yes, oh yes, James. Isn't it wonderful? I do so hope it's the son you want.'

For a moment, his face worked as if he was grappling with some inner conflict. Then he grasped her arm, his fingers biting painfully into her flesh as he almost dragged her in through the front door held open by the butler.

'Good afternoon, my lord,' John began, but he was ignored as James hurried Annabel through to the morning room. He thrust her from him, almost making her overbalance and fall before he slammed the door behind them.

'A son, you say. Of course, I want a son. But' – he jabbed his finger towards her as he said crudely, 'whatever you're carrying in your belly isn't mine, is it?'

Annabel gasped and sank into a chair, her legs giving way beneath her. She stared, wide-eyed at him. 'James,' she said in a strangled whisper. 'I swear to you that this child is yours. How can you possibly accuse me of such a thing?'

James paced the room, stopping every so often to tower over her. 'Dorothea says you've been spending most of your time down in the village. The father could be anyone, but it's most likely Jackson's. And even after I asked you – most specifically – not to go anywhere without the company of your maid.'

Annabel was trembling from head to foot. She felt sick, not with pregnancy sickness now, but with revulsion. 'I – I have taken her with me – most of the time – but when your mother was so ill, she was needed here.'

'You should be here,' he raged, 'tending to your duties in this house, not running around the village consorting with the yokels.'

Now anger surged through her. 'Is that how you view your tenants? Is that how you think of them? And as for accusing Ben—'

'Oho, Ben, is it? How very cosy! *And* he comes here almost every morning, I hear.'

She stood up suddenly. Her head reeled but she steadied herself against the chair. 'You've no right to accuse me of infidelity when you keep a mistress in London.'

They glared at each other and then he shrugged. 'So, what of it? It's the done thing in *my* class of society.' There was no mistaking the accent on the word 'my'.

'Well, it isn't in mine,' Annabel snapped. 'I have been and always will be utterly faithful to you and if you choose to listen to the evil tongue of your sister, then—'

344

'Are you calling my sister "evil"?'

'You're twisting my words. I said she's got an evil tongue. She's obsessed with Theo being your heir and she'll do anything – *anything* – to bring that about.' I'd better watch out, Annabel thought, though this she did not voice, or I'll be finding myself lying at the foot of the stairs and when my baby's born – she shuddered – if it ever is, I'll fear for its life.

Now, James stood very still, deep in thought. Then he came very close to her, looking down into her upturned face. 'You know,' he murmured, 'you are far too beautiful for your own good. I promised Dorothea that I would not consummate the marriage, but on our wedding night, when I saw you looking so lovely and willing to please me, well, what man could resist? Certainly not me. So, I broke my vow.'

'So you did marry me just for my money?' Annabel said bitterly, feeling the tears start behind her eyes. She blinked hastily, determined not to cry in front of him.

He hesitated. Stated so baldly it made him look and feel like a heel. 'It's – not uncommon.'

'In *your* world, no, I guess it isn't. Actually,' she added, trying to be rational now instead of emotional, 'I don't blame you so much as I do my father. His ambition to see his daughter and his future grandson with a title overrode any affection he might have had for me, though,' she added sadly, 'I doubt he has any.'

They stood close together for what seemed an age and then he sighed so heavily, she felt his breath on her face. He held her shoulders, though more gently now. 'Do you swear on your child's life that it is mine?'

There was no hesitation as she said solemnly, 'I do. James, I fell in love with you in London and I still love you – but that's my tragedy, isn't it, because it's obvious that you don't love – or trust – me.' His face twisted with conflicting emotions. Did he love her even just a little? she wondered, staring up into his brown eyes, trying to read the truth there. If not, then why was he so jealous? Didn't that arise from love? Unless, of course, he regarded her as his 'possession', or he was angry because it was she who was receiving all the praise for the improvements on the estate and, it had to be said, the undying gratitude – and yes, even love – of his tenants. Even Eli Merriman smiled at her now when she passed by his shop. And as for Jabez Fletcher, from being so vindictive towards her, he was now her most ardent supporter.

But James was a soldier, she reminded herself. He was the sort of man who probably thought sweet words and declarations of love were unmanly. Even his proposal had been stilted and awkward. She'd given him the chance now to tell her he loved her but when he remained silent, she whispered brokenly, 'I swear to you, James, I have been faithful to you. This child is yours.'

He stepped away and turned and strode towards the door. 'Then we'll say no more about it, but Jackson goes. I'll tell him myself.'

Annabel opened her mouth to protest, even took a step forward to plead with him, but then she stopped and bit down hard on her lower lip. Protest would be futile and dangerous; he would begin to doubt her once again. She sank back down into the chair. Poor, poor Ben. Dismissed – and no doubt without any kind of reference – because of her jealous, possessive husband and Dorothea's wicked scheming that had taken advantage of it. What could she do to help Ben? With a small groan she buried her face in her hands and she was still

346

sitting like that when Dorothea came into the room.

'Mourning the loss of your lover?' she said nastily.

Slowly, Annabel stood up and faced her enemy, for that was what her sister-in-law was.

'I have no lover, Dorothea, only my husband.'

'Well, you might have won him over with your pretty face and your wheedling ways for the moment, but you don't fool me. And I promise you this, your child – if it is a boy – will never inherit the title nor the estate. That belongs to Theodore.'

Whatever tentative understanding had been growing between Annabel and Dorothea was gone in an instant.

That evening after dinner as darkness settled over the village, James strode across the courtyard to Ben's rooms above the archway, righteous anger in every step. Ben Jackson had been born in and had grown up in Thorpe St Michael, working on nearby farms since the age of twelve. At fifteen he had come to work on the Fairfield Estate for James's father, Charles, and had worked his way up until he had been appointed to the post of estate bailiff. He had once courted a girl in the village, but when she had died of consumption, he had devoted himself to his job and the people of Fairfield. It had devastated him to see the estate fall into decline and the lines on his face, which that worry had brought, made him seem older than his years.

James climbed the stairs and entered Ben's quarters without knocking.

'Jackson,' he called. 'Are you here?'

Ben hurried from his sitting room to greet his master with an anxious question. 'M'lord? Is something wrong?'

'You're dismissed.'

The colour drained from Ben's face and he stared at James open-mouthed. 'M'lord?' he stammered. 'Why? What have I done?'

James's glowering frown deepened even more. 'You're spending too much time in the company of my wife. Every day, I hear, you're across at the house *supposedly* consulting her about the running of the estate.'

'That's it exactly. I—'

'You shouldn't need to ask for a woman's advice. Now that you have all the tenants back in place, you should be able to run the estate. Certainly there should be no need for you to see her every day and I won't have it.'

'Then I won't go into the house at all. I—' Even as he said the words, the sorrow at not being able to see Annabel swept through him.

'You most certainly will not, because you won't be here.'

Still staring at his lord and master, Ben shook his head slowly. 'I still don't understand why.'

'My wife is pregnant and rumour has it that it could be yours.'

Now Ben's face was stricken. 'How could you even think that? Lady Fairfield has always behaved with utter decorum and so have I.'

'I've only your word for that,' James snapped.

'So – that's not good enough?'

'You expect me to take the word of a *servant* over that of my sister.'

'Your – *sister*! She's accusing me of this?'

'She has brought it to my attention that my wife has been spending far too much time with you. In the office at the house and driving around the estate, completely unchaperoned. I don't like it and I won't have it. You will leave my employment by tomorrow morning.'

Ben was stunned, yet his care for the estate still surfaced despite the dreadful shock. 'And Home Farm? Who is to manage that?'

James laughed wryly. 'Since my dear wife is so keen to involve herself in the management of the estate, she can run that herself.'

'And you think she won't come into contact with workers then?' Ben said bitterly, understanding now exactly what had brought this about. James Lyndon was irrationally jealous. 'With other *men*?'

'That's not your concern any more,' James snapped. 'Just mind you're gone by first light tomorrow.' He turned on his heel to leave, but Ben, who now had nothing to lose, said boldly, 'You don't deserve Lady Annabel. She's rescued your home and your estate and yet you treat her like this. How can you believe such wicked lies? Your sister's only saying such terrible things out of spite. She wants Fairfield for her son – we all know that – and she'll stop at nothing to get it.'

For a moment, James stood very still and Ben thought he was in for a sound beating. James was taller and younger than he was and, whilst strong from his life of hard work, Ben would be no match for an army-trained officer. But James only turned and glared at him for a long moment before saying quietly, 'I should have let you burn on the night of the fire at Nancy's cottage.' With that he left, closing the door quietly behind him.

Forty-Eight

When he was sure his lordship had left, Ben sank down into a chair trying to come to terms with what had just happened. He had nowhere to go, no relatives left alive to whom he could turn in his dire need. Nor could he go to any of the tenant farmers; he knew they would help him if they could, but it wasn't fair to involve them in this trouble. And trouble it certainly was.

'Oh Annabel, I'm so sorry,' he whispered aloud to the empty room. 'I wouldn't harm a hair of your beautiful head and yet I've brought this upon you.' He dropped his head into his hands with a loud groan. Now he allowed the feelings that he had held buried deep in his heart to surface. There was truth in what James had accused him of; Ben had fallen in love with her, but he was sure he had never betrayed such feelings in her presence. In fact, he had denied they existed until this moment. He only knew that he'd looked forward to the times when he could be with her, when he could see her smile, her violet eyes twinkling at him with mischief, and when he could hear her delicious laughter. And he remembered every single thing about her from the moment he had met her. He had admired her compassion for the villagers, marvelled at her determination and her courage in saving the whole estate and with it, undoubtedly, people's lives.

And this is how the Lyndon family repaid her.

Slowly he rose to his feet with a heavy sigh. He must spend the night packing. He would ask only one favour of one of the farmers; Jim Chadwick, he thought. He needed to borrow a farm cart to drive himself out of the village, but where he could go, he had no idea.

It was gone midnight when he heard a soft tap at the door. A light still burned in his bedroom as he sorted through his belongings. Fearful that James had sent someone – possibly Harry Jenkins – he went to the door but did not open it at once until he heard a woman whisper softly, 'Please open the door.'

Hope and fear in equal measure flooded through him. If she had come to see him, it thrilled him and yet, James's reprisal would be catastrophic. He opened the door slowly and was relieved and yet in the same moment disappointed to see who stood there. 'Jane – come in.'

The young girl stepped inside. Drawing her near to the fire, he said, 'Whatever are you doing here?'

'Miss Annabel sent me.' Her teeth were chattering with the cold and quickly, Ben poured a measure of whisky into a mug and added hot water from the kettle on the hob. 'Drink this. It'll warm you.'

Gratefully, the girl sipped the liquid. 'She's so worried about you. She asked me to come and tell you to go to her grandfather's and to tell him what's happened. He'll help you.'

'Oh, I don't know. I don't want to involve him.'

'She was adamant, Mr Jackson. At least, call and see him. And, she said, you're to tell him everything. *Everything!*'

Ben stared at her. 'You – you all know up at the house.'

Grimly, Jane nodded. 'Lady Dorothea's seen to that. She's telling everyone that the child Miss Annabel's expecting isn't his lordship's – it's yours.' She looked up at him, meeting his gaze steadily. 'But we all know it isn't, Mr Jackson. At least –' She hesitated and dropped her eyes.

'Go on,' Ben said softly. 'There's some that think it's true, are there?'

'Only Annie, but she's always been Lady Dorothea's maid. She obeys her in everything. You heard about the gravy when Miss Annabel first came?'

Ben shook his head and Jane recounted the incident, adding, 'Lady Dorothea told her to do it, so she did.'

They were silent until Ben said, 'Tell your mistress that I will call and see her grandfather, but that I don't want to do anything that might hurt her further. Tell her not to worry about me –' He hesitated, wanting to send more messages, but not daring to do so. He was certain of Jane's loyalty to Annabel, but he didn't want her to be in more trouble than she already might be for coming here so late. Maybe, he thought fearfully, she'd be the next to be dismissed. 'I'll be fine.'

Jane rose and handed him the now empty mug. 'I'd best get back before I'm missed. I share a bedroom with Annie and she'd be only too happy to tell Lady Dorothea I was missing half the night. And if she knew I'd come cross the yard to see you . . .' She said no more but her meaning was obvious.

Jim Chadwick was only too happy to help Ben Jackson, but saddened by the news that he was leaving. 'This is a bit sudden, ain't it, Ben? Has summat happened?'

'Yes, it has, Jim, and you'll no doubt hear all about

it soon enough. The Fairfield grapevine will be hard at work, I don't doubt,' Ben said bitterly. 'I'm saying nothing, but I'd just like to think you'll believe that I am innocent of what I've been accused and – more importantly – so is the other person. Because we are, I promise you.'

'Sounds very mysterious.' Jim started to laugh, but his mirth died when he saw how distraught Ben was. The man hadn't slept at all; he'd spent most of the night packing up his belongings that were now being loaded onto Jim Chadwick's farm cart and the rest of the hours of darkness worrying about Annabel. But there was nothing he could do to help her; he might only make things worse. The best thing he could do to safeguard her would be to get out of her life, but the thought that he would never see her again devastated him.

'Where will you go?' Jim asked.

'I'm going to Meadow View Farm – Edward Armstrong's place – first. I'll leave your cart there. I'm sure Edward will have one of his men bring it back for you.'

'No need,' Jim said, climbing up onto the front of the cart. 'I'm coming with you. You've been a good friend to us, Ben, and I'll not desert you in your hour of trouble, 'cos I can see by your face, it is trouble.'

The two men set out as the first fingers of dawn crept across the fields.

'I'm sad you'll not be here to see the first lambs born, the first crops begin to show. It's not fair.' Jim sighed. 'But that's how that family are, I'm sorry to say. They just think about themselves.'

'Not Lady Annabel. Please don't include her in this.'

'No,' Jim said swiftly, 'I wouldn't, because she hasn't got Lyndon blood in her, has she?'

They spoke very little for the remainder of the journey, each busy with their own thoughts. The yard at Meadow View Farm was already busy with the sounds of the morning milking coming from the byre. At the sound of the cart's wheels, Edward appeared.

''Morning, what brings you here so early?' he greeted them and then his face clouded. 'Is it Annabel? Is owt amiss?'

'Ben's been sacked,' Jim said bluntly as he climbed down.

'Eh?' Edward was obviously startled and as mystified as Jim. 'I can't believe it. Annabel wouldn't do that. She relies on you completely. I thought—' He stopped as he saw Ben shaking his head.

'His lordship dismissed me himself last night and told me to be gone by this morning. I had no choice even though I'm not guilty of what he's accusing me of.'

'And what is he accusing you of?'

Ben too had climbed down from the cart, but was now leaning against it as if he could hardly stand. Shock, disappointment and a terrible fear for Annabel had taken their toll, besides which he had not slept during the night nor eaten since the previous dinnertime. James's bombshell had robbed him of any appetite. He raised tired, red-rimmed eyes to look into Edward's concerned face. 'Have you heard from your grand-daughter?'

Edward shook his head. 'What is it, man? For God's sake tell me.'

'Let's get him inside. He looks as if he's about to pass out.' Jim put his strong arm around Ben. Together, the two of them helped Ben into the farmhouse where Martha at once poured tea and began to cook a hearty breakfast for all three men. Edward usually came in about this time after morning milking when she cooked breakfast for him and for the two young men who worked on Meadow View Farm.

'What's happened?' she whispered to Edward.

'I don't know, Ma, but maybe he'll tell us in a minute.'

'Is it Annabel? Is she all right?'

'That's what I'm trying to find out.'

'Sit down at the table, all of you,' she commanded. 'Breakfast'll be ready in a moment. You too, Jim.'

Ben took a deep breath and said flatly, 'Lord Fairfield came to my home last night and dismissed me. He said that I'd been spending too much time in the company of his wife and that – and that –' his voice broke on the enormity of what he was about to say – 'Lady Fairfield is expecting a child and his sister – Lady Dorothea – has told him it's mine.' His face ravaged with terrible grief, Ben whispered, 'I swear before God and all that I hold dear, the child is not mine. There is not – and never has been – anything between me and her ladyship.'

'That jealous cow!' Jim exploded. 'She'll stop at nothing to safeguard her son's inheritance – or rather what she believes is his right.'

Edward was watching Ben's face closely. Gently he said, 'But you are in love with Annabel, aren't you?'

'I –' the man could not lie, but what he said was, 'I didn't realize it until his lordship came last night. But I promise you she doesn't know, nor ever will. Not from me – and I beg all of you' – he glanced around at the three concerned faces watching him – 'don't ever tell her.'

Edward smiled sadly. 'If it's any comfort, I'd sooner she'd have married someone like you than into that family.' He sighed heavily and, as Martha came to him and patted his shoulder, he added, 'But that was her father's fault.'

'Now, all of you, eat. I'll cook breakfast for the other two later,' Martha said, as she placed plates of food in front of them. 'Ben, try a little, won't you?'

Whilst they ate and Ben did his best to force a little down a throat that was full of sadness, Edward told them all about Ambrose Constantine and his ambitions for his daughter. 'It goes without saying that I'm telling you this in confidence, of course,' he began, and then went on to explain about Annabel's meetings with a young man from Ambrose's works. 'We never met him. For all I know, he might have been totally unsuitable but then again, he might have been a nice young man who loved her.'

'Well, speaking as a happily married man,' Jim said, his mouth full of crispy bacon, 'I can say that I couldn't blame any young man falling in love with her. The villagers – all of us – love her dearly and not just because she's rescued us. She's a lovely young woman who deserves to be happy.' He sighed. 'But it doesn't sound as if she is by the way she's being treated.'

'Pa,' Martha said softly, 'you ought to drive over to see her. She might need you.'

Edward frowned. 'I don't want to make matters worse, but once his lordship's gone back, maybe I could go over then.'

'Perhaps she'll come here to see us,' Martha added. 'After all, she has something to tell us, doesn't she?'

Edward sighed as he shook his head. 'It sounds to me as if all the joy has been taken out of that particular piece of news. My poor girl.'

Forty-Nine

'It's good of you both to offer,' Ben said a little later, 'but I can't stay here. It wouldn't be right. It – it might make things even worse.'

'Could they be worse?' Edward muttered. 'Besides, you say Jane told you that Annabel had suggested you came to us. She knew we'd help you. And she was right, we will.'

Ben was torn. He had nowhere else to go and yet he didn't want to stay with Annabel's grandparents. He feared it might compound the dreadful rumour.

'I know,' Martha said suddenly, 'why don't you go to Jane's father, Mr Moffatt? His farmland adjoins ours and yet is even further away from Fairfield.'

'Now that, Ma, is a brilliant idea. And even more so because Joe Moffatt is in need of a farm manager.' He turned to Ben to explain. 'Joe injured his back last summer and he's not been right since. I've been telling him for months to get some reliable help on the farm and if anyone fits the bill for that job, then it's you, Ben.'

'I'd have to be completely honest with him,' Ben said doubtfully. 'He might not want to take me on, especially as his daughter is Lady Annabel's maid. It might compromise her situation.'

Now Edward laughed for the first time since the arrival in his yard of Jim Chadwick's farm cart. 'Joe

357

won't give a fig about that. If he takes to you, he'll defy the devil himself. Joe ploughs his own furrow, he owns his own land, handed down through the generations of his family, and he fears neither man nor beast. You'll be all right with Joe. In fact, I'll take you there myself. We're on good terms, me an' Joe. And now, Jim, you'd best be on your way. Not a word to a soul about where Ben is. I'll see Annabel later in the week and will let her know how things have gone on. And,' he turned with a smile to Ben, 'I'll be able to keep you informed of how she is.'

Ben gave a wan smile. What good people they were. He didn't know how he was ever going to repay their kindness.

Annabel felt as if she were a prisoner in Fairfield Hall. She dare not go down to the village, dare not leave the house, certainly not whilst James was still here. And even then . . . She sighed. How could Dorothea be so vitriolic? All in the name of her son, who was a charming little boy, far too young to realize what was happening. But as he grew older and his mother instilled into him that he was the rightful heir of Fairfield, what then? Young as he was, the boy already repeated – parrot fashion – that one day the estate would be his.

Despite all the trouble, Annabel was thrilled that she was to have a child, but now secretly she prayed that it would be a girl.

'Did you see Mr Jackson?' she whispered to Jane when they were alone in her bedroom.

'Yes, miss. He's going to your grandfather's, like you said.'

Annabel sighed with relief. 'Gramps will help him.'

James and Harry left later that day. To her surprise, James held her close and murmured, 'Thank you for my son, Annabel.'

She looked up at him, unable to understand his mood swings. One moment he was accusing her of the most dreadful thing and now he seemed to have accepted her solemn promise. Inwardly, she was confused, but she made up her mind to respond to him in like vein.

'What if it is a girl?' she said impishly.

His face darkened as he looked down into her eyes. 'It had better not be. It *must* be a boy. And one more thing before I go, I realize you will want to carry on involving yourself in the running of the estate, especially now with Home Farm, but I want you to promise me that you will take Jane with you everywhere. You understand?'

It was an order, not a request, but with pretended meekness, Annabel agreed. And she knew she would have to comply; if she did not, James would hear about it anyway. The chains seemed to tighten around her.

The news that Ben Jackson had been sacked and the rumours of the reason for it, spread through the village like the proverbial wildfire, though not from Jim Chadwick. Only his wife heard it from him, but Dorothea made sure that Annie spread the word to the village's biggest gossips. But they had both underestimated the affection the villagers had for Annabel and – it had to be said – for Ben Jackson too. He had been a fair and hardworking estate bailiff and they all had reason to be grateful to him and not just in the recent months.

'I don't believe it,' said Lily Broughton. 'It's all

wicked lies. I know we haven't known her ladyship long, but we know Ben Jackson. And he's an honourable man.'

'Aye, but she's a lovely young woman and they have spent a lot of time together,' Dan murmured.

'Now, you listen to me, Dan Broughton.' Lily wagged her finger at him. 'I don't want to hear another word like that from you – or anyone else. If you've got doubts – and let me tell you, you shouldn't have – then you keep 'em to yourself. You hear me?'

'I was only saying it to you, love. I wouldn't dream of talking like that to anyone else.'

'I should think not too.'

'But there's plenty that'll be saying the same thing.'

'They'd better not in my hearing, and you, William, don't you be joining in with any of the gossip.'

'I won't, Mam. I like 'em both but I haven't got a lot of time for either his lordship or his sister. I can't respect anyone who can let an estate like Fairfield get into the mess it did. They're just selfish toffs who care nothing for any of us. But Lady Annabel does. I know she's got a title and all that, but she's like one of us. I certainly won't be spreading such rumours, Ma, you can count on that, but I can't promise not to have a go at someone if they are. And now I'd best get on. Them cows of ours' – he grinned as he thought about the small herd of dairy cows they now had and all thanks to the woman they were discussing – 'won't milk themselves.'

As their son left the kitchen, Lily gazed after him with tears in her eyes. 'He's got an old head on his young shoulders,' she said fondly.

'Aye, and a good heart. He'll do well now. But just

think, without Lady Annabel where would we still be now? Still in yon workhouse.'

'Exactly!' Lily said firmly.

It seemed as if the rest of the small community of Fairfield agreed with Lily Broughton; they didn't believe any of the nasty accusations either. And if anyone did, they were wise enough to keep their thoughts to themselves. Even Eli Merriman, who'd been – and still was – the least responsive to Annabel's efforts to help – said nothing. Nancy shed tears over the news. 'Oh Mam, how could they say such dreadful things about that sweet lady? They're making out she's no better than me.'

'It's Lady Dorothea that's doing it all, whispering into his lordship's ear and no doubt writing letters to him when he's away,' Agnes said angrily. 'And you can guess what it's like for any man when he's away from home hearing tales like that. By heck, what I'd give to have five minutes alone with that woman. I'd tell 'er what's what and no mistake.'

Nancy's eyes were wide with fear. 'Oh Mam, don't. You'll have us all thrown out.'

Agnes sighed. 'No, I can't do anything. That's what riles me, but what I would like to know is what the old lady thinks to it all. She's a lovely woman, though I never did get on with Lady Dorothea when I worked there. What this'll do to Lady Elizabeth, I don't know.'

Fifty

Lady Dorothea entered her mother's bedroom late in the evening on the day after James had left. 'How are you feeling, Mama?' she asked with feigned solicitude.

'Much better, thank you,' Elizabeth replied, a faint smile on her mouth as she eyed the warm fire in the grate, the crisp clean sheets she was lying between and the soft comforting pillows; all thanks to her new daughter-in-law. She was now well fed and well cared for and she hadn't felt so contented since long before her dear husband had died. Even the last years of his life had been marred for them both by their worry over Albert and his wild ways.

Dorothea sat down beside the bed with a triumphant gleam in her eyes. Elizabeth quailed at the look. Whilst she said very little nowadays, Elizabeth was still sharp in her mind even though her daughter thought otherwise and treated her so.

'Mama, I have some news. Annabel is expecting a child.'

Elizabeth started to smile, almost opened her mouth to say, 'How wonderful', but, as her daughter went on, she bit back the words. 'The child is not James's. How can it be, when he is hardly ever here? And besides, he only married her for her money to save Theodore's inheritance. It is a marriage of convenience and in name only.'

Elizabeth stared at her daughter in astonishment. Unworldly though people might view her, Elizabeth understood the ways of men and women. Of course, James had married the girl for the money her father had promised, but if Dorothea believed for one moment that a virile young man like James could – or would – lie next to a lovely young woman without making love to her, then she was a fool. And Elizabeth liked Annabel; the girl had been kind to her and she'd had no need to be. But Elizabeth said nothing. She was dependent upon all the people in this house for their help and her ultimate welfare was in Dorothea's hands, not, unfortunately, in Annabel's.

Elizabeth made no comment but lay back and closed her eyes, pretending fatigue. Indeed, she was weary but not so much physically as mentally tired of all the worry and uncertainty and then the scheming that had gone on in an effort to save the house. They were safe now, and whether they liked it or not, it was thanks to Annabel. But Elizabeth doubted that James would ever see it that way. Certainly, Dorothea would not. They both believed that the title that had been bestowed upon Annabel was just payment for the money they had received.

As soon as the door closed quietly behind her daughter, Elizabeth's eyes flickered open. She felt an incredible weight of sadness descend upon her. How she'd longed for James to have a son so that he might inherit the title and the estate, but now that joy was being sullied by Dorothea's wicked lies. And she was sure they were lies. If only Annabel would come to see her, she could talk to her, but she didn't know how to send word to her. Annie was the only servant who attended Lady Elizabeth now and the frail lady was astute enough to know that the maid was in Dorothea's power.

The hours dragged on but Annabel did not come to see her.

Annabel was sitting alone in her office, staring out of the window, lost in thought. With a strength she hadn't realized she possessed, she was facing the unpalatable facts. She listed them in her mind.

Her father – with Lady Carruthers's connivance – had engineered a marriage to an impoverished member of the nobility to gain a title for her and with the hope – indeed the intention – that his grandson would one day be Lord Somebody Or Other. He had paid off a would-be suitor, Gilbert Radcliffe, whom she might, given time, have come to love and who, she was sure now, would have been infinitely kinder to her than the man she had married. Gilbert's fault had been weakness; he had not been willing to put up any kind of fight for her. But then, she reminded herself, she did not know what dire threats had accompanied the offer of money. Perhaps, in the face of her father's power, Gilbert had had little choice. Annabel liked to see the good in people and she was prepared to give him the benefit of any doubt. In fairness, her father could not have known the circumstances within the Lyndon family. His fault there lay in the fact that he had not bothered to find out what the true situation was and now Annabel was faced with a jealous and possessive husband and an evil sister-in-law who was feeding that jealousy for her own ends. Annabel wrinkled her brow. She'd heard it said that no one is all good or all bad, but at the moment she could not see much good in

Dorothea. Even her ambitions for her son did not seem to arise from her love for him.

Annabel ran a protective hand over her belly as she whispered, 'I will love you no matter what. I will protect you and fight for you always. Though perhaps,' she added with a wry smile, 'it would be better for you – and me – if you were a girl.' The hereditary title of the Earl of Fairfield passed only down the male line and a girl was no threat to Theo's inheritance.

Her mind veered to thoughts of James and Cynthia Carruthers. What a strange world they lived in, she thought, where a married woman – one who was supposed to have been in love with her husband when she'd married him – not only took a younger lover but was also willing to marry him off to another. But that, it seemed, was the way things often happened in their circles. She wondered what had happened in previous generations of the Lyndon family. And thinking of that, the dowager countess came into her mind. Slowly, she rose and went upstairs to Elizabeth's room.

'Annabel!' Her mother-in-law's face lit up at the sight of her. 'I'm so glad you've come. How is the progress on my garden?'

Annabel smiled as she sat down beside the bed. Elizabeth looked much better now than when Annabel had first met her. Her eyes were brighter and her skin was a much better colour. She couldn't blame the frail lady for her first thought being about her garden rather than how the estate fared and the welfare of the villagers. Elizabeth would doubtless never have been involved in such matters, even when her husband was alive.

'We've re-employed the man who used to be head

gardener here, Thomas Salt.' She explained to Elizabeth what had transpired, the new appointments that had been made and the work that was being done. 'They've already cleared the ground, cut the grass and dug over the beds. We'll need you to tell us what you'd like planted.'

Elizabeth leaned back against the pillows and closed her eyes. 'I want it to be just like it used to be.'

Ben's face came at once into Annabel's mind. He had been able to remember the garden as it had once been. He would have advised them, but now Ben was no longer here. How she would miss his guidance and help in so many ways. Now, she would have to rely on Thomas Salt's memory to recreate the garden for her mother-in-law.

Elizabeth seemed in the mood to reminisce and Annabel was happy to listen; she might learn more about this strange family into which she had married.

'Charles had the garden made for me when I came here as a bride,' the dowager countess murmured. 'We were so much in love and he'd have done anything to make me happy – then.'

'So yours was a love match,' Annabel said softly. 'Not a marriage of –' She stopped, unwilling to say the word that might upset the dowager countess and prevent her from saying more. Annabel wanted her to go on; she wanted to hear more about the family. But Elizabeth did not seem to have heard her; she was lost in her memories. Annabel had caught the brief pause before she had added 'Then'.

'You were happy?' she prompted.

'Oh, so happy. The estate was prospering. Charles's grandfather – the second earl – had been a good manager – a good *farmer*.' She smiled. 'They called him Farmer

Bert. His name was Albert.' Her face clouded. 'That's why we called our firstborn "Albert" after him. And Charles's father – Theodore – carried on the good work.'

She paused for what seemed to Annabel an age, but Elizabeth was not to be rushed. It was as if she was speaking to herself more than to anyone else. Annabel hesitated to interrupt her; it might break the spell and halt the reminiscing.

'We were so thrilled at our Albert's birth; an heir for the title and the estate at the very first go. And he was such a handsome little boy. Always merry, always laughing, but a little rascal,' she added fondly, 'even then. And then came Dorothea. She was always a surly child, sulky and jealous of her elder brother's position. She was the ambitious one, whilst Albert just wanted to enjoy life. It would have been better if she had been born the boy and born first.' She sighed and lapsed into a long silence again, but this time Annabel whispered, 'And James?'

'All James ever wanted was to be a soldier. It had always been the tradition in the family that the second son – if there was one – would go into the Army, but it was what James wanted to do anyway. He didn't need persuading. So, as soon as he was old enough, off he went. He's hardly lived at home since.' Now her face clouded; she was remembering unhappier times. 'James had no interest in the estate; he had no need. It was unlikely that it would ever pass to him, but he'd reckoned without Albert's wild ways – behaviour that killed his father.'

'Killed him!' Annabel exclaimed. 'How?'

'Albert got into a lot of trouble drinking, living the high life and – well, you know. Charles paid his debts time and again to keep him out of serious trouble. My husband's health deteriorated because of it. I'm sure of it. And then there was the business of Nancy Banks. She was a sweet girl – a *good* girl – but my son charmed her and – and . . .'

She paused and ran her tongue around her lips. Annabel reached for the glass of water on the bedside table and handed it to her.

'It made matters so much worse because she was our housekeeper's daughter. Mrs Banks was the best house-keeper we'd ever had, but, of course, when it all came out, they both had to go.'

Annabel was tempted to ask why, but she kept silent.

'I think that really finished my husband. He died only months after we heard that the child had been born. The last thing he did was to give Nancy and her mother the cottage at the end of the village.'

'Your husband did that? I'd thought it was Albert.'

Slowly Elizabeth turned her head to look at Annabel. 'That's what everyone thinks, but no, it was my Charles. Albert didn't lift a finger to help the poor girl he'd got into trouble, but Charles gave them the cottage and settled a small annuity on them too. They'd started a dressmaking business and they'd have been all right if –' She passed a hand wearily over her face and Annabel murmured, 'Don't talk any more if it's tiring you.'

'No, no, I want to tell you. This family has treated you shamefully and for that I'm sorry, but I want you to understand *why*.'

Now Annabel said nothing; she wanted to hear it all. Perhaps it would help her deal with the life she had been handed through no fault of her own. And more importantly, perhaps it would help her to understand her complicated husband.

'When Albert inherited the title, we all thought

– believed – he would come to his senses and recognize the responsibilities of his new position. But no, he continued with his riotous life and cared nothing for the estate. He ruined it. He borrowed a huge sum of money and raised the rents for the tenant farmers to such a ridiculous amount that they couldn't possibly make a living. And then he died and James inherited.' She paused and whispered, 'Poor James.'

'Why do you say, "poor James"?'

'Because he'd always lived in his brother's shadow – in Dorothea's too, if it comes to that. She was always the stronger one – the strongest of the three, if I'm honest.'

'How did Albert die?' Annabel asked gently.

Elizabeth was silent for a moment before saying brokenly, 'In mysterious circumstances in London. It was all hushed up and even I never knew the truth, but I suppose I can guess,' she added bitterly. 'I believe he died in a debtors' prison.'

Annabel took her hand and held it. There was a long silence now before Elizabeth went on more strongly, 'James never sought or wanted the title and the responsibility that came with it, but he knew he had to do something to try to save the estate.'

'Marry money,' Annabel said, striving to keep the bitterness out of her voice.

'Yes,' Elizabeth whispered. 'It's what we do.' She turned her head on the pillow and looked straight into Annabel's eyes. 'And now you are to give us a son and heir. You can't know how happy that makes me. And I want you to know, my dear, that *I* do not believe what Dorothea is saying. I *know* that you are carrying my grandson.'

Fifty-One

'Jane – I need to go down to the village and you'll have to come with me if I'm to avoid more tales being spread.'

'I've given that Annie a piece of my mind, but she's under Lady Dorothea's thumb.'

Annabel sighed. At least my mother-in-law believes me, she thought. Aloud she said, 'What about the others? Do they believe the lies?'

Jane shook her head. 'No. Mrs Parrish is so grateful to you for bringing her mother out of the workhouse, she won't hear a word said against you. Luke and the other youngsters, well, all they're concerned about is doing their work and going to The Lyndon Arms now it's opened up again. I'm not sure about Mr Searby, though. I think he's sitting on the fence to safeguard his own position whatever happens.'

Annabel laughed. 'I can't blame him for that. And now, we'll be off. Ask Luke to harness the pony and trap and to drive us.'

Jane frowned. Annabel usually walked to the village. 'Are you feeling all right, miss?'

'Fit as a flea, but I've a lot to do today and I may decide to go on into town later and possibly even to see my grandparents.'

'Then I'll tell them downstairs we won't be in for dinner – sorry, luncheon, I'm supposed to call it.'

*

The village shops were all open now. As they drove along the street, women came out of their cottages to wave and smile and as they passed out of the village, Annabel saw the children playing in the schoolyard. She smiled to see their happy faces as they laughed and shouted. And her smile broadened when she saw Bertie right in the centre of the games. The children had kept their promise to her and now he was accepted as one of them.

Luke drove on to visit each of the tenanted farms in turn. Dan and William were busy in the fields, but Lily made them welcome with buttered scones and a cup of tea. In some of the poorer households, tea was still classed as a luxury but now, every housewife in the village kept a packet of Horniman's tea – just in case Lady Annabel should call!

'You must keep your strength up, m'lady. We're that pleased to hear your wonderful news.'

At Sparrow Farm, Betsy shyly congratulated her and said, 'You'll make a lovely mother, m'lady. See how Eddie's growing now.'

Annabel smiled and nursed the baby, who had been so close to death only a few months ago. Now, he chortled happily and gazed up at Annabel with bright blue eyes.

But when Jim Chadwick helped Annabel down from the trap on their arrival at Blackbird Farm, his first question – when Luke was safely out of earshot – was, 'What's to happen to Home Farm, m'lady?' He had no need to guard his tongue in front of Jane; he knew she was utterly loyal to Annabel, but he couldn't – as yet – be so sure of Luke.

'That's partly why I've come to see you,' Annabel said. 'I wondered about appointing a manager. I can oversee the estate, but I won't be able to manage the

371

day-to-day running of a farm.' Especially, she thought, as I'll soon have a child to care for.

'I'll talk to Dan and Adam,' Jim went on. 'See if we can come up with an idea. Of course, we could' – he went on as if speaking his thoughts aloud – 'manage Home Farm between us. The three of us, I mean.'

'Could you?'

'I don't see why not, m'lady, with your guidance and instructions, of course. There are a couple of good labourers working there already and a wagoner. You don't really need anyone else. I mean, Ben didn't spend much time there. He just made sure things were running all right.'

Tears prickled Annabel's throat as she thought about Ben. If only her jealous husband hadn't been so hasty. Now, he had made her life even more difficult.

After seeing all the farms and completing her business in town, Annabel said, 'Now we'll go on to Meadow View Farm. I want to see my grandparents.'

'Do you think you should, miss?' Jane whispered. '*He* might still be there and I'm not quite sure where Luke's loyalties lie.'

Annabel shrugged. 'It's a risk I'll have to take.'

As they pulled into the yard at Meadow View Farm, Annabel drew in a sharp breath. Her father's carriage was standing there. She felt a moment's panic; her mother rarely visited her parents and she'd been to see them only recently. Was something wrong? Was one of her grandparents ill?

'Jane, run in and see what's happening.'

The girl jumped down from the trap and ran to the house whilst Luke helped his mistress alight.

As she went inside, Jane met her at the door, saying in a hushed voice, 'They're all in the parlour, miss.'

Annabel raised her eyebrows. Martha's best room was only ever used on special occasions. She frowned. Something must be wrong. 'Are they all right?'

Jane nodded but she was clearly anxious. 'Your dad's here an' all and they look – angry.'

'All of them?'

'Well . . .'

'It's all right.' She touched Jane's arm. 'I'll see for myself.'

As she entered the room she saw at once what Jane had meant. It looked as if she had stepped into the middle of a big family quarrel. Her father was on his feet, standing with his back to the fire. 'What's this I hear?' he demanded harshly, without a word of greeting to his daughter. 'You're pregnant with another man's child?'

'How could you, Annabel?' Sarah put in. 'You've brought shame on us all. And after all your father has done for you.'

Before Annabel could even open her mouth, Edward stood up. 'It's the pair of you who ought to be ashamed. How can you even think such a thing of Annabel? Of course the child is her husband's.'

'That's not what his sister said in her letter.'

Annabel gasped and held on to the door for support as her legs threatened to give way beneath her. 'Dorothea? She – she's written to you?'

'Well, I don't suppose you were likely to tell us, were you?' Ambrose said sarcastically.

'Because there's nothing to tell except that she's to have a child,' Edward boomed. 'The grandchild you wanted.'

'Only if it's a boy. I don't want another blasted *girl*.'

There was a moment's shocked silence before Edward, his voice menacingly soft, said, 'D'you know, Constantine, I've never liked you. I knew you for the ruthlessly ambitious man you are, but I never thought until this moment that you were actually evil.'

The two men glared at each other, but it was Ambrose's glance that fell away first.

Recovering her composure and filled with an unexpected calmness, Annabel closed the door quietly behind her and stepped further into the room. She glanced at each of them in turn; her parents' faces were thunderous, her grandfather's angry and distressed, and poor Martha looked close to tears.

'First of all, I have now learned the full extent of your – machinations, Father, to marry me off to a title. It would never have happened if the Lyndon family had not been in such desperate need for your money.'

'We all know that,' Ambrose muttered. 'How else would an earl have looked at the likes of you?'

'Quite,' Annabel said with asperity. 'But the huge sum of money you gave him – ten thousand pounds, I believe – was swallowed up in saving the house and the land. He – and more particularly his dear sister – thought nothing of trying to save the people on the estate.'

Now, Ambrose had the grace to look surprised. 'But he told me –' he began and then fell silent, allowing Annabel to continue.

'I'm sure he told you that your money would solve everything. That your future grandson would inherit not only the title, but also a thriving concern.'

Ambrose gaped at her and then the realization that he had been misled, duped by James's fine promises, sank in. 'Go on,' he said flatly.

'When I arrived there, the farms were run down and neglected. Two were deserted. One family had left, the other was in the workhouse in Thorpe St Michael, along with one or two other villagers. The shops were closed, the public house and the school too. With Gramps's and Granny's help we took food to them and I have spent my own savings to help them. The villagers were on the point of starvation.'

'There was a little babby on the point of death when she got there,' Edward put in. 'Annabel saved its life and several more too, I shouldn't wonder.'

'But who's this Jackson fellow?'

'He was the bailiff and he was a great help—'

'I bet he was!'

'– in getting the estate back on its feet.'

'And your child is his, is it?'

'No, it is not. This is James's child.'

Ambrose glared at her. 'How do you expect me to believe you? Your past behaviour has not exactly been exemplary. Running around the countryside, meeting an employee of mine in secret. It cost me five hundred pounds to be rid of him.'

'Nothing happened between Gilbert Radcliffe and me, nor with Ben Jackson. That's the truth, but I can't help it if you choose not to believe me.' She sat down beside Martha and took her hands. 'I'm so sorry you've had to hear my news this way, Granny, but I swear to you—'

Martha gripped her hand as she looked into Annabel's eyes. 'You've no need to swear anything to me, my love. I never doubted you for a moment.'

'Oh Gran.' And now Annabel did dissolve into tears.

Fifty-Two

Annabel couldn't be sure whether or not her mother and father believed her. All Ambrose would say as they left was, 'Well, if the child is Lyndon's, mind you stick it out and stay there. You hear me?'

'I hear you, Father,' Annabel said with admirable composure, though she was seething inside.

As the carriage rolled out of the farmyard and disappeared up the lane, Edward put his arm around Annabel's shoulders. 'Never mind what he says, my lovely, if you're unhappy at Fairfield Hall, you come to us. There's always a home for you – and your little one – here.'

Annabel looked up at him and smiled sadly. 'The only thing that would make me leave is if I felt my child was in danger. If it's a girl, she'll be quite safe, but if it's a boy –' She left the words unspoken, but there was no need to say more, for her grandfather understood only too well. As they walked back to the house together, Annabel asked softly, 'Did Ben come here?'

'He did. Jim Chadwick brought him.'

Annabel looked up in surprise. 'Jim? I saw him this morning. But he never said anything.'

Edward chuckled. 'He wouldn't. He knows how to keep his own counsel, does Jim Chadwick.'

'Do – do you know where Ben's gone?'

'To Joe Moffatt's place. He's got a job there.'

'Jane's dad? Does she know?'

'I shouldn't think so, but be careful who you tell, my lovely.'

'Oh, I can trust Jane with my life, but I'm not sure about the other members of staff at Fairfield.' She sighed as she dropped her voice almost to a whisper. Luke was a good distance away across the yard, but she didn't want him to catch even a word of their conversation. 'It must be difficult for them. They've got divided loyalties now.'

'Just tread carefully.'

Life at Fairfield Hall settled into a routine. Annabel conducted the business of the estate from her office and if she needed to go into the village or to visit the farms, she always took Jane with her, even to the school, where she delighted in reading to the children, Bertie amongst them. But Dorothea had still resisted Theo attending the village school.

'He'll be going to boarding school when he's eight – to the school James and Albert attended. I hope James will keep *that* promise.'

'Of course,' Annabel said smoothly. 'If you really think that's best for Theodore.' Annabel still read to her nephew most nights. She had grown to love the little boy and enjoyed the precious time she had alone with him. She had begun reading to the dowager countess too. Elizabeth loved books but her eyesight was failing and the print blurred on the page, she said. Secretly, Annabel thought that it was an excuse to have someone sit with her. Not that she minded. She became very fond of the dowager countess and was looking forward to the day when the walled garden would be ready almost as much as Elizabeth was herself. Daily, she asked, 'How is my garden progressing?'

The estate began to prosper. Lambs were born early in March, but Annabel was sad that she couldn't be there to see it. The pigs, too, farrowed in March and calving came in May. And the crops began to grow. There was a feeling of optimism throughout the whole village. There was work for everyone from the children leaving school as soon as they reached twelve to Grace Parrish who, now back in her own home, undertook to clean the school every night after the children left. 'It's something I can do,' Grace told Nelly when her daughter protested it'd be too much for her. 'Don't try to stop me, lass. I can manage it and I need to be occupied.'

The shops thrived now that there was more money about and Jabez Fletcher's smithy was busy from morning until night with either blacksmith's work or carpentry. He was the first to come to the Hall one morning to present Annabel with the first repayment on his loan. Others soon followed and the money trickled back into Annabel's bank account. She was pleased, not because she needed the money but because she knew it was giving the villagers back their pride.

The day came in late June when Thomas Salt asked to see Lady Fairfield. John Searby led him to Annabel's office. The man, so used to being out of doors, was ill-at-ease as he stood in front of her desk, twirling his cap between gnarled fingers.

'Mr Salt, how are you?' Annabel looked up from her papers. 'Please sit down.'

'I'm well, thank'ee, m'lady, but I'll not sit down. I'm

in me workin' clothes. I've just come to tell you that her ladyship's garden is coming on nicely and I think she'd like to see it now.'

'Oh how wonderful.' Annabel said, clasping her hands together. 'We'll arrange it. When would it suit you?'

'It'd be nice on a warm, sunny day, m'lady.' He glanced at the windows. 'It's going to rain this afternoon, so best leave it until tomorrow. I reckon it'll be nice tomorrow.'

Annabel hid her smile. She marvelled at how the country folk seemed to be able to foretell the weather, and invariably, they were right. 'Tomorrow afternoon it is, then. His lordship is due home tomorrow morning, Mr Salt, for a short leave, so we'll arrange a picnic in the walled garden in honour of its reopening. I'll see Mrs Parrish about it.'

The following afternoon was sunny and warm – just as Thomas had predicted. He and Gregory Merriman worked all morning, cutting and trimming in a last effort to make everything just perfect. James, with Harry Jenkins in tow, arrived mid-morning, no doubt, Annabel thought sadly, after a night or two in London with Cynthia Carruthers, but she fixed a welcoming smile on her face. Harry disappeared to the village as soon as he could. Over luncheon, Annabel told James, Dorothea and Theo of the proposed picnic for the afternoon.

'Such excitement won't be good for Mama.' Dorothea pursed her lips. 'She's talked about nothing else since you told her last night. I doubt she hardly slept.'

To Annabel's surprise, James agreed with his wife.

'She'll be fine. I'll get Searby to bring down the bath chair from the attics and clean it. It's one my grandmother had years ago,' he explained to Annabel. 'We can push her to the garden. It's high time she got out a bit. She's been acting like an old lady for too long now.'

'She's a sick woman, James.'

'Nonsense,' he snapped. 'Only because you make her think she is. Keeping her shut away in her room. You've made her old before her time.'

Dorothea gasped. 'Well, if you don't like the way I run the household, perhaps your dear wife had better take over my duties. She's taking everything else from me.'

'Oh Dorothea, don't say that,' Annabel protested. 'You run the house beautifully. I wouldn't know where to start. Take no notice of James, but please let us take Lady Fairfield to the garden.' Now she turned to her husband. 'Your mother was very ill, James, and it has taken her a long time to feel well again, but the garden has given her an interest and something to get better for. She so longs to see it.'

'And so she shall,' James declared and now, even Dorothea did not argue.

That afternoon, it was like an expedition setting out. Nelly, Annie and Jane spent most of the early afternoon preparing a lavish picnic and when John Searby and the new footman had carried it across to the garden, everything was ready. The bath chair awaited Elizabeth in the courtyard near the side door and James himself wheeled her across towards the gate at the side of the stables leading into the gardens. Thomas and the young gardener stood watching, taking off their caps and giving a little bow as the party approached. Even Dorothea had condescended to come and Theo was capering around them like a caged animal let loose.

It was like a grand opening ceremony and when the gate swung open, Elizabeth gave a little cry of delight. As James pushed her into the garden, she looked around her in wonder. 'I never thought I'd see it again and looking like it used to do. Oh, just look at the roses! How hard you must have worked, Salt, you and your colleague.' She smiled at the two men standing together.

'It's been our pleasure, m'lady, and to see you enjoying it will be our reward,' Thomas said and added, with a catch in his voice, 'It's good to be back working here.'

Annabel glanced down to the ground, avoiding meeting anyone's eyes, but she could feel Dorothea's resentful gaze upon her.

The afternoon was a great success. James played an impromptu game of cricket with Theo on the stretch of lawn at the back of the house, inviting the two gardeners to join in. Playing in shirt sleeves, with his brown hair ruffled, James looked relaxed and the happiest Annabel had ever seen him. That night he made love to her tenderly and by the time he left the following morning, no mention had been made either about her pregnancy or about Ben Jackson.

Through the summer months, Elizabeth visited the garden every day when the weather was fine. After her afternoon nap, she would go down to the side entrance where Thomas would be waiting with the bath chair. He would wheel her to the garden, where she would sit and read, or just gaze around her at the transformation from an overgrown wilderness back to its former glory.

'Help me up, Salt, if you please. I want to walk.'

Each day she grew stronger and, just like the garden, in time she was restored to full health. But Elizabeth never forgot the person who had made all this possible.

The summer was a busy and exciting time for the estate too. Farmers had always been used to coping with Britain's changeable weather and the summer of 1897 was no exception, but they managed to bring in good harvests of both hay and cereal crops. From her bedroom overlooking the front of the house, Annabel was able to watch the workers in the fields. How she longed to be with them, dressed in old clothes, her hair tied back as she helped to stook, but her advanced pregnancy kept her close to home.

'You can't go down to the village like that.' Dorothea was appalled to see that Annabel was preparing to be driven down to the village one warm August morning. 'You can no longer hide your condition. *Ladies* wouldn't dream of being seen in public like that.'

Annabel smiled and said smoothly, 'But we all know that I'm no lady, Dorothea. Oh, and just to let you know, I've requested that Nurse Newton should come back for my confinement. She's an experienced midwife too.'

Dorothea turned away, sick at heart. Because Annabel's money paid for everything, she could no longer argue about any expense. She was daily fighting a conflict of emotions. She knew that Annabel's dowry had saved Fairfield Hall and her money had also restored the estate. She had cause to be thankful to Annabel, but her consuming jealousy would not let her admit such a thing. And now there was the coming child. She hoped – prayed – that it would be a girl. For, if it was a boy, even she didn't know what she might be capable of.

Fifty-Three

Late in the evening of 8 September 1897, just over a year after her marriage, Annabel felt the first contractions. Luckily, Nurse Newton had arrived the previous week and had set up a bedroom on the top floor for the confinement. Annabel was fortunate that her labour moved swiftly and her child was born in the early hours of the following day. The baby's lusty cries woke the household, most of whom were awake anyway, awaiting its arrival. Dorothea lay rigid in her bed, determined not to leave her room. She would know soon enough, but the bedroom door opened and Theo stood there, his sturdy frame illuminated by the soft light from the landing.

'There's a baby crying, Mama. I can hear it.'

In the semi-darkness, Dorothea pursed her mouth, screwed her eyes tight shut and didn't answer him. The boy moved closer to her bedside. 'Mama, I said—'

Dorothea's eyes flew open. 'I heard what you said,' she snapped. The boy flinched and took a step backwards.

The door behind him opened wider and Elizabeth, dressed in only her nightgown with a shawl around her shoulders, tiptoed into the room.

'Dorothea – aren't you going to see if everything's all right?'

'No, I am not,' she replied tersely and turned onto her side, her back towards them.

There was a brief, shocked pause, before Elizabeth, in a surprisingly strong voice, said, 'Then Theo and I will go and see. Come along, my dear.' She held out her hand to the boy and together they left the room and went up the stairs towards the noise of the newborn baby.

As the door closed behind them, Dorothea buried her head beneath her bedclothes and muttered angrily, 'It's Theo*dore*.' Even her mother was being influenced by Annabel.

When Elizabeth knocked tentatively, the door was opened by Jane, who had been present at the birth to be at the beck and call of the nurse.

'May we come in?'

'Oh, m'lady! And Master Theo.' Jane's face was pink with pleasure, lit with a beaming smile. She turned back briefly towards the nurse to see if she could admit them.

Elizabeth heard Nurse Newton say, 'Please ask them to come back in half an hour. They can see Mother and Baby then.'

As Jane turned back to relay the message, Elizabeth said, 'We'll do that. Come along, Theo, we'll go down to my room. There's a fire still burning there. We'll be cosy while we wait.'

Elizabeth lit a candle and they sat together in front of the dying fire. But it still gave a little warmth and the early September night was not cold.

'Do you realize that this little baby will be your cousin?'

'Will it? Why?'

'Because he – or she – is the child of your uncle.' Elizabeth was thoughtful for a moment before saying, 'You have another cousin too.'

The boy, now six, though educated solely by his

mother, was bright and intelligent and had been drilled by her in the matter of the family lineage, so he understood about relationships. But she had never told him about a cousin.

'Have I?' he said innocently. 'Who is it?'

Elizabeth was silent for a moment before saying softly, 'Albert Lyndon Banks.'

'You mean Bertie? The boy who came to stay here for a night or two when his house burnt down?'

'That's right.'

There was a pause whilst Theo digested this information. 'I gave him my train, you know,' he whispered, 'but please don't tell Mama.'

Elizabeth chuckled. 'It'll be our secret, Theo dear.'

The boy was thoughtful now and, after a moment, he said, 'But he won't inherit the estate, will he, because I'm older than him, aren't I?'

Elizabeth was silent for a moment, gazing into the fire, lost in her own thoughts and memories. 'He won't inherit,' she said slowly at last, 'because he's illegitimate.'

'What's – ill-illimate?'

'He's your Uncle Albert's son.'

'The one who died who was the earl before Uncle James?'

'That's correct. By rights, though, Bertie should be the heir – he should be the earl now, really, young though he is, because he's the son of the eldest son.'

Now it was getting complicated for the young boy, but his grandmother's next words clarified her reasoning. 'But he can't inherit because his mother and father were never married. That's what illegitimate means. He was born out of wedlock.'

Theo was quiet again, digesting the information, but now he had more questions. 'Am I – illimate?'

'No – no. Your mother and father were – are – married.'

'But I haven't got a father.'

'Of course you have. Everyone's got a father.'

'But he's not here. I don't know him.' He paused and then added, 'Is he dead?'

Elizabeth stroked her grandson's hair. 'I really don't know, Theo. He went away when you were about eighteen months old and he never came back. Do you remember him at all? He was tall with dark hair and a moustache.'

Theo wrinkled his forehead. 'I don't *think* so. I remember Uncle Albert, though. He was fun. He used to carry me on his shoulders, didn't he? And he taught me how to play poker.'

'Did he now?' Elizabeth said fondly. Despite Albert's wild ways and the trouble he had brought upon the family, Elizabeth had loved her firstborn fiercely. He had, as Theo had said, been fun and with his death a bright light had gone out of her life. But now there was another child born into the family – one who might take away Theo's inheritance in a way that Bertie Banks could never do. The child would be her grandchild too – indeed, they were all her grandchildren.

The door opened and Jane peered around it. 'Nurse says you can come and see Baby now, m'lady.'

Elizabeth rose stiffly and again took Theo's hand. They crept up to the bedroom and went to stand beside the bed. Annabel, her cheeks red from the effort of giving birth, smiled at them. Her eyes glowed with happiness as she cradled the tiny bundle in her arms.

'It's a boy,' she said softly, pride mingled with a note of anxiety in her tone. She was not sure how either of them would respond. Elizabeth smiled and nodded with obvious satisfaction. 'The future Lord Fairfield,' she murmured. 'What are you going to call him?'

'I must talk to James when he comes home, of course, but I would like one of his names to be Edward.'

'It's a good name, my dear, but would you consider calling him Charles after my late husband?'

'Of course,' Annabel agreed readily, then her glance went to Theo and she searched his expression for anger or jealousy, but he was looking at the baby's red, wrinkled face with disappointment and all he said was, 'How long will it be before he's big enough to play with me?'

It was two days before Dorothea could bring herself to acknowledge the child's arrival. On the third day after the birth, she ventured – at Elizabeth's insistence – into Annabel's bedroom. She was surprised to see the new mother already sitting in a chair near the window, breast-feeding her baby.

'Should you be up already?' Dorothea spoke before thinking. Then immediately, she was angry with herself; she had shown a concern she was anxious not to express. Annabel looked up and smiled, but her eyes were wary. Elizabeth came each day – twice sometimes – to see her grandson and Theo came as often as he could sneak away from his mother's watchful eye. 'Has he grown today?' he would ask innocently and Annabel would say, 'A little, perhaps, Theo, but it will be a long time before he can walk and talk. I'm sorry.'

The little boy had shrugged. 'But one day he'll be old enough to be my friend, won't he?' His words and the longing in his tone broke Annabel's heart. She touched his cheek with gentle fingers as she whispered huskily, 'Of course he will.'

The household was full of talk of the new baby – the boy who would one day be the Earl of Fairfield; the boy who had usurped Theodore. And now Dorothea had come to see him. She approached, reluctance in every step, and yet she had to see him for herself.

She stood a long time looking down at him. The baby looked up at her with wide, dark blue eyes whilst his mother stroked his downy fair hair. She glanced up at Dorothea, fearful to see the expression on the woman's face. But, to her surprise, her sister-in-law was smiling grimly. 'So – that settles it, then. He's no Lyndon. Lyndons all have dark hair and brown eyes. And,' she added triumphantly, 'Jackson was fair-haired and blue-eyed. James will *have* to believe me now.'

Fifty-Four

It was five weeks before James arrived home. During that time, Annabel wrote countless letters to her husband, begging him to come home to see his son and also to agree to the name she had chosen: Charles, after James's father and Edward, after her grandfather. But no word came and Annabel began to panic that something had happened to her husband.

'I'll have to register his birth. It's the law,' she told Elizabeth worriedly as they sat together one warm early October afternoon in the shelter of the walled garden. The baby boy lay in the perambulator, which the butler had unearthed from the attic. 'If I don't hear soon . . .'

Elizabeth no longer needed the bath chair and she walked from the house to the garden each day with only the support of a walking stick. Now she sat with her hand on the perambulator gently rocking her new grandson.

'Then you must decide the name, my dear.'

'But what if it's not what James wants?'

Elizabeth lifted her shoulders. 'Then it's his own fault. You've done your best. And I must say I am rather surprised and disappointed in him that he hasn't come home. I'm sure Army officers aren't so heartless as not to allow a man a little leave on the birth of his son and heir.'

'Perhaps,' Annabel murmured softly, 'he really believes what Dorothea is saying. Has she written to him, d'you know?'

'I expect so,' Elizabeth said mildly.

Annabel sighed. 'Then that's the reason. He believes her.'

It seemed he did, for when at last James arrived home, he was cold and distant, scarcely glancing at the child and when he did so, it was to say harshly, 'I see that Dorothea is right after all. He does not take after the Lyndon side of the family. Fair hair and blue eyes?' His belligerent glare pointedly took in Annabel's own black hair and violet eyes. 'Now from whom do you suppose he inherited such colouring?'

Annabel swallowed painfully. 'My father has fair hair and your mother told me she used to have fair hair too before it turned grey. And her eyes are still blue.'

'I understand my mother is enamoured of the child whom she believes is her new grandson,' he drawled, his tone heavy with sarcasm.

'He *is* her grandson – and your son, though I presume from the way you are acting that you are still doubting it.'

He shrugged. 'How can I not? You can't deny that you spent a lot of time in Jackson's company. And alone, which is not the actions of a devoted wife or' – he added with a sting – 'of a *lady*.'

'It wasn't my *ladylike* qualities you were interested in when you married me, was it, James?' she retorted heatedly. She was getting very tired of his jealous accusations. Giving birth had left her feeling emotional and vulnerable. And her disappointment in her husband that he had taken so long to come home to see his son was the final humiliation.

'James – for the last time – he is your son. Are you going to believe me or your sister's lies?'

'Are you calling Dorothea a liar?'

'I'm sure she believes what she's telling you,' Annabel said magnanimously, though she didn't feel any understanding for the woman who was doing her best to oust Annabel and her son from their rightful place. 'But she has no grounds for such wicked tales. Ben Jackson was a true gentleman the whole time. Yes, we spent time together working for the good of the estate – *your* estate, which you put second to your army career. It should be you here looking after your lands and your people, not left to a bailiff. James,' her tone softened and she crossed the space between them to stand close to him and look up into his face, 'won't you consider leaving the Army and coming home to look after everything?'

He looked down into her upturned face, meeting her steady violet gaze, the pleading in her eyes as she went on huskily, 'There'd be no need for me to see anyone outside of this house, if you didn't want me to. I'd be willing to live like a virtual recluse, if that's what it takes.'

His expression hardened. 'You should have thought about that before, my dear. It's a little late now, don't you think?' A righteous indignation rose up in Annabel and overflowed as he added, 'Besides, you're only saying this so that you can secure the inheritance for *your* son.'

'So you really won't believe me?' she said. 'Is there nothing I can say that will make you believe the truth?'

His glance went again to the baby lying in its crib. 'Not now I've seen him – no. He so obviously does not take after me or the Lyndon family.'

'And you're an expert on hereditary hair and eye colouring, are you?' she snapped. 'Don't you know that all new-born babies have blue eyes?'

James's lip curled. 'That's an old wives' tale.'

'You're wrong—'

'But I am an expert on who should inherit the Fairfield Estate and let me tell you now, Annabel' – he jabbed his forefinger towards the cradle – 'it won't be him.'

Annabel gasped and stared at him, thunderstruck, robbed finally of any retort. She could not speak and as her legs gave way beneath her and she sank to the floor, James made no effort to help her. Instead, he turned and left the room.

That night for the first time since her marriage when James had been at home, Annabel slept alone in the big bed they had once shared and where, she thought with bitter irony, their son had been conceived.

The following morning, whilst Annabel was washing in the bathroom across the landing from their bedroom, she heard a cry from the cradle that stood at the foot of her bed. She hurried back into the room to see Dorothea standing over Charles.

'What are you doing?' Annabel demanded.

'Just looking at the cuckoo in the nest,' Dorothea remarked with a slow smile.

'He's no cuckoo,' Annabel said moving closer. 'And you know it.' She gazed at her sister-in-law and asked softly, 'Dorothea, why are you doing this?'

The woman thrust her face close to Annabel's. 'Because,' she hissed, her spittle raining on Annabel's face, 'no one is going to take away my son's inheritance. No one. You hear me?' With that she spun round and stalked out of the room, leaving Annabel gazing after her but with her hand protectively on the side of her son's crib.

Annabel didn't see James until the evening. She heard

from Jane that he had been out around the estate all day, visiting the outlying farms and talking to the shop-keepers and residents in the village.

'He even visited Nancy Banks,' Jane whispered. 'Harry's just come back for his tea and he told us.'

'Perhaps he's thinking about what I said; that he should come home and run the estate.'

Jane snorted with laughter. 'Him? Run the estate? I don't think so. I could make a better job of it than him, miss.'

In the early evening, James came to their room, to change for dinner, so Annabel thought. But it seemed that he still had other matters on his mind. He stood in the doorway, his hand resting on the doorknob. With no preamble, no warning, he said harshly, 'I want you gone from this house. Now – tonight. You and – your child.' Annabel turned slowly to face him, the colour draining from her face as he continued cruelly, 'I neither care nor want to know where you go. You can go to your lover, for I'm sure you know where he is.'

That, Annabel could not deny. Had James found out where Ben was? Had Jane let it slip? Surely not.

'You don't mean it. You *can't* mean it?'

'I do. You may take whatever you can carry of your own belongings.'

She could see there was no arguing with him. Dorothea had won. He believed her wicked lies and he was turning his wife and son out into the cold, wet night.

'And another thing. I have seen each and every one of my tenants today and if anyone gives you shelter tonight, they will be evicted too. Do you understand? If you're so concerned about their welfare, you will ask for help from no one.'

393

'But the baby? I—'

'If you really think I care what happens to him, then, my dear, you don't know me.'

The door closed behind him with a slam and Annabel realized bitterly that no, she didn't know him at all.

It was raining heavily by the time Annabel had wrapped Charlie, as she had come to call him, warmly in shawls and tucked him as best she could inside her cape. She packed a small bag with essential baby items, thankful that at least she was feeding him herself; he would not go hungry. The only other thing she took with her was the ledger where she'd kept a faithful record of every penny she'd spent on the tenants of the Fairfield Estate. She didn't want that information falling into Dorothea's hands. There was no knowing how the ruthless woman might try to use it.

No one came near her – not even Jane, which surprised her – and she left by the front door alone and friendless. She was giving up without a fight – she knew that and it was so totally unlike her – but she had the welfare of her child to think of and she couldn't risk him staying in this house another night. Her maternal instinct was at its strongest; she hardly cared what happened to her, but she must keep Charlie safe.

Unbeknown to her, a solitary little figure at a box-room window on the top floor of the house watched her go, tears running down his face.

Fifty-Five

By the time she reached the village street, she was soaked to the skin and cold and Charlie had begun to whimper. He was hungry; it was almost four hours since he'd last been fed. She dared not knock on anyone's door to seek help; she was sure that James's threat was real enough.

The church! She would take refuge in the church for the night, then tomorrow she would walk into town and somehow get to Meadow View Farm.

She had passed by the shops and one or two cottages and the church gate was in sight, when she heard a voice behind her calling, 'M'lady, m'lady, wait.' Annabel shrank against the low wall in front of one of the cottages, hoping that, through the rain, whoever it was who was coming after her would not see her. But the figure came on, hurrying towards her. And then she saw that it was Nancy.

'Oh m'lady, we've been watching out for you. His lordship told us what he was doing and we won't see you put out into the night like this. Not you and your baby. Come back with me. You stay with us tonight and then tomorrow, Jabez has said, he will drive you to your folks' place.'

'I can't,' Annabel said, the rain now mingling with the tears running down her face. 'He will evict you all if you help me. I mustn't involve anyone from the village – or the farms.'

395

'We'll worry about that later, m'lady, but for now, you're coming back with me.' She took firm hold of Annabel's arm. 'You really think that after what you've done for all of us, any one of us wouldn't lift a finger to help you?' And then, strangely, Nancy echoed James's words. 'If you do, begging your pardon, m'lady, then you don't know us at all.'

Without the strength to resist any longer, Annabel allowed Nancy to lead her back along the street towards the rooms above the grocer's shop. Not only were Agnes and Bertie waiting for them, but also Jabez and Josh were there and so, too, was Ozzy Greenwood, the grocer and owner of the rooms now occupied by Nancy, her mother and son. And, much to Annabel's consternation, Harry Jenkins was standing behind them, an anxious expression on his face.

When Annabel had been settled near the blazing fire and Agnes had taken Charlie from her arms and was now crooning to him, Nancy went to Harry and put her hand on his arm. 'You go now, love, and remember, you haven't seen any of this.'

Harry frowned. 'I don't like being disloyal to the captain, but . . .' He stopped and sighed heavily. 'I can't understand why he's done this. He's not a bad man – not an unkind man – usually. He must really—'

'Just go,' Nancy said softly, but firmly. 'And please don't say a word. Not to anyone. If they do find out and there's trouble, we'll all say you left afore Lady Fairfield got here. All right?'

'I suppose – but I don't like it.'

'Nor do any of us,' Nancy said grimly.

Once the door had closed behind Harry and they heard his footsteps clattering down the stairs, everyone's attention turned to Annabel. Nancy knelt in front of her. 'Now, m'lady, you come into my bedroom and get out of them wet things. You'll be catching your death if you—'

'Charlie! Is Charlie—?'

'Your babby's fine. Mam'll see to him.'

'He needs feeding.'

'Then as soon as you're warm and dry, Mam'll bring him in to you and you can feed him in there. Come along now.'

As if she were leading a child, Nancy shepherded Annabel into her bedroom, helped her strip off her wet clothes and wrapped her in a warm dressing gown. 'It were a present from the vicar's wife. They've all been so good to us – everyone in the village – since we lost all our belongings. And you brought all that about, m'lady, so don't you worry about a thing. Jabez and Josh will take you wherever you want to go tomorrow and Jim Chadwick and Adam Cartwright have offered too. *And* the Broughtons, would you believe?'

Annabel's eyes filled with tears. She could hardly believe it, but she was touched by their generosity and their daring. They were all risking losing their homes and livelihoods to help her.

That night, as Annabel readied herself for bed, though she doubted she would sleep a wink, there was a soft knock at the bedroom door. She opened it to find a wide-eyed Bertie standing there with the train which Theo had given him in his hands.

'I thought your little boy might like to play with this.'

'Oh darling.' Tears started in her eyes. 'How sweet of you, but he's too little to play with toys.'

'That's what Mammy said.' He was thoughtful for a moment then said, 'Wait a minute,' before darting into his tiny bedroom. Annabel waited, mystified as she heard him rooting through drawers and opening and shutting a cupboard door. In a moment, he was back holding out a knitted rabbit. 'Perhaps he'd like this. Grandma knitted it for me when I was born. I was holding it when – when Uncle Harry carried me out of the fire. It's the only toy I have left from before. His name's Hoppy.'

Annabel squatted down so that her face was on a level with his. 'But it's yours, darling. Surely, you don't want to part with it, especially—'

'I'd like your baby to have it, m'lady. Truly.'

Unseen by either of them, Nancy had come up quietly behind Bertie. 'Please take it, my lady. We'd really like Master Charlie to have it. I know it's nothing special, but it's been washed and mended since the fire.'

Gently, Annabel took the proffered toy and stood up slowly. 'That's where you're wrong, Nancy,' she said, with a catch in her voice, 'it's very, very special. Charlie will love it and I will tell him when he's older what a very special little boy gave it to him. Thank you, Bertie.'

After Annabel had spent a restless night in Nancy's bed at the young woman's insistence, she was roused by a loud knocking at the back door of Ozzy's premises – the door that led up to Nancy's rooms. She trembled with fear. Had James come to turn them all out? She scrambled out of bed and ran to the window, but in the yard below she saw a gathering of people: Jim Chadwick, Adam Cartwright, William Broughton and his mother, Lily, and several of the folk who lived in the cottages lining the village street. Swiftly, she put on the dressing gown and hurried into the living room.

'They mustn't come in. If James finds out, he'll—' she began, but it was too late. Footsteps were already on the stairs and as many as could do were crowding into Nancy's parlour.

'This is a right how-d'you-do, m'lady,' Jim began. 'Whatever is yon man thinking of? Now, is there owt we can do to help you?'

With panic in her voice, Annabel said, 'You can't – you mustn't – you shouldn't even be here. He'll do what he threatened. He—'

'Don't you worry about us, m'lady. We just want to get you to safety. To your grandfather's farm, I take it?'

'I –' Annabel began, but then she stopped. What else could she do but accept their offer? She nodded miserably. 'I shouldn't let you.'

'After all you've done for all of us, it's the very least we can do. Now, before anyone's likely to come down from the big house, as soon as you're dressed and have had some breakfast, we'll be on our way.'

'Jabez said he'd take her,' Nancy put in.

'Did he? Oh right, then, Nancy, I'll not interfere if it's all arranged. But you just let me know if there's owt I can do. Owt any of us can do, 'cos we're willing.'

'There is just one thing,' Annabel said hesitantly.

'Just name it,' Jim said.

'I'm concerned about Jane. I – I saw no one before I left. And I just want to know that she's – she's all right.'

'We'll find out for you, m'lady. I expect she'll want to come to you and if she does, then I'll bring her.'

A little later, after Charlie had been fed and Annabel had struggled to eat a little breakfast, they set out, with

Josh driving and Jabez sitting beside Annabel in the pony and trap that she had bought for all the villagers. But she had never envisaged it would be put to such a use.

When the trap drew into Edward's farmyard, she almost fell out of it in her haste to see her grandparents. Tenderly, Jabez handed her baby to her and then climbed down himself. Josh stayed with the pony, whilst Jabez went to the back door of the house. His knock was answered by Martha, who smiled widely when she saw Annabel. 'Oh how lovely! We were only saying yesterday that we ought to—' She stopped mid-sentence as if suddenly realizing that something was very wrong. She frowned. 'What's happened?'

Leading them into the kitchen, she held out her arms for her great-grandson and soothed his whimpering. 'There, there, my little one.' Then she turned back to Annabel and Jabez, a question in her eyes.

Annabel sat down in the chair by the fire and sighed. She leaned her head back against the chair and closed her eyes, suddenly overcome with a dreadful weariness. She felt as if she were in a bad dream – a nightmare. Had it really happened? Had James really turned her out?

Jabez was already explaining to a shocked Martha. 'I take it you already know about the accusations that have been levelled against Ben Jackson and Lady Fairfield?'

Wordlessly, Martha nodded.

'Well, it seems that when his lordship saw the little chap with his fair colouring, he didn't believe it could possibly be his son – his family are all dark-haired and brown-eyed, y'know. Well, yesterday, he came round to all of us – every single person in the village – to tell us

400

that he was turning her out – her and her babby – and that if any of us had owt to do with her, he'd evict us an' all.' Jabez sniffed contemptuously. 'Let him try, that's all I can say.'

Martha was glancing from Jabez's face to Annabel's and back again, still unable to believe what she was hearing. 'And you mean he's done it? He's – he's turned her – you – out?'

'Last night – in the pouring rain,' Jabez went on. 'Luckily, we were watching out for her and Nancy and her mam took her in. She spent the night with them and this morning we all rallied round to bring her to you.'

Martha stared at him for a moment before saying quietly and sincerely, 'Thank you, Mr Fletcher.'

'You're more than welcome, Mrs Armstrong.' He looked down at Annabel's white face. 'She don't deserve that sort of treatment. But for her –' He gestured with his hand as he added, 'Well, you know.'

'I do, Mr Fletcher. I do, but you need worry no more. She's safe with us now. We'll look after her and –' She looked down again at the round little face of her great-grandson. 'Do you know, I don't even know his name. When Annabel wrote to us to tell us of his safe arrival she said she was still waiting for James to agree to a name for him.'

'It's Charles Edward,' Annabel murmured.

'Oh Annabel, your grandfather will be so thrilled.'

Edward was indeed overwhelmed to hold his great-grandson in his arms and to learn that the baby boy had been named after him, but more than that his anger was incandescent at James's treatment of his wife.

'This is disgraceful!' he stormed, only quietening his voice when the baby in his arms whimpered. 'Sorry, my little man, but it has to be said. What's to be done about it?'

'I don't think there's anything that can be done,' Annabel said flatly. She was tired, bone-weary from all the emotional upheaval, and now all she wanted to do was to care for her child and lock herself away from the world. 'He says he's going to take legal steps to disinherit Charlie.'

'Can he do that?'

'He seems to think so. The estate isn't entailed to the title anyway, so he can leave that to whomsoever he wishes. Theo, obviously. As for the title, I really don't know how that works.'

Edward and Martha glanced at one another, but it was Martha who voiced what they were both thinking. 'You must come here and live with us. We'll take care of you.'

'Are you sure? You can hardly want a screaming baby in the house again at your age.'

'At our age! Hark at her. We're not in our dotage yet, my girl.' Edward smiled, the anger in his eyes dying. 'Besides –' he gestured with his head towards his wife – 'your gran will be in her element with a little one about the house again.'

For the first time in days, Annabel smiled.

Jane arrived late the following afternoon, with trunks and boxes loaded onto Jim Chadwick's farm cart. She jumped down and rushed towards Annabel, her arms wide. 'Oh miss, thank goodness you're safe. None of us knew where you'd gone. They wouldn't tell us. I was frantic with worry, but his lordship told us that if any of us went after you, he'd have us all sent to the workhouse. I wanted to come, miss, but I couldn't put them all in danger again.'

'Of course not,' Annabel said, hugging her. 'But how have you got away today – and with all my things too? How has he allowed that?'

'He's gone back to his regiment and Harry Jenkins with him. When he'd gone, Lady Dorothea came down to the kitchen herself and told me to pack up everything that was yours. She actually stood watching me all the time I did it, just to make sure I didn't steal owt, I suppose. "I hope you haven't missed anything," she said, "I don't want a trace of that woman left in this house." And then she ordered Thomas Salt to take down your portrait from the dining room and burn it.' Jane pulled a face. 'But I expect she'll hang on to all the money you've given them, won't she, miss?'

Edward put a comforting arm around the girl's shoulders. 'We don't care about the money, Jane, just so long as you're all safe. Now, come along in and have something to eat. You too, Jim, before you go back.'

They sat around Martha's big kitchen table, though none of them could do justice to the tea she placed before them as their conversation naturally dwelt on the appalling events of the past thirty-six hours.

'I still can't believe it all,' Jim said. 'I reckon they're a bit touched, if you ask me, specially her – Lady Dorothea. But I can't understand his lordship believing her tales. But then, I reckon there's a touch of madness – or badness – in them somewhere. Look at Albert and his goings on and the callous way he treated poor Nancy Banks. Mind you, the old man was a real gentleman and Lady Fairfield – the old lady, that is – is a lovely woman.'

'Do you know how she is, Jane?' Annabel asked. 'I was sorry to leave without seeing her – and Theo.'

'She took to her room and refused to come down to any meals and Annie said that Master Theo was crying that much – he'd watched you leave, miss – his mother shut him in his bedroom and told him not to come out until he'd "stopped making that silly noise".'

'Oh dear. Poor little boy. He won't understand why I left so suddenly. He – he'll think I've just deserted him.'

'He'll understand one day, m'lady, when he's older,' Jim promised. 'We'll make sure of that – somehow.'

Annabel smiled weakly, but her heart was breaking as she thought about the lonely little boy and Lady Fairfield too. She'd been very fond of both of them, but she was banned from seeing them now.

'Well, Jane, are you ready?' Jim said. 'I'd best be off. Me cows'll be bursting their udders.'

Jane's eyes widened. 'Oh, I'm not coming back. I brought all me bits and pieces with me. I'm never going back to that house again. If Miss Annabel doesn't need me any more, I'll go home and then try to get work somewhere else.'

'There's no need,' Martha said promptly before anyone else could speak. 'You're needed – and wanted – here, Jane. There's plenty of work for you, helping to care for Charlie and, if you don't mind, working in the dairy, then I can teach you –'

She glanced at Jane's beaming face as the girl said, 'I used to help me mam in our dairy at home. I love the work.'

'That's settled, then,' Martha said firmly.

'So it seems,' Edward agreed, but he was smiling as he said it.

Fifty-Six

There were no repercussions against the villagers who had helped Annabel. Either those at the big house had not heard, or they had chosen to ignore it. Annabel was safely gone and would never – if Dorothea had any say – return. Her name was never mentioned in Dorothea's hearing, though Lady Elizabeth and Theo whispered about her when they visited the walled garden together, Elizabeth to wander amongst the flowerbeds and discuss with Thomas Salt what should be planted and where, Theo to play up and down the paths between the borders, his only playmate now the younger gardener, Gregory Merriman. There grew a special bond between Elizabeth and the only grandson left to her. In their loneliness they drew comfort from each other and it was she who explained gently to the puzzled little boy why Annabel had left so suddenly.

'Grown-ups have silly fallings-out sometimes,' she told him, 'and I'm afraid your uncle James doesn't wish to be married to Annabel any longer.'

'Why? She's very pretty and kind and I – I liked her.' Young though he was, he forbore to say the word 'loved', though that is what he'd felt for Annabel. He was rather afraid he'd loved Annabel more than he loved his own mother, but he felt that would be a wicked thing to say aloud.

'I know, my dear, so did I and I don't want you to

405

blame her at all. Men can be very foolish at times.' She was silent for a moment, remembering her elder son, Albert. Oh, how very foolish he'd been. In a way, this was all his fault. If he had followed in his father's worthy footsteps, none of this trouble would have happened. She sighed and repeated, 'Just so long as you never blame your poor Aunt Annabel.'

It would be several years before Theo saw Annabel again, though Bertie Banks was luckier. He too had been entranced by her and often pleaded with his mother that they should make the journey in the communal pony and trap to visit her at Meadow View Farm. As he grew older, he learned that Jim Chadwick visited the Armstrongs' farm regularly and he would beg a ride with him. His welcome at Meadow View Farm was always assured and he enjoyed playing with the growing Charlie and delighted in seeing that the toy that had once been his was Charlie's favourite possession. He carried it everywhere with him and Annabel told him laughingly that if Hoppy was missing at bedtime, Charlie wouldn't go to sleep until he was found.

Shortly after her arrival at Meadow View Farm, Annabel's parents paid a visit. Her father was incensed by what had happened. 'I have received another letter from Lady Dorothy that you have run away from Fairfield Hall – that you have abandoned your husband and abducted the child.'

'None of that is true, Father. James turned us both out because Dorothea convinced him that Charlie is not his son – just because he has fair hair and blue eyes. I tried to tell him that there was such colouring in my family, but he wouldn't listen.'

'Then you should have convinced him. Women have their ways of persuading a man.'

Annabel glared at him, knowing exactly what he was meaning. 'My feminine wiles were lost on him.'

'You didn't try hard enough. You should have – seduced him.'

Martha gasped and Edward intervened. 'That's enough, Constantine.'

Ambrose rounded on him. 'It's not nearly enough. She'd no business leaving him. Dorothea says he's taking steps to disinherit the boy. He will never inherit the estate or' – he added emphatically – 'the title.'

'Aye,' Edward said, 'that's all that bothers you, isn't it? You're not really concerned about Annabel's happiness – just her status that will reflect glory on you.'

'I wanted a position in life for my grandson and she has lost that by her dalliance with another man.'

'You still believe that after she has given you her word?'

'There's no smoke without fire,' Ambrose muttered.

Until this moment, Sarah had said nothing, but now she said coldly, 'No, actually we don't believe her. People of the Lyndons' class in society don't tell such lies. James would have been proud to have had a son of his own to inherit the title. I agree with Ambrose. He must have had good cause to believe that the child was not his. And like your father says, Annabel, you should have tried harder to convince him.'

Anger rose in Annabel now and she turned to her mother. 'With my "feminine wiles"?'

'Men have their needs. You should have made use of that.'

'His "needs" are well satisfied by his mistress in London. Your dear friend, Lady Cynthia Carruthers. The woman who brought us together in the first place.' She turned back to her father. 'And how much did you pay *her* to bring about the marriage?'

Colour flooded Ambrose's face and he avoided meeting her gaze. 'Ah, I thought as much,' Annabel said softly. 'Well, I am sorry that things haven't turned out the way you wanted and I'm even sorrier that you choose to believe the Lyndons and not your own daughter. But if that's the way it is, then so be it.'

Ambrose recovered sufficiently to jab his forefinger towards her and say, 'You will go back to your husband and take up your rightful place at Fairfield Hall. I will not see all my plans go up in flames because of you. If you don't do as I say, I will disown you – and your son. You will get nothing from me.'

There was a shocked silence in the room. Edward moved to put his arm around his granddaughter's shoulders. Quietly, he said, 'She has no need of your money, Constantine. She has all she needs here. This farm has already been transferred to her name.'

Ambrose looked as if he were about to explode. 'A woman as a farmer? Whoever heard of such a thing?'

'It isn't seemly,' Sarah said with tight, disapproving lips. 'She will be a laughing stock.'

'That she will most certainly not be,' Edward countered. 'She is already taking over the reins and is making a good job of it.'

'And I suppose this feller you had an affair with will be joining you here when the dust has settled.' Ambrose glanced around as if looking for someone, his tone sarcastic as he added, 'Unless, of course, he's already here.'

'No, he isn't.' Edward answered for her. 'Nor will he be. Annabel hasn't seen Ben Jackson since the day he was dismissed from Fairfield.' He did not add 'nor will she' for in his heart he hoped that one day, somehow, Ben and Annabel might be reunited for he had seen for himself the love the man had for her. But for now, he kept silent.

'So,' Ambrose said at last, 'you are refusing to go back?'

'Father,' Annabel tried to reason with him. 'You don't seem to understand. I fear for Charlie's safety. There's no knowing what Dorothea might do.'

'You're hysterical and talking nonsense. I've heard of it happening following childbirth. How can you accuse a real lady of such things?'

'She's not going back,' Edward said firmly. 'She's staying here with us.'

'Aye, that's what you want, isn't it? It's what you've always wanted. Well, if you refuse to do your duty and return to your husband, Annabel, I want no more to do with you. Come, Sarah, we're leaving.'

For a moment, Sarah hesitated. She looked at her daughter and then at her parents, but then she dropped her gaze and followed her husband.

Annabel had settled into her life at Meadow View Farm. She discarded her fancy clothes and wore those of a typical farmer's wife, but she was happy, happier than she'd ever been at Fairfield Hall. And yet, she still ached for her lost love. It was hard to realize that it had not been the real James Lyndon she had loved for she knew now that he was not the man she'd believed him to be. At first, his hints of jealousy had delighted her, making her feel treasured, but they had become obsessive and twisted, born out of possessiveness, not love. Given time, those hurts would heal and now, her only real sadness was that she couldn't see Ben, though she heard through Jane when she visited her parents that he was well.

'Dad and Mam think the world of him and,' Jane told her, 'Mr Jackson asked me how you were. I told him about all that had happened and he said he wished he could come and see you, but he thought it best not to.' With sorrow in her heart, Annabel had to agree. If word got back to Fairfield that she and Ben were meeting, the rumours would not only start again, but might be validated.

The years stretched ahead of her, filled with caring for her child and her grandparents, too, as they got older, and running Meadow View Farm. It was a life with which she could – and would – be content, but there would be someone missing of whom she now realized she had become very fond. Sadly, she decided that she could not see Ben again.

Fifty-Seven

September 1906

'Theo, come here a moment. The new boys are arriving.'

Bertie was standing near the window of the dormitory at the boys' boarding school they now both attended, looking down on to the front driveway at the start of the new academic year. Despite the trouble, Annabel had kept her promise to Dorothea; even though the woman didn't deserve her help any longer, Theo did. He deserved a good education. But the following year after Theo had started at boarding school, Annabel had enrolled Bertie Banks there too, she hoped unbeknown to Dorothea.

'Mama hardly ever visits, but if she does, you'll have to make yourself scarce, old chap,' Theo had told Bertie when he'd arrived at the school, white-face and fearful of the taunts he expected to face. But he had reckoned without the support of Theo, older by six months. Theo was delighted the boy had come and proudly introduced him at once as his cousin. Questions as to the different surname were never asked though one or two of the masters raised their eyebrows and regarded the boy thoughtfully. Whispered talk in the staffroom – out of the hearing of the formidable headmaster, Mr Roper – had revealed that Theo was the heir to the title of

411

Earl of Fairfield and, they presumed, to the estate too.

'There was some scandal attached to that family,' one said, 'but I can't quite remember what it was.'

'All I've read about the Lyndons is that the present earl fought in the Boer War. He was out of the country for months on end, years possibly. God alone knows what happened to the estate in his absence.'

But God was not alone in caring for the Fairfield Estate and everyone on it. When James had known that he was to be sent to Africa, he had employed a new farm bailiff – Jim Chadwick.

'Do you think you can keep an eye on Home Farm and the whole estate as well as manage your own farm, Chadwick?' James had asked. 'You will be well recompensed, but I need someone I can trust.'

The offer had been a surprise and whilst Jim was doubtful whether he'd see anything in the way of 'recompense', he thought quickly what this could mean. 'Aye, m'lord, I'd be glad to. I've good lads working for me on my farm now, so running me own farm alongside looking after the estate'd be no problem for me. And we've got good tenant farmers.'

'That's settled then,' James had said and a few days later when he left to go to war, Jim had chuckled as he said to his wife, Mary, 'Good job he doesn't know what I intend.'

Mary paused in kneading the dough on her kitchen table and stared at him, the question in her eyes.

'I intend,' Jim explained, 'to keep in touch with Lady Annabel. Oh, she won't be able to come here, of course, but I know she'll give me good advice if I need it.'

'Does anyone know that you still see her now and then?'

'Oh yes, but not one of them will say owt. Besides,

I don't see her in person that often, but I see her grand-father most weeks on market day in town. And, of course, I hear about her.'

'But you go every so often to the farm to take her the money. They all know that.'

'That's true,' Jim had said. All those whom Annabel had helped financially were now making regular repay-ments to her, handing their hard-earned cash to Jim Chadwick, chosen by all of them to take the money to Annabel.

'And Ben Jackson? Do you ever see him?'

Sadly, Jim shook his head. 'No, not from the day I took him to Moffatts' farm.'

'Does Ben ever come to market?'

'No, Moffatt comes himself. But Ben's still working for him. I ask after him now and then. And when I do see her, Lady Annabel wants to know everything about what's happening here. She's not forgotten us.'

The estate continued to prosper. The number of live-stock had increased steadily and good harvests had brought a modest income back to Fairfield. New – affordable – rents had been set by James, following Jim's suggestions.

'And Dorothea?' Annabel had asked him. 'She didn't argue with that?'

Jim had shaken his head. 'I saw his lordship and we settled it between us. Proper contracts have been drawn up. Lady Dorothea can't touch us, but his lordship has given her free rein in the house, I understand.'

The big house, he told her, had been rejuvenated, the gardens were now immaculate and he'd heard from the folk working in the house that money had been spent on refurbishing every room. 'John Searby says every-thing's wonderful now, but they all miss you so much.

It's not the happy family home that you would have made it.'

Annabel had smiled wistfully at the compliment. How she would love to see the beautiful house just once more. But there was one piece of news that brought joy to Annabel on the day that Nancy and her mother came to Meadow View Farm.

'I hope you don't mind us coming, m'lady, but I wanted you to know. Me and Harry are getting married.'

'That's wonderful news, Nancy. Do come into the house and tell us all about it. Is Harry leaving the army?'

'No, no, m'lady, he doesn't want to leave the captain, but he'll get home whenever he can.'

When Nancy had told them her plans, she ended by saying, 'I'd so love you to come to the wedding, m'lady, but . . .' She stopped and bit her lip.

'No, Nancy,' Annabel told her gently. 'I'd love to be there, you know that, but I really can't.' The young woman looked relieved, as if the matter had troubled her. 'But I'll be thinking of you all on your big day,' Annabel went on. 'Never doubt that.'

So life had settled down into a routine, the years passed and soon it was time to consider Charlie's formal education too.

'What is it?' Theo said, coming to stand beside Bertie at the window.

'Look. See who's getting out of that carriage over there.'

'Oh my,' Theo whispered, 'it's – it's Aunt Annabel. And who's the boy with her? Surely, it's not . . .?'

'It is. It's Charlie. She must be bringing him to start school here too. Come on, let's go down.'

They clattered down the stairs ignoring warnings from any passing master to 'walk, boys, if you please', and ran out of the front door and onto the driveway, skidding to a halt in front of the newcomers.

Annabel looked at them and blinked. 'Oh Bertie and – and Theo. Oh my goodness!' She stretched out her arms towards them and, without a thought for decorum, they rushed to her, enveloping her in a bear hug, even knocking her huge hat with its fancy plumes slightly awry.

'How you've grown! Oh Theo, how lovely to see you.'

There were tears in the boy's eyes. He hadn't seen her since the night he had watched her walk away from him, down the driveway and out of his life. But he had never forgotten her and since meeting up with Bertie at school, he had asked about her constantly. Bertie, of course, had seen her often in the intervening years.

Now Annabel turned and drew Charlie forward. 'And this, Theo, is your cousin, Charlie.'

Theo grinned at the younger boy, who was looking very nervous. 'How do you do, Cousin Charlie?' Theo stuck out his right hand and shook the bewildered boy's hand firmly. 'We'll look after you, won't we, Bertie? Three cousins all together. What larks we'll have.'

Annabel chuckled inwardly, but secretly hoped that news of any 'larks' would not get back to Dorothea.

'Oh, they're cousins all right,' it was said in the staff-room when it was reported that there were now three boys connected in some way to the Lyndon family. 'Crowstone is the earl's sister's boy, Lyndon is the earl's son, though it's rumoured he's not to inherit, and Banks, well, he's the son of the present earl's older brother who died. Wrong side of the blanket and all that.'

Eyebrows shot up. 'And Roper has admitted him to the school?'

'Now, who in their right mind could resist Lady Annabel? It was she who brought him. And besides,' the speaker lowered his voice, 'I think a handsome donation to the school exchanged hands on his admittance. By all accounts it's her we have to thank for the new library.' He winked and tapped the side of his nose. 'And now her own son is here too.'

'Mm, they'll need watching. I smell trouble from those three.'

But the master's pessimism was misplaced. True the boys were high spirited and mischievous, but no more so than any other boy in the school.

When Annabel had left that first day, Theo and Bertie had escorted their young cousin to the dormitory he was to share with nine other boys. 'You let us know if anyone bullies you. We'll sort 'em out,' Theo promised.

'I expect they might tease me about this,' Charlie laughed, still a little nervous, but he was growing in confidence now that he had the support of his two cousins. He held up the knitted rabbit that Bertie had given him. It was worn now, but worn through being loved and cherished. Annabel had mended it carefully more than once.

The two older boys stared at the woollen toy.

'It's Hoppy!' Bertie grinned. 'You kept him all this time.' His face sobered. 'But I'd keep him hidden, if I were you.'

Charlie settled in quickly. He missed his mother and great-grandparents dreadfully and he worried that something might happen to one of the older ones whilst he was away. But both Edward and Martha, now seventy-six and seventy-five respectively, were still in remarkably good health and Charlie's entry into boarding-school life was undoubtedly eased by the presence of his older cousins. Word soon went around the school: 'Don't touch young Lyndon, else you'll have Crowstone and Banks after you.'

Meadow View Farm seemed strangely quiet without Charlie and Annabel wandered through the house and farmyard for some weeks quite lost without him.

'Tis for the best, my lovely,' Edward consoled her, though he was missing the boy just as much and Martha shed tears every day. 'He needs to go to a good school and be with other boys. The time will soon pass.'

But it didn't for Annabel; it passed all too slowly and she found herself counting the days until the next school holiday.

She had heard nothing from her husband. She presumed he had not divorced her for desertion or she would have known. Nor did she know if he had taken any action about disowning and disinheriting Charlie. All she knew was that it was generally accepted that Theodore Crowstone was the Earl of Fairfield's heir.

Fifty-Eight

Of course, it was bound to happen one day. As Theo had told Bertie, his mother, Dorothea, rarely visited, but when, a year after Charlie's arrival, Theo made the mistake of doing so well in his term work and examinations that he earned the form prize for that year, Dorothea determined to attend the school's Speech Day to see him receive his book prize.

'There's not a lot we can do to keep you two hidden.' Theo wrinkled his brow. 'If it'd been Sports' Day, we might have managed to keep you out of her way, but as the whole school attends Speech Day, there's no chance.' He turned to Charlie. 'Is your mother coming?'

Charlie shook his head. 'No. She said that because you're receiving a prize, she knew your mother would want to come this year and she didn't want anything to happen to spoil your day.'

Theo sighed heavily as he murmured, 'I'd have liked her to be here, though.'

'Best not, eh?' Charlie said softly.

'Should we pretend to be ill?' Bertie suggested. 'Matron'd keep us in the sickbay, wouldn't she?'

'I doubt it, unless she thought you'd got something contagious. Old Roper expects us all to attend even if we have to crawl there.'

And so the three boys took their places with the rest of the three hundred or so pupils in the school's vast

418

hall. Parents and visitors sat at the back. Bertie and Charlie were nervous, fearing a confrontation, but Theo seemed remarkably relaxed.

'Have you got a plan, Theo?' Bertie whispered as they filed into the hall.

Theo chuckled. 'You could say that.'

'No talking,' came the stern voice of their form master. 'Crowstone, you must sit at the end of the row, since you are to go up on stage.'

After what seemed an age, after the school hymn had been sung, the headmaster had given his annual report and the guest speaker had given his address, it was at last time for the pupils to receive their prizes.

When his turn came, Theo marched proudly up to the stage as his name was read out, shook the speaker's hand and received his prize as they had all rehearsed the previous afternoon. Returning to his place beside Bertie, he winked at his cousin.

At the end of the prize giving, the speaker asked the headmaster to allow the whole school an extra half-day holiday, as was customary on such occasions. When Mr Roper smiled and inclined his head, the whole school cheered. When the noise died away, the headmaster rose and instructed the school to be dismissed but added, 'Will the prize-winners and their families please remain behind. Afternoon tea will be provided in the canteen.'

As Bertie made to leave, Theo grabbed his arm. 'You're staying, old chap. And where's Charlie?'

'We – we can't stay, Theo.'

'Yes, you can, you're my family.'

'But your mother . . .'

'There's nothing Mama can say or do about it. And it's high time she knew. We're friends – the three of us – as well as cousins.'

'But—'

'Ah, there's Charlie. Charlie, Charlie – over here.'

'Less noise, Crowstone,' a master hissed, but Theo only turned an innocent gaze upon him. 'I'm just collecting my family together, sir, as the headmaster instructed.' The teacher frowned, but could say nothing. Theo, turning to his cousins, added, 'Come along, let's go and find this afternoon tea.'

Bertie and Charlie glanced unhappily at each other, but trailed after their older cousin. When Theo was on a mission, nothing they could say would dissuade him. Bertie squeezed the younger boy's arm. 'It'll be all right, Charlie.'

But Charlie wasn't so sure.

It had only been during the previous school holiday that he had learned about the family feud. His grandfather had taken him for a long walk in the fields to explain it all to him. 'You're almost ten now, Charlie, and it's high time you understood a little more about your family.' So, very gently, Edward told his great-grandson all that had happened ending, 'But I want you to understand that none of it was your mother's fault. She was wrongly accused of having an affair with another man other than her husband. You know what I mean by that, don't you?'

Charlie had nodded.

'Your mother is a wonderful, caring and loyal woman. She would never have done such a thing, but your aunt is – I'm sorry to say – so ambitious for her own son to inherit that she has spread these scurrilous rumours about your poor mother. And, sadly, your father has believed her.'

Charlie had looked up at Edward and, with a wisdom far beyond his tender years, said, soberly, 'I expect my father didn't really have much time to get to know my mother properly. You said they didn't get much time to spend together even after they were married, did they? And he'd believe his sister, wouldn't he?'

'That's about the size of it, my boy.'

Charlie was silent for several moments before asking, hesitantly, 'Do you think maybe Aunt Dorothea really did believe it or that she was being deliberately nasty so that Theo would inherit?'

'That's a difficult one to answer, Charlie.' Edward knew the answer to that, but even now he didn't want to set the boy entirely against his own father by telling him that Dorothea's lies had fed the man's obsessive jealousy. But he was startled by the young boy's intuitive question. 'Your cousin, Theo – has he said anything to you about all this?'

Charlie shook his head. 'Not about that, no, but he's always asking about Mother and whenever she comes to school he's the first to reach her.' He grinned. 'He beats both me and Bertie.'

Edward chuckled. 'So, there's no animosity between you and your cousins?'

'None at all. We're great pals. Always have been and I don't think anything will alter that,' Charlie had answered confidently.

But now, as Charlie followed Theo into the school canteen where parents waited to greet their offspring, he was trembling. And, beside him, Bertie seemed just as anxious. They were both to meet the formidable woman for the first time that they could remember.

Fifty-Nine

Dorothea was smiling as the three boys approached her, her gaze alighting and remaining on her son. 'My darling boy,' she gushed. 'How proud I am of you. And are these two of your friends?'

Dutifully, Theo kissed his mother's cheek and then turned to make the introductions. 'They are, Mama, but they're also my cousins.' He gestured towards each of them in turn. 'Bertie and Charlie.'

Dorothea's face was thunderous as she stared at them both. 'What – are – they doing in – this school? They have no right to be here, especially' – she glared at Bertie – '*him*! I shall have words with the headmaster.'

Theo shrugged with deliberate nonchalance. 'Their fees are paid.' He paused and looked his mother in the eyes as he added quietly, 'By the same person who pays mine.'

Her face turned purple and she opened and closed her mouth, fishlike, two or three times before grabbing Theo by the arm and hauling him away from the other two boys, but not far enough so that they couldn't hear her words. 'You will not associate with them in any way. Do you hear me?'

'I hear you, Mama, but I'm afraid that is not possible in a school of this size. Besides, they are my friends – my best friends – and I intend it to remain that way.'

Dorothea gasped. 'You are wilfully disobeying me?'

'If you choose to see it that way, then, yes, I am.'

'How dare you?'

'I dare because I know that you have been unfair to both Aunt Annabel and especially to Charlie. He is Uncle James's son.'

'How dare you?' she began again, but Theo went on, 'Just look at him, Mama, really look at him. He's a Lyndon all right. He has brown hair like me and his eyes and the shape of his nose are just like Uncle James's.'

'Be quiet, you stupid boy. Don't you realize what you're saying? You're throwing away your inheritance – everything I've worked for . . .'

Theo calmly raised his eyebrows. He was behaving like a boy far older than his sixteen years. Standing up to his mother was not easy but he had promised himself he would do it. He hadn't wanted it to happen yet, but circumstances had forced him to take a stand now and really, he thought, perhaps the sooner she knew his thoughts and feelings, the better.

But she was still adamant in her scheming. 'You are the rightful heir to the Earl of Fairfield and the estate. Just you remember that. Not that – that woman's bastard. He is *not* your uncle's son. He will be disinherited.'

Theo stared at his mother. 'So,' he said slowly, 'Charlie's not been disinherited yet, then?'

'Steps are being taken, I promise you. But – it's difficult.'

Theo shook his head. 'But I don't want to inherit something that isn't rightfully mine.'

Her grip tightened until her strong fingers were hurting his arm, but he steeled himself not to flinch. 'It *is* yours. I've raised you to know your place in the world. *You* are the next Earl of Fairfield.'

423

Theo shook his head and said softly. 'No, Mama, I am not. I know it and – so do you.' With a mature composure that Dorothea had never seen in her son before, Theo faced her with a steady gaze. She almost flung him away from her and turned away, marching angrily towards the door out of the canteen. As she passed close to a master, she almost shouted at him. 'I wish to see the headmaster. *Now!*'

The three boys, standing together, watched her leave the room, ushered out by a puzzled and somewhat worried master.

'Oh dear, what do you think she'll say to him?'

'No more than he already knows, I shouldn't think,' Theo said, seemingly unperturbed by the confrontation with his mother. He laughed and put his arms around the shoulders of his two cousins. 'Come on, let's go and find some of this tea and cakes they've been promising us.'

Moments later, Theo was piling his plate high with sandwiches and cakes but the other two found that their usual healthy appetite had utterly deserted them.

Over the next few days the three boys awaited the summons from the headmaster, but it never came and at the end of the autumn term they travelled home separately. Luke arrived in the carriage to take Theo home to Fairfield Hall, whilst Annabel came to pick up both Charlie and Bertie.

'Isn't it a bit silly that I'm going right past his door and yet you have to go several miles out of your way to take Bertie home?' Theo remarked to Annabel when they met on the driveway in front of the school. Luke stood a short distance away, embarrassed at seeing his former mistress and unsure what he should do. But Annabel, ever mindful of the awkward position in which the people of Fairfield – and especially the servants at Fairfield Hall – found themselves, merely nodded and smiled at him before turning her attention back to the three boys and their luggage.

'I don't mind,' she said. 'But I'll drop Bertie off on the outskirts of the village as usual. I don't want to cause trouble. Now, let's get these trunks loaded.'

'Mam and Granny would love to see you,' Bertie said. 'You could come to our house. Couldn't she, Theo?'

After the older boy's stand against his mother, Bertie and Charlie had an even greater respect for their cousin. They'd always looked up to him, but now they were in awe of his bravery.

'I don't see why not. It's a free country, Aunt Annabel.'

'I'll think about it,' she promised as she kissed Theo's cheek and held him close for a few seconds. Far from being embarrassed, the boy hugged her in return. 'See you next term,' he said cheerfully, but as he turned towards Luke and the waiting carriage, he saw Bertie and Charlie struggling to lift their trunks onto the back of Annabel's carriage.

'Luke,' he called. 'Give us a hand, would you?' Annabel felt a little thrill as she heard Theo address the man by his Christian name and not by his surname as was the custom of the Lyndon family. Perhaps the boy was already beginning to make his own decisions, even though at the moment it was in small, but to Annabel significant, matters.

Luke hurried forward and lifted the trunks easily. Then he turned towards Annabel. ''Tis good to see you, m'lady. Are you keeping well?'

'I am, Luke, thank you. And how is everyone at Fairfield Hall?'

'All fine, m'lady, thank you. The old lady is rather frail now, though,' he added with a smile. 'Either me or Thomas take her to the garden when the weather's warm enough. She still manages to walk most times.'

Goodbyes were said again and soon the two carriages were bowling down the driveway and travelling for some distance in the same direction.

'Why did Luke call you "m'lady", Mother?' Charlie asked.

'Because I suppose, in his eyes, I am still Lady Fairfield.'

'And are you really?'

'Legally, probably, yes, but at home I don't choose to use the title.'

Charlie and Bertie glanced at each other, silently asking the same question. Shall we tell her what happened? Charlie gave a little nod and together they recounted the confrontation between Theo and his mother.

'Oh dear,' Annabel said worriedly, when they had finished their tale, 'I do hope Theo won't be in dreadful trouble when he gets home.'

Sixty

Dorothea would never forget what had happened. It still rankled and made her nag James all the more to move things forward.

'It's time you took legal advice, James. I don't know why you're procrastinating. Annabel left you. You have every right to divorce her for desertion. And you should take steps to disinherit her bastard son.' James flinched, but Dorothea was not done yet. 'Can't you take it to the courts or even to the House of Lords? There must be *some* way to stop someone from inheriting a peerage to which they have no right.'

James was torn. His longstanding affair with Lady Cynthia had withered and died. They remained friends, but hardly ever saw each other. Now, there was nothing in his life except the Army. He still could not summon up enough interest in the estate to take an active part and as long as Jim Chadwick ran things satisfactorily and the estate was prospering – which he did and it was – James saw no reason to give up the life he loved. But to his surprise, he missed Annabel. Even after all this time, he almost expected her to be there waiting for him when he came home on leave and, despite the relatively short time they'd spent together, he realized that she had wound herself into his heart. He regretted his hasty decision in driving her out and he lamented the fact that he probably had a son and legitimate heir to his title and lands whom he'd refused to recognize. He was sorry that he'd allowed his sister to feed his jealousy with her tales. She had dominated him all his life – indeed, she had dominated both the brothers in their childhood even though she'd been two years younger than Albert. James sighed whenever he thought about it. It was such a pity Dorothea had not been born the eldest boy.

'I'll make some enquiries,' was all James would promise his sister and Dorothea clicked her tongue in exasperation. It was the only answer she ever got from him. Surely, after over ten years of separation something could be done? But the truth was, though Dorothea would not and could not face it, James didn't want to divorce Annabel.

'If you don't do something, James, that boy will fight for his inheritance when he comes of age. His mother will see to that.'

James raised his eyebrows. '*His* inheritance, you say?'

'You know what I mean,' she snapped, though she vowed to choose her words more carefully.

James refused to say more. Instead, he turned away, went to sit with his mother for an hour or so, had a brief chat with his nephew when he arrived home from school that afternoon, and then left to return to camp without another word to his sister.

Dorothea decided not to refer to the argument with her son and she greeted him as usual with the words, 'You have a long holiday before you. Don't let Christmas get in the way of your duty. Make sure you use the time wisely. Chadwick will take you around the estate and make sure he shows you the accounts.'

Theo smiled inwardly, happy to agree to his mother's demands. He regarded himself as custodian of the estate until such time as his cousin could take up his rightful place. It saddened Theo that Bertie, who Theo believed to be the rightful heir, could have no claim on it whatsoever. But there was something he could do for Bertie and he planned to start his campaign the very next day.

Early the following morning, he saddled the horse he used whenever he was home from school and rode down the long drive after breakfast and took the road leading to Blackbird Farm.

'Good morning, Mr Chadwick,' he greeted the farmer as he stepped into the byre where Jim and his farm workers were busy with the morning milking.

Jim, his forehead against the flank of a cow, twisted round to look at him. ''Morning, Master Theodore. What brings you here?' Jim stood up and carefully moved the full bucket of milk away from the cow's restless feet. As he saw the boy more clearly, he said, 'My, you've grown.'

'I was wondering if I might have a word with you, Mr Chadwick, but I don't want to interrupt your work.' Theo glanced longingly around the byre breathing in the smells and sounds of the milking shed.

'We're almost done. The lads can finish off. Would you like some breakfast?'

Whilst he'd already had his at home, the ride had made him hungry again and Theo said, 'That'd be very kind of you.'

'Come along then, Master Theodore, no doubt the wife can find enough for an extra mouth.' Briefly – as he often did – Jim remembered the time when they couldn't even feed themselves let alone an unexpected guest. He thought of Annabel almost every day and thanked the Good Lord for her timely arrival in their midst. Where would they all have been by now, he wondered, without her?

'Please, won't you just call me "Theo"?'

Jim paused a moment before saying, 'If that's what you want.'

'I do, especially,' he grinned, 'as I have a favour to ask.'

Jim chuckled as he opened the back door of the farmhouse and ushered Theo inside, calling, 'Mary, another one for breakfast.'

Mary Chadwick's eyes widened when she saw who their visitor was, but she made no fuss and merely placed more sausages and bacon into the frying pan, cut more bread and broke two eggs into a basin to cook last of all.

'Sit down, Master Theodore,' she said. 'You're very welcome.'

'Theo. Please call me "Theo".'

'Theo,' Jim began, 'has a favour to ask us. Go on, lad.'

'I was wondering if you could find work somewhere on the estate for Bertie Banks during the school holidays. And – and I'd like to help out too. I don't need to be paid,' he added swiftly, 'though I think perhaps Bertie might be glad of the money.'

Jim scratched his head. 'I don't see why not, Master – I mean, Theo. We can always use an extra pair of hands on the estate, especially on Home Farm.' The older man stared at the young boy wondering how much he knew – or understood – about the family feuding.

Theo returned his gaze steadily as he said quietly, 'I don't want to be treated any differently to any of your workers, Mr Chadwick, and certainly not as the future lord and master because – by rights – I shouldn't be.'

Mary almost dropped the plate of food as she placed it in front of him. She turned wide eyes to her husband for his guidance. Jim sat down at the table and picked up his own knife and fork as his two workers came in the back door, removing their boots before they padded to the table in just their thick socks.

Theo ate hungrily. 'This is wonderful, Mrs Chadwick. Mrs Parrish is a great cook but she never makes a breakfast quite like this. I love the fried bread.'

'So, Theo,' Jim said as he stood up when they had all finished eating and drinking a strong cup of tea, 'I'll take you around the other farms and see what's what.'

'Could we pick up Bertie from the village?'

'I don't see why not,' Jim said. It seemed to be one of his favourite sayings.

Theo began work the following day on Home Farm and Bertie was welcomed by Dan Broughton and his family.

'William'll show you around and tell you what he wants you to do. There's not a lot of work this time of year, but if you take to it, there'll be plenty in the Easter and summer holidays,' Dan said. 'And we'll be very glad of your help at harvest time.'

Throughout the Christmas holidays the two cousins worked on the estate whilst, unbeknown to them – though they might have guessed, if they'd thought about it – Charlie, too, was helping out on his grandfather's farm. He worked with the will, though perhaps not quite the physical strength, of a much older boy. And so the three cousins immersed themselves in the country way of life and grew to love it.

The following summer, Bertie begged his mother to allow him to leave school. 'I've already stayed on a lot longer than most village boys.'

'I'll have to talk to Lady Annabel,' Nancy said

worriedly. 'She's paid your school fees all these years. I don't want to offend her.'

So towards the end of the summer holidays of 1908, Nancy and Bertie climbed into the village's communal pony and trap and drove out of Fairfield, through the town and beyond it to Meadow View Farm.

When she saw them, Annabel flung her arms wide and embraced them both. 'Come in, come in. How lovely to see you.'

When they were seated in Martha's kitchen, Nancy said hesitantly, 'M'lady, we can never thank you enough for what you've done for us and Bertie would never have had such a good education if you hadn't sent him to that school, but – but—'

'I want to leave, Aunt Annabel. Mr Broughton says I can go and work on his farm full time. He's got bad rheumatism now and though he still does what he can, William can't cope on his own.'

'And is that what you want to do with your life, Bertie? Be a farmer?' Annabel asked quietly.

The boy's eyes shone. 'Oh yes, Aunt. I never want to do anything else and I never want to leave Fairfield.'

Annabel felt a lump in her throat. How unfair life was. Bertie would have been the perfect future earl and master of the estate and yet he never could be. She raised her eyes to meet Nancy's anxious gaze. 'What do you feel about this, Nancy?'

'He – he's done his best – he's worked hard – at school, m'lady, but he finds book learning hard. He's struggled to keep up with the other boys this last year.'

'I'd hoped Bertie might want to stay on longer – perhaps go to college or university.'

'He'd not be happy,' Nancy said softly.

'Then – if you're sure – I will write to Mr Roper

and tell him you won't be returning in September.'

'Oh thank you, Aunt Annabel,' Bertie cried and without a trace of embarrassment he flung his arms around her.

So, Bertie's future was settled, but Theo's was far from certain. He had no choice but to remain at school as his mother demanded. 'You're clever enough to go to university,' Dorothea declared. 'You could go to Oxford or Cambridge. It would be such a good grounding for a future earl. You must stay on an extra year and try.'

Theo said nothing. Dutifully, he returned to school and suffered another two years. The work was easy enough for the bright, intelligent boy, but he longed to be back home working alongside Bertie on the estate and for the first time in his life, he envied another. Charlie had no choice but to continue his education and he knew his mother would like him to go on to some form of further education. 'I'm not as clever as Theo,' he confided seriously. 'Wouldn't I be better working here on the farm? Gramps says that one day it will come to me.'

'Of course it will, my darling, but a good education is never wasted. At least, stay on until you are eighteen and then you can decide.'

But to the eleven-year-old boy, the grand old age of eighteen seemed a lifetime away.

Late in 1909, to please his mother, Theo sat the entrance examination to Oxford and was accepted at the prestigious university. He began a four-year course in the autumn of 1910 and graduated in the summer of 1914.

On 28 June, the same day that Archduke Franz Ferdinand of Austria and his wife, Sophie, were shot dead in Sarajevo, Theo came home to Fairfield Hall.

Sixty-One

'You know there's going to be a war, don't you?' Theo said to Bertie when they met in The Lyndon Arms after a long day in the fields. It was August Bank Holiday, but farm work on the estate had not stopped; cows still needed to be milked and livestock fed.

Bertie looked at him wide-eyed. 'I knew there was trouble on the continent – Mr Broughton was talking about it, but why should it involve us?'

'It's all very complicated,' Theo murmured.

'And you think I wouldn't understand it.'

'No, no, old chap, I wouldn't think that at all. Truth is' – he laughed drolly – 'I don't really understand it myself properly. It's all come about because of the arch-duke and his wife getting shot.'

'Ah,' Bertie said, hoping he sounded knowledgeable, but the truth was he had little interest in politics and even less in world affairs, which he didn't think affected him. But now, it seemed that the assassination of someone he'd not heard of before the man got himself shot might have a huge effect on all the young men of Bertie's country.

'It's all to do with complicated alliances,' Theo went on. 'The chaps at Oxford were full of it before we came down. Kaiser Bill wants his army to match those of France and Russia and he's jealous of Britain's navy. He's ambitious but we can't let him get too big for his boots. He's been building up his navy and that's a worry for us. He's only just a few miles across the sea. So, for the last few years we've been building more battleships too. He's upset France and Russia by strengthening his army, so we're thrown into bed with *them*. That's the military side of it, but then, there are the alliances.'

Bertie frowned in puzzlement.

'Germany's pally with Austria and Italy. That means that Britain, France and Russia have almost been forced into an alliance together. That's how I see it anyway.' Theo took a sip of his beer. 'And then, of course, there's the size of their empires that's a thorn in old Bill's side. Britain's covers about a quarter of the world, you know.'

Bertie's eyebrows shot up. 'Really?'

'And we're all competing for slices of Africa, grabbing land and wealth by building railroads and plantations. And then, of course,' he went on, 'there's national pride. You've got your larger nations that rule smaller ones and those under someone's thumb – like a lot of the Serbs are under Austria – want their freedom.'

Bertie shrugged. 'I suppose that's only natural. But how's it come to war?'

'I think – and, understand, it's only my opinion – that it's been brewing for years. It just needed a spark to light the conflagration.'

'And that was the shooting of the Austrian archduke, was it?'

Theo nodded. 'It seems like it. He was killed by a Serb and so a few days ago, Austria declared war on Serbia. Now, because of Germany's alliance with Austria, Serbia looked to Russia for help.'

'So that brings France in too, does it?'

Theo nodded. 'Germany declared war on Russia and then on France.'

'And you reckon that'll involve us too?'

Theo nodded soberly before emptying his glass and signalling for a refill. 'I've no doubt about it.'

'So – what should we do?'

'There's a recruiting rally in town on Friday. I was thinking of going. I want to listen to what they have to say.'

'They're a bit quick off the mark, aren't they?'

Theo shrugged. 'A pal of mine from Oxford wrote to say there have been posters up in London since July. He's thinking of enlisting.'

'Then I'll come with you to the rally,' Bertie said. 'But first, it's my round.'

Ben Jackson had not ventured into Thorpe St Michael very often during the years since his enforced departure from Fairfield, but on the morning he heard that a recruiting rally was to be held in the town, his curiosity and some vague ridiculous notion that he might be swept along on the tide of patriotic fervour and volunteer his services, lured him into accompanying Joe Moffatt to market.

The market that day, however, drew little interest and cattle stood miserably in the pens unsold, their owners even more unhappy. The focus of everyone's attention was on the war and the young men – and not so young men – marching off to fight.

'I hope you won't be volunteering, Ben. I can't do without my right-hand man.'

Ben pulled a face. 'I doubt they'd take an old man of forty-eight, do you?'

Joe flicked the reins and the horse moved forward. 'Might have to if it gets serious – and I reckon it will

– but you're right, it'll be all the youngsters who'll go.'

Ben did not reply. He was thinking about Annabel – as he still did every day of his life – trying to work out exactly how old her son would be now. Sixteen, he decided after some mental arithmetic, and he gave an inward sigh of relief. Charlie would be far too young to be accepted into the army. But what about the other two boys, Theo and Bertie? Theo, no doubt, would be kept at home by his mother – somehow she would engineer it – but Bertie might go. Bertie Banks might have to go eventually, even if he didn't volunteer now.

The town was busier than usual and an excitable crowd had gathered in front of the town hall where the recruiting rally was to take place. Every time a man in uniform appeared, they cheered enthusiastically. Joe and Ben stood to one side, but near enough to hear the speeches and see what was happening. Three officers stood on a hastily erected platform and when the first one stood up to speak, Ben drew in a sharp breath as he recognized him: James Lyndon, Earl of Fairfield. He ought to leave now, Ben thought, but he didn't want to be thought a coward by sneaking away before the call to arms had even begun. So he stayed where he was, but tried to keep out of sight from the dais.

James spoke eloquently, his obvious love for the army life dripping from every word. His patriotism shone through and even Ben, who heartily disliked the man, could not help but feel a grudging admiration for such dedication. Even before James had finished speaking, young men were pushing their way to the front of the crowd and mounting the steps into the town hall to 'take the King's shilling'. Each one was greeted with a roar of approval from the crowd. Right at the back, unseen by anyone who knew them, Theo, Bertie and

Charlie stood together. Charlie had driven in with his grandfather, who was at this moment pushing his way through the throng to speak to Ben.

'What do you think, old chap? Shall we do it?' Theo murmured to Bertie, hoping that Charlie would not hear.

'Not now. Not here. Your uncle would try to stop you, though' – Bertie laughed ruefully – 'I doubt he'd make the same effort for me.'

'Right then, we'll go to Lincoln. End of next week all right for you – at the crack of dawn on Friday morning? Will Mr Broughton let you have time off, d'you think, without asking too many questions?'

'I'll try. Where do we have to go?'

'I'm not sure. Probably the barracks on Burton Road. I'll pick you up in the brougham. I'll drive us there.'

Behind them, keeping very still and quiet so as not to draw attention to himself, Charlie listened to every word.

Another officer was now addressing the crowd and James was standing at the back, his gaze roaming over the gathering. His glance, trained to observe, picked out Ben Jackson standing with another man. And pushing his way towards them and greeting them both with a clap on the shoulder was an older man. James squinted. He couldn't be sure, for he had only met him once at the wedding, but he thought the old man was Annabel's grandfather. So, he thought, Jackson was not only still in the area, but also in contact with Annabel at the very least. No doubt they were still lovers, James thought morosely.

Any thoughts of reconciliation died in that instant and he resolved to do what his sister asked and begin proceedings – if it were possible – to disinherit Annabel's son. But his intentions were swept aside when Jenkins met him on the driveway on his return to Fairfield Hall.

'We're to return to barracks at once, sir.'

Sixty-Two

'What on earth are you doing here?'

Theo and Bertie gaped at Charlie who grinned back at them. 'I've come to join up, of course.'

'Oh no, you haven't,' Theo exploded. 'You're only sixteen.'

'I'm seventeen next month and I'll tell them I'm nearly eighteen. They'll take me then. They've taken Eddie Cartwright and he's only a year older than me.'

The two older boys glanced at each other, their faces grim. 'Well, we'll tell 'em,' Theo said. 'We'll tell the officer you're only sixteen.'

'We're not going to let you enlist, Charlie,' Bertie said softly. 'Your mam'd flay us alive if she found out we'd not stopped you.' They glanced at each other again, their shared affection for Annabel surfacing. 'And we – we can't bear to think of her being upset.'

'What about your mams?'

'Don't, Charlie. Don't remind us. We've *got* to go. We're twenty-two and twenty-three. We've no choice.

'Yes, you have,' Charlie countered, determined not to be outdone. 'You work the land. They're saying that maybe farm workers won't have to go. At least you could wait until they bring in conscription – if they do.'

'Oh, it'll not get to that,' Theo declared confidently.

Bertie's mouth was a thin, determined line as he muttered, 'We're going anyway.'

'Then so am I. I want to be a soldier like my father. I want to make him proud of me.' They stared at Charlie as he added falteringly, 'Even if he doesn't think I'm his.'

Theo squeezed Charlie's shoulder. 'We all know you're his son, Charlie. He's a fool to even think . . .' His voice faded away. He was treading on dangerous ground. He sighed as he said flatly, 'Come on, then. We'll join up together. Maybe they'll let us stay together – after all, we are first cousins – and we can keep an eye on you.'

'Wait a minute. Let's think this through,' Bertie said.

'Why? What's the matter?' They were already standing outside the barracks in the city.

'If we go in here, we all might get stopped. This is the headquarters – or whatever they call it – of the Lincolnshire Regiment, isn't it?'

'I expect so. That's what we want to join, isn't it?' Theo was mystified by Bertie's sudden reluctance.

'Well, yes, but as soon as they hear the name "Lyndon", somebody is going to recognize it.'

'Oh, I understand,' Theo said catching on quickly.

'I don't,' Charlie said.

They both turned to face him. 'They'll all know of your father. He's an officer. They'll not let you join for fear of reprisals from him.'

'And they'll likely know about me, too,' Theo said. 'I bet they'd make enquiries before they let me join.'

'And my middle name's Lyndon,' Bertie added.

'So – what can we do?'

The three young men were quiet for a moment before Charlie brightened as he said, 'Would Grimsby be far enough away, d'you think?'

'Grimsby? Why Grimsby?'

'They're forming a new battalion there. I know

because it was in my mother's newspaper. You know she was from Grimsby originally, don't you?' The other two glanced at each other and then shook their heads. 'My other grandparents still live there, I expect, though I never see them. My grandfather is a big trawler owner.'

'Never!' Theo exclaimed.

'Constantine,' Charlie told them. 'You must have heard of him.'

Theo's eyes widened. 'He's Aunt Annabel's father. Good heavens! Fancy that, and I never knew.'

'He's a big name in Grimsby now. Owns a whole fleet of trawlers. Anyway,' Charlie went on, returning to their original conversation, 'the newspaper said that the Mayor has posted notices throughout the town calling on the men of Grimsby to volunteer for a new battalion. Evidently, he has Kitchener's authority. We'd still be part of the Lincolnshire Regiment, but it would be a brand-new battalion and we'd be unlikely to run into anyone connected with my father.'

'What do you think?' Bertie said, looking at Theo.

'Sounds like a good idea to me, unless, of course, your name would be known there – because of your grandfather, I mean. Would he try to stop you going if he found out?'

'I doubt it,' Charlie said bitterly and he explained how Ambrose Constantine had refused to have anything more to do with his daughter and grandson when she had been forced to leave Fairfield Hall. 'Even if he heard about it, I don't think he'd be interested enough to interfere. He's never had anything to do with us. I can't remember ever meeting him, though I've seen pictures of him in the newspaper.'

Theo and Bertie said nothing but they were both thinking how unfairly the woman they called Aunt

Annabel had been treated, and not only by the Lyndons, it seemed.

'Come on, then, if we're going. Let's get the dirty deed done,' Bertie said.

They travelled to Grimsby together and found that they had to report to the Municipal College near to the Town Hall. They were to be part of a newly formed 'pals' battalion'. Lord Kitchener had given his blessing to the formation of such battalions from volunteers from a particular place or background with the belief that soldiers with a common bond would fight side by side, drawing a sense of security from friendships forged. So the three cousins were welcomed when they introduced themselves as such. In turn, they stepped forward to give their particulars. Just as they had feared, when the name Lyndon was spoken, a portly, civilian gentleman, standing behind the recruiting officer, moved forward. He had a curling moustache and was dressed in a smart black suit and bowler hat and sported a gold watch chain looped across his chest.

'What name did you say?' the man barked.

Before Charlie could answer, the captain said, 'Lyndon, Mr Constantine. Why, is there a problem?'

The man stared at Charlie, who, though his heart was beating rapidly, returned his gaze steadily, squaring his shoulders and standing tall. To Charlie's chagrin, it was not his grandfather who argued that the boy was underage, but Bertie, who stepped forward and said, 'He's only sixteen, sir, not eighteen.'

The captain glanced at Bertie and narrowed his eyes. 'Trying to get your cousin out of volunteering, are you? You'd have him believed a coward, would you?'

'No, sir, but—'

'Then stand back and wait your turn.'

Red-faced, Bertie turned away. Their only hope to have Charlie refused now lay with the man still staring at the boy.

The officer now turned back to the older man. 'Mr Constantine – is there a problem?'

Slowly, Ambrose shook his head. 'No – no problem. Sign him up.'

Charlie beamed with delight at him, but the older man turned away without acknowledging him and left the room. Charlie watched him go with a slight feeling of disappointment that his grandfather had not even spoken directly to him. But he was not surprised to see the man present at the recruiting centre; it was just the sort of thing in which Ambrose Constantine, who regarded himself as a pillar of the local community, would involve himself.

Charlie pondered whether or not he should tell his mother that he had seen him, but decided against it. Annabel might see it as a way of preventing his enlistment.

As they stepped out of the hall a little while later, slightly bemused by everything that had happened so quickly, Bertie said softly, 'And now, I suppose we'd better all go home and face the music.'

'Then we'll face it all together,' Theo said firmly. Bertie and Charlie glanced at each other. Whilst they'd be glad to have Theo's company when they broke the news to their respective families, neither of them had any wish to be present when Theo confronted Lady Dorothea.

*

443

They went first to Meadow View Farm.

'Better get the worst one over with first,' Theo said.

'Why's this going to be the worst?' Charlie asked. 'I'd've thought facing your mother would be far worse. She'll go off like a rocket.'

'No, no, I'd far rather face my mother than Aunt Annabel right at this moment.'

They found her in the kitchen of the farmhouse kneading bread, whilst her grandmother sat dozing near the range.

'Oh, how lovely to see you all,' Annabel exclaimed, dusting the flour from her hands. But then she caught sight of their serious faces and realized that this was no ordinary visit. Jane, coming in from the pantry, smiled at the visitors and hurried to make tea for them all.

'Where's Gramps?' Charlie asked. He had always called his great-grandparents by the same names that his mother did.

'In the front room, having an afternoon nap.' Annabel's glance was searching their faces, but she could not guess why they had come. She would never have dreamed of the real reason.

'I'll get him,' Jane offered, sensing that Charlie wanted everyone together. Perhaps she, with brothers of the right age for volunteering, had already half guessed.

A few moments later, yawning and stretching, Edward appeared in the kitchen. 'Hello, lads, what brings you here?' he began and then suddenly his face sobered. He knew at once why they were here.

'Sit down, all of you,' he said quietly. 'Annabel, my lovely, leave your bread making and let's hear what they've to say for themselves.'

'I've joined up, Gramps,' Charlie blurted out, his gaze on the old man's face rather than on his mother's. He dared not, at this moment, meet her eyes.

Edward sighed heavily. 'Aye, I thought as much.'

In her chair, Martha made a little noise in her throat and then covered her face with her apron.

'Joined up?' Annabel's voice was a strangled whisper. 'But – but you can't, Charlie. You're not old enough.' Wildly, she searched the faces of the other two young men. 'Why didn't you stop him?'

Theo felt hcr words like a shaft through his heart and Bertie couldn't stop the tears from smarting his eyes.

'We tried, Aunt Annabel,' Theo said. 'Truly we did, but when we saw he was adamant, we thought the best thing to do would be to join up all together. That way we might be able to stay together. We'll keep an eye on him.'

'You mustn't blame Theo or Bertie, Mother,' Charlie said. 'If you want to blame anyone, then it's my father's fault.'

'Your – your father?' Now Annabel was bewildered as well as distraught at the news.

'I was there when he spoke at the rally in town. He spoke with such – such fervour. Everyone was swept along in a tide of patriotism. You couldn't help but be moved by his words.'

Annabel blinked. She had no reply to this. Soldiering was in Charlie's blood whether she liked it or not. She turned to Theo and Bertie, who were looking stricken by her words. She reached out a trembling hand to them. 'I'm sorry, my dears. Of course it's not your fault. I shouldn't have said that.'

'We do feel responsible, though,' Theo murmured.

'We should have insisted to the sergeant that he was underage.'

'I tried,' Bertie said, glancing apologetically at Charlie. 'But it made no difference. The man just shrugged his shoulders and said, "Trying to get him out of serving his country, are you?" and I knew then it was no use. They were going to take him anyway.'

'You're not to blame yourselves,' Edward, his voice husky, tried to reassure them. Then he turned to his great-grandson. 'I don't know what to say to you, my boy. I've got very mixed feelings. I don't want you to go and yet I'm proud of you. Very proud of you all. Just mind you keep your heads down and look out for each other. That's all I ask.'

Now the three of them could promise that whole-heartedly.

Strangely, it was easier to deal with Dorothea's hysterical anger than with Annabel's quiet acceptance and Nancy's weeping. Bertie had hugged his mother and grandmother but nothing could make it any better, not their promises to take care of each other or to write regularly. In the minds of both Nancy and Agnes their boy was already lost to them.

Dorothea stormed and fumed and threatened, but Theo faced her stoically.

'I'll get James home. He'll put a stop to this nonsense. He'll pull strings. And what on earth have you brought *them* here for?'

'We're going together, Mama. Three cousins, side by side, fighting the enemy.'

'Cousins! Of course you're not cousins, he's Jackson's by-blow. How you've the nerve to bring him into this house, I don't know! You'll be wanting to take them both to meet your grandmother next.'

Theo smiled and said softly, 'I hadn't thought of that, Mama, but that's a very good idea.'

'Don't you dare, Theodore!'

But Theo had already turned away and was leading the way through the house to his grandmother's room, whilst his mother found a pen and some paper and hastily scribbled the wording for a telegram. Then she rang the bell, almost pulling the cord from its holder in her desperation.

Sixty-Three

Because the formation of the new battalion was done in haste, the early training was rather haphazard and the men were billeted in different areas. At first, there were no proper uniforms or rifles, so it wasn't until two months after the three cousins had volunteered that a camp was established at Brocklesby, where the men would live in huts and have enough space to train together properly. At last they had uniforms, although at first they were not the real military khaki that the 10th Lincolnshire Regiment would eventually wear, but surplus Post Office uniforms. However, it gave the men a feeling of being a unit at last. Quite soon the new pals' battalion became known as the 'Grimsby Chums'. They were all from the same area, all from Lincolnshire; they had a common bond and they became 'chums' in the truest sense of the word. They were ready to fight together for their home town, their home county, their country and they were prepared to die together.

'Brocklesby,' Annabel murmured when she heard the news of the training camp being set up, 'I wonder . . .'

'What, Mother?' Charlie asked, but she only shook her head and said, 'Oh nothing, Charlie. Nothing at all.'

*

The 10th Battalion now numbered one thousand men and, two months after the first notices had appeared asking for volunteers, the men marched proudly out of Grimsby towards Brocklesby parkland, their new home for the next few months, to bands playing and cheering townsfolk lining the street. Formal training now began under the leadership of 'old soldiers' from the Boer War, but there was time for games and sports too; football and boxing matches were particularly popular pitting Company against Company in friendly, yet quite serious, combat.

'They say we'll get leave whilst we're training,' Theo said. 'So we'll be able to get home quite often. That'll keep our mothers happy at least.'

'But when are we going to the Front?' Bertie fretted. 'It'll all be over before we get there at this rate.'

But, of course, the war was not over by Christmas as had been expected and the 10th Battalion began to realize that before long they would have the chance to see action. Theo, Bertie and Charlie were in A Company. They trained together, ate together and slept in the same hut and could quite truthfully say to Annabel every time they went home, 'We're still together, still looking out for each other.'

The news comforted Annabel and Martha, but did little to allay Edward's fears, though he kept them to himself. In September, he had begun to read the first casualty lists to appear in the newspapers, but these he kept from both Martha and Annabel. Several local men had volunteered, two from his own farm and one from Joe Moffatt's, and he heard on market day that several had gone from Fairfield village. Whilst volunteers would not be sent out to the Front yet – Edward was wise enough to know that if the war went on, as he sadly believed it would do, at first it would be the British Expeditionary Force who would face action and then, possibly, the Territorials – eventually the volunteers would be sent. And with them, the three cousins were likely to go.

By the time a parade was arranged in May 1915, the makeshift uniforms had been replaced by proper khaki uniforms with Lincolnshire regimental cap badges. They marched from Cleethorpes railway station through the streets into Grimsby arriving at the People's Park gates where the Mayor was waiting to welcome them. Cheering crowds marked their progress and excited little boys ran alongside the marching men as they again passed through the town to the sound of bands playing until at last they boarded a train back to Brocklesby.

'We'll be leaving here soon,' Theo said the following day. 'Let's go into town and have our photographs taken. Then we'll go home to say "goodbye".'

Dressed in their brand-new uniforms the three young men faced the camera, keeping rigidly still and staring into the lens, a fear deep in their eyes that they were unable to hide. They each had one taken standing on their own and then a fourth photograph with all three of them together. Theo sat on a stool whilst the other two stood behind him, each with a hand resting on his shoulder.

'How many copies would you like?' the photographer asked.

'One of each of us on our own, three copies of the three of us,' Theo said promptly, 'and then one enlargement of the three of us.' He held out his hands, measuring in the air. 'About this size.'

As they left the studio and stepped into the street, Bertie asked, 'What's the big photo for?'

Theo was grinning. 'To hang with the rest of the family portraits in Fairfield Hall.'

The other two gaped at him and then burst out laughing. 'They'll never let you.' But Theo only laughed and put his arms about each of their shoulders. 'Each one of us has a claim to the estate. Maybe not to the title, but to the estate, yes. And I promise you both, one day that photo will hang in pride of place in Fairfield Hall.'

On the day before they were due to return to camp, Theo insisted that they should all go together once more to visit their families.

'Uncle James is home,' he told Charlie, 'and I want you to meet him before we're all likely to go to the Front. Did you know he's a major now?'

Mutely, Charlie shook his head.

'Right, we'll start at your place, Charlie, and then go back to the village to see your folks, Bertie, and then lastly, Fairfield Hall.'

'They'll not want us there,' Bertie said. 'Your mother nearly had an apoplectic fit last time.'

Theo only grinned. 'Maybe she'll manage a full one this time.'

Annabel tried hard to hold back the tears as she hugged each one of them fiercely. Theo and Bertie were almost as dear to her as her own son, but she knew now that there was nothing she could do to stop them going. All over the country, mothers were being parted from their sons, and many from husbands and brothers too.

'Maybe,' she said bravely, 'you'll all be back home very soon.'

Edward was solemn as he shook their hands, his face looking suddenly so much older, and Martha wept openly, unable to hide her distress. 'Oh Gran, please don't cry. Give us a smile, eh?' Charlie said, hugging her. But it was too much to ask and Martha couldn't stop weeping for the rest of the day.

Without saying a word, just before they left, Charlie placed copies of the photos they'd had taken on the kitchen table; one of himself on his own and the other of the three of them together. Whatever happened, he knew his mother would treasure them both.

Nancy too sobbed against her son's shoulder, but Agnes's grief was too deep for tears. If their boy didn't come back, what had either of them left to live for? Once, he had not been wanted, but now he was the centre of their world. Whatever would they do without him with only the photographs he had left them for comfort?

They looked very smart in their uniforms as they marched up the driveway as if they were still on the parade ground. John Searby, older and greyer now, opened the front door.

'Good morning, Mr Searby,' Theo greeted him, removing his cap as he stepped inside, followed uncertainly by the other two. 'We're off this afternoon, so we thought we'd come and say goodbye.'

'Very good, Master Theodore. Mrs Parrish will make tea for your friends if they'd like to follow me.' The manservant was trying to give the young man a tactful hint. Theo noticed, but chose to ignore it. Politely, he said, 'That will be lovely. We'll all come down in a few moments, but first, is Uncle James here?'

'In the morning room, sir.'

Theo marched ahead again, 'Come on, you chaps.'

He gave a brief knock on the door and then opened it. 'Uncle James – just popped in to say goodbye.' He turned and said again, 'Come on in.'

The two boys sidled in, unsure of their reception. James rose to his feet from his chair by the window. His welcoming smile faded when he saw who was with his nephew. Bertie he recognized at once, as he'd seen him recently working on Chaffinch Farm, but it was when he looked at the other boy that shock jolted him. The young man standing before him was unfamiliar and yet, very familiar. He had the Lyndon hair colouring and James could see that he had his eyes and nose. The boy was undoubtedly a Lyndon and he realized that he was at last standing face to face with his son.

'Uncle James, Bertie Banks I think you know, but this is Charles Lyndon, though he's usually known as Charlie.'

Father – and there could be no denying it now – and son stood facing each other.

'I'm pleased to meet you, Charlie,' James said at last in a husky voice. 'And you're off to war, I see.' He frowned. 'But you can't be old enough.'

'I'm seventeen, sir.' Charlie spoke with more confidence than he was feeling.

'Only just,' Theo put in. 'He told the recruiting sergeant he was eighteen and they took him despite Bertie's efforts to tell them he was underage. Anyway, we've done our training together and we're off now and we mean to stick together – if they'll let us. We joined the newly formed 10th Lincolnshire. I think they're starting to call it the "Grimsby Chums".' He paused and then added softly, 'Won't you wish us well, Uncle James?'

James's gaze was still on Charlie, but at Theo's question he jumped visibly and said quickly, 'Of course. Of course I do.' He moved towards them and shook each of them by the hand. 'Come back safely.'

'And now I must find Mama and Grandmother.'

This time Bertie said firmly, 'We'll wait in the kitchen, Theo. You should see your mother on your own.'

As they left the room, James watched them go with a heavy heart. Perhaps at this moment, only he, a serving officer, could guess at the horror which all these brave, honourable young men would have to face.

And his son was going to be one of them.

How he wished he had time to put things right, he thought, as he gazed down at the two photos he had seen Theo slip onto the sideboard as he left the room. Still holding the photo of all three young men, James moved slowly towards the desk facing the window. He sat down, pulled two or three sheets of writing paper towards him and picked up his pen.

After a lot of thought, he began to write. The letter took him over an hour to compose, for he had many pauses, several times crumpling the sheets of paper and beginning again. At last, reading through what he had written twice, he folded the sheets and placed them in an envelope, addressing it to *Lady Annabel Lyndon, The Countess of Fairfield – in the event of my death.*

He rose from his chair and, carrying the letter, went out into the hallway and then up the stairs to his bedroom. Only a few moments later, he was asking Luke to saddle a horse so that he might ride into town.

'Is there anything I can do for you, m'lord?'

'No, no, thank you. This is something I must do for myself.'

As he cantered away, James realized that there was not one of his employees whom he could trust to deliver such an important letter to his solicitor for safekeeping. So ingrained were they all with obedience to Dorothea during his long absences that he had not won their loyalty.

The thought saddened him.

Sixty-Four

Brocklesby was to be remembered by the 'Chums' very fondly, when they arrived at their new camp near Ripon, in June 1915. Life there was to be very different. They would live twelve to a tent and undertake musketry courses, hard training on the Yorkshire moors and, of course, drill.

'We're to be part of a brigade,' said Theo, who seemed to be the one to hear all the news first. 'It's getting serious.'

'We won't get so much leave then, will we?' Charlie murmured, silently promising that he would write to his mother more often now they were further away.

'When do you think we'll go out there? To France?' Bertie pestered.

'Steady on, old chap,' Theo laughed. 'You're rather keen, aren't you?'

Bertie grinned. 'I rather thought that was what we'd all joined up for.'

But it seemed the 'Chums' were not yet required at the Front. Over the next few months they moved three times, finally being housed in huts at Sutton Veny in Wiltshire.

'We're getting closer,' Bertie said, as they boarded the train to take them all home for Christmas.

Everyone tried to make merry, but a pall of anxiety hung over their relatives whilst the young men themselves were in a fever of excitement. Rumour had run riot around the camp that in the New Year of 1916 they would finally be going to France.

They agreed that they would say nothing to their families who, after more than a year, had been lulled into thinking that their boys would not be sent into the fighting, that they were being held in reserve – just in case. But the British Expeditionary force and the territorials had sustained huge losses. The volunteers were now needed and the next step would be conscription. Each of them could hardly conceal their excitement and, when they congregated at Meadow View Farm before leaving to return to camp, Edward, Martha and Annabel could feel it, but Bertie side-tracked their thoughts by announcing, 'Emmot Cartwright and I are walking out together. She's promised to wait for me.'

'Oh Bertie, how wonderful,' Annabel cried, thinking back to the solemn-faced, hungry little girl with big round eyes. But Emmot had grown into a pretty young woman who helped her mother in the dairy of their farm. Theo and Charlie clapped him on the back and added their congratulations, though Edward found it hard to say anything. There had been a spate of hastily arranged marriages recently, before young men marched off to war, and Edward found it hard to be sympathetic. So many mothers, wives and sisters would soon be mourning the loss of their young men without adding to their number. Edward sighed. An old man now, he could nevertheless still remember what it was like to be young and in love with the whole of life yet to live. So many of these boys would not have a life to live. However, he smiled and shook Bertie's hand and wished him well, as he did all three boys, but he watched them set off with a heavy heart and did not share his fears with either Martha or Annabel. There was only one person he confided in – Ben Jackson, when he met him on market days.

'How will Lady Annabel take the news when it does come as it surely must?' Ben asked Edward and the old man shook his head sorrowfully. 'I don't know, Ben. She's been very brave up until now, but when it comes to it – I really don't know. How I wish you would visit us. I know she'd like to see you. She asks me every market day when I get home if I've seen you.'

'Does she?' He was heartened to hear that she still thought of him and yet it was hopeless; he dare not visit her, dare not start the tongues wagging again, not even after all these years – at least, not until he heard that her husband had divorced her and, after all this time, there seemed to be no chance of that.

The night before the three boys were due to return to camp, Annabel had thrown a surprise party at Meadow View Farm. She'd invited Nancy, her mother and Emmot and, for a few precious hours, everyone had been able to forget that the next morning their beloved boys would leave them. They had no idea when they would see them again.

When the three cousins arrived back at camp, they were told they were leaving for France the next day on different ships. They met up again in Le Havre, from where they marched to a rest camp. After various moves, which seemed to be bringing them closer to the front lines, they came at last to Armentières at the beginning of February, from where they would go into the trenches and Bertie wrote home excitedly both to Nancy and now to Emmot too that they were now under real enemy fire, but that there was 'nothing much happening here'.

'Thank goodness,' his mother and Emmot agreed. 'Let's hope it stays that way.'

They were in the front-line trenches for a couple of days' 'initiation'. The officer in charge told them, 'We "stand to" twice a day for an hour each time, at dawn and then again at dusk, on the fire step in the front trench with full equipment. In fact, you must wear your equipment at all times, even when you're carrying supplies. Tough, I know, but it's necessary. Just remember to keep your heads down. Any movement seen above the parapet invites sniper fire or even shelling,' he warned them. 'And be especially careful when you're bringing supplies or relieving the front line. The enemy is aware of movement and knows it's an opportune time to shell us. And whenever there's an alert of enemy activity, or during the night, bayonets are fixed. And now, I'll show you where you'll be posted when you're on lookout duty.'

The sentry's position was in a small trench dug at right angles from the main trench and towards the enemy lines where the lookout would listen for sounds and watch for signs of enemy activity.

'That's just to let us know what it's like,' Theo muttered as they made their way back through the winding trench to the support lines. 'Normally, we'll be in the fire trenches for about four days, I've heard. And then a similar time in the support trenches ferrying supplies and ammunition, some time in reserve and then – oh joy – a period of rest. And then we start the whole cycle again. Of course, that all changes if there's action.'

'It's so cold and wet,' Charlie grumbled. 'I don't think my feet have been dry for a week.'

'We'd best have a look at you, old chap. Don't want you getting this thing they call trench foot.'

Theo led the way into a dugout as four huge rats scurried out, disturbed by their arrival. Used to the creatures on the farms, the three young men were not fazed by them, though Bertie remarked, 'They're big buggers, aren't they? Can't say I like the idea of one running over my face when I'm asleep.'

Theo gave a wry laugh. 'One blighter ran over mine only last night. Got his back feet in my mouth. I felt like giving him a bite, but I knew his retaliation would be far worse, so I let him go. Get the brazier going, Bertie. Let's have something hot. But mind the smoke doesn't give us away. Now, Charlie, let's look at those feet of yours.'

It wasn't long before the 'Chums' suffered their first casualty when a private was wounded and suddenly the whole excursion became very serious, made more so at the end of the month when the first fatalities occurred.

Now the cousins knew they were really at war.

Theo and Charlie both kept their letters to their families light and jovial, even when the snow came and it was hard to write with stiff fingers, sitting in a freezing dugout and listening to the bullets whistling overhead, but Bertie wrote home with the truth, telling Nancy and Emmot about the casualties, the comrades they'd already lost and the dreadfully cold conditions, yet always ending with the words. *'But don't worry about us. We're still together and watching out for each other . . .'*

They became used to the ever-changing routine; so many days in the trenches and then so many days behind the lines when they could go to the nearest town, spend time in cafés or at some kind of entertainment if any was available, or even just flirt with the local girls. Theo and Charlie went frequently to one particular café where the two pretty waitresses had caught their eye.

'You go,' Bertie urged them. 'I'll stay here and write to Emmot.'

It was the only time the three cousins were ever apart for long.

I haven't a clue where we are, but Theo (who knows everything) says we're near the River Somme and there's a feeling that something big's afoot, Bertie wrote to Emmot, wondering if his words would ever reach her past the censor, but he wrote them anyway. *You know what I mean. It's like when Aunt Annabel planned that party on the last night. We'd guessed something was up because of all the whispering and the piles of food being hidden in the pantry. Well, it's like that, but we reckon this is going to be a very different kind of party. Ammunition to blow the enemy sky high is being carried up to the front trenches. It's rumoured there's going to be a big push to divert the enemy's attention from the French at Verdun. They've had an awful time. So it looks like it's our turn now. If we could only move forward instead of just being stuck in the same place for months on end.*

During the last days of June, the allies began a huge barrage against the enemy with weapons of all

461

descriptions. On duty in the front line, Theo, Charlie and Bertie stood shoulder to shoulder watching the gunfire and shelling landing on the enemy's trenches.

'It seems such a shame,' Theo remarked. 'No Man's Land looks so pretty sometimes, when the sun shines on the fields of green grass dotted with white and yellow wild flowers and a shower of scarlet poppies. And now we're blowing it all to Kingdom Come.'

Bertie chuckled. 'He's getting poetic now. Just watch he doesn't go over the top to pick flowers.'

'Do you think it's ever going to stop?' Charlie asked. It was the first time the three cousins had been on duty in the front line and it was nothing like they'd imagined, not even in their worst nightmares.

On their arrival, they'd spent some days in the support trenches, ferrying supplies and getting used to the tedious life. They had to 'stand to' at dawn for an hour and then it was breakfast, which might be only a slice of bread and a cup of weak tea. But now, something seemed to be happening. The allied artillery barrage had begun two days' earlier on 24 June in an attempt to obliterate the German front lines and so open up a way for a massive assault.

'I don't know,' Theo muttered grimly. 'I reckon they must be able to hear this back in England.'

'Oh, I hope not. Mam'll go spare if she does,' Bertie murmured. Their patriotic fervour was being eroded by the minute by the incessant gunfire and the nervous tension that permeated the trenches.

'It's the waiting that's the worst, isn't it?' Theo said. 'If only we could get going.' He glanced up and down the short run of the trench where the three of them were standing on the fire step, their rifles at the ready, their steel helmets in place.

'You know what this is supposed to do, don't you?'

'Hopefully kill all the enemy before we get the order to go over the top?' Charlie ventured.

'Well, that as well, but no, they're hoping to breach a gap in the enemy line so that the cavalry can push through.'

'But what about their artillery, to say nothing of tanks? Have they got tanks?' Bertie said. 'Horses against tanks doesn't sound like a very sensible idea.'

'Is anything about this war "sensible"?' was Theo's only reply, to which neither of the other two had an answer.

Half an hour later they were told to stand down but the bombardment continued hour after hour.

'I'll be deaf after this,' Theo muttered as he led the way down into the nearest dugout. 'Now, what are we going to have for dinner, chaps? A nice piece of rump steak from Percy Hammond's shop? Or – I know, what about bully beef and biscuits for a change?'

'Why not?' Charlie muttered. 'Is there any water left?'

'Not a drop,' Bertie said cheerfully. 'It'll be boiled water from the nearest shell hole again.'

'Haven't they brought supplies yet?'

'Doesn't look like it,' Charlie said, scratching his chest.

'Have you got lice again, old chap?'

'They won't let me alone.'

'Come on, off with your kit.'

Charlie stood like some little schoolboy whilst Theo and Bertie stripped him.

'God, he's alive with the little blighters,' Theo said. 'Let's just chuck his shirt. I've got another one somewhere he can have.'

*

'Surely no one over there can withstand that,' Bertie said, as they stood side by side on the fire step once more. It was 1 July and they'd already been awake since four-thirty. After breakfast an hour later they'd moved forward and there they'd waited until, at almost seven-thirty, a huge mine, buried by the Royal Engineers under the German trenches, was detonated, shaking the ground and blowing tons of earth skywards. Two minutes later, the artillery barrage from the allied lines, which had gone on for days, stopped. Fear gripped every waiting soldier's stomach. It was not cowardice – these volunteers were the bravest of the brave. They'd enlisted in a wave of patriotic fervour to save their country, prepared to do whatever it took to rout the enemy, but not one of them could have foreseen the carnage or the horror they would have to endure as they stood at the gates of hell on that summer's morning. Weighed down with over seventy pounds of equipment – entrenching tools, gas helmets, wire cutters, ammunition, bombs, water bottles, field dressings – they'd been ordered to advance at a steady pace to gain, it was hoped, at least two miles of ground on that first day.

The whistle blew, the order came and men climbed the ladders and launched themselves over the parapet and began to climb the hill towards the Germans, who had the advantage of occupying the villages of La Boiselle and Ovillers on the higher ground. Earlier patrols had reported that the enemy's positions had been obliterated. Surely, no resistance could – or would – be offered.

But something had gone disastrously wrong. As the first line, which included the three cousins, appeared over the top of the parapet, they faced heavy machine-gun fire. They walked on, but soldier after soldier fell to the ground. Another line advanced and then another and another, but the slaughter went on.

'Run, Bertie, run!' Theo shouted and grabbed hold of Charlie, pulling him into a shell hole. Bertie tumbled in a moment later, panting and disorientated, but astonishingly, he was laughing. 'You told me to run once before, Theo. Remember?'

'So I did, old chap. But I reckon these Germans are even more fearsome than my mother, don't you?'

'Guess the artillery assault didn't work then,' Charlie muttered. 'Now what do we do?'

Cautiously, Theo poked his head above the side of the shell hole only to hear the ping of a bullet hitting his helmet.

'For God's sake, Theo, stay down.'

Machine-gun fire went on all around them. Another soldier fell into the crater, slithering down the side to lie in the bottom, eyes staring, blood pouring from his chest. The three cousins stared at him and then at each other. He was beyond help. Another rolled in, but he was still alive.

'I'm hit, I'm hit. Oh, Mother, I'm hit.'

The shelling and the gunfire went on relentlessly and now, added to the deafening noise, was the sound of wounded and dying men screaming in agony, lying in No Man's Land where not even the most courageous stretcher bearer could reach them. As dusk fell, the three cousins shed some of their equipment and, dragging the wounded man with them, began to crawl back towards their own trenches. Every so often they lay perfectly still, as snipers' bullets hit the ground round them.

'We should have waited a while longer, until it was really dark,' Bertie muttered.

'There's another crater up ahead. We'll wait there a

while,' Theo suggested, as the moaning of their companion brought another hail of bullets, but thoughts of leaving their wounded comrade never entered their heads. They waited again, and not until the early hours of the following morning did they make it back to the trench, falling in with relief, still dragging the casualty after them.

'Let's get him to the dressing station,' Bertie said. 'You both all right?'

'Careful,' Charlie said, straining his eyes through the darkness. 'There're men still sleeping. Mind where you tread.'

Theo bent and shook the shoulders of one or two men lying on the duckboards at the bottom of the trench. 'Charlie, old chap,' he said softly. 'They're dead.'

'What! All of them?'

In the pale light of the July dawn, they searched among the bodies until they found one or two only just alive. Between them, they made several trips back and forth to the dressing station. When at last they could find no one else who could be helped they retreated into the dugout, white-faced and with dark rings of utter exhaustion around their eyes.

'Let's get some sleep if we can. There'll be more of the same tomorrow – I mean, today – I've no doubt,' Theo said.

The three cousins didn't know it but that day had been the start of a big offensive that would become famously known as 'The Battle of the Somme'. It was miraculous that all three of them had survived those first disastrous hours. As they tried to sleep, Theo said to Charlie, 'Rumour has it that the 2nd Lincolns are here somewhere. Your father's with them, isn't he?'

'I really don't know, but I don't expect I'll suddenly

find myself in the same shell hole with him,' Charlie said, half asleep already.

But strange coincidences happen in war and late that same night, as the three young men huddled together in the dugout, they could hear voices outside and Charlie heard his name called softly.

'Here,' he answered. 'In here.'

A dark shadow crouched at the entrance and then crawled in. 'Don't stand up, chaps,' a voice said, 'I'm here unofficially. In fact, I'm probably being very unprofessional, but I am off duty for the moment and I doubt anyone's going to argue with me anyway.'

As the man straightened up, Charlie gasped and Theo murmured, 'Well, I never.'

Bertie just stared at Major James Lyndon.

'We're very near you. Just to the north outside the village of Ovillers. We've driven deeply into the enemy lines. How about you?'

'Much the same, sir,' Theo said. Both Charlie and Bertie were tongue-tied. 'We've advanced – so they're telling us – but we've suffered terrible casualties.'

In the poor light, James's face was grim. 'Yes, we have too. That's why –' He hesitated and bit his lip. It was hard for the soldier in him to show emotion of any kind. 'I wanted to know that you were all safe.' He glanced round at the three ashen faces. They were exhausted and drained of feeling. There was a long pause before he touched Charlie lightly on the shoulder and said gruffly, 'I'd better be going before I'm missed. Take care of yourselves – and each other. All of you.'

And then, as quickly as he had come, he was gone, crawling out of the dugout and disappearing along the trench, keeping his head low as he found his way through the darkness back to his own position.

After several moments' silence, Charlie murmured, 'Did that just happen?'

'I think it did,' Theo said and yawned. 'But I'm so tired, so very tired, I might have dreamed it all.'

And with that, Theo was asleep on the cold, hard floor of the dugout leaving Charlie kneeling at the entrance trying to catch a last glimpse of his father.

The battles of the Somme would rage backwards and forwards for months and would claim thousands of young lives on both sides. When the long lists of the casualties suffered by the 10th Battalion Lincolnshire Regiment – the 'Grimsby Chums' – began to appear in the town's newspapers, the community realized sadly that they had lost a generation of fine young men and all for the capture of about five miles of ground. But somehow, the Lyndon boys had survived. They had stayed close, watching out for each other and fighting courageously together.

Charlie and his father did not meet again, but in October, word came down the line that Major James Lyndon had been killed on the twenty-third of that month in an assault on the enemy to the east of Les Boeufs and Gueudecourt, when the 2nd Lincolnshire were said to have been 'almost wiped out'.

Theo was now the Earl of Fairfield.

When the news reached Fairfield Hall, the dowager countess took to her bed, overcome with grief, but Dorothea sat down at her desk to write to her son. In the trenches, both Bertie and Charlie began to call Theo 'My lord', but he refused to answer. 'I don't want the title or the estate. They're yours, Charlie. You'll see when we get home . . .'

Annabel received a personal visit from James's solicitor, bearing the letter, which had been left in his safekeeping. She opened it with trembling fingers. The letter was dated on the same day that the three cousins had visited their families in turn.

My dear Annabel,

Perhaps I haven't the right to call you that any more, but I hope you will forgive the presumption as, if you are reading this, you will know that I have been killed in the line of duty. I am writing this on the day I met my son for only the second time in his life. I bitterly regret my hasty and unwarranted action just after his birth, for I can see for myself now that Charles is undoubtedly my son. He is a fine boy and I am so proud of the way you have raised him. He will make a fine soldier and I pray he will return safely to you when all this madness is over.

Annabel, my beautiful wife, I was so wrong to believe my sister's lies. If we had had more time together – you and I – and I had not been so insanely jealous of any other man even daring to look at you, then perhaps things might not have happened the way they did. Dorothea is not a bad woman – I beg you to believe that – but her obsession with seeing her son as my heir robbed her of all sense and reason.

And now I must leave the inheritance in the lap of the gods. Despite Dorothea's pleas and

*threats, I have taken no action to disinherit our
son, so, by rights, Charles should be the next
earl and should inherit the estate too.*

I leave it all in his safe hands.

*My dear, I hardly dare ask for your forgiveness,
but I do so knowing you have a loving and
generous heart. With all my heart I hope that in
the years to come you find someone to love and
cherish you as you deserve.*

James

Wordlessly, she handed the letter to her grandfather
who read it through and then looked up to meet her
gaze. Huskily, she said, 'Gramps, the next time you go
to market and you see Ben, please will you ask him to
come to see me – if – if he would like to, that is.'

Edward nodded. I won't wait for market day, he
thought. I'll go now. He said nothing to either Annabel
or Martha, but he harnessed the pony and trap and set
off at once to Joe Moffatt's farm.

'Where's Ben?' he asked Joe after a cursory greeting.

Joe's smile faded. 'Bad news, is it, my old friend?'

They were all becoming inured to it; every day they
heard of someone they knew being killed or wounded,
or a family they knew losing a loved one. The Somme
was proving to be a slaughterhouse.

'The earl has been killed in action.'

Joe nodded sadly, understanding at once why Edward
had come. 'I'll find Ben.' He turned and shouted to a
young boy who now helped on the farm. 'Find Mr
Jackson, lad, will you?' He turned back to Edward.

'Come into the house while you wait, Edward, won't you?'

'No offence, Joe, but if you don't mind, I'll talk to him out here.'

'None taken. These are hard times we're living in. Did you hear that William Broughton has enlisted?'

'No!' Edward shook his head sadly. 'It'll kill his parents if owt happens to him. Couldn't he appeal? Farming's surely classed as "important war work"?'

Joe shrugged. 'Seems like he didn't want to. Didn't want to be thought a coward, I expect.'

Several young men had gone from Fairfield, including Eddie Cartwright, and Thorpe St Michael seemed to have only young boys and old men left walking its streets.

Edward sighed heavily. 'Where will it all end, Joe?' But it was a question his friend could not answer. Instead, he said, 'Here's Ben coming now. I'll leave you to it.'

''Morning, Edward.' Ben approached, an anxious look on his face. 'Is something wrong?'

'The earl's been killed in action. Annabel heard this morning.'

'I'm sorry to hear that. How – how is she?'

'Ben, I want a straight answer, man to man. Do you love Annabel?'

'You know I do, but—'

'No buts. You're coming back with me now to see her. And I won't take "no" for an answer.'

Ben shook his head. 'I can't. I mustn't. It'd only set the tongues wagging again and . . .'

'Damn the gossips, Ben! Annabel is more important – and she needs you. You're coming if I have to put you over my shoulder and carry you there!'

*

When Edward pulled into the yard, Annabel was watching for him. After only a moment's hesitation, Ben held out his arms to her and she went into them, laying her head against his shoulder and nestling into his neck.

'Oh Ben, what if Charlie doesn't come back?' she whispered.

He stroked her hair but could not find the words to comfort this woman whom he loved so much and had done so, he realized now, almost from the very first time he saw her. He could not offer empty words of reassurance, for he guessed what life at the battle front would be like for all the young, innocent soldiers who had marched away in a blaze of patriotic fervour. Already the casualty lists appearing in the newspapers were growing longer with each day. And now James Lyndon's name was added to that number.

His heart ached for this mother as it did for all mothers. He could even find it in his heart to feel sorrow for Dorothea despite her vindictive treatment of Annabel and her son. Now, both their sons – and Nancy's too – faced a far greater enemy and family feuds seemed petty and insignificant in comparison. He sighed heavily, wishing that the boys had not gone together. Ben didn't believe in 'pals' battalions'. The losses – and he knew they would be heavy before all this was over – would crush whole communities where every street would lose its sons.

Sixty-Five

April 1917

'Bertie! *Bertie!*' Charlie's voice was frantic. 'Theo's been hit. You must come and help me carry him to the dressing station. Sarg has given me permission.'

'Oh my God! Is it bad?'

'Bad enough. He's been hit in the shoulder.'

The two young men hurried to the trench where Theo lay, propped against the side, other men scrambling over his legs as they ran to take up their positions on the fire step.

'Keep your head down, Bertie,' Charlie warned. 'They're shelling us.'

'Leave me,' Theo gasped as they lifted him. 'I'm done for. Look after yourselves.'

'You can't die, Theo,' was Bertie's only response. 'We won't let you.'

They carried him to the dressing station and laid him down gently beside the other wounded being brought in thick and fast.

'I'll get a doctor.'

'Listen – please!' Theo's tone was urgent, demanding. 'I've made a will. It's – it's in my pocket and I've sent a copy to my solicitor back home. You must do the same, you hear me? Make a will, chaps. Promise me,

473

you'll both make a will. And – and –' his voice was getting weaker – 'look after Aunt Annabel.'

Bertie and Charlie glanced at each other.

'We promise – we'll do everything you say – but just lie back and save your strength. You're going to be fine. You've got a Blighty one, old chap. You lucky devil, you'll be going home.'

Epilogue

A door banged making Tiffany jump. They had been sitting opposite the portrait of Lady Annabel whilst the guide told her the story. Outside, the winter dusk had turned to darkness and flakes of snow spattered silently against the window. The door at the side of the room opened and a young man entered. He was tall and slim with brown hair and brown eyes that twinkled merrily.

As he strode towards them, the guide struggled to his feet, murmuring, 'Ah, Mr Jamie, we were just—'

'Hello, Mr Merriman,' the newcomer greeted him cheerfully. 'You still here? No – please – don't get up.'

Merriman? Was he . . .? Tiffany wondered.

The older man sank back gratefully into the chair as the young man he had addressed as Jamie smiled at Tiffany. 'And we have a visitor on this cold afternoon.' As he held out his hand Tiffany got up and found her own hand enveloped in a warm, firm grasp. 'James Albert Lyndon-Banks,' the young man said, 'but I'm usually known as Jamie.' Tiffany could not prevent a gasp of surprise escaping her lips and her eyes widened.

Jamie chuckled. 'I can see that Mr Merriman has been filling you in on the family history.' There was a pause as – reluctantly, it seemed – he released her hand

and asked, 'What brings you to Fairfield Hall?'

Her gaze went once more to the portrait. 'Lady Annabel. I'd heard about her and I wanted to see her for myself.' Her voice trailed away as, once more, she was entranced by the beautiful woman in the portrait.

'And have you heard the whole story?' He glanced at Mr Merriman.

'Not quite, Master Jamie. We'd just got to where the three young men went off to war. The first war, that is.'

'Ah, then perhaps I can continue the tale. It's high time you went home, Mr Merriman. I'll get Perkins to drive you.'

'Thank you, but there's really no need.'

'There's every need. It's dark and cold now and the driveway is slippery.'

'Well, thank you, then, sir. I would be grateful.' He turned to Tiffany. 'Goodbye, miss. It's been a pleasure talking to you.' He gave a courteous little bow and Tiffany was sure that if he'd been wearing a hat, he would have raised it to her.

'I'll just sort out transport for Mr Merriman, but I'll be back,' Jamie said. 'You're not in a hurry to leave, are you?'

'No, no.'

He smiled and his eyes twinkled as he turned away, but he was back in a few minutes.

'That was Raymond Merriman. His grandfather, Gregory, used to be gardener here.'

'Are there any other descendants from Lady Annabel's time still in the village?'

'Oh yes, quite a few. The Broughtons are still at Chaffinch Farm.'

Tiffany raised her eyebrows. 'William came back from the war, then?'

'Yes, he was wounded, but he married and had two children. I think he lived into his eighties. The Parrish family are still here. Josh never went to war. His family have turned the old smithy into a little museum and craft shop and, of course,' he smiled, 'the Jenkins family are still here.'

'Harry survived?'

'He was badly wounded when the earl was killed but Nancy nursed him back to health. He was invalided out of the Army, and they had three boys, two of whom still live in the village.'

'And you're related to the Cartwrights, aren't you? Are any of them still around?'

Jamie laughed. 'Oh yes, they're all over the place. They have Blackbird Farm as well as Sparrow Farm now. Now,' he said, 'let me show you the photographs of the three cousins when they went to war.'

He led her closer to the huge portrait of Lady Annabel and pointed. 'There, you see? We've put the photograph of them right next to her. We know that's what she'd have wanted.' There was a pause whilst Tiffany regarded the faces of the three cousins who had gone off to war together.

'That's Theo seated with Bertie and Charlie behind him,' Jamie explained. The two were standing proudly, almost as if to attention, but she could read the fear of the unknown in the eyes of all three.

'So did he tell you who came back?' Jamie asked softly.

Tiffany shook her head, her glossy black hair swinging. 'No, but he said that Theo was wounded. That's where we'd got to. Did he recover?'

'Let's sit down near the fire.' He led her to the two armchairs again. When they were seated, his face sobered. 'Sadly, no. Theo died of his wound at the Battle of Arras in a field hospital and is buried out there.'

'So, Charlie was then the earl, was he? Or had he been disinherited?'

Jamie shook his head. 'No. Despite his sister's wiles, James Lyndon never took any action to disown Charlie, whom he finally believed to be his son.'

Tiffany frowned, still puzzled by the name of the young man sitting opposite her. She was sure he'd said James Lyndon *Banks*. And there'd been an Albert in there somewhere. So how . . .?

James chuckled softly as he saw her puzzled frown. 'Let me explain. The three cousins made wills leaving the Fairfield Estate to each other – well, sort of. Theo left it to Charlie – just in case there should be any more wrangling – and Charlie willed it to Bertie, for while Bertie couldn't inherit the *title*, he could inherit the estate.'

She began to understand. 'So,' she said huskily, already feeling Annabel's grief. 'Charlie didn't survive the war either and – and—'

'My great-grandfather – Bertie Lyndon Banks – inherited the whole estate and the house, much to the disgust of Dorothea.'

Tiffany smiled. 'I bet!' She paused and then asked softly, 'What happened to Charlie?'

'That was really tragic. He was one of a relatively small number of men killed in March 1918, in one of the very last battles the 'Chums' were to fight in. Sad, isn't it, to think that he'd gone through all that only to lose his life when the Armistice was almost in sight?' His glance now went to the portrait. 'Poor Lady Annabel. She was distraught. She was married to Ben Jackson by then and their son was born only days after she heard the dreadful news. I think his name was Richard, but after Annabel died in the early sixties we lost touch with the Jackson family.'

'Mm,' Tiffany murmured, her gaze still transfixed by the lovely face in the picture.

'Shame, really,' Jamie went on. 'My father can just remember Lady Annabel, but my grandfather knew her well. He adored her and never tired of telling us about her. She was an amazing woman. I only wish I'd known her.'

'Mm, so do I,' Tiffany said, more to herself than to the young man sitting opposite her. His intense gaze was on her face and, reluctantly, she looked away from the portrait to look into his eyes.

Now it was her turn to take up the story, but there was a little more she wanted to know about Fairfield Hall before she did so. 'What happened to Dorothea?'

'When her brother was killed,' James explained, 'she refused to accept that Charlie was his heir. She did everything she could think of to contest it, but when she lost her son, she never recovered from the shock. Poor woman. She committed suicide in 1919, shortly before the dowager countess's death. But the loss of her son, James, and then two of her grandsons, hastened Lady Elizabeth's death too, I think. She was a very brave lady. It was she who made sure that the wills of both Theo and Charlie were honoured and that Bertie inherited the house and the estate.'

'So she openly acknowledged him as her grandson, then?'

'Yes, and she lived just long enough to see him move into Fairfield Hall with his wife, Emmot Cartwright.'

'Did Lady Elizabeth ever see Annabel again? I got the impression they were fond of each other.'

479

'Just once before she died and after that, Annabel used to visit the village frequently. The locals idolized her and she'd never forgotten them. She still advised Bertie about the estate and when he and Emmot had a son, Robert Albert, she was the baby's godmother. They also took steps to have the hyphenated surname Lyndon-Banks made legal. So, here we are. Robert was my grandfather. He only died in 2005, so of course I knew him well. My father now runs the estate, but one day it will pass to me, though I hope that's a long way off yet. My dad's only sixty.'

She smiled at him. 'So, now it's my turn.' Again she glanced at the portrait. 'Annabel and Ben only had the one son, Richard Charles. Annabel and Ben took over Meadow View Farm when her grandparents died. She lost Ben in 1951, but she lived another ten years. Richard took on the farm and married a WAAF during the war – the Second World War, that is, of course – but she was killed in the bombing of the airfield where she was stationed. He didn't remarry for a long time – not until the mid-fifties – and then to someone much younger than him. He and Christine had two sons, Edward, who still runs the farm, and Stephen, who became a successful lawyer in London.'

'Do you happen to know what happened to Annabel's father, Ambrose?'

Tiffany pulled a comical face and laughed. 'Oh, he got his title eventually. He was knighted in the twenties for services to the fishing industry and he'd also made a lot of his steamships available for the war effort. A lot of them were lost, I believe.'

James was looking at her, his head on one side. 'You've done an awful lot of research into the family. Is that why you've come today, to find out about the other side or . . .' He stopped as a thought struck him. 'What did you say your name is?'

Tiffany chuckled – a delicious, infectious sound. 'I didn't.' There was a mischievous pause before she added, 'It's Tiffany. Tiffany Jackson.'

Now it was James's turn to look surprised. 'So you're . . .?' He pointed to the portrait, not quite sure of the relationship, but realizing now that there must be one.

Tiffany nodded. 'I'm Lady Annabel's great-granddaughter by her marriage to Ben Jackson. I'm Stephen's daughter.'

'How wonderful.' He reached across the space between them and grasped her hand in both of his. 'I'm *so* pleased to meet you. Do go on, please. I want to hear everything.'

'My grandfather – her son Richard – lived to be ninety. He only died five years ago, but his second wife – my grandmother – is still alive and living at the farm, though my Uncle Edward and his wife and son run it now. My uncle was born three years before Annabel died. He can't remember her, though he has vague memories of being taken to visit an old lady in bed. Whenever we visited, Grandpops – that's Richard – used to talk about her a lot, but Annabel would never talk about her life before she married Ben Jackson, he said, nor even about Charlie.' She shrugged. 'I don't know why.'

'Perhaps it was all too painful. I'm ashamed to say that my family – the Lyndons, that is – didn't treat her very kindly, even though she rescued the estate. But the villagers worshipped her.'

Tiffany nodded. 'I know.'

'My own great-grandfather – Bertie – idolized her,' Jamie went on. 'She'd been very kind to him and his mother when everyone else shunned them. And it was he who insisted that both Ben and Lady Annabel should be buried here in Fairfield churchyard.'

'And during the night before her funeral the villagers lined her grave with flowers. Is that right?'

'It is. How did you know that?'

'My grandfather told me and he also said that everyone in the village – from the youngest babe in arms to the oldest inhabitant – attended her funeral service.'

'They did. My father remembers that day vividly though he was only eight at the time. But it made such an impression, he's never forgotten it.'

Jamie was gazing at her now, frowning a little. 'Obviously, we're connected by all this, but – but we're not related in any way, are we? We're not cousins, or anything.'

Tiffany laughed. 'No, no. I'm descended from Annabel and Ben Jackson, not James Lyndon.'

'And I'm descended from the wrong side of the blanket.' But his grin told her that he wasn't in the slightest bit bothered.

It was warm and comfortable by the fire and Tiffany didn't want to move, but she had to. Reluctantly, she stood up and James rose too. 'I hope you're not driving far tonight. It's very icy and more snow is forecast.'

'No. I'm staying at The Lyndon Arms tonight. We've come to stay the weekend at the farm' – she grinned – 'for Mother's Day, you know, but when I said I was coming here today, Dad insisted I should stay overnight in the village.'

'Then will you stay to have dinner with us? I'm sure my mother and father would love to meet you.'

Her long, sleek black hair framed her lovely young

face as she looked into his eyes. Unless she was very much mistaken, he didn't want to let her go. And she didn't want to leave.

'Thank you,' she said softly, her dark, violet eyes dancing. 'I'd love to stay.'

As he ushered her towards the door, she glanced back once more towards the painting that had been the focus of their attention and their conversation. 'So, the portrait survived?'

'Ah, now Mr Merriman could have told you all about that. When Dorothea gave instructions for it to be destroyed, his grandfather and Thomas Salt took it down to the village. Jabez made a box for it and it was hidden for years in the church. Of course, when Bertie inherited the Hall, he had it reinstated here in the dining room.'

Again, he too gazed at the lovely woman in the picture. 'You know, you're very like her,' he murmured.

'Oh, I hope so, Jamie. I really do hope so.'

The Clippie Girls
Margaret Dickinson

Rose and Myrtle Sylvester look up to their older sister, Peggy. She is the sensible, reliable one in the household of women headed by their grandmother, Grace Booth, and their mother, Mary Sylvester. When war is declared in 1939 they must face the hardships together and huge changes in their lives are inevitable. For Rose, there is the chance to fulfil her dream of becoming a clippie on Sheffield's trams like Peggy. But for Myrtle, the studious, clever one in the family, war may shatter her ambitions.

When the tram on which Peggy is a conductress is caught in a bomb blast, she bravely helps to rescue her passengers. One of them is a young soldier, Terry Price, and he and Peggy begin courting. They meet every time he can get leave, but eventually Terry is posted abroad and she hears nothing from him. Worse still, Peggy must break the devastating news to her family that she is pregnant.

The shock waves that ripple through the family will affect each and every one of them and life will never be the same again.

ISBN: 978-0-330-54431-3

FOR MORE ON

MARGARET DICKINSON

sign up to receive our

SAGA NEWSLETTER

Packed with **features, competitions, authors'
and readers' letters** and **news of exclusive events**,
it's a must-read for every Margaret Dickinson fan!

Simply fill in your details below and tick to confirm that you would
like to receive saga-related news and promotions and return to us at
Pan Macmillan, Saga Newsletter, 20 New Wharf Road, London, N1 9RR.

NAME _____

ADDRESS _____

_____ POSTCODE _____

EMAIL _____

☐ *I would like to receive saga-related news and promotions (please tick)*

*You can unsubscribe at any time in writing or through our website where you can also see
our privacy policy which explains how we will store and use your data.*

Bello:
hidden talent
rediscovered

Bello is a digital-only imprint of
Pan Macmillan, established to breathe new
life into previously published, classic books.

At Bello we believe in the timeless power
of the imagination, of good story, narrative
and entertainment and we want to use digital
technology to ensure that many more readers
can enjoy these books into the future.

Our available books include:
Margaret Pemberton's *The Londoners* trilogy;
Brenda Jagger's *Barforth Family* saga; and
Janet Tanner's *Hillsbridge* Trilogy.

For more information,
and to sign up for regular updates, visit:
www.panmacmillan.com/bello